for my parents
Judy Rifka   David Reed

A Still
Small Voice

Spring '52

I was born with very red hair.

But it was not red like a strawberry or cherry. It was red like the red of a sun ripened peach.

I was delivered by my aunt at 7 A.M. on April 11, 1852. I can't say for certain if I really do remember that day or if I just have an active imagination. Perhaps it is just something that my people told me—but I know that the sun was soft that morning on the hanging curtains, and that there was a glint of it on the wooden bowl which held the warm water and the sponge of my first bath.

My mum and dad lived in Richmond, in a cottage with white lilies in the garden and green vines on the brick. Mother's name was Ellen Flynt—her maiden name, Penrose. She sewed fancy carrying bags for ladies. Father was Philip Flynt, a cobbler with a shop beside the house. He was a light haired man who matured too quickly, and relied heavily on his wife for picnics. Her eyes were green like mine. That is what I have heard.

DEATH CAMASS

I have heard other things.

I have heard that my mother once grew a six pound squash in the garden, and that she would not cook it. I have heard that my father was not overly concerned with things of a worldly nature, and that at our table, he always set an extra place for wanderers and travelers.

I have heard that my crib was made of young birch and that it smelled sweet like a bowl of fruit. . . .

I have also heard that of those who came to America from Europe, many had set out to escape some extraordinarily trying circumstances. And I have heard that of those who came from China, many immigrated due to similar conditions (though the Chinese especially seemed to endure more hardships in the years to come, with the building of the railroads across the west). And I have heard from some that the Irish brought cholera. And I have heard from others that the Chinese brought cholera. And still others have told me that nobody is to blame for cholera—that sometimes it simply grows, like moss on a rock.

There is a baker, a Mister Joseph Brintons, whose shop was beside the old cobbler's house in Richmond. When I visited there, he told me that when my mother and father were infected with cholera, two soldiers were posted outside of our home. They pushed provisions through the windows, and were given instructions to fire on anyone who tried to enter the house. Mister Brintons does not know under whose authority they were acting, and he is not sure that it was the right thing. But he is also not sure that it was the wrong thing, as nobody else was infected. He told me that in the spring of '56, a doctor named Wickersham stood at the front door shouting instructions to my father, and then to me, when, like my mother, my father became too sick to stand. "Mix salt and molasses into warm water," said the doctor, "and make them drink it." Mister Brintons said that I never fell ill, and that though I was a young girl (just four years old) I dutifully accomplished the doctor's ministrations. He said that by the second day there was a collection of friends and neighbors who stood outside the house holding candles—gathered in prayer. But that is something I do not recall.

My recollection begins with a dying woman that I do not remember knowing. She was pale, and lay under a white blanket on a brass bed. She called me her princess, and asked that I promise to take care of my father, who was downstairs on a bed in the kitchen. I did. He was lying on a mattress on the dining table. I patted him with a damp cloth, and squeezed water into his mouth with a sponge. Over his face, he had a tea towel that he would not let me remove. He was afraid his breathing would infect me. Before sunrise, he too had rested his fingers in his palm, his last breath expired.

I do remember rather well the loneliness of the time that followed. I have heard it was a day. I have heard it was a week. I have heard it was much too long for a child to be alone. And that, I believe. . . .

Many times, the old cobbler's house on Peach Road has been described to me. It was a two story white house with a brick wall in the back. There was a steep staircase to the second floor. The rooms were narrow. The windows were small. I was told that the bricks of the hearth were re-used to build the hearth of the house that now stands on that lot. And I have seen that house—but it is simply a stranger's house, and there is nothing to make me feel that it was ever my own.

Richmond is now regrown—reblossomed, like a flower from a bulb. And when I stood in the streets of the rebuilt town, I did not recognize a single pebble—not a stone, not a shrub, not a tree, not the color of the sky.

And my childhood seemed a long time ago indeed—as I stood there on New Peach Road, and listened to the clop of horse hooves on cobblestone, to children tossing beanbags and jumping rope, to merchants selling flowers, and a man selling popped corn. I listened to the sound of hammering and sawing, and the shouts of men rebuilding—to all those sounds of Richmond from twenty-five years before. And then I heard the echo of ten years before that—of cannon and minié balls whistling overhead, of mad cries, and the long silences when air set still. And from beyond those years, in all the multitude of sounds between me and my girlhood, I strained to hear the sound of my own soft footsteps, and the sound of my own child's brush drawing through my own red hair. . . .

But all I heard was the sound of horse hooves clop on the cobblestone, of children tossing beanbags and jumping rope, of merchants selling flowers and a man selling popped corn.

Even so, since that visit, I sometimes imagine my mum and dad—Mum in a blue dress and a white apron, and Dad with his thin blond hair. They are standing in the slender stairwell with their hands outstretched. I cannot hear their voices, but I read their moving lips.

That's it, Alma, they say to me as I rise from my hands and knees to take my first step. . . .

 The first home I remember having was in the orphanage outside Arlington. There were four boys and four girls. We read the bible and played organized games like Pin the Tail on the Donkey, and Duck Duck Goose. We had clean sheets, which we washed ourselves on the stony bank of the Potomac, and several rabbits which we were not allowed to handle. There were dogs that played on the front lawn. The only other thing that I remember is the yellow dress that I was wearing when I first saw Pastor Miles.

"I think you have outgrown your yellow dress," he said.

I said, "Do you think so?"

It was the July of '59—and like me in my yellow dress, the nation was outgrowing itself. In those days, there was much pulling up of stakes, and digging in of heels. So perhaps the appearance of the pastor was not so extraordinary—although it would prove extraordinary to me, that I would be lucky enough to be an orphan girl who went remembered.

He was wearing a black suit with a white collar, which I imagined was rather hot. I listened to him tell me that he had come on behalf of my Aunt Bettina, who was living in Kentucky.

I crossed my hands, and nodded formally—stiffly.

Standing beside Pastor Miles was the woman from the orphanage. I believe her name was Gravelsham. Her arms were crossed over a stack of papers pressed against her chest. She was looking down at me with a beaming smile. But I didn't know why everyone was smiling. I was much too frightened to smile, and almost too frightened to move.

"And where," inquired the woman, "is Cotterpin Creek?"

Though addressing me, she had inclined her head to the pastor, and he replied with some surprise—

"Oh," he said, and then he spoke directly to me, "it is not too, too far from here. Cotterpin Creek Kentucky is not too far from Frickerham Kentucky, which is not too far from Sudsbury Kentucky, which is not too far from Lexington Kentucky, which is not too far from Lexington Virginia, which is not too far from Arlington Virginia. Alma—may I call you Alma?"

I hesitated. He had straight black hair, which he brushed across his forehead with his hand. He was sweaty. He thumbed at his collar uncomfortably. It was fastened tightly, and he was not accustomed to it. . . .

"Yes," I consented, "you may."

"Alma," asked the pastor, who also began to smile, "do you know about the bluegrass?"

I shook my head.

Miss Gravelsham batted her eyes. "Do you know why it is called bluegrass?"

"It's probably blue," I answered her.

"Well yes" the pastor's voice was not hurried or clucking, unlike the voice of Miss Gravelsham—"it is blue. The bluegrass is blue when a breeze blows over a field of bluegrass, and the green leaves shimmer like the bluest afternoon. Yes, the bluegrass is blue—in May, when it blossoms with the tiniest bluish flowers. Well, that's how I see it, though a great many people see the bluegrass in a great many ways. But one thing about the bluegrass is for certain—it is the finest grass for grazing, which is why the home of the bluegrass is the home of the finest horses. And that is also where your aunt lives—nestled safely in the bluegrass at the bend of Cotterpin Creek, in Cotterpin Creek Kentucky."

Miss Gravelsham tilted her head. "It sounds like your aunt has picked out a quiet and cozy little nook for you, Alma—a safe place to tuck you away. She must be a prudent lady."

"Yes," agreed the pastor, interrupting her, "she is."

By her use of the word prudent, I knew that Miss Gravelsham had meant to scare me—and by interrupting her, I knew that Pastor Miles had meant to tell me that prudent did not mean strict. But Pastor Miles did not reassure me, and Miss Gravelsham did scare me. I turned to run—but the pastor lifted me into his arms and carried me to the coach. He set me down beside it. I looked up. Even the driver was smiling broadly—sitting over the big horses. I would have tried to run again, had there been a place to run.

One of the horses was white and reddish brown. (I would learn a coat like that was called skewbald.) The other was charcoal black. The red and white one did not shy when I put out my hand for it to smell. . . .

"That is Wilma," said the driver, "and the other is Hovington. They seem to like each other, and well, from Cotterpin, it's a haul."

I touched the second horse on the chest.

"Don't worry, miss," the driver allayed Miss Gravelsham, "Hovington is fine with children."

"Bettina," I asked, "she is my father's sister?" And I turned to the pastor, wanting to believe him. I had spoken rapidly, as if to interrogate him, and as I awaited his answer, I tried to make myself firm—demanding. . . .

"Yes," answered Pastor Miles, "she is your father's sister, and she is your aunt—your Aunt Bettina. You have not met her—not that you would remember."

"Her name is Flynt?"

"Yes," said the pastor, "her maiden name is Flynt—she is widowed. She is Bettina Flynt Evans."

The pastor unlatched the carriage door and brought down the stepping stool. He placed it at my feet and offered a hand of assistance, as if I were a lady. So I stepped up. I knew that girls from the orphanage did not grow into ladies. And though I knew nothing of the pastor, or my aunt—I also knew no good would come from staying. And even if it was not proper to judge by appearances, and I was far too inexperienced to make just a few seconds the very basis for a perception that might decide the fate of my entire life (for good or ill) I also knew that, however premature, the time for such a decision had come. So, squinting my gentle eyes, I lowered my brows in a stern way—and I saw that the pastor was tall and strong, more like a farmer than a pastor. As he was helping me into the cab, my hand was still in his, so I saw that his fingers were square and broad—and I could feel that they were rough against my skin. These were trustworthy and loyal hands—hands that would not shrink from masonry or roofing when a friend could use the help. The black leather of the bench was soft and polished. It squeaked some when I moved upon it, and I beheld that this carriage was an upkept thing. The leather top was folded down, and I felt the warmth of the sun on my neck. As the pastor rose into the cab and sat beside me, I smelled that he smelled like a book. I regarded him as he reached into his jacket pocket, removed a pair of spectacles, unfolded them, pushed them up his nose and turned to ponder—to patiently consider with me, through his lenses, what changes this might mean to my life.

And when I saw that it was up to me to set the carriage in motion, I looked away from the pastor—and stared down the dirt road. I said—

"Driver, take your reins."

And I placed one hand over the other on my lap—into the ruffles of my yellow dress. I tucked my chin to my chest and lowered the corners of my lips. I did not turn my head. I did not look back at the lady from the orphanage or the several children that had left their games and straggled to the roadside. But I could feel the sadness of their wide eyes. . . .

The pastor asked if I had anything I wanted to take with me.

"No," I said aloud, "I do not."

And though the driver was perhaps surprised by my audacity, his face turned solemn and resolved, as if on this occasion, it was only natural that a mere girl should have given the word to go. And then, he did take the reins, and cluck his lips once, twice—urging Wilma and Hovington into a trot. Dust swirled up from the clay road. Crickets cleared the way for the horses. A gray powder rose in the warm air—and we rode on the wake of a milky cloud.

Much preoccupied, I began my journey, hardly taking notice as the afternoon passed. The seconds of the day were as transitory to me as were the weeds by the road-side.

I remember only that the air was thick—almost intoxicating. And while drowsy, I was far too affected by the prospects of my journey, and far too wary of my new environment to allow myself the luxury of a girlish fatigue. I can say now that I have seen children in troubled times (and some who have merely endured personal misfortune) who are no longer youthful—but content with the responsibilities that make them adults. Life is a series of obstacles, and children such as that do not look to be nurtured. They are like reptiles, no more than shrunken versions of their elders—in every concern, utterance and gesture. And I often think that, perhaps, I had become such a child. . . .

I sat with my hands folded, making polite conversation when it was required of me—

"Yes sir, we had classes at the orphanage."

"Yes sir, I look forward to seeing Kentucky."

"Yes sir, I like horses."

Eventually, the two men quieted—having run out of questions. They left me to my own thoughts, waiting for a more opportune moment to ease me back into the childhood I held in reserve.

Some hours later, the driver asked Pastor Miles if he thought I ever smiled.

"Yes," Pastor Miles assured the driver, "I am sure she smiles. But do you drink when you're not thirsty? It's good to drink, and it's good to be thirsty, but it is not good to always drink, or to always be thirsty—just as it would not be right to always smile, or to always be happy. Isn't that right, Alma?"

"Yes," I said, "I believe it is."

The day had gone gray. And the sky said it would be starless tonight, and dim tomorrow, and then, maybe, there would be rain. . . .

An ashen sun lowered on the horizon, as Pastor Miles asked if I was hungry. I was not overly hungry, I told him. But he and the driver were hungry, so we soon tied up the horses at a roadside inn called The Summer Blossom. It seemed a clean, respectable house, and as the pastor, his driver and their team had been long on the road, it was decided to remain for the evening. We ate a simple meal of beets, grains and corn. The innkeeper was highly apologetic for having no meat in his kitchen. He offered to skin a rabbit or squirrel, but the pastor declined. For all the modesty of the fare, the inn seemed exceptionally elegant to me, as I had never been in an inn—not that I remembered. There was furniture in every corner of the house—and too many wallpapers to count. In the dining room, the ceiling was an exotic gold and light blue pattern, while the walls were green and purple. There was also a fireplace, and dozens of aromatic candles. Through two glass doors, there was a porch which overlooked an orderly garden. Outside the white railing of the porch, there was a flower plot. After dinner, I sat on a swinging bench and watched a bee, delicately lying on a bed of yellow pollen stalks which grew from the center of a white flower. The bee was so calm, cradled in the essence of that chaste spirit, that I sat on the porch for some time, watching the flower and the bee. As much as half an hour had passed before I was joined by Pastor Miles, who had been inside at the table, reading a newspaper.

Reclining on a rocker, the pastor drew from his pipe and regarded the hazy sliver of moon in the sky, which, perhaps, he believed I, too, was regarding. A plume of white smoke curled up and rolled into the night, as he asked me—

"Do you . . . do you often think of your family?"

The bee shifted slightly in the flower—nestling in the pollen, and lay still again.

"No sir," I answered, "I do not remember them," because I did not remember them.

"Those flowers are pretty," said the pastor, noting my interest.

I believed I understood the bee in the flower—once, at the orphanage, on a day when we children played out of doors, I had been wrapped up in a quilt—in the snow. I'd been there, within that warmth—the cold without. I'd been there, heated by my own breath, and held by the gentle petals of worn patchwork.

"Yes sir," I said, "the flowers are pretty."

He tapped his ash onto the railing, brushed it away, and reloaded the bowl with tobacco from a red leather pouch. Holding the pipe in his thumb and fingers, he asked me, "Do you think things happen for a reason?"

And it was then that I saw the flower was slowly closing. One petal of the five was yielding to the night—folding into its own repose. And I saw that the bee, so still, so ready, had been waiting. Perhaps each night, I thought, the bee returned to this flower.

"Do things happen for reasons?" I said, remembering the pastor, "I don't know."

The pastor relit his pipe, and considered—

"Yes," he nodded his head, "come to think of it, neither do I. Sometimes it is good to think there is always a reason. Sometimes it is too painful—to think that something so dear to us might have been taken away purposefully—and then, it is better to think that there is no reason, or that if there is a reason, it is beyond our understanding."

"Yes sir," I said to the pastor, agreeing with him. *Perhaps this bee is in love with this flower.*

The pastor leaned forward, with his elbows on his knees. His expression said that I had not understood him because he'd been speaking to me as an adult. So he began to talk to me as a child—

"Ah," he said, surprised at the sight of the bee in the flower, "there is a bee there!"

The bee slept as the second petal of the flower closed upon it.

"Yes sir," I told him, "I have been watching it."

"Ah," said the pastor, and minutes passed. . . .

"Alma," he asked, in a voice considered and distracted enough that it suggested to me that he had given up both his philosophical talk, and his childish talk, "Alma, what do you think of that bee?"

And I could see that this was the true man, a man without pretense—and despite my orphan's humor, I felt it was an earnest question, so I endeavored to answer it earnestly—

"The bee? It is . . . well . . . just a worker bee, who has never done much but work. . . . And to the bee, it is a special thing to . . . to be away from the hive all night. But this bee, it very much likes this flower, and it is ever so very fond of it, that this bee thought that none of the other bees . . . no one else in such a busy, busy world . . . no one else would notice if it didn't go back to the hive. . . . No one else would bother, or know—and so the bee decided to sleep in the flower . . . to stay the night. . . . And it loves this flower so much, it will dream beautiful bee dreams. . . . Everything good and fresh—no matter what it's like on the outside, or to other bees. . . . And in the morning, the bee'll wake up and go to work . . . but it'll know it has this secret that makes it special. And all day, it'll remember where to find the flower. And it'll go back, come evening . . . come every evening. . . ."

The pastor nodded his head slowly, savoring his pipe.

"Your aunt is a healer," he said, and packed away his tobacco pouch, "maybe you will learn from her."

"That would be good," I said, "I would like that."

He considered the sky. The breeze stirred. The air was moist, and the night was cooling.

"You know," his eyebrows lifted in a worried fashion, "no one knows how to cure cholera."

And I nodded—*I know.*

We watched the last petals of the flower close over the bee.

"Are you the bee, Alma?"

"No," I said, "I am the flower."

The pastor said, "Ah," and the wind fell down from the clouds. Then he nodded himself, as if both to encourage me as well as to warn me that mine was a challenging ambition, a challenge he knew well—"Alma, is that what you would like to be when you grow up, a flower?"

And then, reminded that I was a mere child, he became amused—"Is that what you would like to do, Alma—embrace the world, and save it?"

"Yes sir," I said, looking at him, "that is what I would like to do. What I will do, I do not know."

The pastor was taken aback, speechless—and he grimaced. "Well then," and he prickled, "it is a rare variety of . . ." But then he held his pipe across his lips and scrunched his brow—and there came a hint of a smile, and his eyes grew bright, and he inclined his head anew—

"Well then, a girl as wise as you—I know that it will not be long until you smile again."

"No," I said. . . .

Whereupon, he began to smile so big, to try so hard, that I thought if I did not smile he might die of dejection. That straining smile on his face pronounced a wish for my happiness that was so absolute, that despite any clumsiness on his part, I could not resist him—and I began to smile somewhat myself, even then, as his kindness had become my kindness—

"No," I said, "it will not be so long before I smile again."

The pastor was a youngish man, and though he knew something of life, his face was not of pure wisdom—instead, the laugh lines at the corners of his eyes were pure goodness and compassion. This was the intuition that guided him. And to see him so, this perfectly imperfect man, hunting for the manner in which he might bring me into a better world, I could not help but relent my lips, my cheeks and eyes, into a glimmer of faith. . . .

And I smiled for the first time that I remember, when Pastor Miles smiled at me.

I began to look down—but the pastor gently lifted my face, and his eyes remarked that happiness was nothing to be ashamed of. . . .

"I am glad you smiled for me, Alma," he said, "had you not, I believe I would have burst into tears."

And I nodded—*I know.*

There was a puzzle in the parlor, and as the evening had grown chill, we burned a lamp and worked on it at the table. It was good we stayed up a little late, as I was unusually anxious. I think the pastor knew that I could not have slept right away, so he let the hour slip his mind—and we worked on into the night. I was quite exhausted by the time we were finished (the puzzle was a picture of a dog dressed as an opera singer), and the thick mattress of my bed was a welcome—even a charmed sight. I could not remember having slept all by myself before, as at the orphanage, we had slept in rows of five, two rows to a room—but because I was so sleepy, I knew that my youthful apprehensions would have no stamina on which to thrive. This was not a darkness that would frighten me, but one that would release me from any grip of cruelty, and receive me with caresses. . . . My bed linen was turned down for me, and the innkeeper had provided a nightgown, a robin's egg blue nightgown which his daughter had worn when she was a girl—twenty years before. It was a beautiful thing, with flowers stitched in silken thread. . . . And, in all that unaccustomed comfort, I fell asleep quite promptly—and my slumber was deep. But as I woke heavily, we were late getting back onto the road in the morning.

Once the horses were set to moving, and we were resumed on our course, I again inquired of the pastor how long a journey I might expect. He answered, as was his way, by saying that Cotterpin was not so far from Frickerham, which was not so far from Sudsbury, which was not so far from Lexington, which was not so far from Lexington Virginia, which was not so far at all. . . .

Black-capped
chickadee

Perhaps Cotterpin Creek was not far in the estimation of the pastor, but it seemed very far to me.

We had been bumping along for several hours when I showed an interest in the flowers at the headstones of a passing cemetery. As Pastor Miles was a religious man, who presumably knew something of cemeteries, I asked if he knew the names of the different kinds of flowers.

"Why yes," said the pastor, pointing with his long arms, "the red ones are roses, the white ones are lilies, the blue ones are violets, and the gray ones are pussy willows." Then the pastor turned to me, speaking resolutely—

"I am glad you are inquisitive, Alma, because I do not plan for us to waste any more time in Virginia."

As the morning progressed, we stopped along the roadside when the pastor saw growing things that he wanted to show me. There was witch hazel, with its curious yellow flowers—he said the oil from the bark of that bush made a soothing lotion. There was white oak, with acorns of shallow cups and knobby scales—splints from that tree were used to weave baskets. The hemlock tree grew in ravines and on the north side of hills—it was a pine tree which made a red dye. There was also a hemlock flower, which was poisonous, and used to kill Socrates, who was a philosopher in Ancient Greece. Pastor Miles told me to tell my aunt about what I had learned—that she would be impressed.

We had packed a lunch at the inn, and we ate in a field by a mountain of apples, where a boy worked with a pitchfork. The pastor said that apples so early in the season would surely be milled for vinegar. The fruits were orange, yellow and green.

Pastor Miles had a fondness for cardinals, and he pointed them out

"That'll be the Cleveland boys," said the pastor. "They like their rifles."

Pastor Miles was grinning good-naturedly, but there was something disapproving about it.

"Oh," I said, and covered a yawn with my hand.

I'd already been told that the Cleveland family had supplied the carriage and driver for my retrieval. It was a payment in barter to my aunt, who had rendered them a service. But the pastor preferred to explain it as a kindness rendered by another kindness. . . .

For a moment, the trees parted and I glimpsed a white castle with red trim. Then the trees closed around it again.

"That's the Cleveland house," said the pastor—

"And it's an ample house for just the five of them. There's Mister Somerton Cleveland and his wife, Doreen Cleveland, and Mister Cleveland's unmarried sister, Caroline Cleveland, who will be your teacher when the time comes, and Mister and Missus Cleveland's two sons. The younger one, John Warren Cleveland, he's not too much older than yourself, while the other's near a man. . . ."

The pastor paused for a moment to hold his chin—

"For the life of me," he furrowed his brow, "I can't put a name to that elder child—I've never known him to be called anything but 'Bugby.'

"Ah . . ." the pastor sighed, giving up on remembering the boy's true name. "There's also the groundskeeper, Stewart Valentine, his wife Cassie, who's a seamstress, and their son Harmon, who's just younger than you, and hasn't yet started school. The slave girl's Natalie, she's eight. Her mother Serena is gen'ral maid and cook. They work in the big house, and live behind it—upstairs of the buggy house."

As we rode onto the Cleveland estate, the first thing I saw was the fencing—there were miles of white fences—high, solid fences. On either side of the walking paths the fences were doubled, explained the pastor, to part spirited stallions.

Then I saw horses. Playful yearlings frisked across a sun dappled pasture of bluegrass. They were muscular and dark, their coats shining with redness in the sun. Most were brown or black, but there was also a bluish horse, which the pastor called a roan, and another two that were lighter—one a light brown called a bay, the second a tannish color with a dark mane, tail, feet, muzzle and ears, which was called a dun. I jumped at another rifle shot—and I saw that the horses were startled but not greatly concerned.

"Those horses're trained for that," said the pastor—"to remain composed in frightening circumstances. These pretty fields aren't just pretty, but full of minerals from rich deposits of limestone in the earth. The water puts the minerals into the soil, which puts the minerals into this fertile bluegrass, which, through grazing, puts the minerals into these horses' bones. And that helps build a strong, light frame—as well as a courageous temperament."

"Pastor Miles," I asked, "horses like that, why don't they just jump the fences?"

"By nature," he answered, "horses are flatland animals, and without a rider urging them on to do so, hardly a one of them is inclined to jump. I don't think they can see too well, when they're jumping, as a result of their nose—"

"And," I added, "they must trust the Clevelands."

"Why yes, that too," agreed Pastor Miles, "I believe they must."

After the carriage turned off the rough dirt road, we bumped onto the short grass between two rows of white fence. Built on half-round posts, the planks were nailed crossways in between. Three up—they were probably high enough to discourage most horses even if they wanted to jump. Around each pasture, the fence was a different shape—all wavy and curving. There were no corners anywhere—just swirling circles, ovals and a few figures that looked almost like eights. Two big white barns had red X's set on the doors. Several smaller barns were set between the pastures—

"Those barns are mostly for hay," said Pastor Miles, "though a few of the family's horses are there, too."

As we made another turn around a group of trees outcropping

from the woods, Mister Ditzler pointed to the outline of the Cleveland house. Then we turned, and it was just ahead—down another lane between another pair of fences. But I remember this path differently than the others—because following that afternoon, I would get to know every blade of grass and ridge on it. I would walk on that grass between those two fences on hundreds and hundreds of occasions—and that's why I remember it so well.

And I like to remember it, because it was so lovely, and now it's gone—

The shadow of the white fence was in the grass ahead of us. The dark lines were made up of the three horizontal stripes of the planks, and the almost endless vertical stripes of the posts. Maybe I got to know that silhouette because it was always so enthralling, especially in the late afternoon sun when the shadows of the horizontal planks were wide and the vertical ones were narrow—even though it was really the opposite. In the real fence, the beams were narrow and the posts were wide. But when the sun was low, below the level of the horizontal beams, their shadows fell a far way onto the grass, and stretched out—while the shadows of the vertical beams were tapered by the angle of the sun, because the sun shone on them from the side. . . .

That was the way to the Cleveland house.

It was a mansion built six or seven feet above the ground—windows to a basement level set me to imagining rows of wine racks and hams. A short flight of wide stairs fanned out onto the front porch. Six columns were lined along the length of the porch. There were another six columns on the porch on the second story. The only thing different about that story was that it had a railing. Even from afar, I could see that the banister on the stairs to the upper porch was a carving of a giant wooden snake. On both the upper and the lower porches, there were rocking chairs, swinging benches, tables, chairs, candles and everything else—I couldn't add up all the windows. As it would turn out, the back of the house was almost exactly the same as the front, except there wasn't a staircase between the downstairs porch and the upstairs porch. It was already plain to see that the house outside was almost as spacious as it was inside. . . .

Looking up at the pastor, I saw that, though he had seen the house before, he was just as awestruck as I was. Inclining his head, he said—

"It is not much like the mill."

And indeed, it was not. Though there was something to the grand outlay that was attuned to nature—it was not so much a gentle lullaby as an august symphony. There was no thought of quiet breathing and restful waking, but of giant cacophonies and tragic finales. It was almost as if, well, I've heard a story told of a tree that held every soul in a whole family, as well as a story of a sparrow that held the soul of a man—and if that tree or sparrow lived safely, so would that family, or that body, to whom that soul belonged—and so it seemed for the Clevelands and their house, that as long as it might survive, and even prevail, so might the Clevelands.

"It was once called Centennial House," said the pastor, "because it would last for a hundred years. The family now calls it Millennium House, because Somerton Cleveland is of the opinion that it will last for a thousand."

For all the contrast to the mill and the frogs, and the kind of temperate life that seemed so appealing to me, the pastor, and what I was already imagining of my sensible Aunt Bettina—still, that kind of life as represented by the Cleveland house was unduly seductive. Even the pastor saw it, in me and himself, and he uttered the caution, "Your house is more like the mill."

And I said . . ."I should hope so."

The horses drew up to the hitching post, and Mister Ditzler eased the carriage to a halt. He stepped down and unloaded the pastor's bag. Mister Ditzler was anxious to get us settled, and to get the carriage to the buggy house and the horses to the stable, as he was impatient to get home himself. Like many who worked on the Cleveland place, he had his own place nearby, where he did a little farming—he and his family raised fruits and vegetables, and kept some livestock.

As the three of us walked up the steps to the house, we heard the explosion of the rifle in the distance. The sky was just darkening. Evening was coming, and though the night was dry, it seemed to me like thunder was coming along with it. . . .

 Glancing at the sky, I reckoned on the weather.

Despite haziness all the day before, there had been a certain brightness, a uniformity to the illumination of the sky. So we had enjoyed the climate as a kind of blessing before the calamity. Then, that afternoon, it had seemed there would be no showers, as the clouds had come and gone. But suddenly, the hot sky was darkening once again, and the air was sighing, *summer rain, summer rain, summer rain—by the time you close your eyes to sleep, there will be summer rain. . . .*

Led by Pastor Miles, and followed by our carriage driver, William Ditzler, I mounted the solid steps to the porch. Mister Ditzler carried the pastor's carrying case. At the doorway, he set it down, the pastor standing aside as he thumped the horse-head knocker.

We waited then, silent with both tension and repose—until the door was answered by a young and stately slave woman in a white dress, apron and hat. I was surprised to learn that this was Serena, whose daughter, Natalie, was just older than myself.

The woman, Serena, brought in the pastor's bag and set it inside the door. We followed, then she dusted her hands on her apron and said, "The Missus'll be with you directly."

She spoke in a clear and educated diction, and I'd later learn that she had been taught to read scriptures and accomplish arithmetic by Caroline Cleveland, who had grown up with her on the estate, and with whom she'd shared a lifelong companionship. As Miss Cleveland was a schoolteacher, she had also helped to educate Serena's daughter, Natalie. Additionally, Natalie had been schooled (in secret) by John Warren Cleveland, who was only two years older than she, and had for her an older sibling's fondness. . . .

It being warmer outside the house than in, Serena closed the door behind us, adding, "Mister Cleveland and the boys—they'll be funnin' in the fields. We've all been expectin' you, and I'm sure they heard your comin', so they'll be about." She bowed politely, and took her leave, having duties to attend in the kitchen.

Until that time, I'd seen nothing of the scale of the Cleveland house, not for wealth or society. Of the architecture, I was impressed foremost by the staircase, which descended from a second landing to spread like a seashell on the first. The foot of it extended to a reception area at the front door. Beyond, the first story divided into a library, a sunken sitting room, and a tiled kitchen—into which Serena retreated. Behind the balcony of the second landing, I could see a line of closed doors, which I guessed were bedrooms.

It was a luxurious way to live, and no detail was lost on me—every wall and ceiling was built of a smooth white plaster. The banisters, the balustrades, the floors and the picture and window-frames were made of a grainy wood that was stained and varnished—all to match. There were furnishings of all kinds—tables, chairs, lamps, wallpapers, statues and paintings. Art, decorating and pleasantries of comfort were to be found anywhere the eye could look, much as it had been at the inn near Arlington—but a thousand times more so. It was a way of life crowded with ease, and free from any moment without distraction—free from any threat of contemplation.

When I first saw Missus Cleveland, she was hurrying down the stairs. Over the years, I got to know a little about Missus Cleveland, and if I had to describe her personality, I would say she was a woman who insisted she be honored as frivolous and worldly, but wasn't always able to quash her natural instinct toward gentleness and thoughtful living.

"Why, hello everyone," she called down, "and welcome!"

Just then, as Missus Cleveland was on the steps, the outside door opened, and without a knock or utterance, we were joined by a smart and sturdy woman whom Pastor Miles introduced to me as my Aunt Bettina. She was a capable looking lady, with strong white teeth, ruddy cheeks, and red-blonde hair, a few shades darker than my own.

the slave girl, Natalie, who brought the stifling porch to life, supplying an armful of white cushions that she fluffed with her lithe arms, and placed on the wooden furniture. I was not introduced to Natalie, but was highly curious about her, as her dexterity made the impression of a bright and spirited girl.

"They all should be arriving any minute now," said Missus Cleveland, as if they were coming from different corners of the world. She explained—

"It's a big property."

We sat down, and with a finesse that was not at all childish, Natalie brought out five glasses, a bowl of chopped mint and a silver pitcher of steaming tea. As her slight hands were removing the tumblers from the silver tea tray and setting them down on the table, the older Cleveland boy arrived—jouncing up the steps to the back porch and shaking the dust from his clothing.

"This is my son," said Missus Cleveland, introducing him to me and smiling. But perhaps, I thought, she was more complicated than she appeared—for in that smile, I sensed cheerfulness, rather than happiness. . . .

Bugby was tall and lank with straight black hair and blue eyes. He had a surprisingly difficult time standing still. His mother took hold of his shoulders to fix him in one place. Still smiling, she tipped her head. "His name is Bugby," and, as widely as she was grinning, I could see what she didn't like—she didn't like the name Bugby.

The moment he shook free of his mother's hold, Bugby hopped back—from foot to foot. He looked like an eager soldier as he bowed to me, saying, "Splendid to meet you, Alma. And it's always a pleasure to see you, Missus Evans. My father and brother will be along promptly."

"What is your name?" I asked the young man.

"Bugby," he replied.

"No, your real name."

"Bugby."

"Oh," I said.

His mother changed the subject. "Bugby, where's your brother?"

"John Warren? He's still out shooting."

"Ah," his mother sighed proudly—"That boy!"

Then Mister Cleveland arrived. He wore canvas gloves and carried a silver bucket full of ice nuggets. He was tall, like his son, but he was also broad. His beard was red, his hair brown and his eyes a pale blue. Without hesitation, he encouraged Natalie to load up our glasses with ice so we could get started on the tea.

With her slender hands, Natalie spooned ice and chopped mint into our glasses. Then she poured the hot tea. The dark liquid rippled over the ice, which was crackling and white.

We all sipped our cool drinks. I had not had tea cold before.

I noticed my aunt was not really drinking hers—she had just a little, then put it down and said politely, "Ah, it is very sweet."

"Yes," said Missus Cleveland, whose face was puffy, "isn't it wonderful?" Her eyes were bulgy and her eyebrows were raised too high on her forehead—that's why she looked so surprised. My aunt told me later that it was from too much sugar.

But I liked my iced tea and was drinking it.

Mister Cleveland watched me sip my tea and nodded his head— "Ice," he told me, "is exceedingly rare."

"Except," I corrected him, "in the wintertime."

Missus Cleveland looked down at her white cushions and said to me, "You be careful with that tea, my dear—there is many a slip between the cup and the lip."

That was when John Warren arrived, slowing his horse from an even canter to a trot. Though not a big horse, John Warren's was a big horse for a boy, or even a young man. And I could see that it was a strong horse—and a fast horse—and on top of all that, even in the storm weather, a composed and well-mannered horse. When the boy bowed his head to greet us, the horse also bowed his head—and knelt to the ground.

"John Warren!" said his mother. "You get that horse up this instant, you know how I feel about your showing off!"

With a lurch, John Warren had his horse on its feet. And the pair of them took half a dozen steps toward us—and the boy rode well, and the horse held well his head and tail—neither too low nor too high. The horse was five years old, almost as old as I, and he and John Warren had just begun their first strenuous workouts—as the Clevelands didn't like jumping horses too young, lest it damage a horse's bones and sense of equanimity. But, for all those things that I would later learn of John Warren and his horse, just then, as a youthful, uneducated orphan girl, who knew near naught of horses, all I saw was a stunning black animal, which seemed great in measure to me, and great in measure to that boy. And as for that boy himself, that orphan girl saw something even more rare and divine than that horse—with his pale skin, his flushed and rounded cheeks. His neatly fitting sweater and breeches. His high boots and thick heels steadying him in the shining silver of his stirrups. The supple leather of the reins that he held in his hands. And his hands themselves—as overdressed and dandy as they were in their cream-colored kid gloves.

His mother introduced me—"John Warren, this is Missus Evans's niece, Alma Kaye Flynt."

It is funny how a child can look like both of his parents, but look markedly little like either one of them. John Warren had his father's frame, which was strong and even—but on his father, that body was brusque and coarse, on account of hard features, red skin and thick hair. But John Warren did not have those features or that skin, or that hair. He had soft features and creamy skin and black hair. And that was because his mother had soft features and creamy skin and black hair—though it was not nearly so attractive on her, and that was because she was quite plump. Somerton Cleveland looked like a soldier, and Doreen Cleveland looked like a landowner, and John Warren Cleveland looked like a prince. His eyes were blue, the same color as the eyes of both of his parents—maybe a touch lighter, as he was no older than ten.

I myself was only seven—and I knew that ten year old boys were not much interested in girls of only seven. Still, I felt his eyes fix on me for too long. I looked up, to regard him. His horse was leaning over the railing—for a carrot Bugby had drawn from his pocket. The horse munched contentedly on the root, not paying much mind to us. But still, John Warren was looking down at me. I was wearing a new pink frock, which the pastor had let me pick out, and which he had paid for with money my aunt had provided him. I was also wearing my blue slippers, which I had also picked out—even though I knew they weren't very practical. . . .

"What's the matter with you?" Bugby asked his brother. "You'd think you never saw a pretty girl before."

John Warren looked away from me and shook his head—as if he'd just been thinking about something else. But I knew that he hadn't, because he looked right back. And for that instant, that one when he could not turn away, he and his horse were transformed—and I did not see the two of them as a fourteen-hundred pound monster, but as a thirteen-hundred and forty pound horse, and a sixty pound boy.

I had a feeling that my eyes were opened huge—too huge to keep secrets—because I could see that he saw in me what I had seen of him. . . .

He was just a boy on a horse.

And I felt my heart would wrap around him, as the folds of the flower wrapped around the bee. And he looked to me, as if he truly were the bee looking at the flower, as if to fold his legs and tuck his wings and love the long night. *Do bees sleep, or do they spend the darkness enjoying the blueness of the white petals, the tenderness of drapery and the sweetness of pollen?* He looked at me, and that was the question that I saw—that anyone would see in his face. . . .

So I just lowered my eyes, because I did not want to embarrass anybody.

Then John Warren pulled up the reins and made his horse dance around in a circle.

"This is caracoling," said John Warren.

Then he stepped the horse back up to the porch and introduced himself—

"Good evening," said John Warren.

His horse was struggling to kneel, as he was accustomed to kneeling for introductions, but John Warren wouldn't let him kneel. "It is a pleasure to make your acquaintance, Miss Flynt, and Missus Evans."

This time, he didn't look at me or my aunt.

"Oh—come John Warren," said his mother, "you know Bettina Flynt Evans," and then she gave Bugby a look. She scowled—and Bugby grinned. And John Warren turned on his horse, hoping to pretend that no, he really didn't know her, and, just a minor incident, he had, as a matter of course, forgotten it. But there was also a grimace and a hint of preparation for the impending disaster.

"Ohhhhhh, John Warren," said Bugby, almost as if he were singing—

"He knows Missus Evans because one day he took it upon himself to collar a nod in an uncommonly appealing tangle of leaves," Bugby snickered, then proceeded with his story, "and he thought it was just a pleasant place in the sun! And, most assuredly, it was not poison ivy, because he knew what poison ivy looked like. But it was poison oak, with which he had not yet been familiarized! As I remember, when I found him, he was still zizzin' like a li'l ol' four year old—but a four year old who was all swolled up like a pig! And no ordinary pig, mind you, but a right fat pig! He knows full well that I rode him over to Missus Evans's house. And he should be thankin' her right now, for flushing his sorry, pussy fanny—and setting him to rest in that brand new bed she had prepared for her niece, Alma, this angelic creature right here, who's so much finer than himself. He should take a close look at her, and think how kind it was of Missus Evans to let his poisoned little corpse curl up there. She might just as well have put him out in the woodshack with the spiders. I know I might have done just that! I know, because I saw him, bloated up like a swolled rat floatin' in a swamp. So he should thank her with that spoiled, poutin' pie of his, because without her, he wouldn't be so graciously returned to his current state of grace. He wouldn't be so puffed up with himself—he'd just be puffed up!"

31

Bugby took a deep breath, as the speech had pinkened and overly excited him—such was his brother's calling. But it was his jovial teasing that flavored the reprimand, and he could not help a little more indulgence of his own—

"You, turn right around—you yellow-bellied lizard! You turn right around and look here, because you know right well who Missus Evans is—and you be polite, even if it was an uncommonly embarrassing moment for a boy of ten—not only because you were helpless . . . but . . . but because you were naked!"

And I could see that just as much as John Warren had feared everything else he would say, that was what he'd feared the most. Bugby smirked, and Missus Cleveland resumed—

"Well, Bugby, that's quite enough . . . but you, yes," she said to John Warren, "you turn your horse around and get back here, and you be a gentleman, because you know Bettina Flynt Evans, even if you'd prefer you didn't!"

John Warren responded as best he could, "Ah yes, of course," but he was still struggling to make his horse turn back, as the horse was just as flustered by Missus Cleveland's reprimand as if she were his mother. Blushing, John Warren inclined his head and extended his upturned palm to my aunt, saying quickly—

"Good evening, Missus Evans."

And John Warren patted the rifle that was fixed to his saddle by a leather carrying case—

"This is a U.S. Model 1841 54-caliber rifle, commonly referred to as the 'Mississippi Rifle.' It was presented to me on my seventh birthday by my father, who told me that a man should have a rifle—and that a man of quality should have a rifle of quality. He says that I can shoot better than anyone on this farm." Then he lowered his horse's head—"My horse's name is Pegasus. My father has bred him over three generations, from the finest of the finest. He is an extraordinary fencer, a capital water-jumper, and very quick."

My aunt said that she'd mistaken Pegasus for an Arabian horse, him being just over fourteen hands high, and with ears so small and pretty. Mister Cleveland proudly replied that Pegasus was bred all in Kentucky, with good stock enough, but surely none Arabian. And as much as he wished to take the credit, he confessed that horses were something like people, and one never knew when a truly exceptional animal would present itself. One might do some right by guess-work—but it was guesswork all the same. He said that John Warren's older brother also had an excellent horse—to see and ride. But Bugby's calico was no more than a common saddle horse—

"And that mare," Mister Cleveland assured us, "she's a remarkable mount."

Pegasus, he was all black, and shiny as could be. His eyes were so brilliant and large! And his muzzle—I held my hand fast to my side, lest I reach out to touch it! He'd a narrow body, sloping shoulders and a long, elegant neck. His hindquarters powerfully built, the length of his body was short—which was fitting for a small saddle. Legs long and fine, his tail was full, fattened by wind and bright with health. His mane was braided, that it would all come to lie on the same side—as well as for adornment.

"Pegasus," said John Warren, "is intelligent, gentle and fast. My father says that he and I can ride faster than any horse and rider in the county. I must be getting him to the stable. It was ever so pleasant."

John Warren caracoled on his horse once again, turned and rode off into the bluegrass. In a bit of a hurry, he dropped a stirrup—but without looking down, in a courtly kind of gesture, he just sort of felt around for it with his foot, and picked it up. The fields verdant and pure, the grass parted as he trotted his horse to the little barn to stable it before the rain. . . .

"That boy will be governor one day," said Mister Cleveland, with bluster.

"Oh, Somerton," Missus Cleveland said dismissively, with a hint of disgust and a forgive-me-anything smile, "why don't you be governor instead?"

✳ ✳ ✳

Chanterelles

"Missus Evans," I asked, "do you think it will rain before we get to your house?"

"No," she answered, "the storm is still brewing, it won't rain until the morning chills the air. And child . . . Alma . . . call me Bettina, or Aunt, or Aunty, or Aunt Bettina."

We walked together on a pine needle path through the forest. It was the first time we were alone together. The woods were quiet, and both of us were a little apprehensive—though she was subdued and I was agitated.

It was not too long a walk from the Cleveland house to her cottage at Cotterpin Bend, but it was long enough. Finally, to fill the silence, I began to tell her the things that I had learned from the pastor. There was still enough light that I could run through the woods by the path and pick out the plants that he had shown me.

"That is the white oak," I said. "It is used to make baskets."

"That is witch hazel—it is used to make a soothing lotion."

"That is hemlock—it is used to make a red dye."

"And that is the poisonous hemlock flower—it was used to kill Socrates, a philosopher in Ancient Greece."

She had been nodding with a puzzled expression on her face, then she finally said—

"You know all that, Alma? That is rather impressive."

"Yes ma'am," I said, "the pastor said you would be impressed."

"Oh, he did?" asked my aunt, and she began to chuckle—"Is that where you learned it?"

"Yes, ma'am," I said, "I learned it from him on the way from Virginia. He told me if I remembered it, you would be rather impressed."

My aunt laughed truly, and I thought that maybe my aunt was a woman who spoke little, but laughed a lot.

"Oh," she smiled, "he told you that, did he?"

"Yes, ma'am," I said.

"Well, you learned it all very quickly. You have a good mind, Alma. You have your father's mind, and luckily, your mother's disposition."

"Do I?"

"Yes."

My aunt's eyes were laughing eyes. In her squint, in her wrinkles—I saw the laughter of every sorrow. . . .

We walked northeast, and the forest grew denser and denser until it suddenly cleared for a field enclosed by a winding brook.

"That," said my aunt, "is the bend of Cotterpin Creek."

I recognized the grass in the field—it was the bluegrass, poised and unmoving in the night.

There was a deceptive turn to the field, and as we crossed it, it appeared that there was no more than forest on the far side. But when my aunt told me where to look, I saw the cottage which was to be my home. Without knowing it to be there, the cottage would have been all but invisible from even fifty yards away. Much of it was blocked by a lofty boulder which sat on the far side of the meadow, just on the edge of the arching creek. The big rock was gray and shiny in some parts, but green with moss in others. There were gray-green lichens too, feathery and ruffed. And there were wide cracks and narrow ones, and small plants sprouting up in between, and ants that walked over the whole stone in neat rows. For a long time it must have been there, watching over the field, and the little cottage just across the trickling creek.

That was my aunt's cottage—a humble cabin with a chimney made of stones and red clay. There was more red clay between the notched logs of wood that built the walls—which were whitened by the sun. The whole house was balanced on a few piles of stacked stones—though the arrangement seemed a careful and maybe even a hardy one, it had a craggy and rather motley appearance.

There was a porch in the front—but my aunt said that was more to keep the water away from the house than to sit on. There were two windows in the front on the first floor, and one in the attic, and one on either side of the chimney on the side of the house. There were also two windows in the back and one on the far side—but I didn't find that out until we stepped through the creaky, crooked door.

Inside, there were so many plants that it was like walking into a grotto in the forest. My aunt had vines, herbs and flowers growing in the windows, and all kinds of mushrooms growing in the corners—and a few varieties of ferns here and there. Dried plants hung from the ceiling, along with dried corn and dried fruits. It all smelled kind of minty, but not exactly. I asked my aunt about the smell, which was a sweet and natural smell, but also medicinal. It cleared up my nose, which I think might have been a little runny.

"That's eucalyptus," said my aunt.

I was tired, and my aunt soon had me installed under the covers of my new bed in my new bedroom. There was one window, which was open, and I lay on my back looking at the sky—it was filled with bright stars, trees and the moon. I had never had my own window. The recent days had brought the first time for many things. My bed was a real feather mattress—and a mattress like that I had not slept on before. The quilt was made of squares of all different kinds of materials—and that was a kind of quilt that I had slept with before—a patchwork quilt. But this one wasn't all mixed up—it had a rich and fanciful pattern. I asked my aunt how she had made it, and she said that she had bought it.

"That boy's a good rider," said my aunt, as she unpacked my few belongings, "but maybe that's a little too much horse for him, really . . ."

She sighed—"Well . . . maybe that's the way it is with the Clevelands—but I think he should be on a true pony yet, and further, I don't think it's right for a boy of ten to be racing around shooting at things. But . . . well, Alma, I don't profess to know everything—and maybe the boys who ride horses and shoot rifles are the boys that stay alive."

My aunt sat beside me on the bed, and pressed her fingers into the quilt, sliding the edge of it to just under my ribs. I lifted my arms for her, as it was an agreeable and comforting experience. Then she went around the bed, to do the same on the other side.

"We'll fatten you up," she said, "don't you worry."

"Are you seeing how skinny I am?"

"No," she said, "you silly child—I'm tucking you in."

"Oh really," I said, "is that what this is called?"

"Why yes," she said, and she looked at me surprised. Then she kissed me on the forehead, and said, "Why yes, that's what this is called."

Then my aunt left the room. She told me to snuff the rush light before I went to sleep. There was a candlesnuffer, and I did right away. I was feeling safe, all snug before the storm. The wind had started to blow, and the air was nippy, and I felt cozy in my quilt. Still, I could not sleep—

For I did not see that boy as a racing and shooting boy. I had seen him doing that, but I imagined him very differently. When I first saw him riding toward us, I saw him, not as he was then, but as he would be during the long summer days—riding through the bluegrass on a black horse. And those afternoons were not racing or shooting afternoons. They were floating afternoons—floating over the passing seconds of the day like a butterfly floating over sweet and shaking violets.

Perhaps it was that he had too much family, and I had too little— or that I had grown up wanting, and he, wanting nothing. But I don't believe it was so—I believe it was that when he saw me, and I saw him, our two souls lightened, and curled up together, rising on a furl as faint as his horse's breath. I believe that what I saw in him was his truest self, and that his truest self was also what I imagined—

Simply, I saw a boy on a black horse riding over the nervous sea of a green meadow.

That was the boy that I had met—the one who lived in a beautiful dream. And I knew that maybe he dreamt his gallant dreams, but mostly, he just sailed through the bluegrass on a quiet breeze. He had his horse and his future—and a long day in the pastures in between. . . .

Autumn '59

Hemlock

Maple

 OAK

Sassafrass

Tupelo
Tree

$\mathcal{I}$ had not expected that a house so large would be so warm.

It was a chilly Saturday in autumn, with winter fast approaching. My aunt and I set out in the late morning for the Cleveland estate, as Missus Doreen Cleveland was entertaining.

We were greeted by Pastor Miles, who was out on the lawn, tossing a stick for a white and brown haired collie. An intelligent dog, who knew friend from foe, the canine greeted us with paws out and tongue extended.

"This is Mack," said Pastor Miles, making the introduction, "the Clevelands' dog."

Shortly, Mack was licking at my hand—his fur was wavy, his ears floppy. Up close, he was ivoryish and reddish. He soon dropped onto his stomach, for a rest apparently, and Pastor Miles set to tussling with him a bit—tickling him just as if to enliven a child.

"On your previous visit, Mack was out with the horses," explained Pastor Miles. "His is a breed of shepherds, and he's a good worker out on the ranch—doesn't frighten horses by barking or creeping up on them. He's got a good manner—and with it, has gained the trust of the other animals."

Pastor Miles took the stick in his hand—"Today, however, Mack is unneeded by the men, and he's entertaining his guests."

With that, Pastor Miles handed me the stick, and I threw it, and Mack went after it—

"My," said Pastor Miles, "that's some throw."

"Isn't he," asked my aunt, "Bugby's dog?"

"That's right," said the pastor, looking out at the running dog, "at about eight years of age, Bugby had badly wanted a dog. His father was quick to provide every reason why a man should not take on an unnecessary burden, yet Bugby was obsessed—and his obsession grew contagious. So he and his mother attended a dog show in Frickerham—where they watched the father of Mack win a sheep-herding competition. There, they were informed that nearby, that dog had fathered a litter of puppies—still fresh on the nipples of their mother, who herself was a looker, and also a champion. The owner had not yet been willing to part with any of the pups, but, as he too was afflicted with Bugby's love for the dogs, the man gave Bugby the pick of the litter. The man said that love like that would give a dog a good life, and that the dog would return that love, and so the boy's life would be likewise improved—and who was he to say no to an im-provement like that?"

Mack returned panting, and my aunt took a turn at a tugging war with him over the stick—and then, having gained the slimy article, she tossed it out to the grass. . . .

"So, with his own hands," resumed Pastor Miles, "Bugby picked out that dog, right out of the litter—and even if Mack doesn't look it at the moment, now that Bugby's gone, Mack tends to desponding. Bugby's off at the South Carolina Military Academy, and that's why we have to keep old Mack entertaining us—because old Mack's the worse for it. Every guest that arrives, the poor dog runs right up to them as if to ask—Did you bring my boy, Bugby? And then he sort of slumps a minute, losing all his energy when he sees that whoever it is has not brought his boy."

Mack returned again, and Pastor Miles set to a vigorous massage of the animal, who just looked up guiltily—*My, this is a pleasure.*

"Such it is with Mack," said Pastor Miles—"He loves without ques-tion. And if Bugby were suddenly to reappear, Mack would not won-der where his master had been—instead, he would just love him all the more. But without Bugby, Mack just waits for Bugby, and without

Bugby, Mack can get more than a little lonely at times—and he can feel . . . well, forsaken."

Still, Mack was lucky to live with the Clevelands, as they led a full and bounteous life.

Despite the enormous grandeur of the house, every day brought unexpected visitors, who were gladly and graciously received. There was always something afoot at the Cleveland estate, whether it be formal dining, evening parties, riding frolics, or riding to hounds with squads of horses, hunters, hounds, horns and a few unlucky foxes, or badgers (though the huntsmen were always quick to say that no quarry had ever uttered a word of protest—and I must say that the Clevelands restrained their dogs from killing healthy animals). This day was an informal spend-the-day party, and it was the first event I was to attend. My aunt had dressed me in my new robin's egg blue dress, and we had hiked through the pine trees that morning. I was not of the social caste of the Clevelands, but I believe I was included because I was pretty—much as an inedible flower is included on a banquet table. My aunt was included because her quiet charm and lifetime of activity made her conversation much sought after in society. Despite a restrained and tasteful manner, there were times when she could not contain her own roaring laughter—and, as her humor could be epidemic and purifying, she had some notoriety in Cotterpin. Even silent, that laugh never left her eyes, or the corner of her lips. Though of an age when one would not expect or encourage suitors, being a widow, she had several. She was popular indeed among the more mature people of the community. Many of the town's families (the Clevelands included) owed their health to my Aunt Bettina and her good works as a root doctor. Besides that, the Clevelands were possessed of some rather new money, for though they had been breeding horses for several generations, it was only as a result of a series of winning race horses, and Mister Cleveland's apparent good hand at it (and his good hand at hiring men who had a good hand at it) that had improved the Clevelands' lot. And while there was a side of them that aspired to a higher kind of living, they were not yet likely to underestimate any of us little people. . . .

As it was still chilly toward noon, the party began indoors. We gathered near the fire to sample cheeses and dried figs from a lunch buffet. There were also beechnuts and wintergreen berries brought in—and they were quite delicious. The shells of the nuts had three ridges around them and the insides were rather meaty. The Clevelands had a silver nutcracker with a handle. The berries were sweet smelling and red. I nibbled the green leaves as well. After all that, a few of the children braved a croquet field set out in the yard, though most of us remained in the parlor to undertake two puzzles mixed together.

Shortly after lunch, a tension fell on the parlor discussions, and Serena, the cook, served a chamomile tea to the adults, which calmed them considerably.

My aunt said that Serena was a West African of Malinke descent—her parents had been interned on the same ship in 1805. A tobacco farmer from North Carolina bought all the children off that boat. In time, Serena was purchased as a mere girl herself. Though her age was not known, one could readily see that she was a good-looking woman, who seemed much more like her daughter's sister than her mother. She had exquisite, chiseled features, and was as strong a young woman as I had seen. It was clear that her daughter would be equally comely—though I had not seen, nor would I ever see, Natalie's father. He must have been a handsome man. . . .

Serena and Natalie enjoyed a favored position over the other slaves on the estate. Serena was the head of all housework and cooking, and as there were at least fifty people on the estate each day, and thirty or forty living there, it was no simple task. Quite an army was required to wait on the Clevelands, as none of them were capable of waiting on themselves. Serena was the all important care-keeper—she supervised almost everything that went on in the house. Ever demanding was her task of food preparation—three meals a day for everyone. And at the Clevelands', food was served hot—never was there a meal of cold gruel and cold tea. Even now, I can scarcely imagine how she managed. Besides daily preparations, near on every weekend there was a dinner party with a sumptuous outlay. I knew that Missus Doreen Cleveland and Miss Caroline Cleveland often helped with desserts and pastries, yet that seemed to me a small subsidy. As I remember it today, I am even more amazed by Serena's industry. . . .

Besides Natalie and Serena, who lived in the buggy house, the other slaves lived in the cabins on the far side of the west slope—just on the edge of the bluegrass pastures. Across from the cabins was the overseer's house. It was three rooms built of logs, and was rough but rugged. I believe the overseer at that time was a Dane named Ragan. I do not remember his family, or even if he had one. It was a position that was never stable, as in the estimation of the Clevelands, an overseer was liable to be too lax, or too severe. Besides that, to take the work was considered a slight on one's character, and the position was much despised. I do not believe an overseer was ever admitted to a party, while a great many of the slaves were in attendance, though of course, my aunt reminded me, they were laborers—

"And not for money."

I remember how her voice was low, but also angry. . . .

Toward midafternoon, John Warren performed some parlor tricks for us children. Even the bigger people were engaged, as he was prodigiously gifted with numbers. He could multiply or divide enormous figures without a moment's pause. If you told him your birthday, he could tell you what day of the week that had been. He seemed to bask in all the attention. But as he advanced in his antics, I began to develop the impression that his performance was for me. When he had risen from his seat, taking his place before his audience, he had been sure to offer me his chair. He'd held out his hand toward it with his palm uplifted, in an easy and chivalrous gesture. And while fixated by his (all too silly) numerological feats and tricks with playing cards, my mind fixed on the hope that he was equally captivated by me. I was sitting slightly behind and to the side of him, and with all the people in front of him, he was continually turning back—asking me to pick a card, or a number from one to ten. I heard one woman, a Missus Esterbrook, the doctor's wife, remark—

"Look at that dress on his little assistant. How adorable! And look at *her*! Just scrumptious! They make a lovely pair."

So, though much abashed by the conjecture, I could not enable myself to let a child's proper humbleness cloud the plain truth—while offering up his chair had seemed to be no more than the gentlemanly thing to do—and it had been that—it was also that John Warren might be assured of my uninhibited view of his ovation.

The stubborn fact was, without the slightest hint of imagination, that it was clear to him, and to me, and to everyone, that we were meant to be together. . . .

And I joined the clapping and chuckling with some clapping and laughter of my own, for I could see that this show of his was not only a presentation of himself to me, but me to his world, and his world to me. And we all got on simply grandly—except for my aunt, who looked a mite piqued in the corner. I went to her, and she told me that it was nothing to be concerned about—she just needed a little water.

Natalie overheard us, and brought out a glass. My aunt's expression was a queer one, and I believed it the surprise of the rapid attendance.

"That slave girl is a fine worker," I said, and my aunt interrupted—

"She is not a worker, as she receives no pay."

John Warren then joined us, having finished with his shaking-of-hands and exchanging-of-pleasantries. His mother had suggested he give a tour of the estate to us children. His invitation to me was a gallant one, preceded by a long and circular swing of the arm.

My aunt assured me that she would be fine when she drank her water, and led by John Warren, I was off with the other children. We rode in the back of a horse-cart, as John Warren pointed out the various animals in the grass, or their various doings on the courses. Sometimes we'd all climb out, for him to show us this or demonstrate that. Even at the reins on our rather undignified cart, he seemed to have no trouble handling a horse—and as he explained the labor of the estate, the business of horses seemed a tender and noble one. A rather informative outing, he instructed us in some of the cautions and cues that might ensure one's safety and enjoyment—

"First thing's to be aware. Next—to never sneak up on a horse. Give warning when you walk behind a horse—run a hand over its back and quarters. And don't tickle a horse—'cause they're ticklish! Always have an idea of what kind of a mood a horse is in—watch their eyes, ears and body, and listen to anything they might have to tell you. When a stallion calls out, that's because he's seen or heard strangers nearby—and that's something to pay some mind. At courting time, when a stallion makes its call—what a terror! That call can make a person pale with fear—and other stallions and grown men alike, I've seen 'em run from it."

Later in our expedition, rather incredibly, just before a cat shot out of the barn, John Warren noted the overall stiffness of the horse harnessed to our cart, saying—

"That means an animal is apprehensive about what's coming up—we'll likely hear her let out a couple of snorts."

And then, sure enough, she did let out a couple of snorts, and that cat scattered out of the barn, and we resumed our course, and John Warren resumed our extensive lesson. When we rode through the pastures, we saw a foal with its tail between its legs, and he explained the behavior.

"That tail means the same as for a dog—fear. It's walking up like that to that other horse because it thinks it's a stranger."

John Warren took a breath and remembered something else—

"*Unlike* a dog, a horse swishing its tail is not pleased, but displeased—and the closer that swish comes to a full circle, the more displeased that animal is. Bad form for show horses—only way we know to break the habit's to keep that horse pleased."

Then the child grimaced, as if he'd said something he disapproved of himself—

"Y'know," he apologized, slowing the cart, as we had by then come full circle around the house, and he meant to hitch up the horse-cart, "I hate the term *breaking*, and men who want to subdue a beast—or any such thing. A horse is not so much to be beat as just properly trained. With good hands and legs, a rider doesn't need whips or spurs. Whoa for stop, a cluck of the lips for go—a horse can hear just fine. No need to yell. Sometimes you might say no. Sometimes you might say yes. Sometimes you might give a friendly pat. As long as you give that horse as best you can, it'll give as best it can. My father says no man who's cruel to his animals deserves that animal—and the animal knows it, and so does God, and thus, no blessing will come that man's way. We just despise any man who kicks his horse—"

And it was just then as we were climbing the steps to the porch that we were joined by John Warren's father, Mister Cleveland, who took leave of several guests and advanced on us merrily—

"And John Warren," he said, having overheard his son, and now boasting proudly, "has very nearly the best hands around—he can handle a horse's reins with as light a touch as anyone," and though I could see that John Warren was gratified in hearing it, and tempted to agree, he became quite red over the whole matter. And his father seemed to take pride in even that—

"Let me add—he's not just sensitive with one hand, but ambidextrous."

Then Mister Cleveland took a moment to explain what it meant to have good hands—

"A horse's lips," said Mister Cleveland, "are rather sensitive, as they are used to gather grass—so good means light—hands that can command without causing pain with the bit. And John Warren's hands are so light that it's almost as if his horse can read his mind—the resistance of his hands against his horse's mouth is exactly equaled by the resistance of the horse's mouth. So, though my son's young, his hands are those of an old man—sensitive and wise. They're educated hands—and for that reason, we don't permit anyone else to ride John's horse, for fear the animal would be ruined. The pair of them work so well together, and are such a responsive and athletic team, that I would not allow anything to disturb that balance."

48

And then Mister Cleveland clapped his son on the shoulder and complimented him yet again, saying—

"And as everyone knows, one can't have good hands without a good seat."

Missus Cleveland then joined us and Mister Cleveland, perhaps in the hopes of returning her husband to the entertainment of his adult guests—though he seemed more at ease with the simplicity and lightheartedness of us children. She warned the boys among us that riding was dangerous, and that they should take care—

"And you girls," she said, "you can ride too." Though indeed, back then, a proper lady could not ride but sidesaddle.

Thereupon, the tour broke up and the children scattered—all but myself and John Warren, who was not so bold as I first imagined. As he accompanied me into the house, he credited his father for all he knew about horses, and his aunt, Caroline Cleveland, with having instructed him in all of the mathematical dexterity he'd demonstrated earlier in the parlor. With afternoon tea, he pointed her out to me— as we were made to drink our tea at a children's table. A great many people were gathered around her by the fire, and I saw that she had hardly a chance to sip the tea in her cup before it went cold. John Warren seemed much taken with her—

"She's a fine scholar," he observed.

After graduating high school at thirteen, Miss Cleveland had spent two years at Doctor Elliot's Academy in Nashville. Subsequently, she had taken employment as a bookkeeper for one of the largest plantations in all of the South—she'd had an office in a bank. Working as a bookkeeper and accountant, she'd then made her way through several bigger cities.

"'Bout two years of that," said John Warren, "she'd wearied of cities, and so, came on home. She knows almost as much about the farm as my father. Their father taught 'em both."

Caroline Cleveland was unmarried (though clearly of her own choice, as she was profoundly attractive, with a delicate frame, auburn hair and stunning aqua-colored eyes) and teaching school at the Cotterpin schoolhouse. Her years of city living had added a styl-ishness to her modest attire. And though the clothing she wore was nowhere near as ornate as the attire of Missus Doreen Cleveland, I do not think there is any doubt that she outshone her greatly. As well as mathematics, Miss Cleveland was well versed in literature, and from what we could overhear, she seemed a deft and sympathetic speaker on a number of popular issues.

"She is," boasted John Warren, with a love and loyalty for his aunt that was rather stirring, "a reader of three newspapers."

I was duly impressed by Miss Cleveland and her green dress. It made the prospect of school a rather exciting one, for if she was to be my teacher, I was sure to learn a great deal. . . .

As the day had warmed, after tea (and toast and berry jam—straw-berry, blackberry and raspberry) many of the boys went outside to play a game called Kill the Carrier. This was accomplished with a beanbag—and was self-explanatory. After that, as there were several courses set out in the grass, they had what they called a Boy's Horse Show. It was so funny to see the boys competing—running about the fields and jumping over the rails in such categories as, Hunters on the Outside Course, or Pair of Hacks. I'm afraid one of the boys in the Jumper Class bumped his head rather badly trying to clear a triple bar. They had so much energy! But even so, they eventually grew tired, and as the day's light grew cautious with evening, they went up to the roof to watch for the flag to lower at the post office. So when they came down, speaking of the event, we knew dinner was near. And shortly, we were alerted to the coming repast by a servant bear-ing a tray of doilies. My aunt told me that it was not considered fash-ionable that season to dine at a table—and we were soon presented with plates. A tray of buttered biscuits and chipped baby beef was served. Then came a tray of coffee, tea and liquor for the adults. To complete the meal, we were offered pumpkin tarts. We had been pro-vided dainty Chinese tables to aid us in our dining, but they were hardly faithful to their duty. My aunt and I shared one. The tabletops were enchanting—landscapes painted in a Chinese fashion—but the three legs were rather unstable. Some of the men were not so fortunate as to even have a rickety trivet table, and would nervously balance their teetering plates on their knees. But, as it was a casual type of formal party, this was not remarkable, and lent a whimsical air to the proceedings. . . .

The cook, Serena, had grown up in that very house with Caroline Cleveland and Somerton Cleveland, and thus, she took genuine pleasure in personally serving the Clevelands their meals. She would say that the Clevelands were her own white people, and she was ever diligent with their care. In some ways, it seemed to me, and to my Aunt Bettina, that the Clevelands had become so utterly dependent on Serena for their everyday needs, and her sage advice, that it was almost as if it were her estate, and they'd been reduced to her favored house pets, or plants. Serena's young Natalie was charged with informing the guests of the menu, and she took to it with apparent enthusiasm. With a friendly smile, she told us that sandwiches and punch would be served later that evening. My aunt said that we would be leaving before that, though she extended her gratitude to Natalie for her charm and hospitality.

After dessert, my aunt and I sat together, sipping our tea near the fireplace. On several occasions, we were interrupted when Mister Cleveland made his way to the mantel to show some guest or other John Warren's many riding trophies. Mister Cleveland was a proud father, as most of the trophies were silver and gold. But the trophy of the greatest stature, placed most prominently on the mantel, was made of pot metal. It was a monstrosity which made Mister Cleveland's pride seem almost comical. In all his great and tasteful home, what should occupy his mantelpiece but an ugly statue of a fat horse—made from pot metal!

Mister Cleveland had attended the Military Academy of West Point and he wished the same for his two sons—

"I always dreamt that John Warren and Bugby would also graduate from that, uh, establishment. But maybe all this, uh, turmoil will resolve itself, allowing Bugby to transfer prior to his graduation."

While my aunt was stuffing me into my heavy jacket (which she had made me wear for the morning and was now making me wear for the evening) she looked back at Mister Cleveland and whispered, with half amazement and half exasperation—

"The things that occupy that man. It seems to me that Mister Cleveland is a little . . . disconnected."

Even so, our relationship with the Clevelands was turning out to be a rather amenable one—and it was only shortly after the Clevelands' dinner that I was first summoned to come calling. Natalie was fleet of foot, and any message entrusted to her would surely travel swiftly. Her long legs carried her to our slumbering cottage just a few hours before dawn on Saturday. We heard her voice through the open window—

"Miss Flynt! Missus Evans!" she called out to us, not wanting to miss any of the event herself—

"One of the mares is birthing a foal!"

As my aunt and I both wanted to witness this arrival, we were soon out of our beds and nightgowns, into frocks and cloaks, and off with the quick girl. Along the path, Natalie told us that the newborn horse would be a brother to Pegasus, John Warren's horse. (Sad to say, the Clevelands would be forced to sell the foal before he was fully grown.) It was latish in the summer for such an event, as horses, like deer, were usually born with the new (best) grass, which came in May or June—but a stabled animal could give birth in all but the coldest of winter. In days prior to the foaling, the mare had been uneasy and cranky—pacing the stall restlessly, as if she were searching for a lost key! It was with her first contractions that she began to lie down and get up—her tail held high. And whenever she rose, she'd look back where she just was, as if her newborn might be there—and she'd just missed it. It was by these signs that the Clevelands had sent for us, and upon our admittance to the barn, the mare was already sweating and reclining—her attention fixed on the birth. Shortly thereafter, kind Doctor Esterbrook arrived to oversee the proceedings, in case of an emergency—though Mister Cleveland was an experienced horse deliverer himself, and hardly needed help. The doctor joined me, my aunt, John Warren, Miss Cleveland, and Natalie and Serena—we stood outside the stall, absolutely motionless, as to move or make noise might risk the mare interrupting the birth. Only Mister Cleveland and Mister Cleveland's man, Mister Valentine, were permitted in the stall—Mister Cleveland to help with the delivery, and Mister Valentine to hold the mare's head, to prevent her from standing up. With John Warren beside me, and the mare there in labor before me, my heart was excited from two sides—and it pumped almost as if I were a horse, huge and mighty. My body was near to bursting with the thunder of it. The birth was a miracle to watch—and the mare, she had wild, wild eyes. Her skin was so very red as Mister Cleveland pulled out the foal by the legs. It had been no more than half an hour—and the foal came into this world just before dawn. From the time of the birth, the mare allowed us people close to her newborn. I took my turn in the stall, as the new mother, now risen, softly nuzzled her foal. She nickered at him softly, using her lips to massage and dry him—and to remove the afterbirth. It was only a matter of minutes before the foal thought to stand, and as he struggled to his feet, we were all just about as anxious as the mare. First, he lifted his head from the side—then he rolled onto his stomach, extended his front legs, and . . . and . . . managed to raise his head and chest. Then up—onto his back legs—then a wobble, and he was standing! All along, the mare was helpless to do anything but nicker, nuzzle and encourage him. The sun outside was rising, and the pink light was coming in through the barn window. And the foal . . . I was able to see the sun rippling on the dark fur of that magnificent animal in that momentous time of life! Soon after, the foal began to nurse, and subsequently, wanted nothing more than to sleep. He was so very sleepy—but'd had such a go of getting up onto his feet that he was disinclined to give up that hard won circumstance. Still, he finally succumbed, as he was quite exhausted. He was surely precious, sleeping on his side—as foals do. And the nap seemed to do well by him, as by the end of the day, he could all but lope about, if not quite run. In days to come, I'd see him standing in the fields behind the front legs of his mother, peeking out at us and the world. For some time, she was nervous about this new appendage of hers, retreating fearfully, even angrily, from just about anything. But by the next week, she'd returned to her gentle self—and the foal was dashing around, bucking and kicking. A stud foal, he was soon to play with others—sparring, racing. Still, the mother and son rarely lost sight of each other—and when they did (as a result of a foal's frolicsome life or investigation of some curiosity) they'd fly hither and thither in a great display of desperation until they were reunited. Having a chance to watch the newborn over the next months, I saw that this particular foal developed a fondness for teasing his mother—ducking behind a fence, and not answering his mother's pleas. And . . . as one must always investigate a whinnying animal (to see who it might be calling out, and to be sure that nobody becomes overly distressed), we'd often arrive on the scene to see that mare whinny and neigh, and run about madly . . . until her foal just popped out, as if to say—

Ah, well, I was right here all along.

At six months, the foal was weaned—and to lessen the separation from his mother, he occupied his time with several like-aged cousins. I was invited to watch John Warren and his family work the weanling—who was just like a child, the way they handled him. In just a few days, he was quite tame. Even so, he had to be watched at every minute, especially when ropes were involved, lest he get himself seriously entangled. (The Clevelands often used string instead of rope, as it would break if the animal got into trouble.) Early on they were especially gentle—he was not really groomed, but just touched, that he might become accustomed to fingers.

And to watch those young horses eat—it was so comical!

As their legs were so long, they had to place their forelegs quite far apart to reach the ground with their mouth—and we'd all laugh at their plight! Well sir, ma'am, they'd seem to suggest rather seriously, if you think it's funny—why don't we just find my mother? It was on the very morning of the foal's birth that *I* first tried mare's milk—Missus Cleveland had glasses ready for my aunt and me, and told us that it was a great health-giving thing—and, she added, the best cure there was for consumption.

So . . . back on that autumn morning, I stood in my cloak, with John Warren beside me, holding my hand—which was perhaps not a normal thing, but a natural one, for the circumstance. . . . The horses throughout the estate were greatly agitated—though they were all back in their stalls, in their barns. Mister Cleveland said it was always better to have a foal born in a barn rather than out-of-doors, as the foal would be more tame. But, for the mare's anxiety, and for that of the other horses, she'd been given her own stall in her very own barn. Even so, from the little barn, which was just a few dozen yards away, we could hear friends and acquaintances whinnying away—Mister Cleveland's gray steed, which was a frighteningly large horse (German stock) and Bugby's calico, which was a lively horse with a good sense of humor (she'd nuzzle or lick just about anyone) and John Warren's horse, Pegasus. . . . My aunt said that animals understood such simple things as love, death and birth. She said they understood them just as well as we did, and maybe even better—

"Human beings," she said, "we think we're so special just because we can stand up and talk."

For all the time I spent at the Clevelands', there was no greater pleasure than being in the barn on that autumn dawn to watch that foal take its first shaky steps—to know that it would soon romp with the other thoroughbreds in the blue-green pastures of the farm. . . . But for all the magic of those instants, I could not—I could never stop myself from wondering at my own astonishment. *Why was I so enchanted?* And over the years, I've come to ask myself other questions. Why does a fisherman stop to watch a lady walk along the dock? Why does an old man feed his pigeons? Why do children lie on their stomachs to watch bugs crawl on blades of grass? Maybe, for some, it is just the moment, to possess an instant as it passes. But I also believe it is the coming of time. For the fisherman, it is the contemplation of a possible future, however remote, with that particular lady. For the old man, it is the surety that his pigeons will come again not only tomorrow, but the day after tomorrow. For the child, it is that the bug will continue to climb, to struggle forward in its objective, even after that child is no longer watching. And for me, and I believe, John Warren, it was to know that we would watch that horse grow, while we stood side by side on the solid ground of the Cleveland estate—with its sprawling white fences, and red and white barns. . . .

Velvet Ant

At the orphanage, the one game we were allowed to play on our own was marbles—and even so, there was only one game of marbles we were allowed to play, and that game was called Crosses. Perhaps it was permitted because it had a slight religious significance. A cross of marbles was arranged in a chalk circle on hard ground. The object was to shoot one's opponents out of the circle, and thereby lay claim to them—and this was called conversion. At the orphanage, with never a lack for opponents, and plenty of time for challenges (as a result of the sparsity of our lessons) I had acquired some skill as a knuckler. In Cotterpin, we played Manhunter. One hole set at each corner of a big rectangle, with a fifth hole set in the middle, the aim was to sink one's marble into each hole (while not being knocked away by an opponent) in a race to become the hunter, who was thus free to clash against any other marble, and pocket it. My marksmanship was deft, and with the few marbles that had been given to me by Sam Ditzler, I was amassing a vast supply. And that was at the expense of John Warren, who was no match for me—especially since he had inflamed my competitive spirit, in asserting that a *baby girl* would be no match for him. He lost good-humoredly however, collecting pointers, then renewing himself to the challenge. And that was inevitably to my benefit.

Often, the stakes could be large, as there might be six or seven of us at a game. The favored marbles (for weight and appearance) had traded hands so many times they seemed to have been owned by virtually every child in the province. They might disappear for weeks at a time, and then return to our circle. Some even disappeared for months, and then returned. Often we'd wonder how far those marbles had gone. It was thinkable that, hand to hand, there were marbles that made their way across all of America, and maybe even into Canada. And maybe even back, all the way to Cotterpin Creek Kentucky.

But because John Warren and I were neighbors, it would often be just the two of us, honing our skills, playing in front of the big rock across the creek from my aunt's cottage. I think it might have been there because of the several good flat areas to play upon, as well as the fact that I had so many marbles. As local champion, I was expected to entertain challenges—and to be a courteous host to prospective opponents. My aunt and I made much iced tea, and a few batches of cookies. Luckily, we had two mulberry trees nearby, as well as a thicket of raspberries and blackberries—so there was much I could offer without troubling my dear Aunt Bettina.

I remember watching John Warren pull down a branch with his lengthening arms. He'd take a fistful of the berries, and while the other children went on gathering their own purple handfuls, John Warren would pinch a mulberry between his lips, and I would pinch one between mine, and at the same time, we would squeeze our lips, and tilt our heads back—the juice running against our tongues, and down our chins.

And the other children would say, "Look at them! Look at them," and tease us for being in love.

Through the autumn of '59, I was not yet attending school, so our games would commence after the other children had finished their classes, and after I had finished helping my aunt gather green things from the woods. And we played without disturbance until one

Sunday at church, a Missus Wigfall, visiting from Frickerham, suggested the game was tantamount to gambling, and stated that her parish had rid itself of the sinful practice. The morality of the children, she said, was at stake, and they should not be forming relationships, which might influence their whole lives, upon such faulty and dissolute foundations. But before Missus Wigfall had a chance to finish, or the pastor had a chance to respond, Mister Nielson called out. It was not polite to call out, or to interrupt when people were making announcements or discussing community things, but Mister Nielson was not a talkative man, and he was old enough to sometimes do rude things without having people judge him for it. His temper had been tested for so many years, and he was so generally right and wise in all things, that when he fell victim to a moment of anger, it was a sign, generally, that whatever he was excited about was far more amiss than his gruff common sense.

He didn't even stand up. He just said, loudly, as he was a little deaf—

"You let those kids and their marbles alone."

Then he spoke to his wife Marie. But his voice was so loud that the whole congregation heard what he said—

"Marie, they're young and like those marbles. They're allowed to like those marbles. They're allowed to amuse themselves. Why can't old people leave young people alone? Why do they always want to take the youth out of the young? They were young once. They know what it's like to play marbles. A sin? Ungpf."

Marie Nielson grabbed his hand, smiled broadly and shushed him, and he grumbled and adjusted himself in his seat. He knew he was loud sometimes—

"Excuse me," he said, "Missus Wigfall—Pastor Miles."

But Mister Nielson had made his point, and in Cotterpin, there was no more talk of ending marbles.

※ ※ ※

Spicebush
Swallowtail

Most children did not begin school until it was decided they could safely make their way to the schoolhouse. I stayed home that autumn, as everyone had agreed that it would be best if I was to get my bearings in my household and in the community before I began my classes. I believe it was thought that the adjustment from the orphanage would be a hard one—though in fact, the orphanage was an emptiness in my life, and it was quick to fill with this new life. Miss Cleveland provided some scholastic guidance to my aunt, who began my education at home—so that I might join my classes with some confidence. As I took to my lessons quickly, and grew an entire inch in just three months (the result of better nourishment) it was resolved that I should begin the winter term.

John Warren was charged with accompanying me on the walk to and from the schoolhouse, and while I was quite frightened the morning of the first day, I already knew many of the children, through marbles, and I was made welcome. It was almost as if, said Miss Cleveland and her pupils, I had always been there. . . .

Miss Cleveland herself was an excellent teacher, and as long as she was teaching my lessons, I knew I would have no trouble giving the proper time to my studies.

Still, there were times when I sat on my bench, looking down at my section of the writing tablet, which was a long panel of wood attached to the back of the bench ahead—and I studied it, carved as it was with a thousand names and messages. And sometimes I looked out the window, or at the shingles of the ceiling, or back to John Warren, where the older children sat behind their desks. I'd look anywhere but at my reader or slate, and think about what I might do during recess, or after school. There were outdoor games like jump rope, and Blindman's Bluff, Bull-in-the-Pen, or stilt-walking—or chase games like Hickeme Dickeme. There was a rather brutal game called Hot Cock, which was played only by the older boys. In that game, one boy would stand blindfolded and receive blows until he guessed which of his fellows had delivered which punch or kick. We younger girls played Hopscotch. The ball games were Tip-cat and handball, which we called Fives. Girls didn't play ball as much as boys, but I was often at it, for though I was no tomboy, I was quite capable with a ball, and often invited to join a game—to even the sides. Everyone had slingshots, even if the girls hid theirs. Many of the boys had bows—and there were some contests at it, as well as shooting contests with rifles. And for the cold, there were indoor games—my aunt had given me a doll with joints and strings attached, so that it might seem to walk freely. It was called a limber Jack, though Miss Cleveland called it a marionette. We all had whimmy-diddle sticks, which one spun into the air by rubbing them from betwixt one's two hands. And we girls had dollhouses, with figurines and miniature furniture, many of which were fashioned by whittling fathers or uncles. (A doll's outfits were made of paper or corn husks.) In those days, many toys were homemade, like poppets of buckeye wood with heads of dried apples. For the classroom, Miss Cleveland had a painted board and pieces for checks. . . .

Remembering those toys now, of more or less amusement, I think of them with a great nostalgia, for children's games change so quickly that they are forgotten within the span of one's own life. And I remember, even then, there were afternoons when I longed for those toys in almost the same way I do today. And yet I also remember looking out the window, to see that kind of white light that said snow. And so came that rarest pleasure, true then and true now, and true for all children—snow.

The winter gave us snow. . . .

It was late in February when I saw my first fat flakes billow in the soft wind. I had seen snow before, but this was my first storm—a friendly blizzard that decimated our humble marble course, leaving us with nothing to do but stare out of windows, and wait for the word from our guardians that might set us out in our galoshes. And when the storm lifted, and left a good deal of clean snow on the ground, we made good use of it—with snowmen (and women) and snowball battles. John Warren and I even constructed an Eskimo igloo with cubes of snow packed from a flower box. It was rather small and delicate— really just a fort. The site was our former marble course—by the bend of Cotterpin Creek, in the shelter of the big rock. It was there that when we were looking at our own freezing breath, we accidentally kissed. We had caught each other's eyes, and leaned toward each other, quite unintentionally. Our lips lingered there, not quite touching, but hot and damp with each other's breath. . . .

And then there was his voice, as soft as the whisper of the soul itself—

"Eskimos touch noses."

"And so," I said, "do wolves."

"It is like a wolves' den," he said.

And I said, "It is."

"But . . . under a meadow of violets," he said.

And I said, "Yes."

And then our lips hovered together—like two butterflies in that meadow, like two butterflies in darkness, faintly caressing each other with a flurry of beating wings. And our breath intermingled—and then our lips met, as delicately as the wings of butterflies in violets.

Like the snowstorm, it was my first kiss, and years later, I would learn that it was also his. It was giggling and innocent, and he said—

"It's dark in here."

"Yes," I said, "it is nice."

"Yes," he said.

And . . . just as no butterfly might be touched, it was not a moment we might discuss—for just as the tiny feathers of a butterfly's wings might be damaged by even the softest brush of a finger, so might a tender kiss be damaged by a word. I have often heard people speak of true love, but for me, it was more of a sense of what was right, like the right amount of cinnamon, or the right amount of wine. And as far as other things I have heard, to say that I was his is not at all a phrase I find accurate, though I might say that I was devoted to him.

And I did not know if I would be with John Warren when we were twelve and fifteen, or fifty-four and fifty-seven, but I knew that I should be. Of course, I knew nothing of the great changes, and the lifetime of rebuilding that our world was soon to undergo. Perhaps I might have seen it in his clothing—in his copper-toed, buckle boots and side-buttoned pants, in his cobalt-colored gloves and maroon hunting hat. But I was merely a girl of almost eight, and he a boy of just eleven, and I knew nothing of our modest love being hopelessly interwoven in events of national consequence. Who could know that the fate of our tender kisses would be a question that tore through the American heart?

"It was so easy," he said.

And I said, "Yes, it really was rather easy, wasn't it?"

"Yes, remarkably easy."

So we had kissed. . . .

But children are like flowers—they are drawn to sunlight. Whatever momentous things they accept, they flee into life—and thus, we laughed. And suddenly tired of kisses, we darted out into the sunlight of that cool day.

And that was the winter and the spring. And the summer, the autumn—and then, the winter again. And being together, in good weather and bad, by ponds and at dining tables, I'd sometimes watch John Warren. I would stare at him, transfixed by his gestures. He would sweep back his hair. He would squint his eyes. He would bite his lower lip, and catch his inner cheeks in his teeth, and hold them there while he was thinking. . . .

Come January '61, there was another blizzard—with fluffy snowflakes and a middling breeze. And as John Warren and I would not let the storm go unseized, we were soon and often out sledding on the slope on the far side of the Cleveland estate. Sometimes we'd take a mule and make our way out to the south hill—to sled there. The hill was almost a small mountain, and therefore, a rather demanding climb—especially while pulling a sled. That's why we usually sledded down the west slope, which was not so tiring, and moreover, not so out of control—as it was rather hard to slow down on a sled, especially when the hill was so high.

I remember one day in particular, a day when we did make the trip out to the almost mountain, a day that was not so fun and free-spirited as usual—

Mister Cleveland and Bugby had made a point of coming out with us on that day—and as John Warren and I did not usually plan things so far in advance, perhaps that was the first thing to detract from the spontaneity of that particular Saturday. That sledding Saturday . . .

Serious, even sullen, John Warren did not seem to enjoy himself at all. He was *trying* to please his older brother and father. But Mister Cleveland said, "Do not try to please us, boy, this is your day. We are here for you, to be with you, on days that you are happy. If you want to make me happy, m'boy, take this happy day from your old papa."

And though John Warren wanted nothing more than to do just that, he was too much distracted. There was a pall over him, while his father and brother were more chipper than I had ever seen them. They were happy the way children are sometimes happy when they are caught at mischief—and have accepted their punishment.

I remember watching them as they stood atop the hill, overlooking the countryside while John Warren and I climbed up toward them—dragging our sleds behind us. We were moving rather slowly, not only for fatigue, but for fear of sledding down that hill again—it was really too big a hill for children our age, and though the actual peril may have been minimal, the perceived peril was great. We'd never have admitted it, but at the end of each descent, we felt lucky to still be alive.

So, slogging through the snow, condemned to a fib of fun, we saw John Warren's brother and father up ahead on the summit. They were standing proudly—maybe even foolishly. And as we approached, I could just hear that Mister Cleveland was saying that there would be no picnic again this year—

"Last autumn just wasn't the same without it."

All bound up in my warm clothing, I turned inward, and took to thinking to myself. For I could see that my aunt was right—that the father and son were proud, and foolish. And yet, as she had also said, I could see too that it was they who were right—that this was as much their country as anyone else's. Mister Cleveland spoke of the Southern man as a soldier man, and of the French as allies, and of one thing and the other. . . . But even as I heard him speak, his reasons and rationales were overpowered by the words of his sister, Miss Cleveland, my teacher, who had said to me—

"My brother knows nothing of warfare, just cockfighting."

I do know that Mister Cleveland was a dreamy man—one who would sit on the hillside, stroking his beard as he had since he was fourteen years old, and puffing his cigar. Still, his whole family looked to him for morality and strength. And what they saw was a man kind in manner, who, wearing a white suit, was sitting on the wet grass. But his voice was inhabited with the authority of God and country. And with grass stains and all, he could reach inside himself and produce something of great authority—even if it did seem a little bombastic. I distinctly remember that way Mister Cleveland had of speaking—and as he stood there on the hill, his son Bugby went on nodding knowingly, and looking up with believing eyes as his father said, "Now, General Taylor, he was a fighting man—to see how we routed the spigs at Buena Vista! Now, son, you'll see your glory too."

And I did not say anything—I did not run to them, and I did not whisper to John Warren that his aunt had told me, yes, Mister Cleveland had been in the Mexican War, though he'd been no more than a cartographer.

Mister Cleveland drew on his cigar—

"Some people say that everything needs to be risked—that a man may protect his way of life."

And though I said nothing, I did continue to think to myself, dwelling considerably on that rather similar thing Miss Cleveland had said to me—

"Sometimes all must be lost, before it can begin anew."

Miss Cleveland had always been dedicated to the betterment of the lives of orphans and widows, and when Mister Cleveland refused his annual aid on account of the institution's steward, Johann Steward, who had, of late, become vocal in his Quaker politics, she became rather enraged. And I remember, after school, Miss Cleveland read me a passage from Exodus, 22:22. Her voice was unsteady, as were her hands. Her eyes were wet—but she was strong, and she would wipe them dry before the tears fell—

> *Ye shall not afflict any widow, or fatherless child. If thou afflict them in any wise, and they cry at all unto me, I will surely hear their cry; and my wrath shall wax hot, and I will kill you with the sword; and your wives shall be widows, and your children fatherless.*

And after Miss Cleveland read me the words, and I turned back to the schoolhouse door, I saw John Warren standing there, blushing, and burning with anger. . . .

But John Warren was a well-behaved boy, as far as his Aunt Caroline was concerned, and he just looked down confusedly. And a little sadly, he said—

"Mother sent me with Florida."

Florida was Miss Cleveland's horse, a fine white mare dappled with iron gray spots the size of silver dollars. I could see the mare out the window—she also had an iron gray mane, and ears, and tail, and feet.

John Warren pushed his foot in a circle on the wood planking, saying to Miss Cleveland—

"Ma thought you looked sleepy this morning."

TROT

Into spring, John Warren and I dedicated much energy to constructing figurines of people and horses and cannons—from a shelf of clay in the creek bank. But our pastimes were soon interrupted, as John Warren was needed at his family's estate. I would often accompany him, and sit with Miss Cleveland on the porch, or stand with a horse who was nipping at the bushes on the other side of a fence—or sometimes even help with this task or that. Of course, I could not spend all my time with John Warren. Yet even when we were not together, sometimes I would feel that really we were together, or that we should be together, and I would climb up the side of the big rock—and from there, watch him and his.

Among Mister Cleveland and the men, John Warren would be out in the grass working the animals—whether jumps, or tricks, or different speeds and gaits. All with ease and grace.

The colts, they'd run tracks—skip logs laid pell-mell, logs in rows, logs half up/half down, half down/half up—then, logs half raised that crossed. Then X's crossing over the ground. And then—those colts would jump. And high jumps—and long ones.

And, rather delightfully, because horses were herd animals, and trained together, they'd often be asked to follow the good example of Pegasus and John Warren. . . .

It was as I sat on the porch one day, looking out onto that field of buttercups, violets, thimbleweed and star flowers, that Miss Cleveland said her brother trained horses in groups to imitate the circumstances of the battlefield, or more accurately—the circumstance of the foxhunting field. And truly, it really did resemble that more than anything—though Mister Cleveland believed foxhunting horses and battlefield horses were the same thing. Animals were instructed to wait their turn, to not get too close, to not fall too far off, to set an even pace, to switch off positions and to never panic—even in rather muddled circumstances, and at a gallop!

And those patterns they ran—they were just so mesmerizing and dreamy!

66

Circles, teardrops, figure eights, wiggly lines and serpentines which zig-zagged between fences. Every afternoon, it was the sure step and the fast step. I never tired of watching the chalk lines wear into worn paths, and the worn paths wear into muddy ruts—whereupon fresh chalk lines were laid on fresh ground. And for all that Miss Cleveland said about Mister Cleveland and cockfighting, it seemed to me that Mister Cleveland did know *something* about horses, and I felt rather lucky to witness the training of his son, John Warren, in what had been his own father's trade. . . .

It was not long after, that Miss Cleveland left the Cleveland estate to live on her own. Mister Cooper from the general store had rooms to let, and as Miss Cleveland was wanting more time to pursue her readings and studies, it had been decided that she would take them. Thus, Mister Cleveland would come up to the porch sometimes, and lean over the railings and talk to me. If I wasn't out with John Warren in the fields, I'd be there alone, as all but me were busy with the work of the estate.

And Mister Cleveland would say—

"Imagine being a horse—and let's say a horse some call chicken-hearted. Now—is it chicken-hearted? Or does he spook at jumps because his rider yanks his mouth? Might he be spoiled by an indulgent rider? Might the fence be too high? Might that horse be unfit? Or cold? Or hungry? Or with a stomach full of worms? Or slow to jump because of weak hocks? Or light-boned—and suffering from overtraining? Might he buck because his rider hurts his back? Might he be too young? Or too old? Is he tired? Or bored? Might he be an exceptional horse—but brought along too fast? Might he tuck his chin because his rider never releases his mouth—is that why he rushes the fence? Might he jump too early because it's his rider who's young and impatient? Might that rider expect too much?"

Mister Cleveland believed that horses, herders, had shy and fragile temperaments. Docile animals, as they were made so by man, they allowed themselves to be ridden—though by natural instinct, their inclination must have been to kill any man on their back. But they didn't, even if they couldn't quite understand why. To Mister Cleveland's way of thinking, a horse might wonder—

Why has this creature climbed on top of me? Why go this way rather than that? Why can't I be free—run with my friends? Why live inside? And when I do go out, why does this man restrain me? And where's the herd? And why perform all these stupid tricks? And why do men hurt me? And why does one man know what to do, while another does not? And why do I understand some men, and not others? And why are some of them heavy, some light? And all this jumping—it's so risky! And . . . why torment me?

You had to treat a horse well, Mister Cleveland would say, not only because horses were timid and sensitive, but because they remembered just about everything that ever happened to them. And if there was something one didn't like (whether that be harm or just a kerchief blowing in the wind) neither would any of the other horses around that horse. One nervous horse could infect another, and so it was with every horse's mischief. The way a horse thought, if one feared the kerchief—why then, there must be something wrong with it! Horses liked things regular and in their place—stalls, routines. No surprises. Handled just the slightest bit differently, a horse might snort as if to say—Sir! Not like that, sir! Mister Cleveland said that the memory of a wild horse served it for food, drink and protection— and that's why a horse's memory was so good. It really was quite amazing the way lost horses found their way home. And even when they didn't, it wasn't because they didn't know the way, but because they were out on a frolic with their friends.

"Horses," said Mister Cleveland, "aren't predators, but prey. And chasing a fox is less in their temperament than fleeing like a fox. Some say a horse is a dumb animal—as a horse, unlike any dog or pig or goat, it'll lack the sense to run from a burning stable. And it's a fact that while some horses might figure to unlatch their stall, most will gaze out longingly upon the field. But horses—even if they're not smart about being pigs or goats or people, they are smart about being horses. Only two things to being a horse. One's good food and water, and the other's good company. In nature, that's all there is to a horse's life—roaming together in search of food and water. So, to think like a horse, a horse well stabled, with good friends and good care—why bother going anywhere?"

They were just like us, horses—good, bad, joyous, despondent. Pegasus, he would rub his head up against John Warren—near every time he saw him. And Bugby's calico—she was so playful! She'd nip at a person's bottom for fun—and then jump back teasingly when that person turned in blushing surprise. She'd pick up the currycomb and toss it about, and she'd always make a person feel accepted—as if, to her, you were just another horse! All ages of horses would play like foals—teasing one another like children at tag. I remember an afternoon when Bugby's calico occupied herself for hours, toying with a piece of rope—

"There," said Mister Cleveland, leaning over the porch railing, smoking his cigar and sipping his coffee, "there you see a horse's natural disposition. And if you can sustain that purity of heart—if a rider can convince a horse that he means it no harm, then that horse will do no harm to that rider. And that's fair not only to a man's way of thinking, but to a horse's way of thinking."

Southern Red Lily

It was on my ninth birthday that the Clevelands surprised me in their parlor. Mister Valentine, his wife and their son Harmon were there, as were Mister and Missus Cleveland—and Serena and Natalie. And John Warren, of course. It was a time of some shortages, and thus, I was already rather pleased with the fabric I had picked out with my aunt. And I expected no more birthday gifts, as a new-made dress was quite extravagant. I had chosen the pattern with Missus Valentine, who was fashioning the dress in trade for my aunt's treatment of Mister Valentine's bad leg. (It hurt him in some weather.) I had managed a covetous peek into Missus Valentine's fine chest of buttons, but it had been decided that I would use the old wood buttons off my old dress, as it would be more sensible.

Thus, I was indeed surprised when Missus Valentine produced her rather extraordinary trunk of buttons—that I might choose among them for my new dress. There were buttons of blue and red and every other color—and silver and gold too. And there were raised castle-tops and blooming flowers, and buttons of leaves and sleeping fairies. And there were buttons shaped like tiny whales, made of whalebone, and buttons of stone, and brass, and shell. And that's what I chose—some nice orange buttons made of seashell. They would be so pretty on my new summer dress—white and orange. And I said—

"Why, my aunt knew!"

And Mister Valentine said, "Why, of course she did, Alma. She wouldn't let you go around anymore with those old wood buttons."

Then the Clevelands presented me with a cherry wood box of Indian beads—enough for several strings.

"They were carved out West," said John Warren.

Missus Cleveland smiled. "John picked them out, Alma."

The beads were of all shapes and sizes and colors, and felt so precious in my pink hands. Some were made of buffalo bone. And though I never did make bead strings of them, I liked them so much on their own, to handle them and consider them and show them, that I have them still—to this very day.

I thanked John Warren breathlessly, and his mother and father for all the fuss, and it was such a nice way to see their family that I couldn't help but feel a little sad that Caroline Cleveland wasn't there.

"Why," asked Missus Cleveland, "what's wrong, Alma?"

I was afraid to say anything. And Mister Cleveland said morosely—"It's my sister." Then he turned toward the window.

And then, John Warren, half laughing, half bursting with laughter—just so full of joy—he said that Miss Cleveland would never forget me, and that she would be moving back onto the estate, and she had a birthday present for me—and he looked back to his father. . . .

And then Mister Cleveland turned back from the window with a box in his hand, and he was smiling broadly, and his wife said—

"Oh Somerton, you shouldn't tease a child like that."

And he looked like he wasn't really ashamed of himself, but that maybe he should be, and he opened the box and showed me the most wonderful candies I had ever seen. I could hardly believe they were for me, and was quite afraid to touch them. There were sticks of striped candy in purple and yellow, and orange and green. And there were pieces tied like tiny bows of ribbon. And there were even some shaped after flowers. And they were all so shiny! I could hardly take my eyes off them.

Missus Cleveland looked at me with her big puffed and pink face, and she said in her jolly way—

"Your aunt doesn't like white sugar too much, but I do. Do you?"

"Yes," I said, looking down and feeling rather guilty about it. "I do too, sometimes."

"Well," said Missus Cleveland triumphantly, "I talked to your aunt, and she said a little sugar now and then wouldn't hurt a child."

And then we all shared the candy, and though I would usually be rather meticulous about taking only a lick now and then, and would thus preserve my candy for weeks and even months, this time I munched the candy with full abandon—as we all did. We munched until our heads were swimming with delight, and on that particular day, I wanted nothing more than to eat it all up—and we almost did too! All but for a few candy sticks which I saw Missus Valentine quietly slip into my satchel. She winked at me when I saw her at it.

For a treat, Serena and Natalie prepared us popped corn in bowls of milk and honey. It was all so wonderful that I began to feel rather faint with happiness—unless my aunt was right and it really was the sugar. . . .

Sometime after dark, it was finally decided that John Warren should walk me home. And as John Warren and I stepped onto the front porch, I asked if it was really true about Miss Cleveland returning to the estate.

"Pa says she will," said John Warren, and he shrugged optimistically—

"I think she will."

Of course, she never did.

We walked a bit, then he stopped and said—

"The horses."

And when I listened too, I heard them astir, and complaining some. Horses could hear, and smell for that matter, so much better than people that it was always prudent to heed their notions. If a horse spooked at an offensive odor, one might expect something— well, offensive. And there was *something* in the air. So we decided to check on the agitated animals. . . .

The stables were built on a slight elevation, for drainage. They faced south for sun, and protection from wind. The construction was a hearty one. Tying rings were fitted to the wall—and the floors were made of flat stones and hard-packed clay, and were always kept dry, for a horse's feet were vulnerable to thrush. The horses, they stood in their stalls—the boxes faced inward, and though horses so situated might sometimes become restless, it was warmer and drier that way. Moreover, the Cleveland horses were always well exercised, and many had windows onto the pastures—wooden slatted for safety and closed tight in cold weather. There were two latches on each horse's door, one high and one low, as the occasional horse understood the mechanism, and would undo the high latch with its mouth—and a horse loose would get into all kinds of molasses! But none were loose. So, as horses had their individual problems we looked in on each individually. John Warren said it might be just one animal that had all the rest out of sorts, and that while misbehavior might cause an occasional stern word or smack on the rump, mostly, understanding was best—to figure out the why of an animal's vices. And, he said, since most every vice could be catching, a handler had to take care not to expose any horse to another's bad habits.

So John Warren went about his task, adding, "Even Pegasus had a problem once. Kicking. Broke my heart to see him with one leg tied up—to see that friend so hobbled. But—cured the malady."

Still . . . in the little stables, everything seemed right enough, and as John Warren looked in on the last horse, I pushed back at the stable door. It opened, then held on something soft—and I peered out and saw it was Mack. Mack the dog. I called to John Warren—

"Mack is blocking the door."

"Oh really?" said John Warren. . . .

"Well—push him out of the way."

And so I did. I placed my hand firmly on that hairy rump and gave a shove—

"Eww Mack," I said, as I pulled back my hand, and sniffed at it from a bit of a distance—

"You're a little mangy."

Mack hadn't moved quite far enough, so I sighed, put one hand on my hip, and the other on the stern of his old body, and gave him another push—this one harder. He gave a short whelp, and turned and smelled my hand himself, and then padded back. . . .

I opened the door, and walked out into the dark night, my eyes now adjusting to it—and then I heard a barking from the house—from way back in the kitchen. It was Mack. John Warren heard it too, and he cried out—

"No, no—don't open that door!"

But I already had—

And there John Warren saw me in the moonlight, through the open door—so far away, and surrounded by three animals, and none of them Mack.

There were not many wolves about—but with all the confusion in our part of the world, that's what those three animals were. Three wolves on the stud farm. Three wolves surrounding one little girl. And these were three hungry, snarling, dribbling wolves. And they were all staring at me. John Warren yelled and banged the wall with his hand. But the wolves ignored him, and one of them tentatively approached me, and nipped at my dress. I pushed down my dress with my two hands and the wolf lost its grip. And then John Warren banged and yelled louder. But the wolf grabbed at my dress again—pulling on it—pulling me toward him. And then I started to scream—and John Warren ran at us. . . .

And I was all eyes as John Warren took the pitchfork, and maybe I should have told him to save himself, but I didn't. I just stood stiff—as rigid as if I were without blood in my body.

And just as that second wolf was jumping at me, John Warren hit it with the pitchfork—and he stabbed it deep. And the pitchfork sank into that animal's side and it stayed there—the handle waving and pointing right up into the air as the wolf curled up gasping on its side.

Then the other wolf let me go, and he went at John Warren, and John Warren kicked at it under the chin with his copper-toed boots—and that beast flipped end over end onto its back! But then the other wolf jumped at John Warren, and John Warren fell. And the wolf was about to bite John Warren on the face. But John Warren had his hands yoked around the wolf's neck, and he pulled back one hand, and he punched that wolf just in the snout, and that brute pulled away. But then the kicked wolf came back at John Warren, and the two wolves descended on him. And there were all jaws snapping and hands flailing for an instant—and I felt my own mouth open. And I heard my own voice. . . .

And then I heard a gunshot. And the wolves' voices, and my own voice—they were all gone. And for just a moment, all was silent. . . .

I turned to see Mister Valentine lower his rifle. He stood just outside the kitchen—he must've grabbed the gun from its place on pegs above that doorway. It was always kept there loaded, as in those days, even civilized people like the Clevelands kept a loaded gun over the kitchen door. And it was a good thing too! He'd blown that wolf clean off John Warren's chest—and in a fit of dust, it had rolled twice, then howled pathetically, and tried to get up once, twice, three times before it gave up and lay panting and crying. The other wolf had run off, and the one with the pitchfork in it soon joined in the retreat. He'd risen and shook, but the pitchfork was fixed in the muscle under his hip, and he ran off with that pitchfork still in him.

Mack had already started out from the kitchen, and fighting mad, he went after the wounded animal. And when that wolf got himself caught up on the water pump, with his pitchfork and all, it was clear indeed that Mack would catch him—so that wolf turned as best he could, and for all his troubles, he let out a snarl that was fearsome and toothy indeed. . . .

John Warren sat up and cupped his hands on either side of his mouth to direct his own voice as he yelled—

"Don't Mack—don't!"

But Mack did. And John Warren needn't have worried, as for such a little dog, Mack made short work of that wolf, even if it was injured. I thought I'd never seen anything so brutal in all my life—the way Mack just hurled himself right onto that wolf's back. And then he bit that wolf on the neck and he rode him, and I'd swear it was so—just like a man on a horse. And finally, that wolf was all kind of bled out, and he fell, and Mack fell on top of him. And then Mack began to chew at the underside of that wolf's throat, to finish the job—until old Mister Valentine had finally hobbled over and nudged Mack away, and told him to sit. (And Mack did too!) And then Mister Valentine used the rifle to put that wild animal out of its misery.

And it was just about then we noticed John Warren was bleeding. He was all but covered in blood, from the chin down. And when poor Missus Cleveland finally came out of the house to see the two dead wolves and Mack and her son so darkened by blood, she let out the most pathetic mewl, and she grabbed at her mouth with her hand—and passed out.

Of course, it would turn out that John Warren had no more than a cut on his lip—just a little V. A scar he would always have . . .

And it was rather a thrill to be on John Warren's arm, as he helped me down the few steps of our country church—just as if we were all grown up! And then we would listen to the people wonder at us—

"Good Lord boy, heard you pulled *her* from a pack of wild wolves."

And my shining knight would say—

"It was only three wolves."

And so . . . I'd sit across from John Warren in school, secretly passing the occasional note (as if Miss Cleveland didn't know all about it). And my afternoons I'd spend with John Warren at the stud farm—or I'd watch him from the big rock, or just think about him.

And Sunday afternoons I'd spend without him.

And how slow those Sundays passed! No work at all was permitted on Sundays, nor was running or noisy play—and the very most I might be allowed was to play with my doll. My aunt spent the day in quiet contemplation, mostly reading the bible. She would read me the stories too—and sometimes stories from magazines or books that had been published back East, though it was not the same somehow as being outside, and secretly, I was not as appreciative as I probably should have been.

But after those ever so slow Sundays came the week—spent at school, and with John Warren and his horses. Sometimes he would come out to my aunt's cottage, and we would help her with the gathering, or the heavier work in the garden. . . .

And then would come Sunday morning, and John Warren and I would sit beside each other at our little church, and I would hear his voice singing—and over his voice, I would hear my own. I remember so well that thickness in my throat and belly—to hear such strong emotions let loose. The hymns we sang were many, but one impressed me rather deeply. So very deeply that even today I can hear the vibrant and rich voice of Mister Nielson, and the sonorous, charitable voice of his wife, and the honeyed voice of Pastor Miles, and the angels' voices of all us children—and the husky, wise and woeful voice of my own Aunt Bettina—

> Rock of ages, cleft for me, let me hide myself in Thee;
> Not the labors of my hands can fulfill the law's demands;
> Nothing in my hands can bring, simply to Thy cross I cling;
> While I draw this fleeting breath, when my eyelids close in death,

Let the water and the blood, from Thy side, a healing flood,
Could my zeal no respite know, could my tears forever flow,
Naked come to Thee for dress; helpless, look to Thee for grace;
When I rise to worlds unknown, see Thee on Thy judgment throne,

Be of sin the double cure, save from wrath and make me pure.
All for sin could not atone; Thou must save, and Thou alone.
Vile, I to the fountain fly. Wash me, Saviour, or I die.
Rock of ages, cleft for me, let me hide myself in Thee.

And though it wasn't necessarily the right thing, when I sang "Rock of Ages," and heard that song, I could not but help to think of America, the all of it—and the big rock that it was, and how the very heart of America must've been the big rock that was just down the ways some from the church, and just across the creek from my aunt's humble cabin in Cotterpin Creek Kentucky.

And where was that in America?

It was the land of the east to the west, and the west to the east, and the north to the south, and the south to the north. . . .

My aunt and I ate from a breakfast table made of thick planks laid in a heavy framework. For its coarse texture, it was a finely made thing, and the surface of it had been long worn smooth and polished by countless hands and meals. In spring we often breakfasted before dawn—so it was there, one morning in the spring of '61, with the new day's sunlight catching every faded knot on our rustic table, as we ate some cut oatmeal with raisins, honey and a little cream, that my aunt told me that some animals love for the course of their lives, while some animals love for only the duration of their meeting.

Pouring me a cup of hot tea, as it was nippy yet, she said in a voice almost melodic—

"A dove will stand with its mate as it dies—and then it will die itself. A spider will merely walk away. The spirits of people are as diverse as the spirits of animals in nature. Some are doves. Some are spiders. One can blame neither. It's just that some animals are free in the air, some are free on the ground or in the treetops, and some are free in the water. Reading the hearts of people is like reading nature—and just as important, if you want to survive in the forest."

That is a day in spring that I will always remember. That day of the sweet smell of dew on the clover. That day of the green and yellow willow leaves unfurling. That day of the tart sorrel's flower of violet and yellow, and its green shamrock leaves—though I gobbled many, I could never eat enough. That is a day that is always yesterday to me—always clearer than the day that just passed. And sometimes it is clearer than the hour or the minute that just went by. And sometimes it hurts around my eyes, and in my chest, as it can be more real to me than the very second, the very instant I find I am in. . . .

John Warren and I had planned for a Saturday out-of-doors—so we decided upon our route, were given permission to make our trip, and after an early start from my aunt's cottage, and a few moments with the Clevelands at their markedly different kitchen table, John Warren and I set out. There was a skewbald pony that I had become accustomed to riding, but it had been decided that only Pegasus should make the journey, and I held fast to John Warren with my arms, and to Pegasus with my legs, as we were bareback. We were light, however, and it was not a jolting kind of riding, and Pegasus seemed quite ready, too. Ears pricked forward, he was listening, interested and prepared for whatever might come.

"Best trained horse," said John Warren, "has one ear and eye aimed back to the rider—one eye and ear aimed ahead to the field."

So, Pegasus let out a rolling snort, a kind of joy of having something to do, kind of relief to be out, kind of "I take pleasure in an active life" kind of snort—and we were departed, riding out to what one would have to call that rather large hill, or rather small mountain which was on the southwestern outskirts of the Cleveland estate. But this time, rather than just sled on the slope, we planned to ride into the highland—to enjoy the day there. We had risen early, and thus, would arrive well before midday—despite our detouring around the fields of the neighboring farmers.

"They're newly planted," explained John Warren.

Unlike most stud farms, the Clevelands had few problems with their farmer neighbors, and wanted none.

At last, we passed through a gate into an orchard, and through another gate—in and out of Mister Nielson's pecan trees. When we sidled up to the second gate, I took time to watch as John Warren placed his reins in one hand, reached over, unlatched the gate, and we rode through. Then, I watched as we sidled back—and John Warren switched the reins from hand to hand, and he carefully closed the gate.

"That field may look empty," he explained, "but Nielson's pigs might have been out, or some goat or other. No pecans this time a-year, but he's a few mules he lets out."

Then we came upon much new, or unfamiliar ground, so we watched for any meandering livestock, holes or slippery spots—especially as we crossed the mountain stream. But for all our caution, Pegasus did grow slightly gimpy. Upon stopping, and an inspection of the animal, we saw that he had picked up a stone wedged between shoe and hoof.

"It's a good thing we saw it," I said seriously, "as he might have bruised his sole."

And John Warren nodded with some concern.

And then we both grinned, for neither of us was much concerned about anything. All our caution, all our responsibility—it was the farce of the utter freedom of childhood. But there was a joy in adhering to that folly, and after we helped Pegasus walk it off, we continued up, progressing back through that same winding stream and the wet ground on either side. Even slogging in the mud, we maintained our care—not charging. Fording the stream too, John Warren kept Pegasus at a steady pace, because if we stopped, he explained, Pegasus could get stuck and pull a shoe or strain a tendon. When the water grew deep, John Warren said—

"Raise up your legs."

And I did—and his legs and my legs were like wings over the water. And then, rather suddenly, I felt that Pegasus was not touching the stream bottom at all. He was swimming! And it was . . . it was . . .

"It's just like we're flying," I said.

And John Warren agreed that it really was.

Then came a hill, and though Pegasus was terribly fit, we did not ride him fast. And sometimes, we even walked beside him, that he might rest.

Toward the top, we found the clearing with the cleft ash tree, which had been designated our meeting place, and we were soon joined by an old mountain man who had finally settled thereabouts. He was a loyal friend to the Clevelands, as they had employed him after he had been mistakenly imprisoned. At that time, he had been badly in need of a bath, let alone a pair of shoes and a shirt and a job, and thus, he was much indebted. Since then, he had married a widow, given up his trade as a wheelwright, and started quite well as a berry grower and land surveyor—for people had been taking land on the highground.

There was an honorable silence that was coming to John Warren with age (all except when he was talking about horses). But the mountain man, Mister Brazleton—age had made him quite talkative.

"Sometimes nature a-does that to us mount'nous types—either that or we're like to a-hardly talkin' a'tall."

Soon, John Warren and I were set down in the grass—as Mister Brazleton went about serving us a meal. I don't believe he sat down once—for he was too dedicated to the tending of his young guests. We had milk, fresh with cream—

"Cold too," he smiled, and I am ashamed to say I was rather surprised to see he had every one of his teeth—" 'cause-a I sunk it in the stream while I was a-waitin'."

Mister Brazleton had grilled venison that morning, and we had several strips of it, which were not gamy at all. We also had a delicious bread of several grains, baked by his wife—and sweetened by her stewed berries. I did not usually eat so much rich food all at once, but in the brisk air on the hill, it felt pure and light.

Mister Brazleton was well familiarized with the area, as was his mule, and the two of them showed us to a fascinating glen with a hidden hemlock grove. It was with great sweeps of a battered felt hat that he directed us, and after ducking several low branches, we dismounted, as the leaves were almost too thick to even tread about, and certainly too thick for any horse. The place was quite enchanted—

"I'da liken it to some garden for angels," said Mister Brazleton.

Once we had reached the top of the hill, we looked down whence we'd come and we saw the grassy lanes through blossoming trees. We saw horses, far away, running through the fields on the Cleveland estate.

"It's a-breathtakin'—that sight," said Mister Brazleton.

And it was too.

Then Mister Brazleton's big smile went small and furrowed, and his laugh-narrowed eyes went big, and he spoke in a throaty voice. It was the kind of voice that held the wisdom of many years, and the witness of many struggles. It was the gruff understanding of untold experience. And to hear him speak, to comment so bluntly on our lives—to hear something like that said by a man who had seen so many springtimes, was to hear a fact. He dug his heels into the earth and twisted his thumbs in his belt loops—

"This day in springtime is your youth, and I feel done honored to behold you two fine children, in a-sharin' it."

I was riding behind John Warren on his horse—my hands were wrapped around his waist, and he took my thumb between his fingers, and pressed the pad of it lightly.

Following a crooked path, we descended the hill, and Mister Brazleton brought us to the stream for a drink. Pegasus drank gratefully, and it was just the kind of water a horse liked—bright and clean. Pegasus had been so very excited that when he lowered his snout to drink, he submerged his whole muzzle—his nostrils well below the surface. Mister Brazleton had one fishing pole, and we set it out with a worm and a cork after we drank our water. We sat on the bank, which inclined steeply into the pond. It was at least ten feet deep, and as clear as day. And there were so many trout shimmering in the water, hurrying this way and that! Their bodies were red, yellow, green, gold and bluish purple. Their shining skin glittered in the afternoon. The pond was surrounded by pink laurel, and the air was thick and sweet with the scent of it. The flowers hung lazy in the day—weighty pink bells with black dots on the inside. The petals were reflected in the water, and when one lay back, the pond was just a pink reflection. At the center of it, one could see the blue sky framed by the flowers. We touched the leaves of the laurels, which were thick and green.

The leaves shook in the cool wind as the hot sun warmed our faces. The three of us were all so happy as to just sit, or to lie around and say nothing. John Warren lifted my hand again, and as we lay under the sun, he brought the back of it to just shy of his lips, and he breathed three words onto the skin—in the warm and windless day. And I took his palm to my lips, and uncurled his fingers, and breathed the three words back. Then we lay there until the sun whispered that we should rise, and we did. . . .

A little ways up the stream there was a waterfall. The water arched down in a sheet, and left a cavern between it and the stone. John Warren and I walked into a dry recess under the waterfall. Behind the water curtain, we leaned forward and let cool streams douse our warm heads. Our hair ran over our faces, and we whipped it back. The cold water ran down our backs—and through our clothing, and down our legs and out through the bottom of our shoes. We dried off with a blanket that Missus Cleveland had packed for us—a blanket we had been sure we wouldn't need.

But we couldn't help but drink from that pool again, dipping in our dry hands and sipping from our cupped fingers. And kneeling there, we looked into each other's shining eyes, as inviting as the water itself, and could not help but release those crystals from our hands—throwing handfuls of water at each other's bright faces. And each drop, flying through the air, refracting every ray of sunlight, was mirth itself—the essence of that spirit. And we smiled and shook our hair, and dried off again, as Mister Brazleton knelt at the edge of the pool himself, drinking and laughing—

"Must be the fountain a-youth!"

Most of the fish just stole our bait, as we weren't really paying too much attention to them, but by the end of the afternoon, we tried a little harder, and we did catch two sizable fish, which Mister Brazleton hooked on a stick and wrapped in a sack. We rode back to the Cleveland estate in the shadow of the hill, with the taste of the day still moist on our lips. There was wind in the trees, and birds were singing. And rabbits nibbled the tips of new grass. And as we had climbed the mountain, so we descended—at a walk. We went easy on ourselves and Pegasus, and sometimes we dismounted and walked beside him, even zig-zagging when the grades were too steep. We allowed Pegasus to follow his own route, and he did so by retracing our steps, very nearly exactly—and thus did he guide himself back to his stall. Toward journey's end, Pegasus became rather impatient, and had to be held back some. And when we dismounted, John Warren teased him for it—

"Such a creature of habit," said John Warren.

And, the long day done, Pegasus puckered his big lips and nodded agreeingly and mouthed his reward—a cube of sugar. Pegasus was appreciative of the occasional treat, and even mounted John Warren would sometimes lean over to offer a dainty—though it was always a rarity enough to be a surprise, and that was for the good, lest Pegasus come to expect it. His workday was done, but Pegasus still needed some attending—to cool down, straighten up and eat. And so, with all the springtime in me, I left John Warren to his chores and bounced down that familiar and welcoming path through the pines to my Aunty Betta's cottage by the creek. . . .

John Warren and I had each taken a trout, and even my aunt, who mostly ate vegetables and grains, seemed to enjoy it considerably. It had a delicate pink flesh, and the corners of her lips were turned up as we ate it. Perhaps it was my talk that was amusing to her—my silly talk of the day.

"And so," I breathed quickly, "after we got back to the Clevelands', Bugby helped us clean the fish, and Mister Cleveland appreciated them as fine fish, and John Warren said to me that he . . ." And then, because of my youth, I was ashamed of those three words that had passed between us—though now, I can see nothing more pure, and I cannot believe those words could have been uttered through two faces more luminescent and innocent than ours were then. Still, at that time, I was embarrassed by our immaturity, and I looked down, as I had often heard adults complain of children. And I knew that they should be seen and not heard, and . . .

"I am sorry, Aunty," I said, "I must be boring you with my chatter— a foolish, chattering child."

My Aunt Bettina smiled ever so slightly. "I remember speaking of my husband Jack like that," she said, her eyes big and shining, "well, not so long ago, not so long ago at all." Then she made a quiet bird's noise, a youthful kind of laugh that almost seemed to escape from her unintentionally. She put her fingers to her lips, to excuse herself—

"And it's not chatter, Alma, but a song, a song from your heart, and to hear it, it is a song in mine."

My aunt lifted her hands to her red hair, and pushed it back over her shoulders—"And when I see you there, sometimes, I am you. I am a red-haired girl again . . . and . . . and . . ."

My aunt was smiling and teary eyed, and she just swallowed, unable to finish her own sentence.

"And," I said, my own voice as clear and bright as a girl's sincerity could provide, "one day, I hope I can be you."

My aunt dabbed at her eyes with a clean napkin—"No," she said, still smiling, but her voice now throaty, "you don't mean that, Alma."

But I did, and I told her, "Yes I do."

My aunt began to cry again—

"Well," she said, "that is a very kind thing to say, my red-haired child."

And whether it was a sweet thing to say, or a childish thing to say, I know that it came to be, as I often hear my aunt's words in my own. And when I write, I sometimes read them. And when I breathe, and look in the mirror, and push back my hair with my open hands, my aunt sometimes greets me—

Alma, that is a very kind thing to say, my red-haired child.

Poison Sumac

It was on a Sunday in the spring of '61. . . .

It was on a Sunday in the spring of '61 when the flower buds waited for water and the limbs of trees waited for the gentle hands of children. It was on a Sunday, when the crispness in the morning air was the greeting of sunshine. It was on a Sunday, when birds made nests and men walked through young fields to see what their crops might bring. It was on a Sunday, when animals looked to their newborns, or lay back and prepared to give birth. It was on a Sunday, when the beavers worked like every other day. It was on a Sunday that my youth trickled out of my breast and ran in runnels down the wooden benches and through the boards of the church floor. It was on a Sunday that I was surprised to learn that spring would go on with one less girl, and one less boy—when I had thought the spring was for us.

It was on a Sunday that my Aunt Bettina told me that I should not associate myself with the Clevelands. . . .

It happened over the course of one morning service—all while we sat in our comfortable congregation, and the world went on around us. I must admit, I could barely keep my eyes open, as usual. That was always my struggle—not as much to listen, as to appear I was listening. But something happened that day—there was a ripple among the parishioners, then there was silence and anger. I do not believe that it was something that happened just in church—I believe it was something that happened inside the church which alluded to something that had happened outside the church. Regardless, it was probably just something caused by a slip of the tongue—maybe something said in the carelessness of excitement. I do not know if it was something said by the pastor, or something said in the pews, that hushed everyone in attendance that morning at our plain wooden temple. But where one minute there had been the pastor's voice, and I had been quietly dozing with my eyes half open, the next minute there was abject silence, as loud as anything I had heard before. And I was wide awake—and frightened.

No one's posture changed—yet somehow, everyone's back was stiffer and more upright in the splintery benches. And somehow—everyone's hands were more folded than they had been before. Every lap was smaller—knees closer together. Every jaw was clenched. The only movement was the rippling of tension in every neck, and the thumping veins in men's temples.

And the pastor turned to Ecclesiastes, 7:9, and read aloud—

> *Be not hasty in thy spirit to be angry: for anger resteth in the bosom of fools.*

$\backsim$

But the pastor's words of forgiveness fell on our ears like water on mushrooms. They simply rolled off—no one heard anything. And when the service was over, we all stood slowly, achingly, and lined up in the aisles to pass through the heavy wooden doors. My aunt had seated us close to the pastor, up in the front, so we were among the last into the day. The bright sun was a shock to me, and I shielded myself from it. Then I felt the hands of my aunt cover my hands, eyes and ears. She turned me to her rugged body and stepped us back into the church.

I couldn't see the commotion, but I could hear it. Through the hands of my aunt, I listened to the shouting men. It was wild shouting—the shouting of men engaged in hard physical labor, or rough play like wrestling or buggy racing. It was the first time I had heard the shouts of men fighting. At first there were just the two men—and then there were the shouts of the other men holding the two apart. After that there was more silence—like there had been in church, but this was outside silence, which was even spookier.

Even the birds were not singing.

The only sound was that of shuffling boots, men untying their horses, and families setting forth on their wagons.

When my aunt lifted her hands from my eyes, I saw a cardinal just outside the church. It was peeking out from one of the birdhouses that the pastor had built. Pastor Miles had once told me that he had to chase the sparrows away so the cardinals could nest there. And he had told me that the cardinal liked the roofs of their houses slanted forward—toward the door.

That is what I was thinking about as we walked toward the road—that, and the fact that the pastor was hurrying from family to family, talking quickly and spiritedly to each—that, and the very last thing, which was that I had heard the shouts of men, but now that I looked around, I saw curiously few young men, or even middle aged men—there were mostly just old men. Mister Nielson had a bloody forehead. It was worrisome to see such an old man with such a bad cut. His wife was patting his head and he was saying, "Oh it's nothing Marie—it's nothing." And she was saying, "You foolish man—you foolish old man."

I realized then that more people had attended church that day than had attended in several months. I thought that perhaps it was because something of consequence had come to pass, and church was a place where people gathered for information—to update themselves on the condition of the world, the state and the community. And what exactly had happened? I asked my aunt.

"Things are . . . changed," she whispered into my ear.

She knelt before me, and fussing with my coat, explained that the congregation was as water spilt on the ground, which could not be gathered up again—and that she and I would not be returning to church for, she stuttered, "for . . . for . . . for a while."

We were the next family that the pastor came to talk to—and he walked along beside us. He took my aunt's hand between his two hands and said, "Bettina Flynt Evans, come to see me anytime—not just Sundays. You can come any day, it doesn't have to be Sunday. Come with Alma, we can make any day Sunday."

"That is what we will do," said my aunt.

"Good," said the pastor, and he hurried ahead to the Nielsons.

But he turned back, and said with a melancholic breath, "We are only without an altar."

And then came the long walk home. . . .

In their clothes of black and white, everyone shuffled along—and most of them clean from their Saturday night baths. Few had carriages, they just held the hands of their children and walked soberly. Those who did ride in their carriages or farm wagons disappeared quickly on the dirt road—and down the hill. The winding road was just steep enough to be a slow way up, and a fast way down. The last carriage that passed us was the Cleveland carriage. Mister Ditzler did not slow Wilma and Hovington. John Warren waved to me but his mother grabbed his hand and replaced it in his lap. Then they disappeared too. But there were still people on the road—probably twenty or thirty. There was Mister Ditzler's wife, Fanny Ditzler, and their son, Flynn, who was only just born. There was Cassie Valentine and Stewart Valentine. There was Miss Cleveland, who was not riding with her brother, Somerton Cleveland. There was Doctor Richard Esterbrook, and his wife Hester. There was Horatio Cooper, his wife Keri, their daughter Susan, and their four granddaughters, Wilma, Martha, Priscilla and Jane. It was funny to think how just about everyone who had been fighting with one another only minutes before was now walking in the same direction. The church was southeast of everything, and we all had to walk north to go home. No one spoke, not amongst themselves and not to one another. Very quietly, my aunt told me that it wasn't anything the pastor had said—he just couldn't help what had happened.

My hand in my aunt's hand, her grip was firm, and it guided me directly down the road. Nevertheless—I turned to look back. It felt so odd to see that shaky little church. When I had last seen it from the road, the hitching rail was thick with dally-slip knots, and there was a row of horses and carriages and country wagons—and now there was naught. I did not know it then, but I would not see so many horses and carriages and wagons outside the church for another ten years.

And it was just as clear as could be, the pastor's voice, as he stood on the roof of the church and called out from the book of Saint Matthew. And all down that church road, every one of us heard the words—

> And seeing the multitudes, he went up into a mountain: and when he was set, his disciples came unto him: and he opened his mouth, and taught them, saying, Blessed are the poor in spirit: for theirs is the kingdom of heaven. Blessed are they that mourn: for they shall be comforted. Blessed are they the meek: for they shall inherit the earth. Blessed are they which do hunger and thirst after righteousness: for they shall be filled. Blessed are the merciful: for they shall obtain mercy. Blessed are the pure in heart: for they shall see God. Blessed are the peacemakers: for they shall be called the children of God. Blessed are they which are persecuted for righteousness' sake: for theirs is the kingdom of heaven. Blessed are ye, when men shall revile you, and persecute you, and shall say all manner of evil against you falsely, for my sake. Rejoice, and be exceeding glad: for great is your reward in heaven: for so persecuted they the prophets which were before you.

Even so, during our walk, it was unclear to me what exactly had come to pass—though it was not so much because I didn't understand, it was just that I didn't want to understand.

But when my aunt and I finally arrived home, she made sure that I understood—

We opened the door to the old cottage. There was the smell of peppermint and coffee. My aunt had been soaking ground coffee beans in water for Mister Nielson, who could not drink coffee, on account of his stomach, but would not stop drinking it, on account of the flavor. So my aunt was taking the acid out for him. She went to the pot and lifted the lid, checking on the coffee extract. It was thick and black, and almost prepared. Two spoonfuls added to a cup of hot water made a cup of coffee without acid. She lowered the lid, and sighed. And that was when she told me we would not be seeing the Clevelands anymore—not on purpose, and probably not by accident.

"I cannot see John Warren?" I asked.

I thought my heart had stopped beating. I thought my blood had frozen.

I opened my mouth and heard myself say, "I think I would like to go to my room."

"Yes," said my aunt, "whatever you would like."

But my room was his room. I remembered John Warren, and how he had been there with his poison oak. I imagined him there, in the care of my aunt—his worried parents and brother gathered around close. . . .

I tried to think about something else.

"Poison oak," I whispered to myself—"poison oak and poison ivy grow from the same vine. When the vine grows in a moist, shady place, it becomes poison ivy. When it grows in a dry, sunny place, it becomes poison oak. Usually that is the case. Out west, there is a whole different kind of poison oak. Poison sumac has little white fruits and red leaf stalks. To treat affected areas, bathe in salt and Virginia snakeroot. For sores, apply poultices of slippery elm and compresses of crushed garlic and sassafras. Administer blood purifying herbs in hot tea. Treat itch with baking soda—"

I suppose my voice trailed off as I watched the shadow of the bayberry-candle shake on the wall. The flame flickered on the wick—and was reflected in the window. Moths flew up against the glass. Their bodies clicked on the smooth surface. They bounced away and began to fall. Then their silent wings caught the air, and they circled to fly back.

Seventeen-year Locust

It is not good for a girl to be deceptive—but I didn't mean to be. I just left my room through the window. At that particular moment, it had seemed to me the easiest way out of the house. And my aunt would never stop anyone from stepping out for a breath of forest air.

I didn't really think about it. I just couldn't help it—

I crossed the creek over the path of stones, and waited for John Warren at the big rock. It is where we usually met, and I knew he would meet me there that night.

The big rock was silvery blue in the moonlight. Because the moon shone on the side of the big rock that faced the field, it looked to me like the rock was watching over the bluegrass. It was watching over me, I thought. The big rock had seen all of it before. I wondered— how many hearts had that rock seen break? How many pebbles of sadness had rolled down its surface? Had it once been a mountain? A mountain eroded by sadness? Or was that how sadness grew? Soil became stones. And stones became great rocks which watched hearts break in fields of bluegrass.

Yes, I thought, that's what happens—for I could feel the soil under my feet turn to stone. . . .

Then John Warren arrived on Pegasus, who was running as fast as he could. And John Warren was breathing hard too, as if he too had been running. Shortly behind him, his father was riding the gray steed. I know that it was so large a horse because Mister Cleveland was so a large man, and it was a better balance for the both of them like that—but all the same, that horse was so very big, and so very spirited, that he unnerved me awfully. It was an abrupt halt from a gallop, and as Pegasus slid to a stop, he seemed almost as disturbed by the gray steed as I was. Pegasus had his ears turned back, listening behind—and that was a nervous attitude for a horse. And hearing that steed grow close, his ears went flat, in just plain anger—and then they grew flatter, and angrier. He had what one might call a crazed gleam in his eye, his mouth slightly open—and that was a look quite dismaying! Perhaps John Warren was fearful too, and Pegasus sensed it. And perhaps Pegasus, who had never been so disturbed, knew from his horse sense better than any of us how true to a torn history this moment might be.

Pegasus snorted a warning—and his nostrils flared. John Warren had always said that a squeal meant anger, and could well be a sign that two horses were fighting, or that a mount was about to throw a rider, or kick—so if one heard that, one had to be rather heedful, lest the animals hurt each other—or you! And so Pegasus began to squeal—something awful! And then Pegasus, he did let out a kick at the air—whereupon Mister Cleveland, not only for his own safety, but for that of his son, was forced to approach most gingerly. Mister Cleveland knew that Pegasus had only one great apprehension—and that was being rode up on by a bigger horse. And in that circumstance, not only might Pegasus kick, but rear. And then—when Pegasus did rear up, it was a terrifying thing, and I thought surely that John Warren would be thrown and trampled—as wild as both horses had become. But John Warren held fast, leaning forward, grabbing the mane, and turning Pegasus' head to the side. So—that mighty horse's body came down. The gray steed had stepped back, and as Mister Cleveland was steadying his animal, John Warren circled his own agitated horse, then sidled up beside me. And though John Warren's horse was wild and great in size in comparison to me, who was so diminutive in stature, I was suddenly unafraid. And in John Warren's eyes I could see that he was full of things to say, and that he had come to me that these things might be said, should they ever be said, for everything was changing so fast that words were like leaves in onrushing streams—mingling and parting and washing away. But all that boy had time to do was look back at his own father, and plead, almost instinctively—

"Don't hate him."

Then Mister Cleveland rode up, and wrested the reins of John Warren's horse from his hands.

And I felt then that my aunt had come up behind me. Having knelt, she'd wrapped her arms around my waist—both holding me back from the horses, and just holding me back.

Pegasus was huffing and snorting, and pulling against the reins, though Mister Cleveland had a tight hold of his mouth. The animal was positively feral with excitement, and having lost the reins, John Warren leaned over on Pegasus' neck, clutching the mane. He lowered his face, and in it was all hope and despair.

And I looked at him with my hope and despair, as all was unknown.

And my Aunt Bettina looked up sorrowfully at Mister Cleveland.

He looked sorrowfully back.

And even if they did not yet hate each other—they could converse no longer.

At a brisk trot, Mister Cleveland pulled Pegasus into line beside the gray steed. John Warren turned back on his saddle. He called out—

"Alma, I'll see you at school."

"Yes," I called back—"I'll see you at school."

But I did not see John Warren at school.

There was no more school for John Warren.

And there was no more Sunday service for me.

The next morning at the schoolhouse, after the bell had rung and we children had seated ourselves behind our desks, Miss Cleveland said that the fathers of several of her students had decided not to send their offspring to our class anymore—but she said that it was really good, because she could pay more attention to each of us.

Seated stiffly behind her table, she pointed her pencil at the board, directing us to the passage she had written—it was one we all knew, but she told us to refresh ourselves, for we would be called upon to recite it.

> *We hold these truths to be self-evident, that all men are created equal, that they are endowed by their Creator with certain inalienable Rights, that among these are Life, Liberty, and the pursuit of Happiness.*

Then she began to sob. . . .

All of us were sitting with our hands folded on our desks, and I thought of church the day before. Miss Cleveland choked back her tears. She let go her grip on the edge of the table, and she folded her hands too. Then she told us in a failing voice that we would start in a minute.

It was sad to see it, because John Warren was among the children who would not be coming to class anymore. And I knew that it was sad, not just for me, but for her, Miss Cleveland, because John Warren was her nephew.

Everyone in the class knew it. But no one said it, no one even fidgeted. We just sat alertly with our fingers knit together, listening to the rain outside the schoolhouse—in the grass and on the rooftop. And although we all had our own worries and broken hearts, we waited patiently for her lesson, because all of us knew that John Warren's father was Miss Cleveland's brother.

As a result of the sparsity of our students, and the quickness we were thus granted in completing our lessons, Miss Cleveland added musical instruction to our daily class. And I remember, in their frames, the windows rattled with wind—and that it was a gray day, when the clouds had seemed to touch the ground. And that it was with some defiance that the first song she taught us was this—

Spikerush

grows in the mars
May - October

God bless our native land,
Firm may she ever stand
      Through storm and night!
When wild tempests rave,
Ruler of wind and wave,
Do Thou our country save,
      By Thy great might!

For her our prayers shall rise
To God above the skies,
      On Him we wait;
Thou who art ever nigh,
Guarding with watchful eye,
To Thee aloud we cry,
      God save the state!

Lord of all truth and right,
In whom alone is might,
      On Thee we call!
And may the nations see
That men should brothers be,
And form one family!
      God save us all!

I could not resist seeing John Warren, and
one pleasant May afternoon, on my way home,
I yielded to the temptation to visit the Cleveland
estate. I went to John Warren's window, but the room was dark—nor
was there any sound within the house. Through the window of the
parlor, I saw Doreen Cleveland playing solitaire with a deck of hand-
painted playing cards.

She was playing distractedly, nervously.

Then I heard a loud "Ho!" emanate out from one of the littler barns. I went to it, and peeked between the slats—and smoke filled my eye. And then I saw men with cigars, puffing. Sitting and standing, the men were piled up in the stalls—the horses moved away. And there was Bugby, and his father, and John Warren—and they had a bird in the ring on the dirt floor. And John Warren held a deep, cock-sized basket in his hand.

And there were at least thirty or forty other men. And most of them were waving money. I saw that Horatio Cooper was there, from the general store, as well as William Ditzler, and Stewart Valentine, and even Doctor Esterbrook. There were many others I knew—and many others I didn't know. And I knew it was in the nature of the cock to fight—and that there was nothing more wrong with a cocker than any other man. . . .

And of the crowd, there was not a single brutal face among them. They might just as easily have been gathered for a prayer meeting. But they were not, and it was a brutal thing, in my estimation. With leather thongs, gaffs were trussed to their claws—and the birds slashed each other. There was blood and flesh—and feathers flew in the barn. The birds were crimson with the violence, and maybe even blind—I do believe they had blinded each other! They were obviously quite exhausted, and were tottering gropingly about, their wings dragging—though still, they struck strong. . . . All in the smoke of cigars. And I saw the men's horses tied up behind the barn, as I left the Cleveland estate.

And as long as that was the house of Mister Somerton Cleveland, I would not again return, uninvited. So I did not return—not for almost a year.

Summer '61

$\mathcal{I}$t was through the spring and summer of '61 that I watched the Clevelands retrain a new lot of horses. Somerton Cleveland had bought out a Frickerham stable, and had paid under one hundred and fifty dollars a horse—for some well-bred animals. All their problems were in their training, as the more experienced men of that stud farm had been called to arms. Mister Cleveland looked on it as an opportunity, as a finished animal might fetch near on three hundred dollars. By this, he hoped to set right the estate, for it had suffered the change of times.

Retraining horses was a difficult task, but Somerton was a man of faith—

"It's never the horse," he'd always said, "it's the man."

Mister Cleveland was of the opinion that one should be not so much a rider as a horseman, one who knew all about the animal and the life. A horseman would know that every horse had its limitations. Each had quirks—one might seem clumsy, but jump well—another might jump a high white fence but never a low log—and yet another might hunt well, but show poorly. Mister Cleveland had always said to be smart, and to be flexible, and that when it did come time to be hard, to be only as hard on the horse as the horse was hard on you. He believed that if it was the horse punishing the rider, that rider was overmounted—if a rider wasn't calm, but anxious, that horse would be anxious too. A horse had an instinct for distress, and reacted accordingly. (Perhaps it was that fine sense of smell.) Regardless, a rider had to be confident, as the horse was an animal averse not only to pain but unsettling emotion. A horse, said Mister Cleveland, should never be exposed to the rage of man. No sensible rider would ever ask anything of a horse in a foul temper, or in anywise cause a confrontation. And discipline, by Mister Cleveland's way of thinking, it should be quick and unfailing. Any hesitation or inconsistency and an animal might not know why he was being punished, or if he did know what he was doing wrong, he might develop a habit of thinking he could get away with it—and that would be the rider's fault. A rider had to be resolute—ask for something, get it. Herd animals did what they were told, one just had to tell them clearly—otherwise they'd become skittish, as they wouldn't understand what was wanted of them. And if the horse didn't know what was wrong, that was the rider's fault too—and no horse should be punished for the faults of the rider.

Above all, Mister Cleveland had always said that a horseman must be honest—

"Never," he'd say, "never take a horse to task for your own mistakes."

And it was from my place on the big rock that I watched John Warren follow the hand of his father, as, with a great deal of perseverance and patience, they set about to re-educating these animals, many of which, by Somerton's way of thinking, had been spoiled, like children—

There was a blue and white horse that kicked—and that was dealt with by a sharp slap on the hindquarter. There were several horses that had to be worked out of bucking—and the riders would thwart that by keeping their horse's head up—or if that horse was already bucking, by sitting deep, leaning back—and holding on! There was a very handsome horse that ran when it should have walked—and the solution was simply to relax that animal. One horse moved from being mounted, and that was resolved by a second trainer holding the horse's head while the first mounted. A few horses would try to return to their stalls, quite in opposition to the wishes of whoever might be their rider—and that was countered with a firm hand and will. A very few of the horses were set back on the longe-line to begin anew.

I knew that Mister Cleveland absolutely hated people who hit their horses, especially on the head, as it made a horse head shy. And it appeared as if several of the horses had been so abused. One could not punish a horse for shying, as that would only intensify the animal's apprehensions. So the Clevelands would just turn the animal away from whatever might be objectionable—or show the horse what alarmed him, and that there was nothing to fear.

And from what I saw, and what I heard, the retraining went rather well—though still, the Clevelands were forced to take on some riding pupils into summer. Some were quite capable already—yet times were to prepare for the worst.

Many years later, an edition from Mister Cleveland's library came into my possession. He seemed to think well of the publication, as the text was accompanied by his own notes. It was a three volume work from 1805, titled *An Analysis of Horsemanship*, by Mister John Adams. One of the sections that Mister Cleveland found of particular relevance advised that a rider should have a forward inclination of body position at the gallop. And Mister Cleveland wrote considerably about the potentiality for using such an inclination for jumping, although I do not remember him having gone so far as adopting one. I do remember that to Mister Cleveland a good sense of balance was everything—in the head and in the saddle. Everyday riding was sitting at the center of a seesaw, balancing at the middle rather than either end. But riding, as he saw it, was never meant to be a comfortable affair—and if one wanted comfort, perhaps reclining on a cushioned chair was a better activity than jumping a horse over a fence. The rider, he'd always said, had to be just as uncomfortable as the horse. To him, it wasn't the rider's comfort that was in the best interest of riding, it was the horse's comfort—and he was near fanatical about making a horse comfortable with that rather uncomfortable circumstance of a mounted rider.

And so—who was John Warren's father?

He was a gentle, gentle man. He was a family man. And maybe he was a foolish man too—but in another time (if he had also been a lucky man) all his life would have been spent loving his family and horses. And all his foibles and political concerns—upon utterance, they would have been met with his own laughter, when he was an old man. . . .

And toward the summer's end, from my perch on the big rock, I could see that he'd taught John Warren and Pegasus to pirouette—a full circle turning on the haunches. All the way around at a canter, the maneuver was quite impressive—and I would clap my hands together, as if they might hear it in the distance. Some people said a move such as that was just physical education and had no true value for a rider. Others said it was how a battle horse might fight a man on foot—the rider's sword circling and slashing at foot-soldiers. And it was after school one day that Miss Cleveland herself said that all the turns from standing were at best not good for too much, and at worst the lessons of sword attacks and battlefield movements—for those turns could not be applied when a horse was moving quickly, as they were too abrupt. But even though it was Miss Cleveland who had said it, and she knew as much about horses as anyone, it was still a hard way for me to see it—for that pirouette was just so exotic, and demonstrated so very much trust between horse and boy. And from my vantage on the big rock, that bond of boy and horse—it was just all that magic.

And though I was not much for disagreeing with Miss Cleveland, with all the time I had spent with the Clevelands and their horses, I couldn't help but ask my aunt if maybe Mister Cleveland didn't know about horses as well as cockfighting, as his were such fine and well-trained horses. I had seen so many horses, but none others like those of Mister Cleveland.

In response, my aunt just grumbled a few words from Ecclesiastes, 9:4—

A living dog is better than a dead lion.

⌒

Rather clearly, I said that I thought Mister Cleveland did know a great deal about horses, and that it was a gift he was giving to his family, and that I was appreciative to see even a small part of it. And my aunt said—

"All that to charge and die."

Like Miss Cleveland, it would seem that my aunt was also rather critical of some of the maneuvers, and as she explained them, they could have no purpose but to maim and kill other men and horses—one such maneuver was to jump and kick back. She told me that could only be meant to kick at another horse—and I feared it was true. . . .

My aunt said that in Kansas she had seen a horse running with its intestines dragging behind it—and another hopping on three feet. She said a horse was a better target than a man. "Bring down the horse," she said—"kill the man. Somerton Cleveland, he's training a lot of dead horses."

"But . . ." I objected, "he *loves* those horses."

And my aunt told me—

"It's not a girl's place to be so contrary."

And I knew that she was right, and I quieted myself—though I so missed Mister Cleveland's horses, and Mister Cleveland's family. The noses of those horses were just as soft as silk—except for a few prickly hairs. And my fingers ached for them. And John Warren . . . I would see him only from afar—riding in the bluegrass. None but an experienced team like him and Pegasus could train on their own like that, and it was rather special to see the one set of horse and rider without so many others—even if it made me ache like a worm for dirt. And though John Warren was some ways off, and I'm not sure he could even see me for the woods and trees, there were still some times when he would stop, look around and wave. . . .

St. John's Wort

And the hot summer went on like that, in a kind of thick despondency. Hide and Go Seek, climbing apple trees, picking blackberries, jumping into piles of leaves and having tea parties—I managed these everyday friendships and activities. All without John Warren. But after accepting one foolhardy dare, I tumbled from a rather high tree, and badly sprained my ankle. The other children helped me back to my aunt's, and she fashioned a crutch—and after I rested for about a half an hour, she sat me in the wheelbarrow and pushed me into town, as that was where Doctor Esterbrook and his wife Hetty kept a small house with a garden and a white picket fence. The doctor examined my ankle and said that I should stay off it for a few days, and that in three weeks I'd be good as new. The visit then turned into a social occasion, as I had yet to converse with the doctor—so he and his wife retired with my aunt and me to the back porch. They served iced tea with crushed raspberries and the doctor and my aunt spoke of Bleeding Kansas, as they had both been there during those difficult years—he had also been to Boston, once, where my aunt had lived for many years. Doctor Richard Esterbrook was an older man—too old to walk far, he said, though he seemed a sprightly sort. He had been in combat with the British in 1812, and his wife said he had fought the Tommies everywhere from Delaware to New Orleans. He said he didn't have that kind of stamina anymore—that his war now was with long distances and flights of stairs. His wife objected that it was not so, as he spent many long hours riding about the countryside to administer his patients—and often in inclement weather. My aunt had once told me that people would gather round Doctor Esterbrook to hear him tell of the Indians, so I questioned him about it. He said their name was the Chickasaws, and that they were a tall, well-built people, with ruddy skin, ink-black hair and big eyes. When they captured people from other tribes, they would make slaves of them—who would then be adopted after only a few years. Doctor Esterbrook had been with the Chickasaws for several years, and he loved them. He seemed pleased with my questions, which were mostly just of their everyday living. . . .

And what an interesting conversationalist he was! He told several amusing stories about a clever boy named Jack. And he discussed with my aunt some of the different kinds of Saint John's wort. There was Big John the Conqueror root, and Little John the Conqueror root, and many other varieties—all of which, for those of a folksy nature, were speckled with the blood of John the Baptist. Farther south, said Doctor Esterbrook, he had seen the root employed in Voodoo magic—and, he laughed, he'd been assured that it was of particular use in gambling. Confessing to a fear he'd had since he was a young man, of becoming outmoded in the country, the doctor explained that he tried his utmost to keep himself abreast of both the new scientific medicines as well as the handed-down botanical ones. Listening to him, I saw this open-mindedness had provided him a rich and interesting life on which to draw. He showed us that he was missing two fingers which had been tangled up in a rope between his saddle horn and a steer when he was a fourteen years old. Though for his dexterity with his thumb and his other two fingers, I am sure that he was more capable than most.

Missus Esterbrook was also highly interesting, and she contributed a great deal to the conversation. She was in touch with the Clevelands, of whom we had heard nothing as of late. I was especially curious about Mister Cleveland, whom I had not seen out with his horses in some weeks. She said that Somerton and Bugby had gone off to fight. They were officers now, a captain and a lieutenant. As they had their own horses, they were serving side by side in the cavalry. Missus Esterbrook, boundlessly active in the community, had been lending a hand to Missus Cleveland, who had not been entirely herself since she had lost her two "oldest boys." Currently, there were as many as forty workers on the Cleveland estate, including all hands and slaves, and it had come time to supply them with clothing.

Concerned that Missus Cleveland was not up to the task, Missus Esterbrook had availed herself. Missus Cleveland was frazzled enough already—attending all there was to attend on the estate, without the added excitement of preparing clothing for the winter. And Missus Cleveland may not have been in a position to hire help, as Missus Esterbrook had heard that the Cleveland finances were not as they had once been, and that the family had told Mister Nielson to sell the foxhounds—though Mister Nielson had been keeping dogs for the Clevelands since Mister Cleveland took up the diversion some six years before.

As Missus Esterbrook launched into her discourse, my aunt sat rather tightly, with her lips closed and her hands locked on her knees—

"Well," said Missus Esterbrook, "as the cold weather will be coming shortly—and as the Negroes especially have been neglected of late, Missus Cleveland and I decided it was important that they should be adequately provided. Now I know, Bettina, that you're not one of them, but a great many in our community think that it's not a time to be troubling with the Negroes—but Missus Cleveland and I agreed that it was, and as my husband and I also help provide for many of the orphans in the Frickerham poorhouse, no one at all objected to our contribution to the undertaking."

My aunt, at times, could be a quiet and stern woman, and such a time was this. Perhaps Missus Esterbrook, both pleasant and insecure in her own ways, believed she was impressing my aunt—but I could tell that my aunt did not think Missus Esterbrook quite as liberal as she thought she was. . . .

"As you know," proceeded Missus Esterbrook, "the task would usually fall to the overseer's wife. But Missus Cleveland had recently been forced to dismiss the overseer and his wife, due to a difference of opinion in the handling of the Negroes. From what I gather, the man employed a whip, so Missus Cleveland told him to pack up his things and go—"

Missus Esterbrook's nurse, Stella, was an august woman. She had been with the Esterbrooks for some thirty years, purchased in Georgia when she was a grown woman, and freed some twenty years before—though, as by state law a freed slave could not remain in Kentucky, her papers were still held by the Esterbrooks. I was later told that she was on call at all times, and even slept in the Esterbrooks' bedroom, should they require attendance in the night. Walking heavily out of the kitchen, Stella carried a silver tray with a white doily that was stacked with hazelnut and honey cookies. Doctor Esterbrook made us try them, even my aunt, who was mildly surprised, and pleased, I think, to learn that the Esterbrooks cooked with molasses, honey and wheat flour.

But I could see that as far as Missus Esterbrook was concerned, my aunt was straining to be polite, as it would do no good to create a scene, or to make enemies of one's friends. But while my aunt knew the Esterbrooks were opposed to slavery, and had even gone to Kansas when the times were dire (and dangerous!), the Esterbrooks were also supportive of the rights of the Southern states to remain autonomous, and my aunt's position was a more extreme one, personally, although she had moved to Kentucky in the hopes that the state would remain neutral, and therefore, she was of a similar mind to them—that no fight should be at her doorstep—and all that was for *my* safety. Still, despite what she wanted for me, she could not bring herself to be a proponent of any wickedness, or kindness, which sustained that peculiar institution.

As I remember, the slaves on the Cleveland estate lived in log cabins just on the far side of the west slope. I know they made some of their own meals, but I do not know how many, and it was by no means all of them. Their rations were meat, grain and corn meal. A large garden provided vegetables. Most also had their own gardens, and hens for eggs. They were given two or three outfits of clothing per year, and several head-kerchiefs. Every few years they were given one pretty suit for the men, and one pretty dress for the women (as well as a pretty apron). Each would have a thick cloak for the cold. Blankets and linens too. I may say as well that they were remembered on holidays with tobacco, drink, special rations and even a few precious days of leisure. . . .

My aunt—she had turned to the mosquito-screen, and through it, looked beyond the porch to the corner—toward the street of the town. She watched people walk. They carried supplies from the general store. And I could tell that as she turned back, she was drawing on her love for me to bolster her reserve in regard to Missus Esterbrook, and her opinions.

"Well," Missus Esterbrook was saying, amusedly, "Negroes, I assure you, come in all shapes and sizes, and it's no simple matter to clothe them. The garb to be made was for every man, boy, woman and girl on the estate—though a great many of the women and girls can sew, and do so, for themselves and their families. But nevertheless, all were provided! And my, I had never seen such an operation! We oversaw a bevy of seamstresses who drew, cut and stitched the clothing. We had cleared a room for the seamstresses to lay out the cloth—a white wool for the pants. We drew the forms of the jeans with blue chalk, and then cut along the lines. The children were outfitted in the most adorable red flannel! The patterns were extremely varied, as the clothing was hand measured for everyone, from the very tall to the very short—from the very thin to the very stout," and then Missus Esterbrook sighed, with self-congratulations—

"Most of it fit passing well."

Though I have not seen anything like it in some fifty years, I have a clear memory of the wool of those white jeans—it was a strong material that turned as soft as flannel after many years of washing. Some of the slaves would dye the material with willow bark or sweet gum or onion peels, thus coloring the white jeans tan, gray or yellow.

"Missus Cleveland and I made absolutely certain," insisted Missus Esterbrook, "that every one of her people had footwear solid enough for the winter."

And I can still hear the clomping of those heavy russet shoes they wore, which were very stiff, and greased often—just to keep them bendable. And it was with the mention of those shoes, and in the glow of Missus Esterbrook's pride that my aunt could not contain herself. And though reservedly, she spoke—

"A few shoes, a few yards of wool and a few stitches of thread is not liberty."

Missus Esterbrook responded, "Well . . . we can't let them freeze—we can't let them starve, can we?"

And to that, my aunt had her answer—

"They are not horses."

The doctor then excused himself rather abruptly, saying, "Ah, this old man is called by mother nature." And thus, he removed himself with a distracted air. It was without turning back that he apologized for leaving me alone in that rumpus. "I'm sorry child—but you can bet your eyes you'll get old."

I asked, perhaps trying to brighten the porch with my own mishearing—

"Bat your eyes and you'll get old?"

"Well, no," he called back, "but that too. Bet. I said bet your eyes."

Then he'd disappeared down the hall. There followed a moment of silence, as the two women composed themselves, then my aunt quietly spoke from the book of Exodus, 21:2—

> *If thou buy a servant, six years he shall serve: and in the seventh*
> *he shall go out free for nothing. If he came in by himself, he shall*
> *go out by himself: if he were married, then his wife shall go out*
> *with him.*

Missus Esterbrook had listened politely, if tensely, and she responded by saying that she believed it was "Hebrew servant," and if her humble memory served her, the scripture followed—

> *If his master have given him a wife, and she have borne him sons*
> *or daughters; the wife and her children shall be her master's, and*
> *he shall go out by himself. And if the servant shall plainly say,*

I love my master, my wife, and my children; I will not go out free:
then his master shall bring him unto the judges; he shall also
bring him to the door post; and his master shall bore his ear
through with an awl; and he shall serve him for ever.

And my aunt, with her hands now folded on the dress of her lap, drew her eyebrows together, and spoke from Exodus, 22:21—

Thou shalt neither vex a stranger, nor oppress him: for ye were
strangers in the land of Egypt.

And to that, Missus Esterbrook pursed her lips, and responded so—

Both thy bondmen, and thy bondmaids, which thou shalt have,
shall be of the heathen that are round about you; of them shall
ye buy bondmen and bondmaids. Moreover of the children of the
strangers that do sojourn among you, of them shall ye buy, and
of their families that are with you, which they begat in your
land: and they shall be your possession. And ye shall take them
as an inheritance for your children after you, to inherit them
for a possession; they shall be your bondmen for ever.

At this (Leviticus, 25:44) my aunt grew rather hot, as did Missus Esterbrook. And I waited, motionlessly, for the doctor's return, for theirs was a discussion I quite dreaded—but I further dreaded that the doctor dreaded it as well, and that he'd abandoned me to that rather raw exchange. And I wished my ankle was not so puffy and stiff, that I might walk, so I too could be called by mother nature.

And my aunt, I could see that she wanted no more of the discussion either—and she looked up and closed her eyes, as if asking the heavens for strength, that she might remain silent—but silent she was not. And when her piercing eyes returned to Missus Esterbrook, my dear aunt could concede nothing—

> *And the Egyptians' evil entreated us, and afflicted us, and laid upon us hard bondage: And when we cried unto the Lord God of our fathers, the Lord heard our voice, and looked on our affliction, and our labour, and our oppression: And the Lord brought us forth out of Egypt with a mighty hand, and with an outstretched arm, and with great terribleness, and with signs, and with wonders: And he hath brought us into this place, and hath given us this land, even a land that floweth with milk and honey.*
>
> ∽

Missus Esterbrook was reddening with the debate, and her voice filled with the strain of it. And to Deuteronomy, 26:6, she retorted with Proverbs, 11:29—

> *He that troubleth his own house shall inherit the wind: and the fool shall be servant to the wise of heart.*
>
> ∽

I was much relieved when the doctor then rejoined us—with his slow, loping walk. But even as he did, intense were the passions—and seating himself, the doctor sighed miserably. My aunt's ears were as bright as I had ever seen them, and it seemed that even her gentle, rosy hair was going crimson. But my aunt had not finished, and her lips, enflamed with passion, and rough with country wind, wrapped themselves around the second book of Philippians, 2:5—

> *Let this mind be in you, which was also in Christ Jesus: Who, being in the form of God, thought it not robbery to be equal with God: but made himself of no reputation, and took upon him the form of a servant.*
>
> ∽

Then the doctor coughed, placed his hand on his wife's shaking knee, to quiet her, and under his breath asked her to speak no more of Ham. And with that, he leaned over rather seriously—

"Would you three like some cookies?"

The doctor held out the tray. And he bellowed, half laughing, half moaning—

"Thank the Lord we are neutral!"

Then he looked around guiltily—"We have all done well to live here, as none of us will be called to draw arms."

With that, he uncorked a bottle of wine, which he produced from his pocket with a flourish. And I realized then that his retreat had been a strategic one. Stella soon followed with a tray of four glasses, and the doctor poured the wine with an even hand. And though we were all tense, we were also somewhat cooled by the gesture, and we toasted—my aunt included. She did not often drink, and until that time, not ever that I had seen. And so, when my aunt consented, I also picked up my glass, clacked it with the others and drank wine for the first time. It was so sweet and prickly! And I did enjoy it. And then the conversation grew polite, merry and finally common, and my aunt and I were soon making our way homeward. . . .

And as she picked us a way through the woods, guiding me, wedged with a blanket into my wheelbarrow, my aunt expressed both an anger and an apology—an anger that Missus Esterbrook could take such a narrow view, and an apology that she could be angry at Missus Esterbrook, who was so much better than most, and was doing no more than making sure people had clothes on their backs and shoes on their feet. And while Missus Esterbrook had chosen not to make an issue of it, the Clevelands were certainly in need, and hers was the neighborly way—and Missus Cleveland was surely grateful for the assistance, as the overseeing of the seamstresses, the shoe-makers, the fabric sellers and all the slaves (and their religious instruction) on top of all the herb growing, garden planting, medicine mixing, cloth spinning, sock knitting, clothes sewing, pig slaughtering, meat curing, chicken plucking, copper scrubbing, vegetable preserving, butter churning, tallow dipping, rug weaving and every other harsh and unromantic chore that a matron had to accomplish in order to help to run a profitable horse farm, was far too much to be expected of anyone. And whatever their own sins, my aunt could not say that wishing ruin upon anyone was righteous. And in the years to come, for all of Missus Esterbrook's shortcomings, my aunt would often take notice of her charitable works. Missus Esterbrook was always there to help her neighbors when they were wanting—and then, when the time came, she and her husband cared for hundreds and hundreds of wounded young men.

And with tears in her eyes, she held the hand of *every* boy that was mortally wounded, until he died. . . .

It was blustery all day. We'd had some cold weather. For almost a week the thermometer had been near zero.

Through the billow of the rolled window-glass of the classroom, I saw Natalie, Serena's daughter, with her svelte arms bent at the elbows—she gestured to me, and walking furtively, sneaked around the side of the schoolhouse. I thought she might have been running her fast run, as, despite the cold, perspiration was dried onto the smooth, dark skin of her forehead. I did not know if Miss Cleveland saw her, but I believed she did. Still, Miss Cleveland turned her back on us students to write a problem on the blackboard. Natalie knew she had caught my eye, and so, seeing her chance, she pointed to Harmon through the window. Pitney saw, and he leaned forward and pricked Harmon with his pencil, as Harmon had been staring off into space, as was his custom. When Harmon saw Natalie, who was peering worriedly in through the window, he raised his hand. Natalie ducked below the window frame as Miss Cleveland finished writing the problem. She chose Harmon to answer it—

"Why, this is a surprise, Harmon," said Miss Cleveland, "you've worked out the problem already? Well, let's have it."

Harmon said he had to go to the privy.

"Again, Harmon?" complained Miss Cleveland, "but you just went!"

Anyone else in the class would not have been granted permission, but there was something about Harmon Valentine, the son of old Stewart Valentine, the Clevelands' groundskeeper, that bestowed him a few privileges. He was at times a very active boy, and at times a very sleepy boy. And if he were not allowed his regular trips to the out- house, he would thrust his hand in the air until he was nearly jumping from his seat. But allowed his trip to the outhouse, he would return, as near as he came to collected. Once Pastor Miles had substituted as our teacher for a week, and we had to explain to him that Harmon had a problem, that he *had* to go, even if it was just for the walk. In that way, he was not like the rest of us—without his occasional respite, he could not keep still. Nevertheless, on this occasion, it was too soon for even Harmon. But, finally, Miss Cleveland let him go anyway . . . and then, he was late coming back! I could tell she had taken a breath to yell at him, and maybe even to thwack his knuck- les with her ruler—before she just sighed and sent him back to his seat. . . . A few minutes later, Harmon folded a piece of paper into a hard square which he passed forward to the front of the room. It went from hand to hand, across an aisle, and then to me in the first row, in the middle. The piece of paper had my name on it, written in John Warren's hand.

Miss Cleveland saw, and gave me a dirty look, but she pretended not to see, and didn't take the note away—perhaps because I was not often prone to such misbehavior. A word of it was written in French, and as French at that time was considered very romantic, my heart gave a rather guilty thump, thump—

Alma,

Rendezvous at the small barn near the woods —after dark.

John Warren

So, after school, I went home, and then, after dark, I climbed out the window of my bedroom, and I went out to the Cleveland estate—to meet John Warren there.

And as I made my way, through the dark pine forest, I thought about John Warren—and how his days must be. From what I'd heard, he'd been providing much care for the family horses—attending several of the chores himself, and supervising many of the other operations—mucking out and the like. As there was no more school for him, his education had been entrusted to a tutor from Lexington, who came out to the estate in the good weather. But even in the warm seasons, the lessons did not take up the whole day—and in the absence of his father and brother, and needed by his family on the stud farm, John Warren had found where he was of use to the family—

And, walking through the pine needles of the path, I thought to the night before, and the last feed—a horse's biggest meal of the day, like dinner for us. And I thought how, after that, John Warren had cleaned and put away the tack, and then, how he'd put himself to bed—or, anyway, made a show of it. And I thought how, back in the stables, the horses had begun to doze—standing in their stalls, all trimmed and in lines—for the Clevelands believed that horses had to look presentable, and not like shaggy goats. For winter nights, a horse clipped would need blanketing—so before the whole estate retired, each horse had been properly covered. And every outfit—I knew that it'd be clean and snug, as a rug slipped under a belly was known to cause panic in an animal—and the Clevelands liked their animals happy. . . .

And the night . . . it was all sleeping and breathing. And in the morning, John Warren would wake—and the first thing he'd set about to doing was watering the horses. And, all through the day, no horse's bucket would ever be empty. . . .

And then I thought of things I'd sometimes think of for hours and hours—about days of work and care—pitchforks and bales of hay and feedings and the sweet smell of bran and sugar beet pulp and ale for horses and a hundred purgatives and remedies and *Missus Allison's Cracked Hoof Ointment* and sweat scrapers and hoof picks and mane combs and fetlock scissors and afternoon training and sudsy baths and massages and . . . and . . . everything. . . .

And I thought how, thus, the night had come again. . . .

And as I walked in the pine needles, I thought of how much time I had spent with John Warren in that little barn, and how many times I would walk in to see all the Clevelands' horses—Pegasus among them, standing in his stall.

He'd like be a little disgruntled at first, his ears back, as that was how he was when someone new entered the stable. But then he'd nicker, as a nicker's how a horse says hi—be it to another horse, or to a favorite person. And with that, it was as if he'd said—"Everything's okay." He was so very gentle that it was easy to forget he was more than a pet, but rather, a spirited stallion—though he'd not even nip a person in jest. It was his personality to hate the scolding word—and almost never have to hear it. He was blessed in that, and also in that he was a great eater, but never seemed to ail from it—to grow fat or colicky. To know Pegasus was to know an animal so playful and fun in his own innocent way, and so very quick even for a small horse, and so sensitive that he might know a rider's wishes even before the rider.

But that night . . . upon entering the stable, Pegasus did not greet me with his questioning eye—as he and all the other horses were asleep. I entered quietly, so none were woken—and as my eyes adjusted, I saw John Warren standing in Pegasus' stall, where Pegasus was lying down. Perhaps Pegasus was warmer in his blanket that way, as it was a rather irregular posture for a grown horse. But it was an easy posture, and as I saw Pegasus breathing, it was as if his whole body spoke of serenity in the cold—a warm heart in a frigid world.

And I watched the white clouds of his breathing plume and disperse, as it was just that cold.

The two stalls beside Pegasus' were empty. I had seen them empty before, but never so empty—the stalls had once belonged to Mister Cleveland's gray steed, and Bugby's calico.

"It's not that I'm afraid," John Warren lifted his head and spoke—"not that I'm afraid to be caught with you—not because I'm afraid of getting in trouble—but because I'm afraid of upsetting my mother. She's so . . . so . . ."

I had heard that Missus Cleveland was in an extremely fragile state, and when I nodded once, and looked down, he knew he need not say more.

"Alma," ventured John Warren, as he was then worried for me, "you are so slight in this cold, shall we lie near Pegasus—he's warm, and . . ."

There was a time when we children would have camp-outs in the stables, but that time was no longer, as horses slept on their feet, and Missus Cleveland had always feared, and quite rightly, that a misplaced hoof might do a child harm. So, custom had become that we children would repose in the hayloft . . . relaxing after a hard day of play, chewing on straw and making plans . . . and more plans.

It *looked* like all the horses were sleeping—but because a horse was always standing, it was sometimes hard to tell a sleeping one. And only as my eyes grew accustomed to the darkness could I see that the animals really were asleep—their heads kind of lowered a bit, sort of sagging, their eyes a quarter closed, their ears relaxed or turned to the side, their bodies wavering a bit, and one of their hind legs tucked up. Once in a bit, the tucked hind leg might switch for the other hind leg. . . . The only horses I'd seen lie down regularly were foals—who slept on their sides, and slept a great deal. But with age they'd lie down less regularly, and then, not at all. It was evidently uncomfortable for them—placing too much pressure on their ribs. Usually, to see a horse lying down—it was a cause for worry. Only a very few grown horses would ever lie down on their sides—Pegasus among them, perhaps as he was so agile, and light. And from all my years around the Cleveland estate, I knew that it was best not to wake a horse quickly, as a horse surprised might kick—and I knew that when a horse did wake, just like a person, that horse might be a bit dopey for a minute or two—and a dopey horse was a *big* dope. And a horse's stall was small, especially for two children—and a horse getting up. But . . . on that particular evening, since, if caught, we were red-handed caught, and breaking rules far greater than the loafing-in-the-stalls rule—and since, moreover, it was that rare and peaceful occasion when Pegasus was lying on his side—well, we just knelt, to-gether, and we risked waking that horse, and we sat, loafed with Pegasus—relaxing into fresh hay pushed up against the wall of the barn. And from just across the stall, we could feel the warmth ema-nating off that reclined horse. And then, Pegasus did lift his head, but only to lay it back down, as if to say—

"What? What's that? Oh . . . it's only you. You two . . ."

John Warren bit his lip and squinted, having great difficulty in bringing himself to deliver his message to me. Finally, his chest grew large, and full of bluster. And he said—

"I won't have to leave."

I pushed a strand of straw across the cold ground, and answered—

"I know."

My eyebrows had been pushed together, worriedly, I believe, and then, I felt my face become open, and almost tranquil—

"But someday," I said, "you might have to."

And John Warren said no—that the French would join the war—that the Union had lost its resolve—that New York itself would join the Confederacy—that—

And I interrupted him to say I was sure he was right. And I thought to myself that maybe he was, too. . . .

There was an emptiness, a silence then, filled only by the cold.

Lying near Pegasus' warm body, I'd an inkling that Pegasus was lis-tening, and considering as well—and then he opened his eyes to look at us—before returning to his doze. Perhaps, I thought, it was no more than that, just as we appreciated his warm body, he appreciated ours. John Warren took my hands in his, and we gathered them all four in a ball—to refuge our fingers from the cold. We turned to lie on our sides, facing each other, and took to whispering. But we didn't whisper like we were telling secrets, or speaking of urgent things, but slowly, and calmly, like there was all the time in the world—like we were talking of nothing important, nothing that could justify a voice louder than a simple whisper—like our words were no more than a sigh in winter. We spoke of friends and school and the weather—of horses and games and neighbors. And then John Warren laid his leg over my leg. And it relaxed there—bent at the knee. And as we were so unmoving, aside from our breathing, we watched his foot rise and fall, ever so scarcely, in time with his beating heart. . . .

"Alma," he said, "I can never leave here—my heart will always stay here," and his voice raised, and quickened, "and . . . I don't think anything is by accident anymore, and watching my heart beat, there—I think that maybe it means that no matter where my feet might take me, in another way, my heart will always be guiding me home. . . ."

His voice cracked—then it stopped.

We were both curled up, and John Warren traced his finger from his foot, up his thigh to his heart. His foot thumping slightly, he said, "My father once said that he would always have one foot here, in this firm soil, in this good grass. And . . ." he clenched his closed eyes, and dropped his face into my hands, "it's true for me, too."

It was scary to me that he said it that way, because if his father had one foot in the bluegrass, I knew where the other one was. Only a few weeks before, my aunt had told me that Somerton Cleveland, along with his son, Bugby Cleveland—each had one foot in the grave.

"I promise" John Warren paused, "I promise—"

And I interrupted him—"You don't have to—you don't have to promise, because I know that some promises are too hard to keep."

But he promised anyway, in a sure and bold and choking and tearful way that a child promises something that can't be promised—"I promise anyway . . . I promise that if I leave, I'll return. I promise that no matter what kind of man . . . I become . . . you and I will be together," and he squeezed my hand, then let go. . . .

He had a package for me—wrapped in brown paper, as if he had thought he might have had to have it delivered. I didn't know what it was at first, but when he handled it, I could see it was my bag of marbles. The package was hefty, as they numbered many. I had left them behind the year before, when John Warren and I had been off on some adventure which did not necessitate them. We had been seeing each other daily then, and it was never even considered that I wouldn't pick them up tomorrow, or the next day, or the day after that, or the day after the day after, or, well . . .

"Here's your bag of marbles," he said.

"I don't need them."

He looked down—"Perhaps if I . . . I could take them with me."

"Yes, maybe," I said, and then I looked down too, suddenly doubtful—"Everyone plays marbles."

My Aunt Bettina and I were not often to town anymore, as it was no longer a place for pleasantries and friendly neighbors. And because the season was well advanced into winter, it was especially desolate. Nonetheless, we attended Mister Horatio Cooper's General Store, as we were in need of nails, fabric and kerosene. As we entered, Mister Cooper looked at us over his glasses—silently warning us not to speak. Two women that I did not know were already engaged in an impassioned discussion.

One said, sharply, "Shall we place our necks under their feet?"

The other answered, almost screaming, "I don't know if I can die again. I don't know if I can hear another bell ring, and another voice say, 'John Frakes is dead. Simon Freundlich is dead.' When I hear that, my own heart stops—and I die too. And I wait for the name . . . the last name to stop my heart."

Then they left, one at a time.

They wore dark frocks and dark bonnets. The cloth was a heavy cloth, but a frugal one, and their kind of life was not divulged by their

120

attire. I did not see their faces—nor did my aunt. She said she might have known them, but she wasn't sure. If she had known the voices, she hadn't recognized them, as they had been so transformed by volume and inflection. She suggested to me that one of them, or even the both of them, might have been visiting, or passing through.

And thus, Aunt Betta and I made our selections of goods, and Mister Cooper filled the kerosene can. . . .

And, as we settled at the counter, Mister Cooper looked down at his hands, which were counting up the coins that my aunt had proffered. I remember that his fingers were shaking. He had white hair and wore glasses. His straight hair was combed back over his head—fixed in place with a tonic. But it fell over his ears anyway. He was thin, but moved quickly and youthfully. The conversation having unnerved him as well, he wrapped the fabric for my aunt in silence, until he said—

"Thank you, Missus Evans, and Alma."

Aunt Bettina was much affected by the discussion at the general store. As we walked home, she spoke to me in a voice mournful and distracted. It was not as if she had planned to speak to me about the emotions that had spilled over at Mister Cooper's, it was almost as if she were impelled to tell me. It was like she had waited, and now the time had come—

"I fear that woman in the store was right." Her voice was sorrowful, and knowing. "I fear that in the breasts of the people—those mature like me—death is alive. I fear that it began in our bodies as simple evil, and now it has lived inside us for too long, and it has grown and taken hold, and it will nourish itself as hatred and sorrow until it has consumed us and our lives are lost, and we are dead."

She told me that William Ditzler had been told that his cousin Sam, the one I'd met in Virginia—he was dead, he'd been killed two days before. And though it turned out not to be true, it was somebody's cousin, regardless. . . .

And it is rather imprinted in my memory, along with the bright sun reflected in the window of our cottage—and the silvery light of the afternoon, and the woefulness of the all-knowing big rock, out across the creek—it is rather imprinted in my memory that later in the day, when I picked up my aunt's bible, and opened it, her book clip was placed at the angry words of the seventy-ninth psalm—

O God, the heathen are come into thine inheritance; thy holy temple have they defiled; they have laid Jerusalem on heaps. The dead bodies of thy servants have they given to be meat unto the fowls of the heaven, the flesh of thy saints unto the beasts of the earth. Their blood have they shed like water round about Jerusalem; and there was none to bury them. We are become a reproach to our neighbors, a scorn and derision to them that are round about us. How long, Lord? Wilt thou be angry for ever? Shall thy jealousy burn like fire? Pour out thy wrath upon the heathen that have not known thee, and upon the kingdoms that have not called upon thy name. For they have devoured Jacob, and laid waste his dwelling place. O remember not against us former iniquities: let thy tender mercies speedily prevent us: for we are brought very low. Help us, O God of our salvation, for the glory of thy name: and deliver us, and purge away our sins, for thy name's sake. Wherefore should the heathen say, where is their God? Let him be known among the heathen in our sight by the revenging of the blood of thy servants which is shed. Let the sighing of the prisoner come before thee; according to the greatness of thy power preserve thou those that are appointed to die; and render unto our neighbors sevenfold into their bosom their reproach, wherewith they have reproached thee, O Lord. So we thy people and sheep of thy pasture will give thee thanks for ever, we will shew forth thy praise to all generations.

It was said Missus Cleveland died of sadness. Her older son and her husband had died in a private home near Dover Tennessee, of dysentery. At first, it seemed we would not be delivered the bodies—that the service would take place without them. The headstones would be laid over empty graves. But then the corpses came. The coffins were closed. Rumor was they were not fresh—that the father and son had been dead some time before their death was recorded officially. It cast the date on the headstones in question—but they had already been set, January 2, 1862, and January 3, 1862. And whether or not the dates were correct, it was believed a fact, and of more importance besides, that the father and son had died one day apart. There was some confirmation that Mister Cleveland's gray steed and Bugby's calico had been killed in an ill-advised charge, and that, as a result of Bugby's advancing sickness, the two horsemen had been left behind. Speculation was that Mister Cleveland had lain beside his son, had watched him die of dysentery, and had then succumbed himself—

> CAPTAIN SOMERTON CLEVELAND
> †
> BORN: APRIL 27, 1818
> DIED: JANUARY 3, 1862
>
> LOVING SON, BROTHER, HUSBAND
> AND FATHER
> MAY HE REST IN LOVE AND PEACE

No more than six feet east was the second gravestone—

> LIEUTENANT AMOS CLEVELAND
> †
> BORN: JANUARY 6, 1843
> DIED: JANUARY 2, 1862
>
> LOVING SON AND BROTHER
>
> MAY HE REST IN LOVE AND PEACE

That was Bugby's name—Amos.

My aunt told me that she was afraid she would not be welcome at the service, but she accompanied me—remaining in the woods as the funeral procession advanced into the graveyard. Because Amos had been a young man, recently graduated from our local schoolhouse where pupils up to eight years younger had sat beside him, nearly the entire population of the town's children were in attendance. He'd left for military academy only two years before, and in one way or another, was fondly remembered by most all of us. As approximately half had been delivered by chaperons who felt more comfortable waiting at a respectful distance, my aunt was not alone at the forest's edge. She was among a whole shadow group of mourners who stood some quarter of a mile off, hidden along the perimeter of cedar trees before the forest. We children were considered perennially innocent, and most households were of a mind to allow the attendance of any child who was thus disposed—as death was a part of life. And poor Missus Cleveland had extended every invitation. It was her wish to have Bugby's classmates and fellows together again. She greeted us all as "angels." She was white as plaster, and trembling. She stood with the pastor and a few of the town's wives. There were virtually no men, just a few of the older ones—Horatio Cooper from Horatio Cooper's General Store, and Mister Nielson, who held the arm of his wife. Missus Doctor Esterbrook was there, but her husband had been very busy as of late—often, she was sorry to report, with a saw. There were no other men between the ages of nineteen and forty-four—only the two dead ones, and Pastor Miles. Miss Caroline Cleveland was not in attendance, due to a situation that my aunt could not abide. Nonetheless, the pastor read Miss Cleveland's condolences aloud, along with several other even more unexpected condolences. Then he began the graveside service. In a murmur, Missus Doreen Cleveland asked the father to keep it short for us, "the little ones." (Perhaps his eulogy at the church was a more studied and lengthy one. I imagine there were not many people in the pews, unless many of those who were there did not proceed to the cemetery, which is also possible.) And while I am sure that Missus Cleveland did not make the request for herself, I believe that the brevity of the father's sermon was more for her benefit than for anyone else's. She was just a shell of herself—all eyes, cheekbones, runny nose and tears. Toward the end of the ceremony, she turned to us children. She held her scarf up close to her neck as she said—

"Well, my loves, you see poor Missus Cleveland very sick."

John Warren was wearing a black suit. He did not wear his copper-toed boots, but fitted calfskin shoes. . . . He did not stop holding his mother's hand—nor did he look away from her. I am not even sure he saw me. I did not call to him, or make myself known—though I had the feeling he felt my spirit, and was thankful for it. I believe he may have smiled at me. But at that moment, his mother's black scarf was lifted by a gust of wind, and I could not see his face. The overcoat he wore was dark—and he had turned up the collar of blue velvet. The sharp tips of his own black hair blew against his eyes. He helped shovel the earth. It thumped onto the coffins. Missus Cleveland tore her clothing and threw dried flower petals into the graves.

When the funeral was over, John Warren walked by his mother's side through the rows of tombstones and crosses, and then on the dirt path that cornered into the darkening woods.

He had grown. . . .

Shortly after, Missus Cleveland was taken to the insane asylum. A Confederate doctor had diagnosed her, and by his authority, her recovery seemed rather doubtful. At the asylum, the attending physician said that her case was highly similar to the case of a woman who'd been in their care for over forty years. But Missus Cleveland did not complete the first night. By the next morning, she had closed her eyes, and gone her way.

Doctor Esterbrook and the doctor from the asylum agreed that it was galloping consumption. But it didn't make much sense to either one of them—that she could have developed it overnight.

Some say that Missus Cleveland just died when her husband and her son died—that when their spirits left their bodies, her spirit left hers—it was practically true that when they took their last breaths, she took hers. . . .

It was as a result of Missus Cleveland's destructive behavior that the Confederate army was alerted (by a neighbor with whom the Clevelands had disputed a property line for sixteen years). A major arrived with a field doctor, and Missus Cleveland was committed. My aunt believed it was too early, though most agreed that it had come the time for that. She had hardly been herself before the news of her husband and son, and after, she'd gone altogether mad. It was told that she had become dangerous, not only to herself, but to everyone around her.

Countless times, she had been found trying to set Centennial House on fire.

Some people of the community, however, were not so ready for John Warren to be without a mother, and, my aunt among them, they planned to petition for her release. But by the time we heard any of the story, three days had gone by, and though my aunt did not spare a moment before she went after Doreen Cleveland at the asylum in Sudsbury, by then, Missus Cleveland was quite dead.

And my aunt, until the day she died herself, was suspicious of that quick demise—and despite the reassurances of Doctor Esterbrook, she was absolutely certain that medical science was the killer.

"She was alive when she went in there," my aunt would state—"she was alive when she went in there."

Doctor Esterbrook would assure my aunt that he had examined the body, and found no evidence of misdeeds—but my aunt was disgusted with the blunt fact—

"She was alive then. She's dead now."

Often, my aunt said to me that it might have been anything—a spoon or glass of water touched by poison. She had heard, and firmly believed, that some of the men who worked in such institutions were of a morose nature—that kind of character that led to the sudden and mysterious death of women. . . .

To this day, that is not a popular opinion, and though I have sometimes shared it, I have rarely voiced it. I do believe that it is equally possible, and woefully so, that it was mere grief, a mother's grief and a wife's grief, that killed Missus Doreen Cleveland.

And thus . . . after completing the morning business of committing the family matron to the insane ward, that Confederate major ate a lunch prepared by Natalie and Serena, then set about to dispatching John Warren to the poorhouse. He had called for his men, and they were to prepare the house for an outpost. A man would deliver John Warren to the poorhouse in Frickerham that afternoon. But Pastor Miles had also gone out to the estate, and he wouldn't let the man send John Warren away. And not even a military man would shoot or fight a pastor—and that's what it would have taken to get John Warren away from Pastor Miles! A message was conveyed to Doctor Esterbrook, who arranged for a lawyer and helped to draw up the papers for Miss Caroline Cleveland to assume custody. Meanwhile, Missus Esterbrook went to Miss Cleveland, who, from Horatio Cooper, let rooms nearby, where she'd been mourning—quite alone. She had not been free to attend the funeral, and perhaps she was mourning that too—having not seen her brother or nephews for more than a year. And the two of them, she would not see again. It was charged to Missus Esterbrook to explain the matter of the third to Miss Cleveland, who had not risen from bed in four days. Miss Cleveland's eyes were glazed, and at first, it did not appear that Missus Esterbrook would be able to rouse the teacher from her trance-like state. It was required that Missus Esterbrook dispense a vigorous shaking to jar life into the catatonic Miss Cleveland—and it was only then that the fight returned to Miss Cleveland's eyes. She'd retired for the evening on Friday—and it was now Tuesday. But while Miss Cleveland was much drawn, she enlisted Missus Esterbrook's assistance in helping her into full dress. The effect may not have been as elegant as it would have been in years before—but it was striking all the same. She wore boots of an untanned leather, tied with thongs. The dress was homespun, in black and white fabric. The white was woven from cotton yarn, the black from a remade silk (the original silk had been scraped with shards of glass—and the pulp was respun into an ever so fine thing). The cuffs and collar were made of a whitened homespun cotton. She had a hat of plaited rye-straw—it had been dyed maroon with the juice of beets. Her gloves were made black with walnut juice. Miss Cleveland had Missus Esterbrook pull the corset so tight she almost passed out. Then she powdered herself, applied her rouge and toilet, packed her bag, and they drove Missus Esterbrook's team to the Cleveland estate. And when Miss Cleveland arrived at the house, she said, "Get your men and supplies out of here. This is my house. And this is my boy." It was said she made an imposing entrance—and the soldiers were much awed by her grace and cultivation. . . .

The major had a black mustache, which he twirled. And even before Doctor Esterbrook arrived, with a letter authorized by Judge McCalister, a birth certificate verifying the identity of Miss Cleveland, and a copy of Somerton Cleveland's will, which, in the event of his wife's death or indisposition, named his sister, Caroline Cleveland, as a beneficiary, as well as the executor of his sons' inheritance if they should not yet be of age—even before Doctor Esterbrook arrived with all of that, the major said, "I am sure you are quite correct, Miss Cleveland. Please accept my humblest of apologies for this grievous error."

The major assigned a man to help guard Miss Cleveland's horses, but, as they were disappearing one by one, the officer eventually offered to buy the majority of them outright. He could not be sure that his men were not involved with the thefts, though if they were, they were clever enough to move the horses out of the area quickly. And, on the other hand, he said that if it was not his men, it was the enemy, and he could not allow such horses to be utilized by the enemy—for they could easily mean his own defeat. The officer was named Major Florian. He paid for the horses out of his own pocket. . . .

And though it should have been the furthest thing from my mind, and despite all of the great losses suffered by the Cleveland family, I could not help but nurture one selfish joy—John Warren would now be in attendance at school, as his aunt was the guardian of his education. Winter break nearly complete, school would be resuming in just a few weeks. And however difficult her life had become, I knew that Miss Cleveland would not give up her classroom. . . . And . . . how sorely I wanted to visit John Warren! But, as the soldiers knew nothing of my aunt and me, and our cottage by the creek, I was not permitted to make the call. Further, the soldiers were in and out of the estate every day, freely conveniencing themselves with provisions from the Cleveland family, and my aunt wanted me, a poor country girl, nowhere near such men. . . .

My aunt said that it was a sad state of affairs—that the Cleveland house was too big a house, and too big an estate, without Doreen, Somerton, Amos or the horses. It was too big a place, she said, for just the slave girl Natalie, her mother Serena, the schoolteacher, Miss Cleveland and her nephew, John Warren. . . .

Aunt Betta sometimes had dreams—not the regular kind of dreams, but dreams of things that would happen.

She woke me on the twentieth of January, 1862— I remember the date because school was to resume that morning. It was well past midnight, but before dawn.

She came to my room and shook my shoulder. She bundled me up, as it was cold, even inside, and set me to gathering foodstuffs. She instructed me to pack some pecans, dried cherries and a jar of pickled pigeon. She wrote a note which she attached to the pigeon and cherries. It said not to eat too much at once.

"Alma," said my aunt, "go out to the garden and collect some winter greens. And see if there are any carrots."

She was gathering some popping corn, dried barley, rice, beans, oats and hominy as she sighed, "I'm sorry that we won't have much in the way of fruits and vegetables, but in a manner, maybe it's for the best, because it's all so light to carry—and there's water almost everywhere. A boy brought up so close to the woods will know the water that's good to drink. And there will be fruits and vegetables anyway, as spring comes."

After I had gathered up some yams and cabbage from the garden (there were no more carrots) my aunt had me help her make a pile of batter cakes, which we wrapped up and packed in a basket with several jars of preserves. We added the packets of cherries, nuts, beans, rice, corn, barley and oats to that, together with a few other odds and ends—and finally, for all the haste, and my persistent questioning, my aunt told me what I was to do with it.

She said, "Take this basket to the Clevelands'. Place it on the steps of the front door. I would go myself, but I am too old, and too slow. Run Alma—as much of the way as you can. Do not take the path. Let no one see you. Here, take my shawl, you'll be warm in it. Be sure to keep your head covered. The soldiers will see your red hair."

My aunt wouldn't tell me more—she said she wasn't sure about anything. Then she began to doubt herself, and that I should make the trip. So I took her shawl and the basket and I did run. And I placed the provisions as she said.

At the Cleveland estate, I didn't see any soldiers, so I lay down on the hidden side of a knoll, and peered down through the white fence to the house—which was blue and gray in the early morning light. I was bundled up in my aunt's purple shawl, and since I had been running, I was warm enough, and with the cold air to breathe, and the great emotional drain of the morning . . . I plummeted into sleep.

When I woke, it was to a voice screaming. I saw the basket was gone. The voice was Miss Cleveland's—

"John Warren! John Warren! Where are you?"

She was running out of the house and down to the barn—he and his horse were gone. Then she ran off, down the road, screaming, "John Warren! John Warren!"

There were still a few horses on the place, and Stewart Valentine had been working with them in the big barn across the white fences and the grass.

Stewart Valentine was an old man with a bad leg—when he was a young man, working on a ship, it had been wound up in a rope when a sail went up. But he could ride a horse if he had to, and he galloped down the grass trail on a cinnamon Morgan, while clutching the bridle of Miss Cleveland's horse, Florida, who galloped beside him. He was yelling to Miss Cleveland that Pegasus was gone—that wherever John Warren was going, he was taking his horse with him. Shedding her shoes and petticoat, Miss Cleveland ran—and she didn't stop running when Stewart Valentine rode up beside her. And, the horses galloping, it seemed like they were all running, as fast as they could, when she mounted that horse. The horse was saddled already and as she pulled herself up, I was sure that she would mount sidesaddle—as I had not seen a grown woman ride but sidesaddle. But I was quite surprised to see that leg of hers swing right over to ride, not sidesaddle—but full on! I had never seen a woman ride a horse like that! Then, with a sudden change of direction, Miss Cleveland's horse applied a flying change, switching her mount's lead leg. And then, from the canter, came the full gallop, and riding astride, she left Mister Valentine and his mount far behind, racing ahead as Mister Valentine turned down the pine tree path—that they might cover both directions. And, with all my admiration and sorrow for Miss Cleveland, I lifted my head off the dried grass to watch as she and Mister Valentine rode off, searching for the boy John Warren. . . .

"John Warren! John Warren!" I heard her voice calling out, "We're looking for you."

"We're looking for you. . . ."

But as much as I loved Miss Cleveland, and as much as I loved John Warren, I did not look for him. I did not stand up to call for him—I just held my fists in tight balls, clenched my teeth, breathed hard and did not wipe the tears from my eyes.

I just lay crying on the frozen ground. It was the start of a warm winter day. The kind of day that melted ice and winked at spring. I lowered my face to the cold ground and could not believe it was the start of such a day.

The boy John Warren was gone. And I knew he would not be seen again. . . .

It was the kind of thing that made time take notice, and after I had cried, and rose onto my knees, and then my feet, I turned my head, ever so slowly, and the clear morning revealed itself—

It was cold and breezy, but the sun was bright, and the forest had opened its eyes—opened its eyes for a moment of sharpened consciousness to interrupt the long night of winter slumber. Squirrels, chipmunks and rabbits were out of their burrows for fresh air, a brisk run, and a taste of buried plunder. And even the unkempt Cleveland estate had the somber smile of a moment of peace—the front door and the barn door were open, Miss Cleveland's petticoat blew against the white slats of a long fence. . . . And all was still, calm, as if to maintain that lie—*nothing will change here for a hundred years, nothing will change here for a thousand*. But it was already so different, and as I thought about how my aunt's basket was gone, I was rather quick to accept its loss, to think, ah, it's only a basket—and even the weaver of that basket knew it would eventually be lost. And then, as I began to shiver (as I had sweated in my feverish sleep, and now, the cold wind was blowing in my half adjusted shawl) I began to consider all the other things I had lost. My hands were shaking—so I thought of lost hats and mittens. And I thought of how at first it had been upsetting, and then I had gotten used to it. I expected to lose pens and pencils, and even writing tablets and the occasional notebook. Sometimes they were found, but sometimes I hardly even looked for them. It just wasn't worth any time at all—wishing for a lost bag of marbles. Losing things—it was the kind of activity that practice made perfect. And now that I was growing accomplished at losing the common kinds of losable things, it was getting easier for me to lose the larger ones. *Ah*, I thought, *the basket is gone. But that is all right, I have lost a whole family, in Richmond, which is a town in a whole state I have lost.* And as for the strangeness of the empty Cleveland house, the family estate now left with only one member of the family, a dog and four ghosts—that one member of the family being Caroline Cleveland, that dog being Mack and those ghosts being John Warren, and who he might have been, and his deceased mother, father and brother—and as for the strangeness of that suddenly unfamiliar plot of land, it was only strange because at one time I had assumed it was mine. John Warren and I had already lived out our lives there, having picnics, riding sleds, playing games, and all along knowing that we would one day live there to raise horses, and we would give great parties out on the lawn, where the children would play and fall in love. . . . And, we thought . . .

And, what we thought—all that was lost too. And the Cleveland estate was lost, to me.

Or, perhaps, I considered, that girl was lost—that orphan girl from so long ago. Perhaps I was the fifth ghost of Centennial House, standing in a life that no longer belonged to me. *John Warren's Alma . . . she's lost too.* I breathed hard, and the cold air stabbed my nose and lungs as I thought. . . . *And John Warren, after he found the basket, did he find me? Did he kiss me when I was sleeping? Did he think not to wake me, thinking I would lie here, dreaming, until the day of his return? Did he think he would return a tall, polished soldier, and I would be as shining and upright as his own sword? Did he think that when his lips touched mine, I would wake, and then we would be together?*

But then I knew he did not dream like that, as he too had grown accustomed to losing—and I knew that he did not dream like that, because if he did, he would have woken me to this fine dream. He would have said, "Everything will be dandy." But those words were not so easy to come by, not if you thought your home, your family and your future, all was lost—just like a scarf in the woods, just like a mitten sunk to the mud at the bottom of a pond and frozen under the ice. Just like a moment, riding a horse across the grass. . . .

Of course, I had assumed that it'd not be long before Miss Cleveland freed her slaves—but she did not. And truth be told, despite her long opposition to the institution, she fought bitterly to keep them on when the estate came into her possession. She even went so far as to hire the Clevelands' former overseer, Ragan, to recapture a group that had escaped. She explained it to me one day after school, "I'll free them when the fighting's over." I was standing in the empty classroom, doing some reading and helping her care for the class animals, which needed attending. And thinking about what she had said, it seemed like a practical thing to me—as the times were woefully hard, and it would be better, safer for her people if they had work, food and lodging. But later that evening, when I told my aunt, she reminded me that Somerton Cleveland had always said that he would free his slaves when he and his wife died. And he didn't. And that was the thing with slavery, she said, it would gradually corrupt one's soul until the right thing to do was a very distant thing to one's sense of logic.

"Aunt Bettina," I said, "I believe you are wrong."

"No," she said, "Alma, I am afraid I am not. If those people want to stay on there, working for food and lodging—that is up to them to decide."

That was the biggest fight I ever had with my aunt, and that was the extent of it. But for me, storming into my room, it was a sort of a tantrum. Miss Cleveland was so perfect, and I knew . . . I knew, well, that she treated her people well, and they wanted to be there, and . . . I knew it wasn't right, but I simply couldn't believe that Miss Cleveland would ever do anything wrong. . . .

And I stayed on in my room, and slept without eating—but even so, by the time I closed my eyes, I knew that indeed, Miss Cleveland was wrong, and my aunt was right. And so I told Miss Cleveland, after school the very next day.

I said, "You always said you would free them, and I think you should, even if it is a bad time to do it."

Miss Cleveland looked up at me, a little puzzled, and a little sad, and she finally said, "We have a difference of opinion then, your aunt and I."

"And me," I said, "Miss Cleveland, me too."

And I can say now, without shame, and retaining my sense of fondness, that my worship of Miss Cleveland did not abate, though I did develop a sense of our human frailty—our imperfection. And with that knowledge came the patience to wait for what was just, and the forgiveness to bestow when the time came to bestow it—for judgment was not mine to make. If it was to be made by any, it was by those that had been slaves to the Clevelands for all that time. And of course, it was not to be made by them, as soon enough, every last one of them would move on. So, perhaps Miss Cleveland was too easily forgiven, and perhaps there was no legal penance that she had to pay, other than a monetary one—but there was a moral penance in the years after the trouble, when she worked for the Freedmen Bureau, giving classes in reading, writing and arithmetic. It was at that time that Miss Cleveland repented. Nearly four years had passed when a fight broke out between two boys in our class, one claiming that freedmen were Americans, one claiming they weren't. I was older by then, and I was standing by Miss Cleveland when the one boy said to Miss Cleveland—

"But you owned slaves."

And Miss Cleveland looked at me, her face screwed up in an ugly way, and she said, "And Andrew, we treated those slaves as we'd have the devil treat us. . . ."

Now—it was true that Caroline Cleveland had grown up in a world of . . . well . . . a kind of a vanity, and even, at times, a grotesque cruelty—but it being a contradictory world, hers was also a world of deep awareness and daily kindness—and those were the traits in her, which, in her adulthood, she chose to nourish. And beyond that, she was a woman of internal perseverance and character—as she would not go from a blossoming Southern girl to the flower, fragile and dewy, of a Southern belle—and from there to life-long wet nurse. She would not win a man through batted eyes and flirtatious chatter. She would not encourage, flatter and confide. She would not choose from the best of the moths she had attracted with the illumination of a bright smile. She would not be such a candle. She would not be such a woman—and she would not have such a man. And whatever weaknesses of her upbringing that she combated through her life, that was always to her credit, and the credit of her family.

I could tell that it was a rather painful thing for Miss Cleveland to sell her horse, Florida, but she was offered a good price, and she was greatly in need of the money, and every horse was so much work, and it was a good officer who wanted to buy Florida, and as she said—

"I will not cry over a horse."

And if she did cry, I didn't see it.

It may have been a kind of turning point for her, as over the next months, I spent a great deal of time with Miss Cleveland and the horses. The stud farm was really just too much work for her and her people, and I tried to make myself of use as she set about reorganizing. She had sold the most valuable stallions, and was roughing off a good many of the other horses, that she might put them to grass, thus lessening the expense of keeping them. I'd have much opportunity to observe the horses in this more natural state, grazing and playing—and I learned about their personalities. Besides being an easier way to keep a horse, Miss Cleveland said it was sometimes a good thing to let an animal take a break, as horses could get barn sour, and too dependent on routine. She expected the situation would last no longer than a few months, though it would turn out not only to last longer, but to be the first of a series of changes that would eventually divest the Cleveland estate of every last resident—horses and people alike.

The first thing Miss Cleveland had to do was even the field—and several of the slaves helped us to flatten out the ridges and pack the soft spots that had recently come about. There were even some holes, as one or two of the fences had been pulled and re-arranged—and those holes were filled in. Next, Miss Cleveland and I set about to free the new fields of any dangerous weeds—and sure enough, we did find some deadly nightshade and chokecherry. . . .

To set the horses out was a simple thing in itself, as horses, quite plainly, liked the company. By their very nature, horses were happiest in a field of others. They'd shuffle about in groups of twos and threes—friendships close. Between some, there might be as much love as between mother and foal. An animal disposed to friendships, one mare became nearly inseparable from Mack the dog. They were rarely seen apart, but unfortunately, that horse was sold the next season, and Mack suffered for it.

The males and females were usually kept separated, except for horses that Miss Cleveland wanted to pair, and that took a fair share of organization—a man to help the stallion, a man to help the mare, and a man to generally facilitate the operation. But what I remember most about those pairs, and pairs of friends, is how they would stand head to tail, tail to head, whisking flies off each other—and how they would stand side by side, gently massaging each other's withers with their lips and teeth. And just to think of it makes my own neck and shoulders yearn for a soothing hand. . . . And they were always nipping and sprinting. One friend playing with another—not because times were hard, but because there was now so much more time to play. . . .

Horses, their lives seemed dedicated to these loving attentions—that and having a life of enough food and enough sleep. Even at night, they'd sleep for a while, eat for a while—sleep for a while, eat for a while. One of them always seemed to be keeping an eye out. (Just in case some lion might venture by!) And, as they slept on their feet, the whole of them would sometimes scatter at the approach of a coyote, or such. An open barn was emptied of all but straw, with the one side almost completely exposed, so that no animal could get trapped—and occasionally, a horse or more would retire to that barn for some treat of grain or a sheltered sleep. But in the warmer weather, the preference was definitely for the naked air—and who could blame them? The air was so fresh, and rich, and full of the smells they loved. And when they woke with the morning—they'd just lower their heads to set themselves about the serious task of grazing. There was one ridge in particular that they all seemed to favor—and in their spare moments, they liked to walk up there, to admire the fine view in this direction, and the fine view in that. . . .

For grooming, sometimes they'd flop onto the ground, let out a good breath, and roll in dirt soft and dusty. They seemed to just adore this occupation, especially when they were sweaty—and it did seem to keep them dry, and to scrape off bugs and the like. In spring, it seemed to help them shed their winter hair.

We'd still need to check on the horses—and Miss Cleveland did so with her people every day. They'd attend to hooves, and take care with rugs and blankets. She kept the animals trimmed from the stomach up to the harness line, as this was a good clip to prevent too much sweating and loss of condition, yet still keep out the cold. It was a shame in a way to have all those animals out, but the horses themselves didn't seem to mind it, and they had their workouts—though perhaps not as strenuous as before. Tails were never clipped, as it was a horse's device to battle flies. For their coats, we couldn't really scrub'em down, just sort of brush them off and get rid of any mud, as a horse at grass needed its natural oils to keep warm.

So—out I'd go with Miss Cleveland, in the afternoon, and I learned in a glance to see that a horse was healthy—the ears would flicker, the coat would shine. And the legs, they'd be cool to the touch. . . .

Autumn '63

$\mathcal{I}$t was as if Harmon Valentine were the spirit of us all.

In our spooky schoolhouse, with no more than six or seven children at a time, there were so many empty desks and benches that we all grew rather jittery through the days—although the games we played were glum. A ponderous anxiety infused us all—all except for Harmon, who took that pure jitteriness and transformed it into pure expression. And rather comical expressions at that! Sometimes Harmon would run across the yard and right into a tree, and as he collapsed, he'd say—

"My uniform is gray."

And then he would lay his hands on the ground and he'd push himself up and fly across the yard right into the side of the schoolhouse. And he'd crash and collapse again onto the ground, whereupon he would sit up with his bright eyes and say—

"My uniform is blue."

And I would say. . . .

"You're a weird one, Harmon."

But we'd all be laughing, because it was funny—even if it was in a *weird* way. I remember rather distinctly how even indoors, Harmon would make himself the clown, running into room corners and jumping into them—*thud*—just as if, by that, he might disappear right into the wall!

Harmon was a boy of unkempt agitation. And through all the day, he would rock the school bench, which perhaps would have been funny too, and perhaps would not have been a problem, were I not

143

sitting on the same bench as Harmon, and were Pitney Zooks not sitting behind us, trying to write on that swaying ledge fixed to the back of that swaying bench!

Miss Cleveland was growing rather disgusted with Harmon, really. Even if it wasn't on purpose—what he was doing. He'd just set his feet on the floor and set to rocking. And I'd look up with my fists clenched around my pencil and my lips pursed. And Pitney just groaned—

"Harmon, quit!"

And then, Miss Cleveland finally decided—

"Okay. That's it. The three of you—get up."

And then Miss Cleveland adjourned our lessons for the afternoon and we children helped move two of the benches and two of the older children's desks out to the shed. And then we spaced what was left—all evenly. And then Miss Cleveland sat Harmon, Pitney and me at our very own desks! We were not so old as the children who sat there before—but the places were empty, said Miss Cleveland, and the time was therefore right. I was so very proud of that desk! It was hardly used at all, and the wood was smooth as silk—or *almost* so. The feet were iron—cast in the shape of paws. It had a groove for pencils, and a hollow for books and the like. My feet hardly even touched the floor. And I was only eleven!

And Miss Cleveland was right, by the time we were all done, the schoolhouse did look much better—and not nearly so empty.

Miss Cleveland woke to the sound of a scratching coming from outside the house. She went to the west window, and saw faces floating in the pine needles of the tree by the house. They were soldiers perched in the branches. They were men, peeking in—through the closed window, through the thin curtain.

She heard the peal of musketry. Several rifles were fired, just outside the house. There were whoops. She backed away from the bed, and looked through the north window—there were men in front of the house, firing their weapons into the air.

Then there was a banging at the door. Miss Cleveland hurried down the stairs, wearing no more than a robe. Luckily, Stewart Valentine was up and about, as he had seen the men coming, and had known their intentions. When Stewart Valentine had woken that evening, some of the slaves had already made their way into the house, and were walking around in the late Mister and Missus Cleveland's finest clothing. One couple had been arm in arm when Stewart Valentine came upon them. The man had tipped his hat, the woman had curtsied—then they had left, laughing. Miss Cleveland would later say that she could not blame the slaves, and regarded the matter as a joke of fate. It was said the clothes fit the couple perfectly, and in the end the slaves took surprisingly little. And, added Miss Cleveland, what they did take—it was better they should have it anyway. It belonged to them more than it did to the Union army. And as the slaves themselves felt that very same way about it, and wanted not at all to be subjected to torture and theft at the hands of the Union army, they did not linger on the estate. For fear the soldiers would come, over the past few weeks, Miss Cleveland and the Valentines had already hidden some provisions and all of the firearms—burying them out in the fields. But they had not been prepared for the thoroughness of the raiders, who would take not just sustenance, but everything. The soldier on the other side of the front door said he was to search the house for guns—although in the end, none were found, and none were taken.

Miss Cleveland refused to allow the soldier entry. Finally, he kicked down the door. Stewart Valentine barred the threshold. But the soldier swung his gun like a billy-club—cracking old Mister Valentine across his face. His cheek tore, he lost two teeth—and he fell. Then Miss Cleveland barred the threshold. She was shuddering—shaking all over.

The soldier was a peculiar man, in some ways very modest—in some ways, not at all. He said, "I didn't think twice about hittin' that'un, but I won't lay a finger on you, as I have a womun at 'ome." He blushed—

"I may shoot you though."

"You do it, then," said Miss Cleveland, standing firm. "A man who would shoot an unarmed woman is the lowest kind of creature alive, and I would rather be shot than stand with such a man."

"Well," said the soldier, "you mayn't respect me, but you'll fear me," and he raised his gun.

Miss Cleveland stared down the barrel—it was a long, smooth barrel.

The soldier stepped toward the door, but Miss Cleveland didn't move.

"Well, miss, I'm aiming to kill you. Let me in and maybe I won't."

She said no.

The barrel did not waver. She smelled gunpowder on it. She realized that it had just been fired—he'd been one of the men firing out in her own front yard.

"I'll shoot," he said.

She answered—"I know."

There were other soldiers behind him now, and Miss Cleveland was unsure if that would make him back down, for shame, or fire for certain, for bluster. The men didn't try to stop him, but just said to her, "Let 'im in. Ain't gonna do no good not to."

But she didn't let him in, and he fired his rifle.

She heard the report. She knew the bullet would enter her head. . . .

She fell beside Stewart Valentine, who was scarcely moving at all. Regaining consciousness, seconds later, she saw that the men were in the house. She herself was unharmed, but she heard a yelping. She remembered that Mack had been barking. Stewart Valentine had wanted him in the house—and Mack had been on the stairs. She rolled her head to look at him. He was shot.

One of the soldiers grabbed Mack by the leg and dragged him into the yard, as, despite his mortal injury, Mack was still trying to bite the soldiers, and furthermore, Mack was bleeding on a carpet that the soldier had been trying to roll up—to take.

Mack was a good dog, and a loyal dog, and he died in the front yard, growling. The body disappeared, and Miss Cleveland hated to think that Mack had been ground up and fed to the animals of those prowlers and thugs.

At that range, Miss Cleveland knew that the soldier could not have missed by accident. She must not have seen that the gun was pointed at Mack, behind her. Even staring down the barrel, she had not seen it—that's how close it had been.

The soldier who fired the rifle returned to her, and asked if she was now afraid of him. She said she was not. And the soldier swore an admiration for her, and went about his business, which was stealing. . . .

There were twenty or thirty men in the pantry, tearing open the cabinets and drawers with their swords. Miss Cleveland had roasted several ducks lest Stewart Valentine's fears come to pass. She had stashed them in the kitchen safe, but the soldiers forced it open immediately, and were soon devouring whole birds, ripping them with their hands and teeth as they went about the remainder of their duties. They charged the pantry, hoping for whiskey, but all the casks had been broken, and the alcohol had drained through the floor. (Stewart Valentine had done the deed, as when he saw the soldiers, he thought the whiskey would place everyone in jeopardy. It was a good thing that he was delivered to Doctor Esterbrook before he could be questioned.) Natalie and Serena were standing in the kitchen when the soldiers charged, but each of them had undergone a startling transformation. Natalie, a tall and upright girl, suddenly had become crooked and weak-minded—she stood with her eyes crossed, her feet pigeon-toed and her mouth open and drooling. Serena, her mother, a comely young woman, of a natural appeal equal to that of her young daughter, had also slumped—she had dusted her hair in flour, and wizened her face, and she was suddenly an old woman, just barely able to hobble from here to there. . . .

Thus, the two slave women went unmolested—though the house

itself was not so fortunate. Everything closed was opened. All that had even the slightest use or worth was taken. And everything else was destroyed—envelopes of children's hair, and correspondence of great-grandparents. The soldiers made off with all the eating utensils, silver and tin, and absolutely anything else they had a whim to acquire. Some of it was left lying in the front yard. They drank up a few crates of old blackberry wine. Several of the raiders even had lists from back home, from wives or sweethearts. Miss Cleveland secured one, and years later, showed it to me. It was written in the hand of a woman, an uneducated one—

Silky gluvs
Silky dress
Purl neklas and purl ear-rings
Purty pin

The soldiers would even take the chain from the well bucket, which would prove a great hardship. They seemed to have a dislike for crockery and dishes—as all that was not taken was shattered. The last horses were also taken. It was good that many had been sold already. In the previous months, Miss Cleveland had gathered all that remained of the family fortune, converted it to gold and buried it in the woods in cans—over the coming years, Miss Cleveland would sometimes go after it, alone, with a rifle. She would shoot at anyone who followed her. And she would try to hit them, too. . . .

Miss Cleveland was nursing Stewart Valentine as the soldiers climbed into the kitchen attic where she had stored ten bushels of meal, which they took. Miss Cleveland asked that they leave enough for her and hers to eat, and they poured her a few handfuls which she wrapped up in her dress. They spilled some rice on the floor. She gathered it all up, along with some scattered grain and beans, hoping she might wash it off later, and grind it into meal. On her hands and knees, she begged them for more, but they said they needed feed for their horses. They wanted men's clothing, and they took everything that had belonged to John Warren. When they took the clothing that had belonged to Amos, Somerton and Doreen Cleveland, Serena cried out to the soldiers— "Dose dead people's clothes, dose dead people's clothes," and a few things were left.

After the sitting room was cleared of all valuables, the remaining servants and workers were gathered up and ordered into it. A guard was assigned to them. When the bedroom was likewise emptied, Miss Cleveland was allowed two handmaids, Serena and her daughter Natalie, who helped her to dress. The soldiers had left Miss Cleveland only the plainest things.

When the officer arrived, Miss Cleveland informed him of the peeping toms. He said he would investigate the matter, and if the tale were true, the men would be disciplined. On his belt, the officer wore a whip—the kind worn by the whippers-in of a foxhunt. . . .

The officer then assigned her another guard, a man whom he'd had with him. The officer seemed a gentleman, though he had allowed the estate to be ransacked. He said they were his orders.

"Robbing a schoolteacher?" asked Miss Cleveland.

"Those are my orders," he said.

After the night was over, the soldiers did not leave, and they did not let Miss Cleveland or her people leave. They were kept under guard, and locked in the upstairs bedroom. Word was that Miss Cleveland had turned to Serena to ask—

"Am I a coward?"

Thus, Miss Cleveland's predicament—and added to the other unpleasantness, it was told that Miss Cleveland and her people were not being properly provided for nutritionally. What was being served to them was of a grievously poor quality, and the soldiers in charge seemed almost to enjoy the quandary of this fine lady—eat slop, or be starved. "O'," said one, "how the mighty have fallen!" By the third day, there were only four men on duty, and no officer, and in that capacity, no one to defend her. After five days, my aunt could no longer suppress her concern, and she darkened my hair with a temporary wash, so it would not stand out, and she bundled me up, to look fat and young.

My aunt would have preferred not to go at all—and not to bring me at all. But she could not let herself stand by while Miss Cleveland and her people withered to nothing, and she would not leave me alone—so she took me with her. We walked all the way around to the far side of the Cleveland estate and approached it from the southwest, so that it might appear we had come from that direction. When the three soldiers sitting on the porch first saw us, and called down to us, it was ever so tense and frightening for my aunt and myself, not only because the soldiers all had their rifles by their sides or across their laps—but because my aunt had brought her pistol! It was sewn into her rabbit-fur hand warmer, and though she knew the Union was fighting "her fight," they didn't know that, and besides, we had all heard stories of soldiers, on either side, that would justify the discharge of a firearm—not for the battle between North and South, but woman and man. And thus, we stood fixed—her hands in her hand warmer.

The chickens were loose in the yard and a fat soldier raised his gun, lazily, and shot at one—evidently, they would shoot at them as they had a mind to, as several of those that had been hit were lying dead and rotting out on the lawn. A few chickens that were shot were still alive, and suffering—gasping and bleeding.

There was an awful smell about, and looking up into the field I saw two dead horses and a dead cow. The horses were swelled big, but the cow was swelled out to the size of a shack. I couldn't even see where the head had been. It was hazy with flies. We'd be told later there was a dead pig too—it had been dropped in the well to spoil the water. There were tatters of Centennial House anywhere one looked—house windows, curtains, portraits. . . .

"All that waste," called out my aunt, "and people are starving inside!"

"No one's starving, ma'am," said the loudest of the three, "they eat no worse than we eat."

"Well," said my aunt, "I've brought some food."

"Oh," joked the smallest of the men, who was polishing his rifle, and sniffing continuously, "just leave the girl anywhere, we'll baste her right nice."

"Shut up, Slevin," said the loud one, "and go git them pies."

When the man, like his comrade, saw the pan-pies stacked against my chest, he was quick to react. He jumped up and bounced down the steps. We could smell the man even before he arrived—and I handed over the stack of four pies rather hesitantly, almost frozen by my own disgust.

Slevin took the pies and began to unwrap them, demonstrating how he would dig in with his hand.

My aunt spoke to him like an angry mother, "They aren't all for you, Slevin—here, these two are for you and your friends—these two are for Miss Cleveland and hers. The two vegetable pies are for them. The rhubarb-strawberry, and the surf'n'turf—those are for you."

"Look," said Slevin, calling up to the loud man, "she's feedin' us poisoned pies! She's a 'tarnal witch, Ebner! She's a—"

Ebner replied, "She ain't no witch, you fool, and those pies ain't poisoned. She's just trying to overfeed us, that's all."

"Hey," said Ebner to my aunt, "what's that meat pie?"

"Squirrel and turtle," my aunt answered.

"Yeah," said Ebner, miserably, "that's what we call surf'n'turf at 'ome too."

"Well," considered the fat soldier, who had shot at the chicken, and hadn't yet spoken, "overfeedin', that ain't bad. Slevin, take them pies, and bring up the leafy ones for the prisoners—she knows damn well we don't want those—and don't tell Judd about these others, okay. If we want to," he snorted, "we can always save him a sliver."

Slevin embarked on his errand, and my aunt and I backed toward the southern woods, and luckily, as the soldiers were a decidedly lazy sort, not a one of them, besides Slevin, would lift a toe to do anything. . . .

It was only a few days later that the Cleveland house was claimed as a military post, and other dwelling arrangements were made for Miss Cleveland, her servants and the Valentine family.

The big house was occupied by a military clerk. He wore thick glasses, and spent each day reading popular books, while sitting behind a desk he had moved onto the front porch. He was awaiting additional supplies.

It was a peculiar thing, but Miss Cleveland was not a day without a horse. That would be a blessing in the years to come, as it would enable her to look after the Cleveland estate without living there. For the time, she had retaken the rooms she had let from Mister Cooper. Town was some distance from the schoolhouse, especially on foot, and since the soldiers had arrived, it had become not entirely of a nature to support a lady—thus, it was hoped a new domicile could be arranged for her shortly. At first, Miss Cleveland was not decided on whether her guard had been assigned to prevent her escape or to protect her person. Mister Cooper offered the guard some whiskey to help him resolve the matter. The guard wavered, but then would not drink it. He said, "I try, ma'am, sir, to be a other kinda man." And then, over the night, he seemed to grow sympathetic to Miss Cleveland's cause. He sent a request to the lieutenant, explaining the matter of the distance of the schoolhouse. The lieutenant responded by returning to Miss Cleveland her riding carriage. It was pulled by a mule, who, even after a half a night's rest, was too exhausted to move. Come morning, he simply would not budge—and would have no part of the carriage, or even the harness to the carriage. But not having known of the gift mule, Miss Cleveland had already roused, with ample time to walk the hour and a half to the schoolhouse—classes had already been interrupted for two weeks, and she would not have them interrupted any longer. Her guard, whose name she learned was Mitchell Pope, was a man with children, who were also attending school that Monday, though they were very far away. Miss Cleveland said she hoped another good man would accompany that schoolteacher to her schoolhouse. Mister Pope said regretfully that he didn't know he was a good man, and he wished the man back home a better man than himself. . . .

In those days, men loved their horses, and when a horse's life was threatened (either because it was injured, or because resources were so limited as to prevent proper care, or, in many instances, both) a man might set the horse free that it might recover or die on its own. Though the latter was more likely—it was a less sure death than a bullet, and many of the men argued, less cruel than a death at the hands of its own master.

And when Miss Cleveland and her guard approached the school-house, such a freed horse was there—eating the bluegrass.

Miss Cleveland was no stranger to horses, and Mister Pope was much surprised to witness the horse's capture by Miss Cleveland's dexterous toss of a lasso. The horse, strange to say, did not resist, but merely inclined his head and returned to his meal of grass. He was a gentle horse. He whinnied at Miss Cleveland's touch, then seemed to appreciate it. He did not, however, take to the soldier, and would not let him approach. It would turn out that his hatred of soldiers was universal, and no man in uniform could near him—not until his dying day. The most conspicuous feature of the horse was his powdery tan coat and black feet. He had intelligent, luminous features and eyes. But it was the deeply grooved scars on his back that told tales. He had been branded many times, and it was no longer clear if the first brand had been U.S. or LA., for Louisiana. In his new life in the service of Miss Cleveland, he would often be referred to as Yankee, and often, Reb, depending on the nature and temperament of the speaker.

Through the years, he'd show that he had acquired some battle-time habits—such as digging grass out from under the snow, which must've been useful for a wild horse in the winter. And, to look at him, he'd been better off as a wild horse than a soldier's horse. His body spoke of the conflict itself—and Miss Cleveland took his pulse, placing her hand on the horse's leg, just above the pastern. Then she checked his breathing—reading the rise and fall of his ribs. Following her diagnoses, that there was nothing too seriously wrong with this animal, he was treated for several weeks by Stewart Valentine and William Ditzler. The worst malady was thrush—that foul smelling infection. It was cured by paring away the rot, and packing the cavity with *Mabeline's Thrush Mix*. The saddle sores were treated with salt, water and alcohol, to harden the flesh. The horse had some scratches, grazes and cuts on his legs from his life in the forest. They were cleaned and treated—dressed with herbs and powder. Few needed bandaging. Though his legs seemed fine, for all his hardships, the muscles and tendons were also treated with a hot poultice. A few bruises were treated with witch hazel. He was also cured of a cold, which had been the cause of a thick oozing from his nose. The mange and ringworm took a salve. . . . And what emerged from all that treatment was a stocky horse—but at least one could say his legs were not too long, or weak in appearance. And it would turn out that he was a good worker, though only for Miss Cleveland, and sometimes Mister Valentine or Mister Ditzler. He was a jibber at other times, refusing most every type of labor, and having a generally bad attitude. He was excitable in company, and I'm sorry to say it, a horror to look at—with his knobby legs, all full of spurs, splints and curbs. He was also guilty of dishing, with his forelegs swinging out in a funny way when he walked. . . .

So, he was not exactly a handsome horse—but even so, he was stately in his own bold way. And perhaps it was a noble disposition that allowed him to realize, in one way or another, that he was indebted to Miss Cleveland for his very life. An animal could surely know something like that, and an animal could surely have a noble disposition. And he loved her so, and was such a fine provider and gentleman to her. And while it may have been true that he was missing an entire ear, a portion of his scalp, and had a great hole in his other ear—he was alive when many others would not be alive. And he was a horse tested by man, land and travail. Such were his good looks. Perhaps he had been pretty as a foal.

For all those years the Clevelands had loved their animals, it was just as if the sky had looked down, and said that this family will never be without a good horse.

✳ ✳ ✳

I could no longer believe in Santa Claus.

I so wanted to still believe. But when it came right down to it, I had never been one too easy to fool—and I was fooled no longer.

Pig's Bladder

I knew that the talk was Santa was not coming this year—and that if he did come to Kentucky at all, he would not get around to Cotterpin to well nigh February. And I knew that it was not because of a blizzard in the North Pole, as some of the younger children said, but because of a failure in the distribution of the post office. Nothing was getting out of Frickerham. That's what I'd heard—that everything was so backed up that even had they the men to keep up with what was newly piling up, it would take at least a month to sort out what had already piled up. Such was the privilege of a slightly older girl— to be permitted the overhearing of adult conversation. . . . When I informed my aunt I was well aware of the matter and that she should not worry of the gifts for me, as a warm house and warm food were quite gift enough—she just looked into my eyes and nodded rather disheartedly. Still, it was to be hard for the little ones, as many had been without for some months. Clothing. Flour. Sugar. Not to mention toys and sweets. I heard Mister Nielson wish that Santa would bring him just one cup of coffee. Even my aunt and I were suffering some shortages—mainly milk, eggs and butter, as we did not keep chickens or cows, and we Flynts did not churn butter, but depended instead upon the barter of my aunt's medicinal recipes for those supplies. Yet there was always someone to trade for something, and even into winter, there were the late vegetables and greens to be had, and with the first frost, Mister Nielson butchered his pigs—so we did not go hungry. . . .

Still, some of us children were becoming rather sick with the dispirit of it. Among the all of us, we could not find even one ball to bat about! So I suggested we walk out to Mister Nielson's, as surely he still had his ponies. But when we arrived, Mister Nielson woefully reported that both his ponies were sick with horse sniffles, and that while both would be back to new in all but a few days, when they would be delighted to ride us, they were rather crabby today, and in no mood for it. So, we children all collapsed despondently into the fallen leaves. And we looked up at the mild December sky, and Mister Nielson asked—

"No ball?"

And we answered miserably—

"No ball."

And then Mister Nielson rather excitedly told us to wait right where we were, and he went into his house, and came out not a moment later with three balls in his hand! Why, he had very cleverly blown up three pig bladders and tied them off as balls!

And we ran among the bare pecan trees—bouncing, kicking, throwing and catching.

And then in the afternoon, he made us all a special treat, and we sat around his stove as his wife delivered to each of us a pig's tail jammed on a stick. And we held them into the fire—and they sizzled and the fat dripped off them. And we sucked and chewed that fine roasting flavor from them until we sat back like princes and princesses indeed! We pitched the bones into a bucket, and helped Mister Nielson when he threw them to his hounds.

And Mister Nielson said—

"And those hounds, they know it's a special treat, as pig tails are but once a year!"

And we children quite understood how those hounds felt about it, for we still had the taste of that sweet meat in our mouths—and when we went home, it was to a dinner that filled us—and to a sleep that engulfed us. . . .

And Mister Nielson—even if it was in his own gruff and old-times way, he really did know what was best fun for a child.

Even so . . . by dawn of the day before Christmas, there was no sign of the post—nor Santa Claus, for that matter. And so my aunt and I hiked down to the big valley pond on the other side of the Cleveland estate, and gathered up three bundles of young willows (one for her to carry, one for me to carry and one for her to carry) and returned to our cottage. And then we made two rocking chairs— one little one for me, and one big one for my aunt.

So we would have Christmas after all!

My aunt worked on the big chair—and I, the little. And as we worked, my aunt showed me the way to fashion a country rocking chair—

First, we made the seat—a square of the willow sapling woven with bark. Then we split another sapling and curved the two halves of it to make a seat back, which we attached to the seat. Then we wove bark onto that. Then, likewise, we made the arms, and wove bark onto that.

Then, for the last, we split the curved willow tree that we had taken, and we attached two legs to each chair side, and fixed it to the chair seat.

And in evening, we sipped hot cocoa that my aunt had secreted away, and we rocked in our rockers, and it was a merry Christmas after all. . . .

And it was a white Christmas too! When we woke in the morning, there was a dusting of snow on the ground, so my aunt and I gathered it from corners in the garden where it had blown deep. So we had pans of snow. And the molasses and sugar and cider that we had boiled together and stirred into a goop we poured into the snow and it hardened into brittle cider candy. My aunt wasn't much for candy, but she seemed to enjoy in my eating it.

As she said—no child should be without Christmas candy.

And then I gave my aunt the one gift I had for her—an apple so stuck with cloves that it might impart a spicy and fresh aroma to the air. And my aunt gave me a pair of mittens that she had knitted for me—

"Aunty," I said, "I didn't know you knitted."

"First time," she admitted—"in some fifteen years."

But she knew how anyway, and they were very pretty mittens—all red and orange.

And my aunt seemed to like her apple so much—the way she smiled when I smiled at her, I thought it was the most wonderful Christmas ever—even without Santa Claus. Even if I could not help but miss him. . . .

It was about then we heard twigs snapping in the cold—and a shuffling in the bushes. We went to the window, and from the half of the bush we could see, my aunt could tell that it was a 'possum or squirrel, or something or other tangled up in there.

So we threw on our shawls and stepped into our untied boots and we went out—and lo and behold, that something or other was old Joe Sharpless from the post office!

"I'm after my hat." He smiled, and reached out again, "I can't quite reach it."

Now my aunt, she was a bit bigger than Joe, so she just went right over to that bush and plucked that hat right out.

"Why, here you go, Joe."

Joe took it, dusted it, replaced it on his head and explained—

"Nasty wind."

"Joe," asked my aunt, with a curious smile on her face, "what are you doing all the way out here on Christmas Day?"

"Well," said Joe, readjusting his hat, "well I'm uh . . . out to the Nielsons'. Nielson and I go way back, y'know."

"And you weren't going to stop in on us, Joe." My aunt put her hands on her hips and clucked her tongue.

"Why," he said, "an old man would be an imposition."

And to that, my aunt said—

"Joe, I'd bet you'd like a cup of real coffee, and sweetened with brown sugar. Not white, but not molasses. That can be our Christmas present to you. I bet not even Horatio Cooper has any sugar left."

And old Joe was all the whites of his big blue eyes—

"No ma'am, I know for a fact he don't."

"Well then," said my aunt, turning Joe around, "in you go!"

And Joe Sharpless said—

"Yes ma'am!"

Inside, Joe sat down and my aunt set to his coffee, and packed up a bit for Mister Nielson as well, that Joe might deliver it. And Joe looked at all our presents—unwrapped and gathered around a wreath set apart from the fire.

"Hungh," he said, "looks like you two wouldn't have needed Santa Claus . . . even if he hadn't come."

And my aunt looked at me regretfully and I said—

"I know there's no Santa Claus, Joe."

"Well," Joe sighed, "it happens younger and younger every year."

And Joe stroked his white beard—

"But I sure wish I could explain that to Santa, when I saw him, not five minutes—"

And even though I knew it couldn't be, I said—

"Really? Joe? Really? You saw Santa? Oh, where Joe? Where?"

"Well," said Joe, very matter of factly—"right outside, coming off your porch, I believe—I thought he had surely been here for a cup of hot tea."

"Out on the porch, Joe?" My aunt's smile went grand—

"Alma, why don't you see if Santa left anything out on the porch."

And I did. And Santa had. Or old Joe had. I knew that it was probably old Joe. He had probably gone to Frickerham, and sorted out all the Cotterpin post, and set back to deliver it on Christmas day. But I wanted so to believe in Santa, and there was a glimmer of hope inside me that did.

"What did the reindeer look like?" I asked.

And Joe described the sled and the reindeers, and even Santa himself (though I knew what he looked like) all very finely.

And then I went to the packages, and Joe teased—

"I believe he said that all he brought you was a switch."

And I said—

"That isn't true, Joe."

And it wasn't.

For me, there was a new pair of flannel underwear, which, until we washed them, made me laugh and laugh, and could not be worn—for they made me absolutely mad with itchiness.

There was also candy for me—three red and white peppermint candy canes. Joe told me that they weren't really canes, but shepherd's staffs, or big letter Js, for Jesus. The thin red stripes were for the nails on his hands and feet—and the thick stripe was for his suffering for our sins. I agreed with old Joe that it was very meaningful, though it gave me the heebies, anyhow.

And for my aunt, there were the dried figs and oranges I had ordered from Horatio Cooper.

I began to ask, "Why how—"

But old Joe interrupted, shrugging his shoulders and exclaimed—"That Santa!"

My aunt ate one of the oranges and we saved the peels, that we might make orange candy of them. It was an ever so exotic fruit. I had never seen one before but at a country fair.

There was also a gift from the Esterbrooks—a whole two pounds of butter! The molds of berries and grapes in bunches were all wrapped individually, and near frozen solid, so as long as the weather kept chill—that butter would do us for winter. . . .

Joe stayed on for just a few minutes longer, and my aunt dished up our rather modest fare, as times were such, of bean porridge flavored with salt pork. But old, kind Joe, he said that salt pork was like cream to him.

And when we saw him off, he called back—

"Santa needed a helper," as his wagon was yet filled with undelivered packages. . . .

So, it was a marvelous Christmas—and we had butter! Even if, into January, we did run out of everything else. It finally came to where my aunt and I gathered more willow trees and barked them and we wove ourselves a fish basket. Still being winter, to set our trap, my aunt had to hike up her skirt, and wade and work barefoot in that ice-fringed stream. But set it she did—where the water ran steep and fast into the marshy lake. And though the water flowed right through that willow bark basket, the fish did not—so we always had fresh fish.

We planted early, and with the good weather, we thought we'd soon be past the hardships—and provided by our own garden.

And we were just about to begin our harvest too, when a flock of wandering soldiers descended on our garden, and devoured every last stick in it—and in less than two hours! We did not leave the house, and they, quite fortunately, did not enter it, so we were never to know whether they were wearing uniforms of gray or blue. . . .

And when the rain came on and flooded near on everyone else's gardens, my aunt and I, in our own private and proud way—we thought we might be hungry until our next crop. We'd have only what we could gather wild from the forest. And one night, late, I woke and went out to the hearth, where I saw my aunt melting bits of lead in a deep spoon. From the spoon, she poured the molten lead into bullet molds, and she said to me—

"We have a rifle."

And we did. But I hardly knew my aunt to use it—or that she was so fine a shot with it that she could hunt. But necessity made her fit—and my aunt could hunt—and the next day, we went out for geese—and the geese went—

Monk, monk, monk—kwanck, kwanck, kwanck.

And my aunt, she shot them right out of the pond, and right out of the air. And I played the loyal hunting dog, and gathered them up—until we had seventeen birds, and I could no longer carry their sacks, or even drag them, without her help. And my aunt and I agreed that it was somber in a way—but it *was* us or them. And it wasn't nearly so somber when we marched them into town and traded them for the supplies we needed.

And we had geese with mushrooms and geese with wild grains, and geese with wild onions, and geese with wild sage, and geese with wild everything. . . .

And when fall came, we went out for geese again—and ducks too! And we Flynt women—we never did go hungry. We ate every day—

even if it wasn't always what we wanted to eat, and even if it was somber to fall birds. As my aunt explained it, she'd often seen me running up and down the creek—from rock to rock. To run on rocks, one might never know where the next rock would be—one might never know the next place one might plant one's foot. But one had to believe, because one had to run strong and fast, just in case that next rock be far away—just in case one had to jump. And so, that was how to run on rocks without falling. Run fast.

And that really was what it was like making do just then—it was like running on rocks. . . .

Virginia Deer

Nobody knew exactly when the Union left the Cleveland estate, but sometime that winter, it went its way, leaving the doors and windows open to the fields.

As it turned out, the dog Mack was not killed. The day he had been shot, the bullet had caught him in the hip, and though it had appeared a fatal shot, it was not. How serious the wound had been, in fact, was not known—as no one could get close enough to Mack to find out. Mack had dragged himself into the woods, where he had lived for more than a year. Mack was not a large dog, but he was large enough to hunt, while small enough to feed himself. I had heard about him from Miss Cleveland and Mister Nielson, along with several other people who had passed through the old estate. Harmon and I once went out to have a look. Mack didn't recognize either one of us, or maybe he did, but he wasn't friendly anymore. Mister Nielson had bred foxhounds for twenty years (the hounds were sold in Virginia, Kentucky and Tennessee) and he said that he was sure that Mack had recognized us, because if he hadn't, he would have attacked. Mack was lying on the terrace when we saw him. He came down and barked something fierce. And we didn't get any closer. Later that winter, I saw Mack again—this time with a rabbit he must have burrowed out of its den. The rabbit was limp and bloody, and at first I had thought it was a cloth or a plant. Mack was eating it. He was in the bluegrass across the creek—next to the big rock. Then, in early spring, I saw Mack fishing tadpoles out of the creek.

I began to agree with Mister Nielson, that Mack recognized me, but was not a friendly dog anymore—and that it was because Mack had known me in a former life that he just barked, and didn't really bother with me.

Then my aunt told me I should be especially careful of that dog, because it had killed one of Missus Nielson's chickens and gotten into Mister Nielson's smokehouse. Luckily, as the fall hogs had not yet been slaughtered, there was close upon nothing in the smokehouse but a ham or so, and the oak, sassafras, hickory and meat cobs that Mister Nielson had been drying for the next smoking. And Mack wasn't about to go after any of the live hogs, as they were about 250 pounds, and he couldn't have been much more than fifty. Mack did make a mess of the hogs' nuts (peanuts and pecans) probably going after the field mice—but that was nothing of consequence. Still, my aunty said she would shoot Mack if he ever got too close to our house. But Mack never did. And Mister Nielson wasn't so upset about the chicken and the ham—partly because it was about to be roundup (first frost was near) and after all the hogs had been slaughtered, there'd be more pork than anyone knew what to do with. The hams, of course, would keep, and one could pickle the ears and knuckles and some of the joints, but all the rest had to be made into sausage, or just plain eaten—every kind of internal thing, like brains, livers and intestines, which, in those days, were battered and deep fried, and called chitterlings, or Kentucky Oysters. Chit'lins inspired in some people a great enthusiasm, and inspired in others something much closer to nausea. Regardless, there was a regular festival of pork around that time of year, and Mister Nielson wouldn't miss a little ham. (My aunt and I did not take up Mister Nielson's offerings of such pork—all except the cracklings, for which she had a weakness. They were a chip made from the pig lard, and baked into bread.) And as for that lost chicken, it was too old to eat besides—and Marie Nielson would have more chickens come spring, and it seemed to the Nielsons scant payment to have a dedicated guard like Mack out at the Cleveland place. And Mack was dedicated, just lying out there on the terrace most of his days—going after anyone who came too near. All that for just a dragged-off chicken and ham—maybe Mack had somehow sensed, in that wolfish kind of way, that he was no enemy to the Nielson place. Though Mister Nielson knew that Mack had gone wild, he said that if Mack's family came home, he would be a family dog again—and we all wanted that to be true, as there was nothing better on this earth than taking a walk with an old dog. Mister Nielson said that's what Mack was hoping for—that's what he was dreaming of. He said when Mack shook in his sleep, he was being shaken by the boy he had grown up with. And when Mack's feet jerked in a slumber, he was chasing a stick thrown by the man who fed him each day. And that boy would be Amos "Bugby" Cleveland. And that man would be Somerton Cleveland. And of course, neither of them would be coming home. But Mister Nielson said he knew hounds, and he knew dogs, and he knew that dog wouldn't hurt anybody who didn't have it coming. Miss Cleveland sometimes went out to the estate with a few bowls of corn mush. Mack didn't mind her much. He just growled over his bowl, let her go about her business and occupied himself with his unexpected meal—eating it and then lying down to digest it. Miss Cleveland said that she hoped the estate would survive another winter—but that she couldn't look after it as she should—it was just too dangerous. So, as she had her horse and carriage, she kept on at Mister Cooper's, and left the estate to old Mack, who, Miss Cleveland estimated, was going on thirteen years old. . . .

It was a somber joy that descended on our town—a sigh that said, no more houses will burn. And empty, alone, aside from old Mack, the Cleveland estate re-

laxed into a serene evening—an evening tense but hopeful. The spare rooms yearned for velvet covered couches—velvet unstained by tobacco spit, and unburned by the embers of cigarettes and cigars. The cupboards yearned for grains and sweet preserves. The storerooms yearned for hams. But then, the Cleveland house did burn down. Perhaps the house was sleeping when it happened—perhaps it was itself dreaming of the Cleveland family, sitting by a warm hearth on a cool April evening.

Some insist bluntly that it was arson—evil-doers in the night. Others said that fires could start in hay sometimes, for no reason at all. In summer, winter, autumn or spring—a rat runs across the top of a tool rack—a sharp pick falls onto a flat stone sometimes used to set under the wheel of the carriage—a spark sets light to a corner of hay powder—the powder sets flame to two dry leaves—and the house is burned.

Still others said it was Doreen Cleveland, returned from the dead to do the deed. . . .

And then there were those that had a more definite idea. The previous winter, the estate had been utilized as a munitions storage and depot. And along with a few empty canteens and loose cartridges, there was spilled gunpowder all mixed up with the dust in the yard. Added to that, the dust and gunpowder was all mixed up with percussion caps, which could have fired from a horse hoof, or anything—even something like a rock kicked up by a carriage wheel.

But no one knew who might have been visiting the Cleveland estate—Miss Cleveland said it had not been her. And no one knew why someone would be visiting the Cleveland estate—Miss Cleveland said there was nothing left.

Fearing it was soldiers, leftover ones, and maybe even gone-criminal ones, people were afraid to go to the Cleveland place—and even though the blaze was visible from a distance, and everyone knew where it was and what was the matter, no one dared venture to the estate to put out the fire. A few days later, Mister Nielson went after the dog Mack, and found the canine's body near the ashes. He had shed his mortal coil. He wasn't burned, but gagged to death. Mack wouldn't leave the old place, and had died there.

Perhaps, said Mister Nielson, it was best.

When Mister Nielson brought Mack to Doctor Esterbrook to have him look at the corpse, the doctor said Mack's hip had been shattered by the bullet—broken in three places—and it was a miracle he'd survived at all.

Every day, boys and girls were visiting the ruins of the Cleveland place. It smoked for well nigh a week. Then it stopped smoking, and the children stood at the edge of the woods watching grown men pick through the ashes. The children knew they were dangerous men, and did not dare disturb or compete with them.

And just as, every day, the children visited the ashes, every day, they were told not to. "There are all kinds of ruffians about," said Miss Cleveland herself. I did not visit the ashes, as much as I wanted to, because every evening, my aunt glowered at me and asked, "Have you been to the ashes?" I told her I had been there on that first day, but that I had only stood at the edge of the woods. Even so, she was not happy, and I knew not to do it again, especially as I expected her glowering question to come at the end of each evening. So I knew not to go there, just so I could shake my head and say, "No." Eventually, I heard from the other children that the coarse men were gone from the cinders, and each child would turn up with pockets full of melted spoons and broken teacups. It seemed that the few remaining relics of interest were left in the kitchen—there was certainly nothing left of any value. It was around then that my aunt just began to glower at me without saying a word—and I would answer, "No, I have not been there." But I was exceedingly curious, and it seemed safe to me, as all the jewels of the ruins had been picked away—and then I realized that my aunt didn't want me to go there, but that the reason she wasn't asking anymore was that she didn't want me to lie if I had been there. So finally, even though it wasn't entirely with permission, I could resist no longer, and I walked from school to the Cleveland place with Harmon Valentine. Harmon Valentine had grown up with the freedgirl Natalie, and she met us outside the school. For the time, she and her mother, Serena, were living with Fanny Ditzler, and helping out there with the farming and her new baby, as William Ditzler had been called away. And when my aunt glowered at me that night, I did not answer—and my aunt nodded, and that was the end of that. She had known it would happen. She had feared it. And now she smiled—because it was over and I was safe.

Harmon and Natalie had been out to the Cleveland place before. But neither one of them had found anything worth keeping. Because I knew the house almost as well as the two of them, who had both lived there, I helped in the picking—figuring on where Missus Cleveland's room had been, and where Mister Cleveland's room had been. Harmon found half of a tortoiseshell comb—and Natalie found an empty perfume bottle. She also found some ribbon. Over toward the mantel-place, I found a hardened pool of pot metal—it was John Warren's big and ugly riding trophy, the only one that remained. I imagined the others were all pilfered by the bandits.

It was a dull drizzling day—and I picked up the lump of metal, brushed it off with my sleeve, and returned it to the hearth, which still stood among the ruins. Once upon a time, said that trophy on the shelf of the fireplace, there was a boy here who rode horses. Then I went to where John Warren's room would have been. I pulled the planks of roof aside and there was his bed—soaking wet and mildewed. It was spooky that, so moist and marshy, it still smelled like fire. Even John Warren's room was pretty much picked through—but under the bed, I did find a lump of glass melted into a metal cup. When I found it, I fell through the rotting and jagged floor and cut my leg. Harmon and Natalie helped me climb up out of the hole, and I was glad I had not fallen deeper. Another boy had fallen as deep as the cellar, and his father had been called upon to fish him out with an A-frame and a rope. When I had a chance to look closer at the cup of glass, I saw that the glass was not smooth, but bumpy. There were globules in the cup—like a thimbleful of half melted hail. They were marbles. They looked like they were in the bag when they melted, and when I turned the cup upside down, the marbles dropped into my hand. The lump of glass was cracked through, but still held together, and I showed it to Harmon and Natalie—and that was what I took home.

But then, when I had left Harmon and Natalie, as I was crossing the creek to my aunt's cottage, I did not want to take the glass inside—not because I didn't want my aunt to see it and to know where I had been, but just because I didn't want to. So I stood on the rocks halfway across the stream, and I took the lump out of my leather satchel (which I often carried to gather herbs and flowers and such on my way home from school). The glass was heavy in my hand, and as I weighed it, not knowing what to do with it, I saw a wide flat stone up the stream. The rock faced me, and without thinking, I threw the glass and it shattered on the surface of the rock—then the glass splintered out and rained into the creek. And then a funny thing happened—in the sand of the rushing stream, the glass disappeared. It was all gone. I remembered that years ago, at the mill at Frog Falls, Sam Ditzler had told me that those very marbles were just sand from a stream. And now they were shattered, and over the years, as the broken marbles ground and smoothed themselves on the sand of the creek, they would shrink, chip, crack and break until they were nothing but grains of sand, again. . . .

After visiting the ashes of the Cleveland estate, I sat in the back yard—in my aunt's garden patch. I did not often sit there, but, as it was nearly summer, much was ripe or in bloom, and I could not resist doing something pleasant, yet rare, and maybe a trifle circumspect. . . . So I sat, with the trees surrounding me—the forest trees beyond. And nearby—the apple, peach and pear. My aunt grew the best garden in town, or I thought so, and she didn't work nearly as hard on it as a great many others. Rather than an organized kind of a garden patch, she believed in a wild one—contending it took up less space, had less weeds and insects, and used less water and manure. She believed she could put things in the shade or in the light, all depending on the height of the other things around them. Others said she just had a wild inclination. Regardless, there was corn, squash, parsnips, carrots, turnips, beets, artichokes and red-hot radishes. There were several different kinds of potatoes, as well as sweet potatoes and yams. There were onions, shallots, chives, garlic and several other spices and herbs (and a whole second garden patch where she grew her healing varieties of plants). For green—there was cabbage, lettuce, spinach, asparagus and cucumbers. For beans—there were green beans, butter beans, black-eyed peas, crowder peas, blue-hulled peas, whippoorwills and tiny lady peas. There was a great deal more—too much to remember all at once, and besides that, like just about everybody else's garden patch, the crop changed yearly, for variety, as that was nearly all we ate—which was also why there was so much. Any extra would be bartered with Horatio Cooper, and between that and my aunt's remedies, we were never wanting. During that time, the boy Pitney Zooks would sit on the porch fashioning brooms, while my aunt and I would roast parched holly berries, along with parched rye, acorns, beets and sweet potatoes. (Just as Pitney had seen the lack of brooms as an opportunity, so had my aunt and I seen the lack of coffee—we had a number of recipes for substitutes, which we prepared according to season.) And then we would all go into town, to trade upon our labors with Mister Cooper—for store credit or supplies. Pitney Zooks was a boy who attended school with me, and it was around then that the entire community began to take notice of his industry. Besides brooms, he also fashioned cork from cypress knees. My aunt was rather fond of Pitney, and asked after him often. . . .

And I was thinking about that, and other things, and anything not to think about the splintered marbles in the creek, when I heard a crunching of twigs along the side of the house. I thought it might be my aunt, returning from the necessary, but when I turned, it was to see Natalie approaching—

Natalie was tall and slight, as she was growing into a pretty young woman. Over the years, I had come to regard her mother, Serena, as a woman with stores of unsaid wisdom, and it was at that moment that I saw in Natalie the image of her mother—though perhaps fresher, and less sorrowful. The image of Natalie on that day is forever fixed in my mind—she wore a white dress with a pattern of cherries and strawberries. Her sweater was a rust-colored wool that buttoned up the front. She had the perfume bottle in her hand—

"Alma, may I come 'round? I had an idea." Then Natalie took the burned ribbon from her pocket and tied the open bottle to the Mulberry tree. "It's for haints. I was afraid we might'a brought some back from the embers—and there are plenty a haint bottles danglin' at home."

"Ah, yes," I said, "what does it do?"

"Well," she said, "a haint flies in there, and then it can't fly out. This here comely, red bottle—it'll fetch any haint that you might have about. You might put up some others though, if you want."

"Thank you Natalie, I might"—and I did over the years, I made myself a bottle tree—"it's pretty there, all lit up in the tree." The sun was reflected through it, and it was pretty. Natalie had placed it rather perfectly.

My aunt brought out some iced tea and Natalie and I sat on the porch and talked. I was duly impressed by the knowledge she had of her family. It was much more extensive than any family history I had ever heard.

"Well," she said, "Nanna and I saved up all winter, from weaving baskets, and her father's uncle, the one who used to be a preacher, his sons were soldiers, for the rebels, and they been given some land in Tennessee—and Nanna's uncle, he's a man who welcomes anyone who loves Jesus, and . . . well . . . we thought a goin' down there, and weaving baskets."

It sounded like good sense to me, and I told her so—and that was when there was what Natalie called an omen, though neither of us understood it at the time. It was a great number of birds that passed overhead—passenger pigeons—and the sky was darkened for almost an hour. My aunt came out to see it, and she told us that when she was a girl they would sometimes darken the sky for a whole day, or even two. Natalie and I didn't believe it, but it was a nice story, and a nice thing to think about, because we all liked passenger pigeons, as did most people. They were a good-tasting bird, and besides that, they were sociable, and strikingly fine featured, much more so than any ordinary rock dove. They were long and slender, with a pointed tail, a pinkish body, and a blue-gray head. They were so many of them—spirits in the sky. And that was the omen—though we didn't know what it was then, and now I do know. That species, on this day in 1919, with every other great calamity and loss, is killed to the very last animal. My Aunt Bettina, as a girl, saw billions upon billions of them—and she swore that estimate was no exaggeration. I have seen them die. They are hardly remembered by my children's generation—and my granddaughters and great-granddaughters will see none. They had a pretty sound to the flutter of their wings. . . .

And that was the omen.

And it was true, that perhaps we might have known that we were hunting the species to death—with the railroads, we'd all seen car after car of them, stuffed to brimming. So, it was true that perhaps we might have known the birds would not survive.

And it was also true that Natalie, Harmon, my aunt and myself (all of us that day), we might have known that it would be the last time Natalie would be among us. We might have known that after that night, neither I, nor Harmon, nor anyone else from Cotterpin Creek would ever see Natalie or Serena again. And they did not go to Tennessee—as Cotterpin received doleful letters from their relatives there. Some said they went to one of the all freedmen townships. But

171

I did not hasten a guess, for truly, I did not know what fortune or ill befell them.

They had simply disappeared.

And though I couldn't say it so succinctly then, after supper, and more importantly, after Natalie had gone from us (for the evening and forever), I was back on the porch thinking about dreams lost. So many dreams had been lost—and maybe for the better. And mine too—they were included. It was a hard thing to face. But what had I dreamt of until then?

Well, it was a dream and also a memory—

The Clevelands' porch was two stories high, and on both sides of the house. And that porch was just full of cozy nooks, shady arbors and lovers' lanes. And that was what I had dreamt of, and still dreamt of—being in love with John Warren there. And, I am ashamed to say, I also dreamt of living in that house—in that life with the flowers and leaves of the persimmon tree fallen on the planks of the porch. And the fruits of that tree so abundant they would lie uneaten—oozing, sticky and syrupy. And I dreamt of the horse chestnuts, in their spiky green husks, and of when they dried to brown—with the swirling and polished wood of their shells. (That kind of wood was much like the wood of the furniture in that house.) And there were also muscadine grapes—threaded through the beams on the upper porch. And there were sassafras trees. . . .

The sweet smells of Centennial House—that was my lost dream. The wisteria would hang in clumps over the balustrades of the porch—the clusters purple and dense, the leaves dark green, and rose-red when young. In spring, I remembered, the smell of them was so caressing and kind that it seemed, in a manner, that warmth did not come with the season or the sun, or the maturing moons, but simply with the blossom of flowers.

And there had been honeysuckle, and I had imagined John Warren and myself sitting there for our whole lives, inhaling the perfume of those trumpets. Some were orange, I remember, some red, some white—all stamens yellow. We would have taken them to our lips, and they would have given us their nectar. And to that there would have been added the blossoming of the azaleas, and the camellias, and the boxwood and gardenias and crape myrtle and day lilies—because I would have planted them. And the thick air would be so robust with the love of all those flowers that one's heart would burst to just meander down that porch—filled with every fugitive from Eden.

And those were the kind of dreams that had probably brought my grandfather from England, and had sent my aunt to Kansas. They were not bad dreams—though perhaps they were the kind of dreams that one should give up. They were the kind of dreams that one had of working for only an hour a day—or for only a year of one's life. Those very well might be dreams that brought about some good ideas, and some spurts of hard work—but in the end, they weren't very realistic dreams, and one could only be disappointed, in oneself and everyone else, if one continued to pursue them.

But that dream house would be hard for me to give up, and I imagined, even harder for John Warren to give up. The truth was, that house was burned, and that landscape was gone—as were, I thought, all those other dream landscapes that had been inside that house. There must have been a hundred and one paintings burned, or stolen, maybe. . . .

And thus did darkness fall, and then I could hear the homely mockingbird, whose whispering song was so longing. It was singing the song of the cardinal—but better. Better than I had ever heard it before. And though the night was full of uncertainty, I was sure this mockingbird loved, even if it wasn't singing its own song. It was still a sad song. It was still a lover's song. And another mockingbird would know—would know that this was no cardinal. And when the mockingbird dropped the song, I waited, for I knew it would sing another.

It might be the song of a warbler, *weesee, weesee, weesee, weesee,* or a veery bird, *whree-u, whree-u, whree-u,* or a teacher bird, *teacher, teacher, teacher, teacher,* or even the sound of a cricket, or a frog.

Or maybe it would just make something up, out of all those other songs. After all, they did that sometimes.

173

Roasting Ears

That autumn, many of the town's children who had not been in attendance returned to school, and it seemed to me that Miss Cleveland's classroom was not only more cheerful than it had been, but more important than ever. So it was a sad fact that circulated, as the town heard that Miss Cleveland was entirely out of money. The little that had remained of her family's once vast estate had been spent on property taxes—and she was lucky to have been able to pay it. Mister Cooper's niece had arrived from Atlanta, and over Mister Cooper's objections, Miss Cleveland had quietly settled her back rent with him, packed her trunk and carriage, harnessed the old battle horse and moved out to the schoolhouse. Mister Cooper talked to the people who came into his store, and it was shortly arranged that Miss Cleveland's living conditions would improve. A date was set aside, and soon came the morning that Cotterpin Creek would build a new room onto the schoolhouse. The room would actually be divided into three rooms. There would be a kitchen, a bedroom and a modest library. It would not be large, or what Miss Cleveland was accustomed to, but it would suffice for the time, and Miss Cleveland was not the kind to complain.

The day for the building came, and as the townsmen arrived, they unloaded their tools and lumber from the horse-carts. Everyone was donating some goods, though Mister Cooper was donating the most of it.

The labor began, and the morning advanced with the little folk often cautioned for their exuberance. They were soon put to work themselves. At first, they helped by leveling the ground with shovels, then they fetched tools, coffee, and were set about a few other various errands. And then the children were reprieved, and they returned to just playing on the site. They ran up and down the slope with their arms outstretched. They had tried valiantly to contain their nervous energy, but finally, they just couldn't, and it had been suggested they exert themselves in a game of Blind Man's Bluff. It was a wise woman indeed who suggested they play on the hill, as not an hour later, several of them were taking naps with their heads on the laps of their mothers. Several others sat tranquilly, singing to themselves, or discussing matters of the world with their peers or elders.

Throughout the day, there was always the steady hammering and sawing emanating from behind the schoolhouse, and the occasional figure would pop up on the roof with some piece of work to carry out. The carpenters took to their tasks stoically, double checking their measurements, then proceeding decisively—all speed and efficiency. They were old men and boys. But they seemed powerful as they worked, as frail as many of them were. Their bodies were made serious—made strong through their sufferings. The young men were energetic—the old were experienced. And lean muscled and tense jawed, they all worked side by side—though some of them were men who had not seen or spoken to each other in five years. Many had been sworn enemies, and were still gravely opposed. But those who had come had come to work, and they had come for reasons of their own choosing, and they had no intention of failing at what they had set out to do.

The few women who came sat on the bench in the schoolyard and watched—that is, until evening. The day had started early, and for tomorrow, there were just odds and ends left to attend. But for all the somberness of the men, among the women it had been decided that this gathering was somewhat of an occasion, even a celebration, and as the day wore on, they arrived with comestibles. Marie Nielson had a tablecloth and some cruets which she set out on the picnic table, and as Miss Cleveland still had some of the belle in her, she admonished her girl to keep the linen white—"And the casters, make sure they're polished and well filled." Of the food, there was one of Mister Nielson's special sugar-cured pecan hams (his hogs had free range in his pecan field to eat all the pecans they could put snout to), which was brought by Marie Nielson, as well as a number of different recipes of fried chicken—fat fried, oil fried, spicy, plain, flour dusted, corn meal dusted. . . . Of course, there was also every variety of corn bread—there were hush puppies fried with onions, mushrooms and spices, and there were hoecakes, and even some spoon bread pudding. A few of the women had gone home to cook the corn bread, and then had come back, as many of the men expected corn bread hot. (There was molasses to spread on the cakes and bread too.) A kind of patriotic arrangement of beans—red, white and blue—was quickly disarranged. I do not remember in particular, but there may have been some turnip greens or parsnips—perhaps some corn was roasted in a fire. Missus Valentine had made a great burgoo with squirrels, whole hens, potatoes and the like. Stella, the Esterbrooks' nurse, supplied several platefuls of carrots stuffed with deviled eggs, onions and peppers. Her recipe was quite a marvel, and she exchanged it with Marie Nielson for her raisin sauce recipe, which she served with her husband's heavenly ham. Eventually, I would acquire the recipe myself. It was this—

Marie Nielson's Hot Raisin Dressing for Her Husband's Hams

Cream 1 half fist butter with 1 grab mustard, 1 grab brown sugar, 1 grab flour, 2 big spoons molasses, 4 sprinkles cinnamon, 3 sprinkles salt, 2 pinches cloves, and paprika to please. In second pot, bring 2 medium cups water, $1/4$ medium cup clover honey, and 4–5 big spoons of vinegar to a boil. Stir contents of second pot into first. Add one medium cup raisins and one handful dried cherries. Simmer until fruit plump.

During the work, there had not been much social interaction, but when the food was ready to be served, an amnesty was made. The men fixed the last tiles on the roof as the sun lowered. They climbed down the ladders and packed their tools into their horse-carts and farm wagons. Then they hung their hats in the brambles, and quietly ladled food onto the plates that had been set out by their wives. They divided into groups, and some whispered. The few who laughed by accident looked around guiltily then went back to their drumsticks, and their raisin pie.

For housewarming, I made Miss Cleveland a present of a new flannel pincushion and needle book. I'd had a good bit of trouble putting on the bead fringe. It would be the first thing she would put in her new house, she said. Almost everyone had presents for her. Mostly, they were just practical things, and not pretty at all.

Over the next few weeks, I spent a good deal of time with Miss Cleveland, sharing in her fortunes and misfortunes. For all the costly belongings she'd had and lost, she was always a majestic woman, with more grace and elegance than any deprivation could test. After class one day, it must've been the second week of September, I walked with her back to the old Cleveland estate, and helped her to gather up the chickens that had been living in the woods all through the summer. There were two roosters and eight hens. We also noticed some carrots and radishes that the Union had left in the garden, and after we had the chickens packed into the horse-cart, we harvested what there was of the crop. Miss Cleveland had been lodging her other animals with the Nielsons, and Mister Nielson was sorry to report that someone had stolen her last pig, the blue-spotted sow, which was a real shame, as he had planned to couple her with the Valentines' animal. But there had been some good fortune, as Miss Cleveland's cow had given birth to twins. And finally, after digging around for some considerable time, we found Miss Cleveland's mother's silver tea set, which Miss Cleveland had buried in the yard. It was a challenge to find that tea set, for while it had been set in a wooden box buried directly beneath the hackberry tree, that had been in September '63, and by September '65, no tree remained in the yard. Nor was there a trace of that tree—just ashes. For weeks, Miss Cleveland had found no more than minié balls, rifle parts and buttons from Yankee and Confederate uniforms.

At the end of the month, it was learned that Miss Cleveland was not in the possession of dishware, and consequently, was taking her meals on a half a turkey plate. Her utensils consisted of a bent knife, a horse-trampled spoon and a one-pronged fork. She was drinking from a dried gourd. It sounds very comical, though I am sure it was very trying. Mister Cooper offered her anything from his stockroom. At first, she would take nothing, insisting that, from the forest, she had chosen several logs of hard wood, out of which she had nearly carved a bowl, a plate and a rolling pin—all with a jackknife. But Mister Cooper also insisted—so she took a pot, a frying pan, a glazed metal dish (which was deep enough to also employ as a bowl), a glazed metal mug, and a rather clever set of utensils (knife, spoon and fork) which fit together. Mister Cooper would take no pay and had offered her a good deal more in the way of kitchenware, but not only did she refuse it, she was determined he be recompensed, so she helped him arrange his incoming and outgoing transactions in a log—up till then his system had consisted of a pen and a crate filled up with scraps of paper. Miss Cleveland made the columns in the logbook herself, with a light pencil and a ruler. Mister Cooper said he was glad to have it—both the logbook and the improved system of accounting. His wife, Keri Cooper, wondered that he had finally done it, when she had been after him to advance his finances for more than twenty years.

Horse Skull

It was a sad day in fall.

It was the kind of day when one thought about how far the autumn lessons had already advanced. It was the kind of day when one feared that all of life would be another chapter in an arithmetic book, or another hundred years of European history, or another two hundred spelling words. I knew that all that was very nice, to keep track of one's commerce, to know what had happened so one might see what would happen, and to be a proper speller—but it also seemed to me, on this kind of October day, that life was lacking that thing which made learning worthwhile.

It was one of those days that I did not feel hungry enough to count another apple. . . .

It was one of those days, cold and damp, that was not at all summer anymore—and as I walked home from school, my shoes and feet got all icy and wet. It was a slushy, disagreeable afternoon—and I worried about my aunt, who was out in the forest, and who was not as healthy and as young as I was.

The route home was lonely and seemed longer than usual that day. When I saw the little cottage by the creek—now shiny with the early frost—I was warmed inside as if I were already close to the embers of the fire.

As soon as I walked into the house, I changed into a pair of dry boots. I had several pairs because Aunt Bettina said you could never have too many boots. They were all well cared for—rubbed with tallow to keep the leather soft and the foot dry. I thought maybe my aunt needed a fresh pair too, so I picked out the old pair from next to the fire, tied the laces together and slung them over my shoulder.

My aunt was just up the creek gathering the herbs she used to make her ointments and remedies, so I skipped out into the gray day with the boots flopping to and fro on my shoulder.

But outside, on the other side of the creek, I noticed something curious. It was a stranger sitting against the big rock. He was turned to the sun. But when he saw me, he shook his long hair over his face, and he raked at his thin beard, as it was thick with dirt, and he looked down. . . .

I picked my way across the creek, carefully hopping from stone to stone. I didn't want to get wet.

"Who are you?" I asked the man.

He was a young man. Maybe even, I thought, just a boy. From far away, he had looked grown-up, but up close, he was nearer to Bugby's age, or the age Bugby might have been—I guessed about nineteen or so. I was thirteen. I knew boys who were nineteen, from town, and from school, as I'd seen those who had graduated grow up. But this boy was not like those boys. His blue and gray clothing was torn and worn out. He was shaking. His face was smeared and dark. Though brown with the woods, he'd a brick-red beard of soft hair—the kind that some young men have. He was so frail that I could see his skeleton through his hands, and around his eyes, and then I saw that he'd been crying—that's why he was shaking. The tears had made white streaks on his cheeks. His skin was pale and soft under the dirt.

When he finally answered, even for his long hair, I could see the tears running off his chin, and hear the crying in his voice. . . .

He said, "I am a soldier."

"Were you a drummer?" I asked.

"No," he said, "I was not a drummer."

"Must be," I said hopefully, "it was not so long."

He looked down—

" 'Bout four years."

"Are you crying?"

"No," he said, "I am not."

But I could see that he was.

I asked, "Where are you coming from?"

"Oh, over there," said the soldier, pointing over his shoulder.

"Oh," I said, "and where are you going?"

"I don't know."

I asked, "Could you go home?"

He said, "I have been home."

"Oh," I said . . ."then where will you go now?"

He answered, "I will go to Lexington, maybe. But probably not. Somewhere farther, I think. Somewhere very far, I think."

"Oh, where is that? A big city?"

"Yes, maybe. You think a big city?"

"Yes, well, I know it is very far away, and I have often heard that a young man should go to a big city to make his fortune."

"Have you heard that?"

"Yes."

The young man was rubbing his feet. They were blue like chunks of ice. He began to wrap them in rags, which he was pulling out of his pocket.

"Well," he said, "it is too bad it is very far."

His feet were blistered and bloody.

"But," the soldier resumed, "I have these dry rags from my pocket. The wet rags that I was wearing wrapped around my feet are now in my other pocket. So, the next time I stop, they will be dry—from the warmth of my body. And then I can take off these rags, which will by then be wet, and put them back into this pocket—to dry them off. It is a fairly good system, for what I have available to me. I have come a very long way already with this system. But I must say it is really too bad that I have a very long way to go."

"You mean," I asked, "you have no boots?"

"No," said the soldier, wiping his eyes and smiling, "I have no boots. But at least it is not winter. I have seen men without boots in winter, and that is very hard."

I dropped my aunt's boots into the grass.

I said, "I have an extra pair of boots."

"No," the soldier sighed, "those are not my boots. They are your boots."

"No," I said, "they are much too big for me. They are my aunt's boots. She is grown all the way—and a big woman. I do not think you are grown all the way yet. You are still too small. You should eat more. Let me see your foot," and I measured the bottom of his foot to the bottom of the boots. "Yes, they will fit. And they don't look like a girl's boot."

"No," said the soldier, wiping his nose and his eyes again, "they do not. But won't your aunt mind?"

"No," I said, and I sat down and began to thread the laces through the old boots. "She won't mind. She has new boots and these are old boots, and you need them much more than she does. You need boots to put on your feet more than she needs boots to put by the fire. I was going to bring them to her right now so her feet could be dry so she wouldn't catch a cold. But you already have a cold, and this way, your feet can be dry. And then I can just go back and get her a different pair of boots from the closet, and her feet can be dry too. My aunt says you can never have too many boots. I guess this is why."

"I see," said the soldier. "Well, please thank your aunt for me."

"Oh," I said, and I finished lacing the boots, "I will."

And I handed the soldier my aunt's boots.

The soldier finished wrapping his feet with the dry cloth, then pulled on the dry boots.

"I am only sorry I don't have socks," I said.

"It's all right," said the soldier, "I have rags."

The soldier lifted his knapsack and slid his canteen over his shoulder. Then he pushed himself up the rock and rose unsteadily to his feet.

"Are you okay?" I asked.

"Yes," said the soldier, "I have to be getting on."

"Oh, yes," I said, rather correctly, "but why didn't you tie your boots?" Then I noticed that the soldier's fingers were too swollen to tie his boots. "Oh," I said, "I see. . . . Well . . . you just hold on for one short minute.

"Do you like this field?" I asked.

"Yes," said the soldier.

"I do too," I said. "I have always liked this field."

I tied the soldier's boots. I tugged the knots tight, so they wouldn't come undone. But I didn't make double knots, because those would be hard for the soldier to untie.

When I was done with the first boot, I began on the second. He began to tuck his trousers into the first. "So the bugs can't get in," he explained.

"Oh," I said.

After I knotted the boot and tucked in his pant leg, I stood up.

The soldier looked away—"Thank you very much."

I said, "You're welcome."

Then the soldier took the first step of his long journey, and I turned back to the cottage for another pair of boots.

We were just a boy and a girl in a field in late fall.

Some would call it early winter, and some would have called us a young man and a young woman. And some would say, in better times, we'd still be playing marbles. And some would say, in better times, we'd still be stealing kisses. And some would say we were about the right age to get married. And some would say we were much too young for that.

But whatever anyone would say, we were cold and alone—and that boy or young man or soldier, much more than me, was far too cold and alone for his age.

He was shivering freely as he walked. It was clear to me that even he didn't know if he would be returning to the life he'd left behind, or if he'd never be going home.

I had turned away from him—and it was then, as I was looking away from that thin and hungry young soldier, that I recognized him. And turning back, I knew it for sure when I saw him walk.

"Where," I asked, "is Pegasus?"

The soldier stopped walking. But he did not face me to answer— "In heaven, if there is a heaven for horses. I know they say that there isn't. But if there is, he is there."

"Will you work with horses? There is work everywhere for men who know horses."

"I do not know that I can ever look at another horse."

"Oh."

"It is nothing against the horses."

"I know."

"It will be . . . just . . . just . . . some time."

"Yes," I said.

He squinted and grimaced and bit his lip, all at once—

"I mean, if you could have seen the look in his eye. If you could have seen it. After so much, I . . . I . . . ." Then, the soldier took a deep breath and sighed, as if summing up all he had ever known about horse and man—

"I mean, I asked him to trust me, and I did this."

"Yes," I said. . . . "I understand."

And after a few minutes passed, I thought of us children, and I said of the horses—

"They were innocent too."

This was met with silence . . . as this soldier thought himself neither innocent, nor a child, and when he finally did speak, it was not so much to answer me, but to resume what he had said—

"We . . . we treated men like horses."

Why had I not recognized the boy in the man? It was his long hair, which had been short. It was his tall body. It was his thin body. It was his beard. It was all that pain in his face that had said he was older than he was. It was all those things which he had not been. . . . It was those things which had deceived me. And it was only as he crossed the old marble course that I first recognized his gait. It had been near on four years, and while the boy had been plump and foolish, the man was lean and cautious. My heart was thumping as I realized that someone, all at once, could change so little, and change so much.

I stepped to him, reaching out my hand to move the hair away from his face—but he moved away from me. He was facing to walk southwest—in the direction of his family's property.

"Don't go there," I warned him, "to the house."

He answered, "I have already gone."

"Oh, yes," I remembered, "that is too bad."

"Yes, it is."

"Four years can be a long time," I said.

"Yes," he agreed, "it can."

It was uncommonly cold, and along the edges of trickling water of the stream, there was forming a fringe of ice.

"Oh," I said, trying too hard to make light of something much too heavy, "now you are an orphan too!"

"Yes," he agreed, but it was not lightly, "I am also an orphan."

I held my breath for a moment, then I released the bottom of my lip from between my teeth—

"Will you stay?"

I don't know why I asked, because I already knew that he would not stay.

"No," he said, "I cannot stay, I am here . . . to . . . to tell you."

I said, "Oh," and I looked down—but then I looked up again.

We watched a chipmunk climb back into a burrow under the roots of the pine tree.

"It's hibernating already," I said.

"Alma," said the soldier, no longer able to wait to say what he had come to say, "I am breaking my promise to you."

"Yes," I replied, "I know." My voice sounded old like his, and serious—"You are breaking your promise, but I understand. I have also broken promises."

I did not say what promises, though there was really only one— and that was to my mother. I promised her that I would take care of my father. I knew it was a promise that I could not keep. But that did not make the not keeping of it any easier.

"I know," I said to him, "that sometimes we break promises."

The soldier began to walk again.

"John Warren," I called out, "John Warren Cleveland! Can't I see you? Won't you turn around?"

But he did not stop walking. He did not turn around. And he did not clear the hair from his face. Instead, in a jerky and hobbling kind of way, he began to run. He jumped over a fallen tree branch and shouted—

"You know, Alma—Alma Kaye Flynt, that I cannot."

The autumn was yielding to winter, and with the panic of getting things done before the coming of the cold, there came much regrowth and activity in our community.

Bobolink

A new Cotterpin was rising up at the railway station. Many of the old-timers who came to town only once every few seasons were rather surprised to find that the former Cotterpin was near abandoned. They would make their way to the new collection of businesses by the railway station, and be confused by their whereabouts. Just standing around, puzzled, they'd remark that this might be Cotterpin, but they didn't recognize where they were. . . .

The one business spared destruction or impoverishment was Mister Horatio Cooper's General Store—that being due to what some called shrewd business practices, and what others called pure greed. It was funny to see that store, still thriving where other buildings were just broken windows and open doors. But when new businesses began to sprout up around the railway station, Mister Cooper was finally forced to move as well. I wasn't sure that even Horatio Cooper could sell the old building on that plot of land. It was no good for farming or horses, and it was no good for trade, as the activity was no longer there. Still, I knew Mister Cooper could afford it.

Embarking upon my first walk to Mister Cooper's moved general store, it felt to me like both a farewell to the past and a greeting to the future—so I detoured through that familiar and now worn-out Cotterpin—that melancholic hamlet. But as I made my way down Main Street, so dilapidated as to be almost unrecognizable, the picture I saw was a surprisingly sad one. Only the Esterbrook house had survived the turmoil. All nearer Main Street was picked apart or burned. There were several heaps of bricks where houses once stood—though even those heaps of bricks were quickly disappearing into re-use. Over the years, I had seen so many familiar faces on that friendly old street, but now, there was just a handful of dismal looking faces—gathering up those few things they could find. Some dragged filled-up wheelbarrows. The wind was sighing ruefully through all the empty windows and doorways. Shutters creaked— like the crying of the very sick, or the mortally wounded. By winter, not even a vestige would remain—due to the pilfering of building stones, bricks, lumber, doors and windows. Such things were in great demand, especially among people who couldn't afford them—and it was hardly a crime to help clean up the mess. Even wood too ruined to employ in building would surely be taken for firewood—and so, by the following spring, I imagined there would be little more than a muddy field.

Perhaps the Esterbrooks, having lived in a town house, would be better off thinking themselves living in a country house, or a house in a future countryside, rather than a ravaged township. The course of nature for the land thereabouts would be—ragweed and lamb's quarter and the like—then milkweeds, thistles and perennials—which would bring butterflies, meadowlarks and bobolinks. Then would come shrubs and vines—and catbirds, and quail. . . . And that's when the forest would creep in—seasonal trees taking root with the help of squirrels and birds. Of course, that might be fifteen or twenty years in coming, and the land might already be filled by pines. But I imagined the Esterbrooks would take up some of the planting—and they did too, and with a good deal of relish. And though that land would never become a forest again, it did indeed become countryside—I'd say, within twenty-five years. And though that was not during their own lifetimes, the Esterbrooks did have a chance to see it coming. . . .

And, as I detoured through the old town, it was my inclination to call upon the Esterbrooks, as I had heard told that the last of Missus Esterbrook's charity errands had proven to be an exceedingly depleting one. It had been several years since she helped Miss Cleveland with the clothing of the slaves, yet now it was being said that her acts had returned to her in the guise of a shipment of dead soldiers' uniforms. The clothing had been forwarded to her almost by accident, through a series of mishaps that led from a large Tennessee hospital to her unwanting doorstep. Still, she had taken in the crates, as cloth was scarce. She had hoped the fabric might be dyed, restitched and employed as garb for the children of the Frickerham poorhouse. But when she opened the crates, the clothes were a-crawling with lice and vermin, so much so that it looked like sand—a million grains of sand, with legs. Some of the eggs, she said, were as big as sesame seeds. Stout and knowing, Stella, the Esterbrooks' nurse, was competent and able in all enterprises—and being a Southerner of three generations, was an expert destroyer of almost every vermin and blight known to the South. But upon witness of the infestation, even Stella wondered if the clothing should be kept. Missus Esterbrook had ordered her to rid the soldiers' uniforms of lice, and Stella just wasn't too sure she could do it—

"Dose tings, dey cleber and bile. Dey hide in ebery stitch and seam—and you bile dem all day and all night and all day besides, and dey still alibe and crawlin'."

Missus Esterbrook told her to do whatever she had to, and Stella did it—washing the clothing, rewashing the clothing and rewashing the clothing—and then drying it. But not just drying it in any ordinary way, but drying it with the hottest iron anyone had ever seen—pushing the edge of it deep into every seam. Stella went after the lice—smashing them and their eggs with her powerful thumb. And then she washed the clothing again, and ironed it again—and as much of it had shrunken in Stella's boiling baths, the attire needed no more than patching, buttons and dying to be of use at the orphanage. And of course, when Missus Esterbrook and Stella had done the work—that was a great boon. But nevertheless, the fruit of her labor must have been a bitter fruit indeed, as Missus Esterbrook offhandedly remarked to my aunt how she had been right to doubt that charity she had undertaken, all those years ago, and how this new chore reminded her so much of that work at the Cleveland place. Missus Esterbrook, like many others in the community, stated that it was almost as if all that clothing she had made for Missus Cleveland's slaves had come back to her as soldiers' clothing. And now, it was infested with vermin—as if even the original task had been a wretched one, no matter how fine and generous the clothing, no matter how fine and generous the intention. . . .

The Esterbrooks' house was just around the bend of the old avenue, and as I turned into the yard, I saw Stella out in back—doing three things at once. The laundry was washed and she was soaking

The first thing I saw was Horatio Cooper's General Store, which was not only moved but expanded—it was so close to the railway station that the cars could be loaded and unloaded directly into his storeroom. As a result of his side industry, the lumber business, he had been badly needing an expansion. He was building a new mill, which would be completed shortly. It was almost by accident that he had found himself in that lucrative trade (though not everyone approved of his clients). Nonetheless, he was the sole supplier of lumber to the area, and as his costs were fair, he was a daunting foe to any out-of-towners who wished to launch a rivalry. They might as well just move on to the next town, and set up their occupation there.

However, many new people were moving in, including what my aunt called a few opportunists. Among them was a lawyer named Pimpernickel. He did not seem to be an evil man, but my aunt did not like the look of him. Simply put, he was a soft man, an obese man— a gluttonous and inactive man. And my aunt was disapproving of that particular combination of excesses. He was not simply plump, or rotund, or even hearty—he was just enormous. And it was no mystery how he became so—my aunt and I saw him eat a whole ham by himself. (To wash it down, he drank a swill bucket of Julep—the bucket so plentiful, and emptied of all but mint, that I mistook it for a salad.) You would think that a man who consumed so much would be well nourished, but he wasn't—his nails were brittle and splitting. He also had jowls, which my aunt said were from spoiled intestines. His hairy eyebrows were severely scrunched and angled down—like he was scowling. And that, said my aunt, was from too much meat. He had thick lines on his head from excess liquid, and a swollen nose, which my aunt said meant his heart was wet. His skin was oily all over. Besides that, my aunt knew that all his internal organs were gone bad because he was as fat as a fat pig. In fact, he resembled a pig, and not just because he ate like a pig, and ate a lot of pig, but because he drank like a pig and smoked like a pig.

The other intemperance that he was plainly guilty of was his attire—he was dressed to the extreme of fashion, and added to that he wore several showy gemstones. My aunt said that a man in a dandy's clothing was not much to her liking—and in current circumstances, such garishness was certainly hard to fathom.

So, with men like that being the newcomers, and the bringers of progress, maybe it wasn't so surprising that the town's regrowth was not exactly a joyful one. It was a disconsolate rebuilding, filled with whispering and memories—whispering of changes and unresolved bitterness—memories of things gone that could not be forgotten. And of course, there were also rumors. There were rumors that the Cleveland estate had been divided into lots, at least one of which was sold—and that was a rumor borne out. The sale had been handled by Mister Pimpernickel, and the word was that he had organized his office with that engagement in mind. He was just returned from Canada, where he had lived for the past seven years. He had worked in finance, and was said to have made a great deal of other people's money. Some said that all the trouble in the nation had been caused by men like him—men who wanted to make up reasons for themselves to be able to take things that weren't rightly theirs.

Still, in early autumn, something good seemed to come of Mister Pimpernickel—a new family moved onto the first lot off the Cleveland estate. It was just down the creek, and my aunt and I were quite curious about them. We soon had a chance to make their acquaintance, as they attended Sunday service. They were named Mayfield. The wife was Willa. The husband was Frank. They were clearing some of the woodland for farming. My aunt and I also had a chance to meet their young son, Loren, and their daughter, Nora Mae, who was very near my age, and had a sweet look.

Yuletide '65

$\mathcal{S}$ometimes the world turns on a simple kindness, like giving an apple to a man who is hungry, or giving a pair of boots to a man who is cold. I often think that without that day in the woods, my soldier could not have returned to me—and that it was providence that I mistake him for a stranger. He had to be *any* young soldier, and I had to be *any* young girl—for the thing that kept us apart was not each other, but the great gulf between the hearts of all Americans.

Perhaps slight acts like that are the basis for all forgiveness—all salvation. Perhaps from those small gifts, one can bestow and receive even larger gifts—and that is how the human heart can heal and grow. . . .

Twenty-seven days following that young soldier's visit, my Aunt Bettina was in Frickerham—having been called to an outbreak of whooping cough at the poorhouse. Still too young to join her, I looked forward to that time when I would be of use, that I might feel my life expand outward, out of Cotterpin—as I knew that the spirit I held grasped in my breast was not a small one. Throughout the whooping cough crisis, I had been lodged at the Mayfields'—as, quite apart from any medical emergency, Nora Mae and I were becoming fast friends. After three days, the hard rain finally subsided, and I was permitted to return to my aunt's cottage—for as much as I was enjoying my time with Nora Mae, I was anxious to see my aunt and to sleep in my own room, in my own bed. (It might have been a relief to the Mayfields too, as they lived in a dugout, yet.) Earlier that afternoon, Mister Nielson had seen my aunt on the road, and she'd sent word that I might make my way home, as she'd shortly be home her-self—she had only to stop in town to return the horse carriage to Mister Cooper, and to resupply herself with sweet potatoes, Kinsey's linden honey and flannel—as she'd exhausted those resources in Frickerham. Mister Nielson had told as much to Mister Mayfield, upon Mister Mayfield's visit to the Nielsons' to help patch the roof—and by the time Mister Mayfield returned (I was thirteen years old, and for several years, had been walking to and from school, and all around the community, quite unsupervised), he allowed me to ven-ture back to my aunt's cottage in the woods, saying that if my aunt wasn't home by dusk I should come back straightaway. . . .

Though my aunt had promised him that I was of a quite indepen-dent and competent character, and I could see that Mister Mayfield was of a naturally easy-going disposition, he was not so with other people's children—so I thanked him for his hospitality, and pledged to make assurance double sure that I'd be safe—and then I set out, onto the path through the red cedars, thinking to prepare my aunt some tea, rice, squash and maybe some spinach. . . .

I was wearing my raincoat and galoshes, and as the ground was particularly muddy, I walked through the cedars, pines and gin-berry junipers, looking for no more than the next place to put my foot. The land between my aunt's cottage and the Mayfields' (and the old Cleveland estate) had been cleared by loggers some forty years be-fore—and all that had grown back since were pines—and a few trees from stumps. Of course, it was pretty anyway, but sometimes it had that feel of mire and land unloved—and this was one of those occa-sions. Thus, it was a breathtaking sight when I came to the clearing of the big rock. The yellowed grass was matted down, after so much rain, and the creek behind the rock was higher than I had ever seen it before, as the water was now rushing down, full force, from the mountain.

It rained so once or twice or so every year—and sometimes, the creek would rise up like that. In such weather, the water became quite difficult to cross, and I was sure that Frank Mayfield had not meant that I should attempt it—he simply hadn't known the danger. I thought to turn around, as the nearest crossing was the rope bridge at the Mayfields', but then I thought that maybe I could pick myself a path, as it looked to me the water would be yet higher tomorrow.

I could not see much in detail, just the outline of things against the rain—all that white. I saw foam at the bottom of the big rock. And as I tramped toward it, over the flat grass, that was when I saw the body—sprawled out in the rain. It wasn't foam. We were quite blessed to have the Mayfields as neighbors, for we were always supplied of Willa Mayfield's marvelous butter—but at that moment, my small hands just opened, and I dropped the tub of butter that I had been clutching—and in great sucking steps, I ran across the grass in my big galoshes, with my arms waving and my black raincoat sailing out behind me. And there was the rain and the wind—and there was my very own soldier.

And though I was nowhere near as knowledgeable as my aunt, I could see that he was extremely sick with pleurisy—wet lungs. His fever was high, and he had been bleeding from the mouth and nose. He was barefooted, his feet in no more than wrapped rags.

There was so much rain on his wan, anemic face, that I knew that he could not feel my tears. . . .

When I took my hand away from his forehead, to try to warm his cold fingers, he woke, and his tremulous, blue lips parted. At first, he made no sense at all, but then, his thoughts seemed to clear, though his eyes were as wild as before—

"Ah, I knew you would be here. But, well . . . not so soon. Petals of the same . . . Always spring . . . Perhaps snow too . . . but . . . always be in bloom . . . Funny to think of it—I believed my brother was dead when he was alive. I saw him at the railroad tracks, and he led me . . . us . . . me and the other soldier, back from the tracks to . . . to . . . the big rock. I could not have found it without Bugby. I suppose he was able to save the other soldier. . . . Bugby saved him. . . . Ah, Bugby. I had expected that I would have to wait so long to see him—the length of my own lifetime. But now I see that I'll have to wait the length of his lifetime. And you—I thought no matter how long it took me, I'd surely return to you as the man I should have been. Now I see that you too have died young, when I thought your life would be long and happy. What has brought you here, Alma? I do remember my own sickness—but why would a child like you be stolen from the bosom of life? Are you Alma Flynt? I must say, that for my sake, I hope you are, and for her sake, I hope you are not. Are you Alma Flynt? Or do all angels look alike?"

"My soldier," I said, "you are not dead."

"Ah." He asked, "Then, where is my brother?"

"He is dead long ago."

"Ah yes, I suppose he would be."

I saw that the creek water was rising, and I thought about it—about the difficulty of crossing with a whole soldier. There came sleet—then hail. I saw the balls of it, on the surface of the rushing water, and bouncing—rolling across the ground.

"Oh," said he, finally, and dizzily, "then I am alive?"

"Yes," I said, "you are alive."

"Then we are here," he asked, "by the big rock?"

"Yes," I said, "we are here."

"Will you bury me here?"

I did not reply.

He asked again, "Will you bury me here?"

And I said, "I will."

He sighed, relieved. I had started to tremble myself. But when he looked up, I did not believe he could see me. His eyes were rolling, as if he was blind with fever—"And where," he asked, "is the other? The other soldier?"

I replied, "I do not know. I have not seen another soldier."

"Ah," his red and swollen lids lowered wearily "then he . . . then he is dead."

Previously, my soldier had hid his identity with his long hair and beard. This time, his hair was cut and his beard trimmed. But I had known it was him even before I saw his face or hair—even from a great distance—even, somehow, before catching sight of him. It was as if, traversing the wind-whipped grass to the big rock, I'd a sensation so strong that I saw him across time and years—and now I was so close as to see clippings of hair matted to his brow, cheeks and neck. And, as he turned away to look at a bare tree, I saw his hair—spiky, dirty and clumped—and that trimmings of it clung to the shoulders of his wool suit—and that the fine hair on the back of his neck was much too long.

Then . . . I saw his hair style as a rather rough approximation of what it had been so many years ago.

"Did you," I asked him, "cut your hair for me?"

"Yes," he answered. Then his lashes batted, and his head rolled to the side, and his eyes were closed—and he was unaware.

Looking up, I saw that the water was still rising. The creek a flood wash, to cross it was noways a consideration except one or two days every few years—but this was the first of those two days. And while crossing by myself was question enough, crossing with an insensible soldier was an impossibility. I was not big enough, or strong enough—and I was angry at the orphanage because I knew it was their fault I was small for my age. *They did not feed me enough. They did not feed me enough.* I gripped my hands, the rain squeezing out of them, because he was just too heavy—I tugged at him, and then I feared that by trying to convey him, I might even be the cause of his premature death, as I was afraid I'd slip and lose him in the water. He'd rush downstream, and no doubt the flood would treat him brutally, if not drown him, in his poorly state. . . .

And because I estimated a death by drowning faster than a death by exposure, and I wanted that soldier to live for as long as possible, I curled up beside him on the wet ground—curled up around his cold body, to keep him warm. We were under the outcropping in the big rock, and behind the wind. But it was still cold, and in a thick mist, the rain still found us. So—I curled up with him and shivered for several hours. The light dimmed—the sun set. The rain fell harder—rolled off the big rock and onto our bodies. With my raincoat, I covered us as best I could, and I breathed with him. . . .

And finally, my aunt arriving, returning from her trip—she found us thus.

It was dark, and the sun had still been in the sky when I lay down, so when I saw my aunt, I thought it must have been two hours, maybe three. I was trembling hard when I sat up. Then I heard my aunt calling to me—she was halfway across the field.

"Alma! Alma!"

Then that old lady ran, dropping her bag and perambulating faster than I had ever seen her perambulate, and certainly faster than I could run myself, though I was a very fast runner. She knelt by me, and put the back of her hand against my forehead. And upon perceiving that I was merely cold, she turned to the soldier. She rolled him over, and while I had told my aunt nothing of my soldier's previous visit (not for secrecy, just propriety) she seemed to know everything, without a word or an instant's reflection. It was in her shoulders, in her hands which she pressed under his shirt to feel the temperature of his chest. I could see it in the clarity of her look, the focus of her pupils—without widening her eyes, without even a blink, my aunt had recognized my soldier.

It was almost as if—as if she had expected him.

My aunt lowered her two hands, and with them, she held that soldier's face. He had a badly bloody nose, and was covered in that blood. She turned to me—

"He'll die, but you'll hold his hand when he does."

I did not think. I just saw that the creek was an angry monster—there was huge water, roiling up. And I thought we might not even be able to get our soldier across it. And through all the turmoil of the storm, there was a stillness inside me, almost as if my own circulation had stopped—as if my own heart had stopped beating. . . .

And as I looked at my aunt, knowing all of my life would now consist of before and after this moment, I saw that it was true for her as

200

well—that just as something had changed in my eyes, something had changed in hers.

My aunt regarded me, and then the sky—and I saw that she was clenching her teeth—and her mouth was open against the rain and the wind. . . . Though she knew of it, when my aunt saw our young love, it had surprised her (as it is with young love, ever fresh) and she was so moved by it that she could curse the natural world, which was the love of her old age.

And I never saw her curse before, and I never saw her curse again, but she swore at heaven—

"Damn you! Damn you! By my oath, you will not take another!"

For the weight of emotion, I could not keep my eyes open, and I closed them, and I heard the rain, and then I fell to the wet soil—my hands out flat, my cheek in the black mud. . . .

And when I opened my eyes, and looked across the blowing leaves, and through the glistening twigs, and the bouncing balls of hail—I saw my aunt ford the creek. The water was even higher than I had thought it was, and it was still rising—and my aunt lowered herself into the water, carrying that soldier over her shoulder—like a great sack of onions. Her legs were straddled, and though she could not see where she placed her feet—not through the white water, which was at times as high as her chest—she walked with a gravity that tied her to the center of the earth. Several times she slipped, but she did not falter—and her long hair swept downstream with the white water, but still she walked, like a stolid mountaineer. My aunt, she was a stoic hero—she had cried her tears, she had survived her terrors, and now, simply, she would surrender no ground to defeat. She would walk through a thousand storm washes—she would carry a thousand boys. She had lived long enough to know that she could not let one more die of cold. All of her life had prepared her, and I could almost see whole months and even years of strain expended in those brief moments. My aunt was sixty-four then. And to watch her—it was like Samson, holding up the temple. Her last power—and her greatest act of strength, not just physical, but celestial. It had taken a lifetime for her resolve to cure—for her to find the force to challenge the sky, to lift herself up and fight the storm.

And thinking back on it, I often wondered if that momentous act was not a defying of fate—if it was not the five, ten, twenty years of a force that had been reserved for her old age. I sometimes think now, that in her great act of determination, she somehow turned on the spigot to the essence of life. And it spilled, it gushed with a full effervescence. And it shined on her then, because she demanded it. . . .

There are moments when old people can be much stronger than young people could ever be. It is like all that strength just gathers up somewhere in their bodies, awaiting true need. They may not have quickness, or longevity, but they have a lifetime of labor, and a lifetime of spirit. They understand that some moments cannot be lost to fate, and they will wedge themselves between their families and misfortune, as wood may be wedged in the jamb of a door. She was . . . I do not know how to describe these monumental seconds except in terms of small things, like the black water, like the wet folds of her purple shawl. I do not know how to describe her but with the million balls of hail that sought her from the sky. They struck her. The torrent blasted her. And she was . . . she was silver with the storm. . . .

And when she had crossed the creek, she carried that soldier to the house, and then she came back, crossing the creek again—this time, for me. She did not even look at her bag left lying in the field—she just lifted my body, as if I were no more than a newborn babe. Though I was small for my age, I was still thirteen, and too old for that, but she scooped me up like nothing, and held me to her chest, and she told me to hold on to her—and I did. And the water had risen even higher, and I was wet up to my chin, and my face was wet from the waves, and the water was so cold that I reminded myself to breathe—

Breathe, you must breathe, Alma, you must breathe.

And then we had crossed, and we dried off by the fire, and we dried our soldier by the fire—and then I changed. And while I changed, my aunt sponged our soldier clean and dressed him in long-johns and socks that had once belonged to her husband. And then I came to the fire, and I finished setting out the cot, and making a bed of the cornhusk mat—and then we laid our soldier upon it, and covered him with a quilt. . . .

And then my aunt changed, and the soldier coughed up more blood onto his clean and dry long-johns.

And, as I would come to learn it in the years to come, the story of how my soldier came to rest at the big rock, it was the story of—

House wren

A refusal to pledge the oath to the Union.
The discovery of gold figurines—an assortment of molded mice,
    in full evening-wear.
Greed and anger.
Another soldier.
Detainment in the cold cellar of a mansion—with vermin
    scuttering over one's back as one slept, and fleas and flesh bugs
    all the time.
Lies.
An Irishman with a good heart.
A plan.
An accusation of poison and a denial—and an invitation to switch
    bowls.
Bittersweet in the mush.
A keeled-over Irishman.
Hot coffee to a soldier too sick to walk.
An escape.
A masquerade as milk boys, while walking down a long hall—
    enduring mockery in rags.
A cattle car.

And running.

And dying.

And running and running and running. . . .

And that was when my aunt had rescued him—and after he was settled by the fire, my aunt told me that back at the poorhouse in Frickerham, she'd heard of two escaped soldiers, and she thought my soldier might have been traveling with a companion. So, taking a dry coat, and a dry pair of boots, she readied herself for another battle. And the wind whistled as the door opened, then slammed closed.

And I knew she would be out searching in that weather for much longer than wisdom would advise.

And I knew she was much too old for that—but I could not leave my soldier. . . .

It was the cold that had caused his disease—that was the only condition required, as pleurisy often attacks those with the strongest and most vigorous constitution. He coughed often—his lungs swollen and sore. And he shivered—sometimes with chill, sometimes with heat. He clutched his ribs, as if they were in great pain—and he lay curled up on his other side. His sleep was restless—his cheeks, red. And sometimes he retched before he coughed his short, hard cough. The mucus that came up from his lungs was yellowish, and there was blood in it. . . .

I administered to him a half a teaspoon of crushed pepper berries in a half a glass of water sweetened with *Kinsey's Purified, Clarified Honey*. I set warm bricks and vinegar cloths to his feet—and laid hot flannels to the pain in his torso. His heartbeat slowed, and I believed this calming to be an auspicious thing. To help clear his lungs, I employed a tincture of honey locust and herbs. My aunt had feared that he would die—that he was too sick. But I had fortified myself against that eventuality—and I would not let him die. I would do all that could be done, give all the care that could humanly be given—and I would sit by his side, and watch his troubled breathing until this sickness was quelled. . . .

And I would keep my lip from quivering, and keep my tears from falling, and my breath from bursting my own chest . . . and I would not let him die . . . and I . . . I . . . I would hold his hand in case he did. . . .

Columbine

When my aunt returned, it must have been toward two or even three in the morning. She'd found no other soldier, nor any trace of one—though she'd been out searching for more than six hours. The snow had turned to ice, and her skirt was frozen stiff. . . .

I was still awake, and my eyes were on her when she opened the door. I rose and helped her to dry off and set her wet clothes by the hearth. And though I knew that she was tired, and that I was tired, neither of us wanted to sleep. It was almost as if, as rich as it was with exalted hopes and gloomful dread, this time was too nourishing to the spirit to abandon.

So we sat awake, though tired, to speak of that which we had not spoken. . . .

She did not seem sick, as I had worried she would be, but rather, sturdy—almost vital with exhaustion. Still, her every energy was spent, and by the lines in her face, she seemed older now, by five years, or maybe ten . . . or maybe, by just one more great occurrence in a lifetime.

Sitting at the fire, we pushed the toe-toaster, and ate the toast with peach and raspberry preserves, and tupelo honey. And we watched my soldier, as my aunt spoke of her mother, come from England, as well as her grandmother, and her grandmother's sisters. And then she spoke of her own brother, my father. And among her aunts was a woman named Kaye, after whom I had been given my middle name. And . . . she spoke of us Flynt women as mourning doves, or primary colors. She spoke of her own true love—and years in Boston, and some in Kansas. And she spoke of the loss of her husband, and the misdiagnosis of a doctor, and the loss of her own child . . . a son.

The fire was gold and blue. And my aunt and I, we conversed with much contemplation, and deep breathing, and application of handkerchief. She sat with her hands on her knees, and her whole body went stiff, and she held the tea towel readied—

"I'm . . . I'm . . ."

She'd begun to say "I'm sorry," but she stopped herself—"Perhaps if I had sent for you sooner. I might have . . ."

Then she caught on her own words, dabbed at her smile-wrinkled eyes with a kerchief, and admitted to me (and to herself, maybe) that there was no evading the passions in one's blood. In hers. In mine. No matter if that was precisely why one wanted to hide oneself away. And then my aunt—she laughed in her wry, wise way, and joked that to make a list of one's nightmares, it'd likely be the course of one's life. . . .

And I felt myself arch the brows over my reddening eyes, and tilt my head, to listen. And my aunt gazed at my soldier—his white face. She reached out to close his lids, which were lifted slightly. His breathing was just hardly audible. And—she said that nobody could find a child's innocence and hide it. She said that she'd thought she could capture it, protect it—cherish it as if it were her own. Then she went to the kitchen—to pour herself another cup of tea. The pot empty, she cleaned out the tea ball, refilled it, fetched more water for the pot and returned to me. And, in the light of the hearth and a breath of wind that whispered through the timber, she spoke slowly, dreamily—as if quieted by the onset of internal clouds—

"We are like bees in tornadoes. And all of our morality and aspirations are lifted into the swirl like leaves into a twister. And we see naught but the few breadths ahead of us, and the chance to push our wings against the air another time. And, however pure or maligned our intentions might be, sometimes, it is as if there is no great demon, whipping the land, changing the countryside—there is just the struggle."

The tea steeped, and when she sipped it, she said, surely, that she knew the difference between selfish and unselfish things, and that right would prevail, and that to prevail was the very nature of right—for a thing could be right only because it would prevail—

"But sometimes, we are so lost and dizzied to the squall, that it seems like all is struggle, and only struggle. And sometimes, we are so blinded by our own puniness, and it seems our passions are so insignificant that we battle against the storm without purpose, and we are left exhausted and directionless. And we question faith, and hope. For, we ask ourselves—what in divinity could just shrug at our lives, and say that sometimes we win, though wrong, and sometimes we lose, though right?"

And then I asked my aunt about her late husband—

And she told me she'd learned that when a body died, one had to take from it what was best—that one should make their life a lesson. Make it so they died to teach that most important thing that they could not teach in life. One had to ask what it was their death was meant to mean—and receive their sacrifice as their gift. Then my aunt, she lowered her head, and I saw a stray tear splash in her teacup—

"I had so much love to give. And my heart—it was opened to all alike. . . . Not until my Jack was departed—did I learn how much the world could need my widow's love."

And in a pensive way, my aunt was amused at that—at having called herself a widow.

I asked, "Is that when you became a root doctor?"

And she said, "Yes, it was."

And she told me that her mother, my grandmother, had first learned the forest as a girl in England. And what my Aunt Bettina had learned from her was the basis of what she'd come to know. It was after my aunt left Kansas that she made a study of roots across the nation—and a profession. By her mother, she'd been introduced to such works as *Leech Book of Bald*, *Herbarium Arpuleii*, Bartholomaeus Anglicus's *De Proprietatibus Rerum*, *Banke's Herbal*, *Grete Herball*, *Gerard's Herbal*, John Parkinson's *Paridisus*, and the same author's life work, completed at seventy-three, *Theatrum Botanica*. There were also other English works, somewhat more recent and easier to come by, such as *Cole's Art of Simpling*, and *Mary Dogget her Book of receipts*. Most of these were provided by my aunt's mother, my grandmother, from her own collection, and several in turn from my grandmother's family back in England—which is how I maintained my connection to my English cousins, with whom I exchanged some letters, and over the years, seeds. But some of the volumes my grandmother had merely remembered, or heard of, and my aunt'd had to hunt them down on her own, and several of them she copied out herself—just sitting down for a couple of days and transcribing them into a notebook. Those would be *Poor Man's Friend*, *Turner's Herbal* and *Lady Sedley and her receipt Book*, which are right beside me on the shelf, written in my Aunty Betta's warm hand. Besides that, my aunt also added some books of her own, books of a more American caste—*Joyfull Newes out of the newe founde worlde*, by Nicolas Monardes, John Josselyn's *New England's Rarities Discovered* and *The American Physitian; or a Treatise of the Roots, Plants, Trees, Shrubs, Fruit, herbs, etc., growing in the English Plantations in America*, by William Hughes, and so her researches went on and on (she learned much over the years from the Indians, and those who had been among them), and so went my own researches, and the study of my own additions, like *Wright's 3000 Receipts*, *Mackenzie's 10,000 Receipts*, *Christison's Dispensatory*, *Chemical Times*, *American Chemists* and one hundred and one others.

(I know now that Gillian, Sue Anne's Gillian, is interested in my dusty notebooks and mildewed library—just dab at the mildew with a light solution of lemon water and bleach—and she's welcome to have the lot of it when the time comes—I can't help but be delighted in her interest in my funny pastimes. For safekeeping, I put my aunt's journals in the trunk under the porthole window. And that trunk— it's sitting here now, waiting for you, girl, in the frosty light of this old attic.)

So finally . . . our voices grown sticky, my aunt begged pardon— that she was just an old braying goat. An old used-up widow—so romantic that she took seriously a child's puppy love . . .

And trembling wildly, I folded my hands into my lap, and endeavored to formulate my thoughts, my words carefully—not to overstate things, or to presume knowledge of things I could not yet understand. And—I told her that *I* didn't think she was an old goat, or a used-up widow—or that mine had been a puppy love.

And even so, I said, I might stay alone, if I had a mind to—

"For yes, you are alone—but you don't seem to mind it. And Miss Cleveland too, she is alone—and I know there is nothing wrong with that."

And my aunt answered slowly, shaking her head—that no, no, she supposed there was nothing wrong with it—and then she dabbed at the corners of her eyes, and said—"Even if I am just some old hen, who knows less now than she ever did—I'd swear it, Alma, I can see your future."

Then my poor aunty tried to smile. . . .

And I could see that she wanted to cheer me up, because I too had grown emotional. My hands white knuckled, I was wringing my frock. But through her own upset, her eyes were sage and warm, and she touched her fingers to my chin, lifting my face to hers as she assured me—

"Yes, I can see your future, my little chickadee. I see it in my mind like a painted picture—a thrilling life, full of faraway places, and undreamt of things."

The night went on, even after we had finished talking, and we absorbed the heat from the fire and considered—and I realized that nothing stops, though conversation might. . . .

Outside, there was the sound of the creek, and the water blowing off the branches of the trees.

And my soldier was gasping—making noises. Grumbling and grunting as though he were listening to something—answering to a conversation in his mind. . . . With nothing more I could accomplish, I sat back in my chair and massaged his hands and feet, to keep up the circulation, as his extremities were ice cold. Otherwise, it was up to him to get better, and despite my aunt's fears, I was growing to believe he was no longer a boy—he was a soldier now, and would not die easily.

The remainder of the darkness was spent staring into the fire. It was a hypnotic and enticing thing, yet also a scary thing. And when I relaxed into my soft chair, pondering volcanoes, and other fiery things in the earth, I sank my chin into my chest and began to feel nauseous—wondering if my soldier would die.

I watched his stilted breathing subside, and expire, and then, he did die. I was there alone with him, as my aunt was out on the porch, grappling with the firewood. That was when my soldier stopped breathing. I watched his chest cease its rise and fall. But then, only a minute or so passed, and it began again. My tears had been pacific tears, and kindly tears—and I pressed them over my cheeks with the palms of my hands. My soldier's breathing had begun again—making a ragged but steady climb. And thus did the health of my soldier seem to improve—with a kind of dogged struggle into the bottom of a valley, and then, back out. . . .

As my aunt explained it—that soldier was simply too young, and the disease forgave him. She stood in the doorway of the porch, her eyes riveted on him as she spoke bluntly, as if they were true words come from a dream—

"He was too young."

He was too young for the kind of bad blood that insisted on retribution. Too young that corruption should swallow him whole.

Too young—as all children are innocent.

And then . . . my aunt and I spoke of seemingly superficial things—of local things, and how this or that person might persevere. And I thought then that these sentences were of passing consequence, and I let them go by, like milkweed in the breeze. But now that I think back on that faint impression of the words that came and went, I only wish I could faithfully recount them. All of us of that time forgot about those little things to get us from there to here—and now the only thing we wish is that we remembered, for it was the birth of a nation.

My soldier's eyes would sometimes flicker, and there was the sound, all night, of my aunt chopping wood out on the porch. She was like some kind of heavy, melancholic woodpecker—sentenced to her labor. And no matter how I tried, she would not let me help, for though she was toil-worn, and it was obviously too much for her in her deteriorated condition, she did not want me to handle the ax while I was sleepy.

With dawn, the sun rose into the window, and there was light in our dark house. I slipped into a tumble of thoughts and things very near to dreams, but not quite so—and only a few hours later, I woke— abruptly. My aunt had nearly prepared our breakfast. When she set the flapjacks in front of me, I saw that the fire needed more wood. I stood, but my aunt eased me down, her hands on my shoulders—

"Eat those hot."

And because I was a child, and because hungry children eat, and because I knew it was of no use to argue, I sat down to eat. . . . But then, my aunt was just so exhausted, dragging her poor, old bones out to the porch, that I began to beg her to let me do it.

"You're tired," I pleaded.

And she snapped at me—"Sit down!"

Then, as if it were just the most natural thing in the world, my soldier just sat up, wiped his eyes and went out to the porch to chop firewood. . . .

My aunt and I were utterly flabbergasted, and it was almost breathless that my aunt whispered—

"He must've heard me, fussing out there all night."

Then he returned, with a look on his face both distracted and determined, and he wordlessly unrolled the wood tote, threw a few logs onto the fire and went back to sleep.

✳ ✳ ✳

Buck Bean

It was still early when my soldier woke again, and my Aunt Bettina administered a vegetable purgative of buck bean, mountain flax, poplar bark, ginger and gentian. Following that, a violent purge for which I retreated out to the back porch, my soldier slept through—and then, he woke again.

My aunt had turned in, for a mid-morning nap, but I was awake—and there by his side. The first thing my soldier did was to whisper my name. And then I whispered his. But the peace with which he had said my name was quite opposed to his dismay upon hearing his own. His eyes opened wide, though his brows angled downward, as did his lips—and he rolled his head on his pillow and looked at the fire. He was pouting, his mouth compressed in a surly way—as if by saying his name I had uttered something terrible. As if I'd reminded him of something he wanted to forget. His whole body had gone limp, almost as if he were a wet doll—though he was sodden, not with water, but with guilt and remorse. . . .

His body was so heaving that when he opened his mouth, he seemed barely able to speak. It was as if it were his very first word—all over again—when he asked for "Miles," Pastor Miles. . . .

But it seemed we would not be able to deliver him his wish—for though the storm was quieted, we could not leave him alone with the Union soldiers about (as my aunt had heard talk of them). So, it was something of a miracle when, in the rain—there materialized Temperance Flowerdew and his cobbler and tin cart! His name was one that much suited him—not so much "Temperance," as he had a rather flamboyant nature, but "Flowerdew," as his lips were so red they appeared to be rouged! He liked to reminisce about the days when he was a young beauty—but for all the time anyone could remember, he had been driving that cart in circles between Frickerham and Cotterpin. He was just coming from the Nielsons', he called out, as he tied up his mule—but he still had pots. It was likely he'd stayed the night at the Nielsons', not only for the storm, but for his work on their shoes—leathers often needed an overnight soaking, and it might be a day to make a new pair of boots, besides. Thus, it was rather good luck to hear that he had already stopped at the Mayfields', and was next off to the church, where he might fetch Pastor Miles for us.

Still, he was rather disappointed when my aunt told him we'd need no work on our shoes. She did purchase a few pie pans and a grater, that nothing might seem amiss—yet Temperance was a rather insightful kind of curious man—and he just couldn't understand why he wasn't being invited in, or why we should have such a need of Pastor Miles. He was also a rather fun-loving and innocent sort of man, and as he stood at the door collecting his payment, he made a feint to peek inside—up over my aunty's shoulder—and then, ever so quick, as my aunt moved to impede him, he ducked to look under her arm.

And he saw that soldier. . . .

And he stepped back as if he'd been struck in the head, and stammered, "Oh dear. Yes, I see. Pastor Miles. I heard . . . Well, of course . . . I haven't seen anyone. . . . No, no, not me. I've seen no one."

And as Temperance Flowerdew climbed up into his cart (waving away my aunt's payment for the pie pans, as if to say—*Oh, there's simply no time dear. No time at all!*) he said—

"Don't you worry about a thing, dearest ones. Believe old Temperance when he says he can keep a secret."

And it was true, when Pastor Miles arrived, not an hour later, not even he knew why he had been called upon.

"Why," he joked when he saw us, "I haven't rode at a gallop since . . ."

And he clucked his tongue and shook his head—

"That Temperance! Had me so riled up! Now what's the problem Bettina? Bad roof in a storm? Temperance wouldn't even let me get my tools. Said you . . ."

And that was when Pastor Miles, in at the door and removing his sheepskin coat, saw my soldier at the hearth, and he merely whispered (Job, 5: 7)—

Man is born unto trouble as the sparks fly upward.

Now, I retired to my room—but houses then were small, and though I didn't mean to be listening . . . well, I was not old enough to know how to ignore it. And I listened some, and filled in some (for there was much I couldn't hear), as my soldier stuttered in a frail and heaving kind of way that he had nothing and wanted nothing. A fresh start, maybe . . . But he wished . . . wished . . . wished he had something for . . . And he choked as he exhaled, and gasping, or maybe crying, he wished . . . he could . . . a new life. . . . He couldn't. . . . He was too . . . well, too . . . How might he . . .

And Pastor Miles, he did not condescend—did not speak as if to say his life had taught him so and so and so and so—it was as if, in the face of all that experience, he could not charge his own with that burden. Pastor Miles, he was not an insistent man—not for God or himself. But his voice—it was a beautiful and manly and decent voice. All at once—luxurious, flowing, firm.

And . . . when he spoke from the first book of Samuel, 2:6, I heard that voice as if he were sitting beside me—

> *The Lord killeth, and maketh alive: he bringeth down to the grave, and bringeth up. The Lord maketh poor, and maketh rich: he bringeth low, and lifteth up.*

And then my soldier, he spoke of honor—and no honorable thing to do. . . . But Pastor Miles, he interrupted with Ecclesiastes, 7:15, gently reminding my soldier he'd already decided not to die—

> *All things have I seen in the days of my vanity: there is a just man that perisheth in his righteousness, and there is a wicked man that prolongeth his life in his wickedness. Be not righteous over much; neither make thyself over wise: why shouldest thou*

destroy thyself? Be not over much wicked, neither be thou fool-
ish: why shouldest thou die before thy time? It is good that thou
shouldest take hold of this; yea, also from this withdraw not
thine hand: for he that feareth God shall come forth of them all.
Wisdom strengtheneth the wise more than ten mighty men which
are in the city. For there is not a just man upon earth, that doeth
good, and sinneth not.

$\backsim$

And though I was a young girl, and young girls are all eyes and no
bodies (and, all eyes hankering!), I thought crossly to myself that I
wanted nothing from my soldier but laughter. And then, I began to
smell the honeyed air, and it was such an intoxicating and overpow-
ering smell, my own demand seemed paltry. So I decided that what I
really wanted, it was no more than laughter, and that . . . that . . . that
he share with me, every single year, the smell of the linden tree.

Still . . . I feared he wouldn't believe me, or that he would believe
I believed myself, though I'd not be nearly so easy to please as I supposed. It infuriated me some—so I knew not to speak of it. I thought
he might yet have a few big notions in his head—even if they had
killed his father, his brother, his mother and nearly him, too. . . .

And I folded my arms—and thought of how I should go have his
father tell him to give it up!

And then I remembered where I was, and when I was—and that his
house and his father were gone. . . .

And my soldier and the pastor, they spoke of the Cleveland estate—and of the taxes on it. And my soldier asked the pastor if *he*
would save it. And he said yes—he would.

And my soldier . . . he laughed again, and his mirth calmed into
something so considered it was gentle—like a much handled scrap of
felt. And the world went quiet for him as he made more
wishes . . . wishes that he could erase time, that a loving look could
make all that'd passed meaningful. Wishes that someday, it could be
so. And his peaceful manner was so heartfelt and eternal!

But . . . there followed nothing of that domestic serenity—of felt worn soft. Instead, I realized that tenderness had only been a sigh of tranquility, for my soldier's emotions were as shifting and wild as the bow of a sailing ship in a storm. And even if he didn't want it to be so, my soldier was plunging into an anger, a fury—

"But now . . . now . . . now, when I see a hill, I see a hill where my father carried my sled. And that sled is now burned. And when I see a pine tree, I see a pine tree under which my brother's dog used to nap in the shade on hot afternoons. And that dog is now killed. And when I see a patch of dandelions, I see a place where my mother once set silver on a tablecloth laid out on the grass, for a picnic. And that silver is now stolen. And my father is dead. And my brother is dead. And my mother is dead. And I cannot stay to watch their murderers take all that should be mine. I cannot stay to watch the scalawags and carpetbaggers take this land. It is not my country anymore. . . ."

And I knew what he meant to say was that it was not his country anymore—it was mine.

And I thought how, through this trouble, there were men who could be courteous and friendly till they turned around and killed you. And then I heard motion—a-wild—and the pastor saying—*easy soldier, easy. . . .*

In due time, that settled, and my soldier spoke, his voice trembling—

And though I strained, I could not hear what he said. . . .

And then—I heard the wind and rain return, and I thought to reheat the compresses that lay on my soldier's sore chest—the compresses and flannels that I had prepared myself—and then I grew angry myself. And I thought—*I have lost a family too—and you also have an aunt, who loves you.* And I looked out the window as the sky cleared—and I imagined my soldier and the pastor staring out through their window, across that same creek, as Pastor Miles said (2 Samuel, 22:2)—

The Lord is my rock, and my fortress, and my deliverer.

⌒

It must've been a quarter of an hour before I heard the sheets rustle. And such a silence followed that I imagined my soldier, having just rolled over, staring up—at nothing at all. And, almost as if it *were* nothing, or they were the first words of a conversation, he said—

"There were so many people on the road."

The sheets rustled again, and I imagined him sitting up, ever so slightly, as he spoke of the poor condition of the roadway, as it'd been much traveled—all able-bodied men at arms. And he spoke of seeing them that passed, and how most everyone's life had been so much harder than his own—and how most would lead lives that would always be harder. . . . There were so many kinds of a person on the road, walking or riding along in either direction. And as many whites as there were, he said, there were just as many slaves—or those who had been slaves—heading for Southern cities or up North to find work. He said the funny thing about that was—he knew his family was gone, and not to look for them, and that his aunt would not leave Cotterpin—so, the only faces he found himself looking to were the brown ones. And the only people that he was looking for were Natalie and Serena. Among all those faces—those two! Of course, he didn't see them. . . .

And my soldier's voice, it went singsong, kind of giddyish, as he said that some of the Rebs were going south, some of the Yanks north—though just as many Rebs were going north, and Yanks going south. It was like a dancing wheel—dizzy and crazy. If you are up the room, you must dance down. Down the room—you must dance up. A Yank might ask a Reb for directions—and get them. And he didn't know how the soldiers could do it—when, surely, they all would have killed one another if the fight were still on.

"Matter of fact," he said, "I took directions myself."

And then my soldier spoke of the slaver, Ragan, and having

chanced upon him. And then he spoke of how Ragan had always been a competent man, who carried out his tasks—and how he and his comrades in the cavalry had all had such men in the employ of their families. . . .

And then . . . came the wrathful words. And then—words too muffled to hear . . .

And when it came time for Pastor Miles to speak, he did, from Ecclesiastes, 9:11—

> *I returned, and saw under the sun, that the race is not to the swift, nor the battle to the strong, neither yet bread to the wise, nor yet riches to men of understanding, nor yet favour to men of skill; but time and chance happeneth to them all. For man also knoweth not his time: as the fishes that are taken in an evil net, and as the birds that are caught in the snare; so are the sons of men snared in an evil time, when it falleth suddenly upon them.*

And then my soldier confessed to a very terrible thing. A thing so terrible! He and his gents of the cavalry! And as he and the pastor turned to talk of rage and salvation—I heard my aunt, banging about with the firewood. And though I'm sure the hearth did need the wood, I also felt strong emotions in that ruckus—thoughts unspoken, but deeply felt. . . .

And Pastor Miles, I heard him turning the pages of a bible (one that he'd leave for my soldier) and he spoke from Ecclesiastes, saying that there was a time for *everything* under heaven. And he spoke of Job—that *anyone* might be tested. And finally, my soldier sighed, as erratic as he was, with a kind of understanding that gave a hint of him as an older man. The conversation had become one without words, and that tired exhalation, it was as if to say—

No, I don't know where the sin might lie. Perhaps with Ragan, or perhaps my father and men like him—or all such men who carried just enough sin that they did not discern the burden of it. *I don't know anymore that one man in particular—no matter how oily his skin—I don't know that any of us bore a greater weight.*

My aunt, she was a healer, and pain always pained her. And she was not accustomed to keeping her peace when there was a sighing body at her own hearth—but keep it she did. And stoke that hearth she did. If a bit noisily . . .

And when the fire was hot and aside from its crackling there was naught, Pastor Miles spoke from the book of Psalms, 118:24, for all of us—

> *This is the day which the Lord hath made; we will rejoice and be glad in it.*

~

And though I did not expect it to gentle the temper of our cabin—it began to do just that!

And my aunt prepared relaxing tea, and my soldier—he drank it. And she took the rocker in from the porch, and angled it behind him in the cot, and massaged his temples—and he drifted into sleep. And by then, I was beside him, and I could see it was a deep sleep. . . .

The fire was settled, my soldier's chills had subsided, the storm had quieted and the evening was warming. But I did not want to leave the hearth, so my aunt fixed me up with my rocking chair, and a blanket. And I slept too. Through my sleep, which was a light and confused one, there was the murmur of Pastor Miles and my aunt, speaking in low tones. Sometimes he tapped his pipe. . . . Late in the afternoon, I heard the pastor making off—and then there was only the sound of my own rocking chair—*rickity-rick, rickity-rick, rickity-rick*. . . .

I found myself swaying in the middle of the night—my legs were softly pushing against the floor, and my soldier, awake, was watching me.

It was then, in middle of night, that my soldier asked if I would play marbles in spring.

"I'm a little old for marbles," I said.

But he asked that I promise, and because his memories of playing seemed so fond to him, I finally did. I could tell it had agitated him, and that it would help him to go back to sleep if I promised, and when I promised, it did. So he went back to sleep. And then I went back to sleep. . . .

With dawn, my aunt came to me, and woke me matter of factly, asking if she should prepare a solution of onion and peppermint juice, and a pot of tabasco tea.

And I looked at her funny, because it had not occurred to me it might be time for such, and I said—

"No thank you, I am not ready for that."

And so my aunt nodded once, and returned to her bedroom.

Morning come, we enjoyed a fine breakfast—one healthy for my soldier. We had wheat flapjacks, with maple syrup and the butter from the Mayfields (which had been fine in the cold). But my soldier was very hungry, so we also had oatmeal and raisins, along with a little honey and cream. (And, as that boy was also very slender, my aunt did not mind fattening him up!) Then we had some warm cider—all out on the wooden bench we set by the big rock. After the storm, it was uncommonly tranquil, and though it was nearly December, the sun was warming the field. We had been inside so much that it was especially enjoyable, even if it was nippish, and we were bundled good and tight.

Realizing it was Thanksgiving, we drank peach tea, ate bread with jam and watched the sky through the bare trees. There came a beauty to the spare day, not just in the silvery big rock and the winter grass and simple fare of our repast, but in the moment itself. It was inspirational, after all that had been so agonizing and exposed, that we could just sit, like a kind of a family, drinking peach tea and talking about the size of crickets in various parts of the country—and the difference between the sound they made, and the sound made by small frogs. . . .

"Might we shave your beard," I suggested rather suddenly, guiltily looking up at my soldier—

"And, do you still have your wolf scar?"

"Why Alma!" said my aunt.

And my soldier smiled with big eyes, and he nodded once, as if to say he would always have that scar, and my aunt laughed, saying, "He might need that beard this winter."

And I said, "I know, but I haven't seen him—"

And still laughing, my aunt interrupted, "But Alma, he'll freeze his face off!"

And just then, my soldier began to laugh, and he said—

"Why, you'd never get my father to shave off his, but me, I don't think I like my father's bea—"

And then my aunt held up her hand—she'd heard something, and it wasn't a frog or cricket either. Then my soldier listened, and heard it—and he said he knew it was soldiers, having listened for and listened to the sounds of soldiers over so many years. We were quick to gather up our things—as a Thanksgiving picnic would not impart that austerity and deference most favorable to our well-being. I thought at first they might find us, but had hardly opened my mouth when I saw the smoke rising from our chimney. . . .

We could hear the soldiers, scraping, bumping and complaining in the woods—and they hastened us in our preparations. After taking in our bench, I cleared up our breakfast table, and then my soldier's bed and supplies. If the soldiers were looking for him, his capture might mean an indefinite imprisonment, or worse—as those were times wild with greed, foolishness and secrecy.

My aunt was swift among the tonics she had bottled and stacked in the cupboards. She gave my soldier twelve vials filled with her distillates and sealed with wax—one for right then, to liven him up, and one for later, when he should want to sleep. In addition to the two more for waking, and the two more for sleeping, there were six others, all the same—one of which he was to take each day, that he might stave off his sickness in what would surely be less than ideal circumstances. She made him drink one of those too.

Meanwhile, the soldiers had arrived outside—they were at the hitching post, tying up their horses.

My soldier changed into his washed clothing, as he had been wearing only the long-johns, thick socks and cloak that used to belong to the husband of my aunt. Shedding the cloak, he then dressed—retying his tall boots. With his new socks and long-johns, even if he had been sick, this time he was prepared for the cold. With his cloak—he did not look like a soldier. His youth had returned, and he looked too young for the battlefield. . . .

He turned to me, and I turned to him, to say good-bye. But then, we both just knew that he would stay.

I said, "Stay."

And he said, "I will."

Perhaps we were foolish children, and perhaps our mistake was our armor—like a seashell against the ocean. My aunt's lips were held tightly, and she looked away, not speaking. Then my soldier went out to the porch.

"Until they're gone," he said, "I'll be here."

And I said, "Yes, until then."

Out of the corner of my eye, I saw my aunt shaking her head, skeptically, ruefully, and then I knew that somewhere inside me, and somewhere inside him, we also knew that this was farewell. . . .

I saw he had his bible.

And . . . I stepped around, out onto the porch—and I lifted my palm, and took his warm neck—and his hand took my neck, and we kissed for the second time.

It was not a long kiss, but a deep kiss, and . . .

And I am reminded of a tree that I saw growing in Richmond. It was a grand tree that had taken root over the troubled years, and had uplifted and overturned a whole brick patio through the course of its life.

And that was the kiss—a sprout grown from the pore of a brick. A thing so delicate—a thousandfold more delicate than a teacup or a matchstick. With just two gentle leaves, with just one watery root, it was the kind of thing that, over the years, would simply insist. And with a persistence so tempered and gradual, it would crack that brick, lifting away the two halves and taking to the soil.

Then it would ease more compliance, and lift countless bricks, and grow under the patio, not so much despite the bricks, but because of them—because there'd been a great void in the earth, without life or roots. . . .

And that's how, out of the ruin of old Richmond, that sprout had grown, without nurturing or expectation, into a tree.

And that was how that kiss took hold in the two of us. And that was how it grew.

And that was how that kiss began to grow—when we parted.

My soldier said, "I'll be out on the porch."

And I said, "Yes."

And he said, "I have the feeling it will only be a minute."

And I said, "Me too."

And then, when that child was hid, my aunt opened the door.

Bark.

Beetle

The soldiers were still out front, fiddling with their horses. And these men were not horsemen. Some of the men were still riding up, and one was sitting so way back on his horse that that horse must've had a sore back indeed! Another rider hung on his horse's mouth, steadying himself by it—and ruining it. It was plain to see the horse was losing all feeling in his mouth—with the result that the man just tore it up more and more. It was hard to just look on without saying a word—and to allow a horse to so suffer. In fact, all of the horses were very nervous, for, simply, these men didn't know what they were doing, and the horses were ill at ease with the inexperience. Many say horses are nowhere near as bright as even a dog or cat, and while I'm not sure that's true, for I believe horses are just smart about being horses—just as a man would make a dumb whale—I do know that horses are herd animals, and need to trust their leaders, and, in other words, need to have confidence in their riders. But these men inspired no such thing. From where I stood, I bit my lip and laid my hands flatly on my thighs to prevent myself from fixing all the twisted straps, mislaid saddles and badly set stirrups—too long and too short. The men were so close to one another on their horses, and riding up on one another from every angle, that I was afraid that just about any moment, any horse might kick. The best I could say about any of them is that one of the riders was rather light, so he probably wasn't hurting his horse too badly. I could hear one of the men speaking to his animal—"Damn ya, c'mon, jusda liddle maw . . . aw, damn ya—damn ya, ya win, a'ready—I ain't gonna led ya rub me off wid dat tree, I see wad yer dinkin'." It made me sick to see it, the way they sat on their saddles like kitchen chairs—slumped, leaning and crooked. No, I thought, these were no horsemen—and then I saw that all the horses bore Alabama brands. . . .

And while it seems a rather unfair thing to report, as the men themselves were such a sorry assortment, I'm afraid the horses were little better. They too were a sorry lot, even if they were battle horses—as these soldiers, having no knowledge of horse, had managed to acquire for themselves the very worst that was available—and in times like those, that was a rough looking horse! Some of the beasts looked like they'd barely be good for another mile. There was one horse that was distinctly jugheaded—that big oafy head like a watermelon in his rider's hand. There was a ewe-necked animal, who stood staring at the sky, paying hardly any attention at all to his miserable rider, who was tying him to our hitching rail. There was a bull-necked animal, all short and stumpy-like—and there was a mutton withered horse, whose saddle was fixed far too tight, for were it not, that saddle would be likely to slide right off! There were horses knock-kneed, bowlegged and swaybacked. Legs were swollen, lumpy and splintered—bone spurs all everywhere. One mare had eyes so deeply set and close together that were there not a great need for horses, I was quite sure she'd have made a visit to the butcher by then, as pig-eyed horses were often considered meanspirited, and hardly worth the trouble. Of course, a great many of their problems were not their fault at all, but the result of poor handling. (Their hooves, especially.) Over the course of the conflict, Doctor Esterbrook had put three horses down—one had lost its sight from moon blindness, one suffered a serious case of ringbone which had circled all the way around the hoof, causing lameness, and the last was a victim of sweeny (a draft horse gone paralyzed in the shoulders). Mister Nielson had also put an animal down. He'd found the mare in the woods, in winter, and she was beyond what any man could do for her—her ailment was simple starvation. A few horses were caught and treated successfully. The Ditzlers had cured one colt with a blanket, a laxative and meals of bran mash, grass and hay. Frank Mayfield had cured an animal of a bad case of colic—he'd found the horse, in a field, pawing at the ground, lying on his side, and nosing and kicking at his belly. It appeared that several horses had been moving together—perhaps in transport, and this animal was just too much trouble to stop for. Mister Mayfield healed him with a blanket, care and no food for twelve hours. . . . And from their look, several of these horses would be similarly abandoned, and with a good blessing, similarly rescued. Still, for the time—there they walked, with their halting, sick gaits, their wavering bodies, their swinging knees and unmoving shoulders—and, added to that, the unsightly, unhealthy effects of the men behind the reins—flexed heads, high heads and stretched necks. . . .

As the last of the soldiers tied up their horses, one said to another, "Ya flat'ead paddy, da's na'how ya tie a knot ta one'a dese dogs."

And then the man looked up, and, upon seeing my aunt, he looked down, ashamedly. And it was at precisely that moment that I could see that though these soldiers were very foolish and very greedy, they were not of the intention of harming any women. . . .

The soldier who had spoken approached. From his pocket, he

drew a piece of paper, which he unfolded. It was a wanted poster, with an etching of my soldier. But it was not the boy I knew—it was a beady-eyed killer of a boy, one who was smiling—cruelly.

The soldier was almost bashful. "We're on da'unt fer dis murd'rer and traitor. 'Ave ya seen da likes of 'im?"

"No," said my aunt, "I can honestly say that I haven't seen anyone like that. And if he were here, I would have seen him."

The soldier looked at me as I joined my aunt in the door, and I just shook my head—*no.*

"Well," said the soldier, "we're searchin' dese naybhoods 'cause dis oder dhug," and he held up another drawing—" 'e was found dead right 'round here, could be even kilt, and we jus' wansda make sure everyone's safe as kin be, as dis fella 'ere is a genu-ine desperado."

Another one of the soldiers chimed in, " 'E kilt dat oder fella by stealin' 'is boots—'e was barefoot when we found 'em, and dat's what—"

The first soldier cleared his throat, and said, "Dat's correct," as he had meant us to think the murder was a more spectacular one than that. But my aunt and I nodded, as if acutely impressed and frightened, even if we knew that my soldier hadn't stolen my aunt's boots— though it did set me to thinking that the other boy had died because he hadn't any. And what had happened to my soldier's boots?

"If only . . ." I sighed, "they had both had a pair of boots."

"Yeah," the soldier coughed, "well, dey may be 'ard ta come by if you're a disagreeable sort, and wanted by da law. Dis one 'ere," and he rattled the page, " 'e's a regular t'ieving wido'maker—wanted fer questionin' 'bout some stoled gold. Looks like 'e kilt'a trader by the name Ragan. A child, 'id in the woods, saw 'im and 'is uglies pickin' over da stiff."

Though the soldier wasn't an educated man, he had somehow become a corporal—and had obtained orders to search all the houses in the area. His name was Shipton. As there was no advantage would come from debate, my aunt consented, and suggested she make some cocoa for the corporal and his four men while they were at it.

"Da'be kind, ma'am," said Shipton, "we won't meka mess. We be from frog'n toe—got 'ouses like dis back dair—"

"Excuse me?"

"New York," said the soldier.

And my aunt looked at them a bit skeptically, as if to say—

Really?

For it was being said of New York that it had hardly even been in the trouble—and of those who were fighting, it was right there in New York—and for the Confederates!

And so, one of the other soldiers piped up, to say, "Ain't even a po'bastad da'wansa get kilt for no shine. Dem splibs, dey—"

And Shipton interrupted him—

"We be gud republ'cans 'ere—volunteers like, fer da-gud."

And my aunt looked at Shipton long and hard, and considered him. And Shipton, he looked at the others, scraggy pirates that they were, and he considered them. And finally, he amended—

"I be, anyway."

And my aunt, she sighed as if, well, she might believe *that*. And then, grinning a big huckster's grin (but an evil huckster's grin) Shipton said in a way almost charming, almost endearing in a lost child kind of scalawag way, "We ain't in it fer da-gettin', but da-gud, if da-gettin's gud—ain't dat right boys?"

And they sniffed and grumbled—and one patted his pockets, as if he suspected that one of his fellows might have lightened his burden.

And my aunt just picked up my hand, and she held it tightly—

"Well," she said to Shipton, "New York and Kentucky—they were both neutral."

And there was a tense silence for a moment, before Shipton conceded—

"Kud say so, ma'am." Then he added, apologetically—"D'ain't nothun' nice 'bout anyadis. We just poor sams, tryin' ta make our stake."

And he was true to his word—his men didn't make a mess, and they were polite (polite as they knew how to be), and when my aunt

227

asked them to remove their boots, as they were tracking mud all over the house, they did it. The bootjack was there by the door, and they'd hold it there on the floor with the one foot, and hook their other boot into it, and then repeat the task on the other side, and then hand it off to the next man.

And with so many men, it all took some doing. . . .

Eventually, they asked if that was a back porch, and we said yes, and they went out there. We followed, but by that time, my soldier was gone. He knew those woods well, and to flee into them, I knew that he would not be sighted or caught in them—not with such a lead as he had taken.

There was a candleholder on the wall—brass with some cut glass—a kind of half sconce, half luster. And upon witnessing one of the four soldiers slide the object off the wall and into the deep pocket of his coat, she burst out—

"You put that . . . that thingamabob back! You think I've spent the last ten years of my life fighting for the likes of you, so you could steal from me!"

Shipton apologized, and told his man to replace the candleholder.

"I'm sorry, ma'am," stumbled the man, "I'm sorry . . ." while the corporal said, "Maxy, you get dat ding back in dair!"

As Maxy produced the item, Shipton said excitedly, " 'Ere it goes, ma'am," and then looked down, and rolled his head woefully, " 'E got no manners, ma'am—'e got no manners."

Maxy went back into the house, and replaced the candleholder on the wall—my aunt muttering, "Stealing my . . . my thingamajigs . . ."

But another soldier was still out on the back porch, staring into the wood—"Ay Shipton, what'if we be da bens 'ere, and dat gip's off inda drees?"

Then I stood, along with my aunt and the three soldiers and the officer—all staring into the woods.

I read the broken branches—guessing that my soldier had departed in the direction of Virginia—to enter the Union there, if he was still of a mind to, though he may well have gone farther south.

With all of his anger, and these men after him, I thought that was probably the most likely—that he'd go to Louisiana, or Florida, or somewhere like that. . . .

Then one of the quiet soldiers asked if he saw tracks. We all walked out into the garden, and he was right—there they were, clear as they could be—fresh, and stamped into the mud of the wet ground.

"Dang," said the soldier, "dose ain't from no boot."

And that was when I realized that my soldier had crept out over the yard, backward, on his hands and knees, with his fingers pressing five toe prints onto the hind tracks, and five toe prints and a heel onto the forepaws—to fashion the tracks of a black bear.

Shipton sighed, "I ain't seen none 'round 'ere, but dose bear tracks, sure," and he looked sorrowfully up at my aunt and me—" 'E been right up to the porch." He looked around the corner. "Yep, right dair, he jumped off and gone back inta da woods."

And I saw that my soldier had not only covered his tracks—but he'd made two sets, one coming, and one going. For one of the sets, he must've walked in the knee prints back and forth—making the toe prints on his second pass. . . .

Without pause, my aunt stood back with her hands on her hips—

"You know, when I came back here from Kansas, I didn't think I'd ever see another bear. But this little ol' black bear has been a real nuisance, oh, for more than a year or so—and I have dozens of traps out there that'd take a man's leg clean off—and they're not doing a whit of good! But you're some solid men, with some fine guns, maybe you could take your rifles and . . . well, that's good meat, and Alma loves bear meat, and I could sell that—"

"Whoa ho," said the quiet soldier, "I ain't goin' after no bear—not 'less 'e's wearin' a gold watch."

"Well," sighed my aunt, resigned, "Mister Nielson was planning to come out with his rifle and . . ."

With that, Shipton and the other soldiers retreated into the house. Their socks had gotten wet, as they had walked into the garden without shoes. My aunt said they should dry them off by the hearth, and she served them the hot cocoa. I was still standing out on the porch when I heard one of them tell a coarse joke about a bear.

My aunt had stepped outside, to place their wet boots in the sun.

Maxy told the joke whisperingly—"So dis bloke goes 'untin' for bear, an' 'e's da 'ard way sort so 'e's 'untin'em wit an iddy biddy pistol. So 'e shoots da bear an'da bear walks up to 'em an' says, 'Unter, I ain't dead, so now I'm givin' you a choice—eider I eat ya or sod'mize ya.' So da bloke drops 'is pants, leden da bear 'ave 'is way, an' den da bloke goes 'ome an' gets 'imself 'is 30 cal'ber. Den 'e loads up an' comes back ta da woods an' shoots da bear an'da bear ain't 'urt so 'e grabs 'em ans tells 'im again, 'Get ate or get sod'mized.' So 'e drops 'is pants again an'da bear 'as 'is way an' den da bloke goes an' buys a 58 cal'ber an' comes back an' shoots da bear an' da bear grabs 'em an' says, 'You ain't 'ere fer da 'untin' are ya?' "

And I don't know if it was accidentally that my aunt walked in just then, hearing the punch line and the laughing, or if she had been waiting on the porch to make her entrance at precisely that moment. Regardless, that was when she went back into the house and said to them—

"Put on your stinking socks and get out! I have a child in this house!"

And then Shipton apologized again, and my aunt accepted the apology, and the soldiers all made funny faces at one another as they dunked their hoecakes and drank their hot cocoa—as if they had been scolded by someone's mother. Then my aunt gave them some bowls of corn mush, which she had been preparing. And they sat there eating it, and dipping their bread and sipping their hot cocoas—just like children. Shipton said it made him think of the orphanage, and I felt something for him, intermingled with the fear and hatred—for I saw that he could well have been a woefully unlucky child. My aunt gave them each another hoecake, and as the cakes were cold, she suggested they toast them with the toe-toaster by the fire. Then, drinking their cocoa, and munching their toast, the soldiers were suddenly drowsy, and sitting around the fire, reclining in their chairs, they were disposed to taking a restful afternoon—napping at the hearth. . . .

I had taken the blanket off the rocking chair, and I sat out there—rocking on the porch, looking at the garden and feeling the woods.

I sat there, warm under that old woolen blanket. . . .

I sat there, and grew accustomed to the tough and grainy fabric. . . .

I sat there, and looked through the branches of the bare trees. And I thought of autumn and winter, and spring and summer and autumn. And I thought of how all leaves fall.

I sat there, on that crisp winter day, knowing there would be more lonely snow this winter than ever before. It would be a snow too heavy for igloos or sledding—a snow that demanded to just be watched, from a chair by the window. And on a giving day, it might invite me to lift the pane, to trace a line on the sill and then to lower the pane again.

And then I sat there, and there were just the winter things—the air, the woods and the sky. And for a while, I thought about the winter, about its voice and body.

And then, rocking on the porch on that crisp day, wrapped in my thick blanket, just as the animals were nestled in their lairs, I quit thinking about the winter, and I was the winter—my quiet breathing, my limbs, my eyes. . . .

Diving Beetle

When I came back inside, late that afternoon, I felt the stare of the soldiers linger on me, and it made me anxious—and a little nauseous. But then, the soldiers didn't stay too long, as I was obviously becoming sick (I went out to the creek to throw up) and they didn't want to catch anything. My aunt said it might be "flu-tartka fever" which was highly contagious—

"Yes," she said, "I'm sure you've all had it, it's harmless for women and children, though it can be a tremendous misfortune for young men—swollen groin, resulting in what I've heard is a just extraordinary pain, accompanied by a discoloration—blueness, yellowness and redness—as well as glandular dysfunction as a result of the pus."

My aunt had said this rather starkly, as if talking about the garden, and I did not know exactly what these ailments were—not then—though of course I do now, so I can appreciate the humor of her steps to rectify what she saw, probably rightly, as an exceptionally serious situation—for now that she knew my soldier was safely away, it was time to rid ourselves of the unstable element in these soldiers.

Shipton asked my aunt if she was joking—

"Ma'am, ya wouldn't be misleadin' strangers, would ya?"

"No," she said, "I'm not." Then she folded her hands, gathered the sides of her lips and opened her eyes wide—"Would you like to stay for a dinner of rice and cabbage?"

I could hardly keep from giggling at that, as rice and cabbage was not too tantalizing a dish. The men also knew that, and they were still not sure that she was serious—but my aunt had a way of staring that was both fierce and passionate, and she stared down each one of them, until he looked away, and believed her, or at least, *feared* she might be telling the truth about the fever.

"Look 'round 'ere," said the quiet one, "she gotsta be some kinda granny doctor—*could be* somthun' 'round 'ere. *Could be.*"

My aunt had gone out to the potato hill, and picked out a few, which she had tossed into the coals of the hearth. She told the men they were cooked for them, and the soldiers poked them out, and with a rag that my aunty gave to them, they wiped them of ashes, that they might eat the skin. And then they gathered up their things to depart—a little sadly. They had dried off, and though they were still sleepy, they made their way quietly, thanking my aunt for the cocoa, mush and potatoes—and the pleasant afternoon at the hearth.

"Happy Danksgiving," said Shipton, and as he stood in the door, he handed my aunt a tightly wound package from his pouch. It was a prized kind of package, as it had been wrapped with extreme care.

"Why thank you," said my aunt, a little puzzledly—and Shipton asked that she open it.

My aunt did, and inside, she found two dainty maple candies, one molded into a maple leaf—the other, a flying bird.

"One fer you and one fer da girl," he said, and with great, round eyes, he gestured to us, "Ead 'em—maple syrup never hurd no-one."

And in a kind of a mesmerized way, my aunt offered from the package, and I took one, and we both ate of the candies. And they were delicious. I had never had a maple candy that melted so like cream and honey. And I could see it in my aunt's face too, and she began to say—

"Why—"

But Shipton answered her, still in his sad way, "I know, ma'am. Dey be good. My ma's ma and pa, dey made dose. Up Nord, sap ran sdrong lasd'yere."

And then Shipton turned, and turned up his hand in a kind of backward way, and he walked to his horse. My aunt shook her head, and I shook mine, and then we closed the door on Shipton and his men. . . .

Tidy Tips

My soldier's visit had only lasted three days, but I remembered them . . . like crystal in clay.

One morning after winter, toward the coming of spring, I sat by the window in the parlor, and through the green shoots of my aunt's herbs, and through the dew gathered on the glass, I watched the big rock, and how it cradled and released the sunlight. It would hold the sun embraced in a crevice or cleft, and then the dimple would slip into shade. . . . There was moss on the low perimeter—green and appreciative of this premonition of springtime. And the rock beckoned to me, as it had beckoned my soldier, months ago.

The whole nation had been divided, and stitched up in a sorry kind of way—like a doll ripped apart and sewn up with thick black yarn—beans leaking out. The whole nation was limping, sullied and worn. And as there had been no rain, when I went to the big rock I walked, as we all walked, on ground that was cracked and parched. And, all the while, I thought, there had been this rock by this creek where the water ran, and even in a dry spell, there was moss a-growing. And nothing ever changed about this big rock, except that it moved—sank, oh, an eighth of an inch or so every seven or eight years. . . .

But with the country so split, one would expect that even the big rock would be struck by lightning. And I had dreamt that it was—but that didn't make it so. It was still the same big rock—born of whatever cataclysm that had brought it there. Did it roll down the mountain? Did it arrive from the top of a volcano—blown into the air? Was it once a mountain itself? Was it just the tip of an even greater stone, or stone ledge? Was it all the soil around it that was new? Had it been there, that big rock, when the field by the creek was the bottom of the sea? Had it seen other nations divide? Had it been whole for so long?

Maybe, I considered, it wasn't a natural tendency that all great things should break. . . .

That was when I went outside. I rose stiffly, slowly, and I took my aunt's hand shovel to dig out the thawed ground of the marble course—just to keep that promise to my soldier. And with purely a sense of compromise, rather than fun, I found the gold mice.

First I found the boots—two of them, and I thought—why would they be buried here? Then I heard a shaking in one of them, and I pulled out the leather inside, and there beneath, under a strip of metal, pressed into the heel—there was a sack—just a circle of un-tanned leather threaded along its perimeter with a cinched thong. Inside, were three of the mice. Inside the other boot, were four. All were very dirty, though the gold shone. . . . And I could imagine my soldier cutting sacks from that untanned leather (perhaps a rabbit he'd hunted himself). And I could imagine him placing the mice inside those sacks, and fashioning his boots to hide them, and burying them there—on that day almost five months before. Maybe he dug with his swollen hands (into the cold and wet and rocky ground), resting when the pain in his fingers pierced him. And then, maybe he removed his boots from his swollen feet, and pushed the dirt over them, and sighed, and sat back—and unwrapped the rags on his feet, and replaced them with rags from his pocket. . . .

I ran through the woods, to fetch Nora Mae, and when she saw the gold she said I should buy dresses and hats with it—that I could buy everything I could ever need right away, and never have to shop again. It seemed a fanciful suggestion to me, but it was a pleasurable diversion to speak of how many silk dresses and lace-up gloves those shining mice might buy.

It was, by then, early afternoon, and when I decided what I wanted to do with the figurines, Nora Mae and I went to my aunt and showed her the treasure. Then we went to visit Miss Cleveland at the schoolhouse. As it was a Saturday, we were fortunate to find her there.

I was nervous walking along with all that gold, even though no one knew I had it, except Nora Mae. Still, I was afraid that I would somehow give it away. I knew it was silly, because I had never had any problem with thieves in the woods, but I couldn't really help it—being afraid. So I held the bag close to my body, under my jacket. . . .

I knew that even if it was in a roundabout way, my soldier had told me that I could keep the gold if I wanted it—and I could have. But I also knew Miss Cleveland would repay me a million times over (and she did too—especially when I was starting out on my own). And I knew that whatever my soldier had said, that gold should go to saving his father's land. Nonetheless, because my aunt had been more silent than usual (and though Miss Cleveland seemed much overwhelmed, and pleasantly so) I knew we all had some reservations about the Clevelands' land being regained by those ill-got spoils. I made sure that Miss Cleveland knew of the origin of the gold, but she took it anyway, and without pause. I cannot say that I was disappointed in her, as it was near enough to pay all the loans and taxes and fines that were warranted against the remaining estate, but I did understand why my soldier wanted no part of it. Miss Cleveland seemed to understand as well—although I think it hurt her rather deeply. But perhaps I was no less wrong, having so admired the lifestyle of the Clevelands in the days before the troubles. To think about the past, we were all no more than phantoms of who we had been. But, while I was much admiring of Miss Cleveland's strength and perseverance, there was something in her that seemed to be clinging to a shadow cast by the moon, when the sun was rising. . . .

Recounting to Miss Cleveland the tale of her nephew's visits to Cotterpin Creek, I suggested that he'd wanted no contact with her while he was at my aunt's cottage because it was unsafe. I explained that he feared the soldiers who were investigating him would turn their inquiries to her—that they'd believe she had a stash of gold, and they would lawfully rob her, as the result of accusations made against him. And Miss Cleveland nodded, saddened but accepting.

Everyone expected—hoped for letters from my soldier. But he had not promised to write, and we did not receive them. With the wealth he had provided, Miss Cleveland managed to save the final parcels of land—in the Cleveland name. She had hoped by correspondence to inform him of that, and to find him—but she did not. It was rumored he was living in Florida, but his whereabouts were not known—and that was an enormous state! I was of the impression that he did not write because he was no longer a child—that he had not the time for such nonsense as letters. But still, we wanted them. I wanted one. And it was a needle in my body—that want. But I imagined the past was a similar pain in my soldier. I thought of that needle not as a sewing needle, but as a compass needle. . . . It was the needle of a compass—set free to cut in our bodies. And why did he not write? Why did we not find each other? Because the needle did not point from him to me, or me to him—but just north.

Away from both of us. Away from home.

Soon after, Miss Cleveland was enlisted to teach for the Freedmen's Bureau. On a Thursday after school, a tall, well-dressed man of African descent entered the classroom. He was of Northern manners, and spoke in an accent of that region. His name was Lawrence Henry. He had traveled from Frickerham, for that was the locale of his jurisdiction, to ask if Miss Cleveland would teach a Saturday morning class. There were six freedmen commuting from Cotterpin to Frickerham for such improvement, and he had been led to believe she might avail herself of the task.

Mister Henry was college educated, from Kentucky's Berea College. His wife, Stanhope Henry, was a schoolteacher who had a classroom at Swell Junction, near where Cotterpin Creek joined the Frickerham River.

Standing there, upright and neat in the doorway, wearing a tweed suit, and leather shoes, with a fine pen in his hand—that was to be the only time I would ever see Lawrence Henry. But I had heard my aunt foretell of gentlemen such as that—and when I learned he was married, I was sure that his wife was equally refined. . . .

And when Miss Cleveland answered, it was after several minutes, and she said, "Mister Henry, that is a sixth day from my week—but I could not say no to you."

And Mister Henry said, "I am aware of that fact, Miss Cleveland."

Over the next several years, without ever seeing the Henrys, I heard much of them in the community—some good, some bad.

But I grew accustomed to the unwarranted criticism of people, and like my aunt, became a staunch, if quiet supporter of those efforts in educating. And for as long as there was a need, Miss Cleveland taught her class—and I felt the aura of the Henrys, over in Frickerham, leading their lives, and contributing their graces to the uplifting of our province in America.

And Miss Cleveland, for some ten, some twenty years (long after she had given up the tutelage of her schoolhouse pupils) continued to grant her energies to a cause in which it took her almost that long to have a passionate belief. And even then, when she no longer taught classes, she carried on in that cause, in one way or another, for the remainder of her years.

It was writ on her gravestone in 1904 that she was—

A Neighbor to All People.

Spring '67

*A*lmost two whole years had passed, and I'd tried to forget about the stormy days with that young soldier. . . .

I had been busy with reading and arithmetic, and helping my aunt gather roots and herbs and other things from the forest. And more importantly, I had been busy growing up—and where we children had been living in that Eden of Leapfrog and potato-sack racing and Tag and jumping rope and Cat's Cradle, we were now embarking upon the thrill and worry of young adulthood. . . .

Suddenly, Pitney was more than just a solid boy who liked to climb, but an apprentice carpenter. And Harmon was no longer a boy with a dreamy demeanor who was expert at tracking salamanders, but the kind of person who might spend a warm afternoon counting branches, or ladybugs, or even the number of leaves that fell from an oak tree— he might still be holding a salamander, but he would say how many of the spots were orange, and how many were black. There was also Dahlia Swanson, who was extremely talkative and liked to show off. Her family was new to the community—her father, a maker of fine cabinets. He had settled in the area on account of the good hard wood there was to be found. And then, there was Nora Mae, my partner in fishing, my deskmate at school and my ally in all things.

It seems now, as I look back on the hours of those days, that they were long and pleasurable—leisurely moments of just breathing. But I also remember that back then, they seemed just interminable, even filled as they were with school (all attended except Pitney, whose studies were incorporated into his apprenticeship) and work, and chores.

As I remember it, we seemed to have hour upon hour of idle living, and we spent most of our time out at the lake—catfishing.

It was really not much of a lake—but just the marshy pond which gathered in the valley on the other side of the Cleveland estate. Nor was it much frequented by the older set, for the mosquitoes, though with my knowledge of herbs we were quite capable of keeping the bugs away. All close to the same age, and from nearabouts, the five of us would congregate there to loaf on the bank—lying on fallen trees, and sitting, slumped, on the flats of the tree trunks. We'd be fishing, and talking, and fishing, and sometimes swimming, and then Pitney's mother would ring the bell after him and we'd all go home.

For fish, we had spudheads down in the marsh—they weren't as sizable as some others we'd heard about, but they were about the ugliest catfish around. Usually, we had a few cane-poles, hooks (or bent pins), sinkers (or rocks) and worms (or some rotten liver). And we would just let that bait set on the bottom, and once it started moving, we'd let it go five, or ten, or fifteen feet (depending upon its speed) and then we'd give a steady and even kind of slow pull, hoping that fish had swallowed that hook—because these fish didn't ever bite, exactly. So—it was a kind of fishing that didn't promote excitement, just a patience which some might go so far as to call lethargy. Pitney Zooks was the master of a true-to-life art that his father had taught him, and sometimes we'd get to watching him at that. What he'd do is lie in the water (when it began to be warm, late in the spring) and just reach in and snatch a fish right out. He'd sneak up on it, and then just grab it by the mouth—and that was the art of noodling. And when he reached into a log, or under a rock or the like—that was called grabling. And when he would lie on his belly and slowly edge his hand right up under a catfish, and stroke that fish's belly until it was mesmerized, and then just pick that fish up and take it—that was called tickling. And it was a concentrated thing, and an admirable thing, when Pitney just hypnotized a fish onto a dinner plate. . . .

Even my aunt would batter and deep-fry a catfish now and then.

242

And though it seemed a rather slothful way to spend a spring afternoon, my aunt was of the mind that perhaps at that stage in life, one needed some sloth—that being lazy was a good thing, that we were absorbing our new bodies and minds like lizards absorbing the sun. I suppose if I must say, I was sought after in my own fashion—and, as I was much the same as any other girl of my age, my authority was most likely the result of my aunt being a root doctor, and my having garnered some knowledge from her association. Valerian root was quite smelly. Stone root was a mint leaf with a lemony scent and little yellow flowers. Chamomile had little white flowers. Saint John's wort had yellow flowers too, but with black dots. Purple cone flower had a purple flower. Columbine had a five spurred leaf with red and yellow flowers that drooped. Squaw weed also had yellow flowers, as well as heart shaped, rounded leaves—and it was especially important to women with bad menses. Bloodroot was a white poppy which grew low to the ground, had leathery leaves and was ever so red on the inside. (It was rather critical that I be able to find bloodroot, because that was what kept away the mosquitoes at the marsh.) Every day I was learning more about the ways of the forest, and healthy living, and how one might apportion nature's remedies. Thus, I was of use in a practical way, and was generally included.

I have a memory of myself in those days. Or, perhaps, it is only an impression—I am a pale faced girl with red lips. I am wearing a white dress with a sash at the waist, and I am standing straight, and with my wide eyes, looking directly ahead. My chin is lowered ever so slightly. There is some red in the sash of my dress, and my hands are folded. I am wearing light blue shoes.

I believe that is what I wore at church on Sundays. . . .

But I also remember that there were times I was not included, that I would stay at home, preparing remedies with my aunt, specifically because a plan had been made without me—and those were times when Dahlia and Nora and Harmon and Pitney were up to the no good things that young folk are sometimes up to—pushing over outhouses (sometimes with people in them) or toppling cows, or soaping windows, or worse yet, smearing them with candlewax. Halloween especially was a time that I'd stay home—as that was the time for the older children to coax the younger children into the mud of the marsh. And those children would flee all the way home, covered from toe to neck in leeches! (I once helped poor little Trumble Ditzler, who was so embarrassed, I found him outside my window, well after dark, when he should have been home hours ago. He'd stretched a few of those leeches, but they hadn't come away—so I poked them with the hot end of the poker, and they'd just sort of seize up and pop off.) There were other times when I'd be called upon to free a child who had foolhardily accepted a dare to lick the frost off a water pump—I'd use slippery elm tea . . . hot. So, I don't think anyone thought me naive, though perhaps, for my disapproval, there was a bit of the square Mary in me. Mostly, I believe that from my years in the orphanage, I had already seen too much unkindness, too much unneeded sorrow, and it was understood that I wished to be spared these coarser pleasures of human nature. . . .

At the marsh, we'd spend our afternoons in every combination of three or more—Harmon, Nora Mae and myself, or Dahlia, Pitney and myself, or Nora Mae, myself and Pitney, and so forth. It was on a day with Nora Mae, Dahlia and myself, with a fishing pole set lackadaisically in the water, that Dahlia threw a rock out into the woods, and said to me—

"You know, Alma, you should really quit leading Pitney on. You're such a flirt!"

I was much taken aback, and silent.

The fact was that Nora Mae was a much better friend of Dahlia's than I was a friend of Dahlia's—though it could not be said that Dahlia was a better friend of Nora's than I was. So Dahlia was often the third one out—but still, Dahlia was the fiery one, and as that behavior was not always to my liking, and being often busy, I took my turns out as well. . . .

Dahlia had just finished braiding Nora Mae's hair, and Nora Mae turned around—

"That's not true at all, Dahlia, you're soft on Pitney, that's all."

"No," said Dahlia, "he's death on me, and Alma's just getting in the way."

I believe I was reddening, and I know Nora Mae was— "You know that's not true, Dahlia. Alma just doesn't want him." Nora put her hands on the ground and turned to me. "Isn't that right—isn't that right, Alma?"

"Yes," I said to Dahlia, the tips of my ears burning. "You can have him, Dahlia."

Dahlia stood up, and clapped her hands along the front of her peach-colored dress—it was an expensive dress. She said, "You don't have to give him to me—he's already mine."

Dahlia was always a little too exuberant for me, and Nora Mae agreed. Under her breath, Nora Mae muttered that Dahlia was a cracker, or a gumbo, or a mucker, or some such silly thing, and they all but came to blows over it. I could see it in the way they were standing, and glaring at each other—Dahlia had stepped out of her shoes. Luckily, it was then that Harmon arrived—meandering down to the creek for some pallin' around. Despite his flights of fancy, he was a good old Kentucky boy when it came right down to it—with that boyish type of arrogance and goodwill all rolled together.

"Why are you girls always fighting over me?"

Nora Mae and Dahlia were quick to agree that he was not the cause of any dispute, nor was there a dispute. We three walked home soon after—and when we came to the pine woods, Harmon walked with Nora, and Dahlia and I went our separate ways. . . .

As summer came, I helped my aunt gather herbs and flowers to dry out and use in the wintertime. It was on a sunny day in the middle of August that we noticed two men in glasses taking careful measurements of the field by the big rock.

My aunt had heard that the two men were surveyors, and that they were parceling another lot off the old Cleveland estate. The two men weren't very talkative, so my aunt and I didn't talk to them.

Just a few days later, a crew of men arrived from a nearby town.

The men put up tents in the field and began to build a house. They were not educated men like the surveyors, but they were friendly men, men who talked about their families—some of whom lived just back in the town, some of whom were quite far away. They were hard-working men and didn't have much time for play or long conversations. My aunt made an arrangement with them to take care of their food and look after their health. She fed them good clean meals hearty on vegetables, and when any of the men began to cough or sneeze she prepared them a remedy. Some of them were in poor health, and their ailments were much improved by the end of their labors. The foreman, Mister Monroe, did not mind my aunt's rates for her services, as under her care, the men were both easier to get along with and more productive. Thus, he said, my aunt was really saving him money. It was an interesting way to look at things, I thought. . . .

Sometimes, I would converse with the men when they were washing their clothing in the creek.

And some of them would joke with me—Alma, my dear, what are you doing for the next forty, fifty years?

And I would tell them I was busy.

And some said that they'd come back and check on me in two or three birthdays.

One of the men had a banjo, and though I did not hear him speak one word (not once in all the months he worked on the house), he sang at night. He had a beautiful voice—and perhaps that was because he used it for only singing. My aunt would sit on the back porch and listen to him. Nobody could see her back there—none but me. She would rock in the rocking chair slightly, and she would smile and wipe her eyes. . . .

Minnie Minton, I am wounded,
And I know that I will die.
By strangers, I'm surrounded,
There's no loved one kneeling nigh.
And I fain would hear you whisper
In the twilight cold and gray.
But I only hear the tramping
As the armies march away.

The men had all been soldiers, and some of the time, they all sang together. And their woeful voices were like the howls of wolves—

Do they miss me at home—do they miss me,
At morning, noon, or night?
Is there a lingering shade all around them
That only my presence can light?
Are joys less invitingly welcome,
And pleasures less hale than before,
Because one is missed from the circle,
Because I am with them no more?
Because I am with them no more?

They were sound men, but sad men, and though all were kind and gentlemanly with me, it did seem that some of them might be angry men—and that was an unhappy thing to see. It was not anything they said or did, as they were all men who valued their own civility and honor, but sometimes, it was just the way a man would swing a hammer, or set about sawing an innocent board. . . .

Since the very day my aunt had taken our cottage, a section of our back porch had been collapsed, and one Saturday, with some spare lumber, the men not only repaired the porch—but added several feet to it at that! It took them no more than a few hours, as they were all working together. They did the work both to thank my aunt for her kind care, as well as in trade for her fixing Max Vicar's broken leg.

Max Vicar was tool boy, and as he was lame already, it was no surprise when he fell off a supporting beam and broke his leg. All of the men were rather fatherly to Max, as, during the conflict, his rifle had back-fired, leaving his vision in a poor condition. He wore thick glasses. One of his legs had always been a little shorter than the other, which accounted for his limp. Even so, until he had broken his leg, he had gotten on admirably—he was no stranger to hard work. And even when he was not working, he could be found somewhere, reading a rather thick book. He was studying for the cloth—and was hoping soon to enroll in seminary school. The men respected his aspiration, and when Max broke his leg, they fetched their own tools, and Max sat by the creek and read his books—and he did his builder's work by answering questions, and writing letters home, as most of the men were illiterate, or very nearly so.

I too spent many hours with Max, asking him questions. We would sit by the stream and discuss things of a theological nature, and though I often worried I was detaining him from his studies, he too seemed to enjoy the company. He was not so much older than me, and in another time, perhaps our ages would not have been so great a divide. I often felt that my questions were rather unsophisticated to him, but he loaned me books, and I read them, and I kept asking the questions—as theology was a fine challenge for my young mind. Max, with his grace and quiet politeness, always entertained my in-quiries seriously, and I developed a great respect for him. I hoped it was a mutual respect, but I am afraid his respect for me was more based upon my enthusiasm than my conversation.

And besides all the questions I had for Max Vicar, I asked a num-ber of questions of the men themselves—

Who did they work for? They were not sure, they said—they had been hired by the foreman, Mister Monroe, who had been hired by the lawyer of Cotterpin Creek, Mister Vachel Pimpernickel—and no one knew who had hired him. It was a man from the Northeast, they had heard—a mature Irish man who owned dance halls. And, I asked, why were they building the house for the Northeastern man, the mature Irish man who owned dance halls? For him to live in, they supposed, but they weren't sure. And, I asked, what kind of a house would it be? And how would it look in the sunset? And how would anyone get across the creek? And if they built a bridge, what would it look like? And—and I had so many questions, I told them, and . . .

And they said they would build a great big house. They said that it would have two stories, white columns and a porch—in the front and the back. They said the porch in the back would be a nice place to watch the sunset. They said they'd put in a wood stove, and a dozen glass windows. They said they'd build a little wooden bridge for carriages to cross the creek. They said that each railing of the bridge would have two arches, shaped like a heart. And they said as soon as they finished, they would go home. . . .

And they did everything they said they would do.

And they left before the weather turned cold.

And the big house by the big rock was locked up and empty all winter.

white Chapel cart

It was quite a surprise when my aunt received a letter from Max Vicar, the tool boy from the previous year. It was his leg that she had set, and, in his letter, he informed us that it had healed quite well. He also wrote of his father's improved fortunes, and, as a result, he extended his gratitude toward my aunt by sending her a notice, and passes (as well as an arrangement with a carriage) for attending the May Fair in Frickerham. The plans were all made for two—my aunt and me. He remembered us fondly in the letter, and we in turn remembered him as that awkward but studious boy who had spent all his time reading for the seminary—sitting against the big rock with the creek running along before him. I did not think my aunt would be inclined toward such a gesture, but she was, and the carriage was confirmed, and I informed Miss Cleveland that I would be taking off from school—and thus, the trip was made.

The day was of ample distraction, and we saw some fine farm animals, and some rather exotic animals such as Cashmere goats and Berkshire hogs, as well as some rather unusual animals—like two-headed turtles and miniature horses.

There was also a grand figure of a freedman wrestler, who defeated all his challengers with enormous ease and good humor. We saw girls running for smocks—and a donkey race in which each contestant rode his neighbor's donkey, the resulting sport being quite merry and unpredictable. There was a competition of old women—the one who made the ugliest face won a supply of snuff. Then we saw a competition of climbing a greasy pole—the winner retrieved a leg of mutton stuck onto the top. There was also a race that was run by men in sacks—it was for a wheel of cheese. The sacks were fashioned up to the men's necks, and hopping like that, when one toppled, so would many others—thus, the winner was not the fastest man, but the most cautious. By the time of the pig-catching contest, my aunt and I were already feeling quite peckish, and we snacked on sugared peanuts (hot) and iced tea. Within sight, we watched three soaped pigs set loose in a pen—all the contestants trying to grab them by the tail. The winner was a boy of no more than fifteen—the runners-up were a pair of brothers of nigh the same age. They were all rather muddy. The victorious youngster was given a side of bacon—the runners-up divided a second. . . .

In the afternoon, a kite contest had kites from all over—some were quite immense, and built in unexpected shapes. Many were ingenious as well—one looked like a giant worm, and was dyed in multiple colors—black from walnuts, tan from sumac berries, blue from wild indigo, pink from pokeberries, yellow from sedgegrass and green from pine needles. The kite was made by a girl and her father from Frickerham. They won the blue ribbon, and a share of the contestants' fees, and deservedly so!

There were also some fine examples of crafts from local people—basket makers, weavers and quilt makers. . . .

And, despite my every expectation, my aunt enjoyed herself

tremendously—more so than even me. And it was such a pleasure to be with her—we were like two young girls, running about at the fair. We tried a new drink called Root Beer, which was the cause of some debate, as to who had originated it—this kind was called *Puffer's Root Beer*, and was simply made of sarsaparilla. Other kinds, evidently, had different recipes. Aunty Betta was not ordinarily an enjoyer of things sweet, but as of late, she had been increasingly free with her delights, and, along with a pound of taffy, we had a barrel of it brought to our carriage. We even danced some. I danced with the children in the children's circle, and with my aunt in the grown-up circle—and not only did I learn a great deal, but I exhausted myself rather completely. And after dining on potato salad, roasting ears, barbecue quail and watermelon, by the time we were homeward bound, I could barely keep my eyes open.

For several miles, there was a kind of bedlam on the road, as all the horses and carriages had set out at once. I could see that everyone was comparing wagons, but even so, my aunt and I had nothing to be ashamed of, as our Rockaway was quite comfortable and fashionable. My aunt took the facing seat, and I spread out on the back seat, and after we pulled the curtains, and my aunt rolled up her sweater for me to use as a pillow, I was soon sleeping soundly in the swaying carriage. . . .

Starflower

I was growing to be a more independent girl, and as soon as I came home from school, I liked to throw my satchel onto my bed and run outside to the big rock where I would meet Nora Mae.

But on a day in late May, my Aunt Bettina ran to the door to call me back.

"Alma!" she called, "Alma, I picked up a letter for you today at the post office!"

I had never received a letter before, so my aunt and I sat out on the back porch to read it.

It was from Mister Pimpernickel, the town lawyer.

Dear Alma Flynt,

*I have of late received an inquiry on your current
employment status. It has come to the attention of my
client that you are not only of a responsible stock but are
in a position of geographic consequence.*

"What does that mean?" I asked.

"I think," said my aunt, "that means someone wants to hire you to
do something around here."

"Oh," I said.

You were recommended highly by Willa and Frank Mayfield.

"Nora's mum and dad?" I asked.

"Yes," said my aunt.

*As you know, your property is adjacent to the recent
construction in the acreage beside the formidable boulder.*

"The new house in the field by the big rock?" I asked.

"Yes," said my aunt.

*The house, being empty, is in need of a caretaker. The
responsibilities will be minimal yet indispensable. The pay
will be modest yet fair.*

The letter went on in the same mumbo-jumbo, but my aunt and I
decided it meant the owner of the new house wanted me to look in
on it now and again—keep out the animals and watch for leaks. I
didn't mind having a little extra money. And my aunt said it was fine
with her as long as she didn't end up doing it.

"No," I said, "I'll take care of it."

"Okay," said my aunt, "I'll talk to Mister Pimpernickel."

And I went out to the big rock to meet Nora. I was afraid I was late. We were going to go find Nora's little brother, Loren, who wanted help in letting his pet frog free in the pond. . . .

I had a lot to do.

I had to go to school in the daytime. And in the mornings I had to clean the blackboard for Miss Cleveland.

I had to make sure that the new house by the big rock was taken care of. And all through the spring and summer, I would check for termites, leaks, broken windows, mice, raccoons, birds and every other kind of problem.

I had to gather things from the forest—herbs, mushrooms, flowers, barks, mosses and all kinds of other things that grew in the woods. The reason I had to gather my aunt's supplies was that my Aunt Betta could not walk so well anymore. Every day, my aunt taught me something new about the forest. I could make a spring tonic of bloodroot, or cure an ailment of the stomach with sassafras or black snake or calamas—or regularize the intestines by the administration of jimson or blackberry root, or redroot. I could alleviate sore kidneys with stone root, or eyes with slippery elm, or hearts with heart leaf—or lungs with crab apple bark. For coughs there was mullen. For bad blood there was dandelion root. There was buckeye for rheumatism. Larkspur for hair troubles. Persimmon bark for salves. Pennyroyal for bedbugs. Butterfly root for the troubles of women. And wild comfrey for the vitality of men. (I gave some to Nora Mae that she might make a tea for Harmon Valentine—she was much smitten by him, and it was only one of many ways that she set about to stir his ardor.) And there were redbud roots to clean the teeth. And, well, a hundred others. . . .

And of course, besides all the things that I had to accomplish, I had my friendships to pursue. I had to swim, fish, ride Mister Nielson's ponies (and his wife's bark swing) and dream up grand parties with Nora Mae—we planned masquerade balls that we fancied we'd throw at the Frickerham opera house.

I did my very best to look after the big house, but it was a very big house, and there were a few things I could not do.

I could not stop the sun from shining in through the windows and making funny marks on the floor.

I could not stop the dust from gathering.

I could not stop the cobwebs from growing.

I could not stop the winter. . . .

And I could not stop the new house from turning into an old house. It no longer smelled of freshly cut wood, and the pine grew gray. And I worried that so abandoned, that house could not be maintained.

So, with the help of my aunt, I wrote a letter to Mister Pimpernickel.

Dear Mister Pimpernickel,

Thank you for giving me this job. I am trying to do the best I can. But the sun is coming in through the windows and ruining the floors, walls and ceilings. Also, there are a lot of cobwebs, and there is a lot of dust. I could do an even better job if I could buy some curtains for the windows, a duster for the dust, and a broom to get the webs off the ceiling. Please ask my boss if I can buy these supplies and he'll pay for them.

Sincerely,

Alma Flynt

A few weeks later, Mister Pimpernickel forwarded a letter to me.

Dear Alma,

My client is indebted to you for your various exertions, and thanks you for bringing these conditions to his attention. He has instructed me to initiate an account for you at the town store, so you might purchase whatever you require. He also suggested a doormat, a candleholder and a few candles. In addendum, I believe that firewood would be a wise thing to have on hand. Have Mister Cooper at the town store arrange its delivery.

On a lighter note, your employer forwarded a personal request. Though he cannot predict when his business will allow him to make a visitation, when he does, he will surely need a genuine pair of country boots. He is a city man, who likes to keep in the current fashions, so, adding to whatever else you need, he has requested that you please order for him a proper pair of country boots at the start of each season. He has expressed the hope that your practical nature will behoove him well in the selection of such footwear. His boot size and several catalogues from the preferable shops in his vicinity are included herein. He requests that you choose something appropriate for the local terrain.

A cautious man, he wishes to inspect your acquisitions. Unfortunately, he is also a busy man, without the time for frivolous trips to local shops. Upon your selections, we will arrange at the post office and the shop in question for one boot to be sent to his urban domicile, and one boot to be sent here, to his country retreat. As he is not a wasteful individual, one pair of boots per season shall suffice.

Thanking you for your loyal services,
Attorney at Law,
Vachel J. Pimpernickel

I was glad I could buy what I needed for the house, even if the whole thing about the boots seemed a little funny. But it didn't bother me. I had heard that city people were like that. The catalogues had come all the way from New York City, which I had heard was a very big city, filled with people who were a little funny.

I was worried that I was doing a little too much decorating, but no one seemed to mind.

In fact, everyone was distracted by the allure of new things. As many had suffered years of deprivation, a spirit of the covetous had captured the population like a fever. The winter over, it was spring—and there was so much to see. The new town by the railroad tracks had grown and risen to a major trading post, not only for the outlying district, but for areas farther south, and some farther north. There was much needed in the lower states, and whatever those states had that was of value to the Northern states was promptly directed North, and sold there. . . .

The former Cotterpin Creek was entirely a ghost town, occupied only by beavers, birds, squirrels, field mice and (on weekends and holidays) children with bold and adventurous natures.

Horatio Cooper, the store-master, had bought up the old town—and said he was sure he'd think of something to do with it. Mister Pimpernickel had already lined up some prospective buyers, and the land would surely appreciate. . . .

Mister Cooper's lumber business was still thriving, and he had finally moved it to the new mill. There was plenty of labor about, and though most of the men were not steady types (some were going north, some were going south, some were going east, some were going west) Mister Cooper had an eye for the honest-day's-work-for-the-honest-day's-pay type of wanderer. A great many of them took the chance to gather themselves up before moving on to better things—and one or two of them found a new beginning right here in Cotterpin. Mister Cooper still spent his time behind the counter at his general store. He had a new sign on a hefty piece of lumber, with heartily sculpted letters—

HORATIO COOPER'S
STORE FOR EVERYTHING

And it really was a store for everything. There were more painted signs all over the outside of the store. Signs like—"Home Brewed Ale," "Licensed Dealer in Tobacco," "Spirits," "Meat Dried, Salted and Pickled," "Lumber," "Hardware," "Houseware," and "General Esoterica." I myself charged up chairs, lanterns, rugs, bolts of colored cloth and all kinds of stuff at the town store. Mister Pimpernickel supplied Horatio Cooper with the new catalogues, and from them, I ordered a new pair of boots at the beginning of each season—a pair for spring, a pair for summer, a pair for autumn, a pair for winter—and then I ordered them all over again.

I received nine boots at the town post office.

The postmaster, Joe Sharpless (who'd taken to saying he was as old as the U.S. post office itself), he was much chagrined by this odd pastime. But just like everyone else, at the end of our exchange, he smiled and nodded his chin and said—

"Thank you very much, Miss Flynt."

The big house was a nice place to be alone when I felt like reading, or had some difficult homework on which to concentrate, or when I just felt like sitting at a window and not doing anything at all.

Sometimes I dried out my aunt's herbs on the back porch of the big house, and sometimes, after school, when Nora Mae would come calling for me, my aunt would send her up to the house, saying, "Why don't you go looking for Alma up at the new house? Tell her to be back before dark."

Sometimes Nora Mae and I would close our eyes to pretend that the house was a castle, or a ship returning from a long journey. And then we would talk about what finery and adventures we might witness. But usually, because we were getting to be young women, we would just sit around to discuss and kid about young men, or talk about the more serious things that young women had to talk about. . . .

And as the year wore on, it became a time of reflection, as it seemed that our childhoods were suddenly drawing to a close. Though Miss Cleveland's schoolhouse was only the one classroom, there were two groups within that class—the lower school and the upper school. From the lower, a handful would graduate at twelve or thirteen—or even eleven. Miss Cleveland was opposed to graduation at eleven, although those children were often needed at home—and a good many of them would further their studies in one way or another. The whole upper school consisted of only Nora Mae, myself, Dahlia Swanson and Harmon Valentine, who was too dreamy to be much good for physical labor. With the spring of '69, I was near my seventeenth birthday, and no longer a student, but a teacher's assistant. I was studying for my teacher's qualification, and in two summers, I planned to test for my higher levels in Frickerham, for I was thinking at that time to earn my certificate, and teach school. Miss Cleveland assured me I would have no trouble passing the test (and indeed, when the time came, I did pass, though I never did teach but to substitute for Miss Cleveland when Pastor Miles grew too old for such trouble). Neither Nora Mae nor Harmon would be returning next fall, as it had come time for them to contribute to the betterment of their own households. Dahlia Swanson was planning to take two years at Doctor Elliot's Academy, the finishing school that Miss Cleveland had attended.

It was not uncommon that one might continue one's schooling at seventeen, or even eighteen, as schooling could sometimes be irregular, especially if the family was returning from the West, as some were in those days. The previous year, there had been a girl who stayed on through her engagement, that she might continue to study for her higher levels. Like me, she planned to earn her teacher's certificate, as a teacher could earn upwards of twenty-five dollars a week, which was quite a lot of money.

Nevertheless, of us older children, I would be the only one staying on for the fall term. . . .

And I remember one afternoon, sitting with Nora at the big house to look over her notebook and reminisce. There were pages and pages of assignments we had copied from the blackboard, like "Qualifications for a teacher," and other pronouncements on life—though I must admit, those are proverbs that I have mostly forgotten, and those that I do remember, I am sure I remember inaccurately. We had also copied poems from the board, like "The Destruction of Pompeii," or "The Dying Year." I do remember one poem called "Farewell," perhaps as much for content as for seeing it that day. It was written in Nora Mae's fine hand—

Farewell

Oh I love not that word, whose unlimited power
Can shadow with gloom friendship's sunniest hour,
For it comes like a blight when our joys are in bloom
And recklessly robs them of half their perfume.
It beguiles from the eye of affection a tear,
Tis the pitiful knell of delights that were dear.
I could roam through life's wilderness friendless and lone,
Uncared for by many and cared for by none.
But to meet with a being while journeying on,
Who attracts and delights and forever is gone,
Oh this, this were more than the spirit could bear.
Did not hope while expanding her pinions so fair
Softly whisper of sunshine round purity's throne
Where friends are united and farewells unknown?

I remember being ever so affected by that poem, and touching my hankie to my eyes upon reading it—and, I read it many times in the years to come. I am afraid I do not remember the author. But I do remember the impression it made on that melancholy and romantic afternoon, for as we pored over those lines, I thought of my soldier. . . .

There was a paragraph that Nora Mae had copied out of a book, and written very small on the end paper. It spoke of "romantic vicissitudes" and "overtaking," and "vivid fancies," and I could see why Nora Mae had written it so small. Even so, her penmanship was quite remarkable—it was as refined as the line of a river, or the breeze in the wake of a sailing ship. Nora liked to sketch miniature beehives, loaded up with bees—so they would proliferate in the margin, as they too were ever so small. . . .

And then, once the book had been graded and returned to her, down on the bottom margin, in letters too small for any but the very young to read, she would copy out romantic couplets (so guiltily!) in her fine hand. They were lines copied from books hidden in her mother's linen.

And I recall the one of them, the last one of her notebook—

Love is a smoke rais'd with the fume of sighs;
Being purg'd, a fire, sparkling, in lovers' eyes.

And I remember also, that she and I talked of Pitney Zooks, and his fancy for me. Nora said that Dahlia Swanson was after him, but I was of the opinion that Dahlia was just too bossy to interest him. Pitney would never like her, I told Nora—

"She's just too bossy."

And though I liked Pitney and all, when, only a few days later, he leaned over to kiss me, I turned away. We were out at the pond, and I moved closer to the water, as if to watch Harmon and Nora Mae, who were swimming, and just out of sight behind some trees. It was not something I had to think about—I just did not want to kiss him.

I knew that I had said good-bye to my soldier—but good-bye had been enough. . . .

Pitney had blond hair and a sturdy construction. His eyes were direct, and when he did something he only did it once—it was like that with him, whether it was with carpentry or schoolwork or catfish tickling. Yet his caution was a variety of impatience, as, not with banging a nail, or writing a sentence, or catching a fish, he didn't like to repeat himself. Doing things twice was a wasted effort to him, and he sat back, speaking, as he did, briefly and consideredly—

"Is it John Warren?"

"Yes," I said.

Pitney had known John Warren as a boy, in fact, John Warren and Pitney's older brother had been quite good friends all those years ago—and Pitney was silent for a long time then. . . .

And I thought that silence had always been a part of his charisma, that he could walk you home and not say a word at all—and yet, you would have the feeling that the conversation was all encompassing. And when I thought about it, I knew that this was the most I had ever heard him talk at once. And, as I hadn't kissed him, I was gladdened, for I knew I could not lead such a silent life—it would be too frightening a thing. But I was also made nauseous, for at the same time, I knew that I could lead a quiet life—and that it could be a divine thing. And then, finally, Pitney Zooks said—

"You know, Alma—he's never coming back."

And just then, I knew Pitney was right—I knew that if I were to live a complete life I would have to release, to forget my soldier . . . but . . . but . . . being a resolute child, I also knew that I never would, and I began to cry.

"I know," I said to Pitney, "but . . . but . . . ." And then I could say no more, for that was all the explanation I could muster.

Pitney Zooks, however, was a practical young man, who was not impressed with such weak reasoning. To this day, he's always remained a gentleman to me, but I saw that my lack of reason left him puzzled, dejected and disappointed—and not just a disappointment in being turned down, but a disappointment in me. . . .

Pitney's face was all screwed up when he said, "Why, sure, Alma—what you say . . ."

And Pitney would still call after me sometimes, as would Harmon and Nora and even Dahlia. And of course there were other boys—none in school, but a good number of them working already—either learning trades or farming with their families. But Cotterpin was a smallish town at times—or I felt so—and as Pitney was as fine a specimen as Cotterpin had to offer, I remember that I was not exactly as sought after as I had been, and, said simply, the boys didn't bother me so much anymore.

Or perhaps, the more honest way to say it would be that they didn't bother *with* me so much anymore.

It was late for my aunt to sleep in. But it being a Saturday, I warmed the grits and brewed the coffee. When she was still dozing, I went in to wake her. I put my hand on her shoulder—

It was cold, and she didn't wake up. I set forth for the Mayfields', and they sent for Doctor Esterbrook and Pastor Miles. Everyone visited through the day, and many sat with my aunt and me through the night. Missus Esterbrook and Willa Mayfield took to the kitchen, and prepared food for near upon twenty-four hours—braised duck, stuffed eggplants and mushrooms, and pastries with fresh fruit—strawberries, pears, peaches.

My aunt was left in her bed, and I did not leave her. I do not know how I had missed it for all those years—but I saw that Pastor Miles' black hair had gone white. As we sat, awake and talking quietly, he held my hand in his.

"She is going to a good place," he said.

"Is it far?" I asked.

"No," he said, with tension in his face and ease in his eyes, "it is not too, too far."

And Doctor Esterbrook sat beside my Aunt Bettina, reading to her from the bible. There were a great many people coming in and out, and giving me their condolences, but I was scarce aware of them, and not until the break of day did I clear my eyes of tears, and my throat of sobs, enough that I might see or speak. . . .

Out by the hearth, people drank coffee and wine and recounted stories and fond recollections. It was almost a feast—a solemn celebration through a night, a day, and a night, though I hardly saw it and I hardly ate—only what Pastor Miles would eventually apportion for me. It was late the second evening of the wake that he filled a dish and sat me down out in the parlor rocking chair—and when I told him I was not hungry, I thought he too would cry, so I tried to eat what he had provided me. . . .

There had been a kind of a cheer when I had exited my aunt's bedroom, and there was a kind of a cheer when I took my first bite. I believe it was just a spoonful of creamed corn. It was not long then until daylight—and the procession of the funeral. I was now convulsing less, and managed to sit up in the carriage. Still, I felt so thin and weak that each step of the horses was a pain to me. But I would not look back, and I would not fold or slump onto the black leather of the carriage. It was the same carriage as I had ridden from the orphanage. And it was the same man, William Ditzler, at the reins. And it was the same man, Pastor Miles, who sat beside me—

"It was a good trip here," he said, and his eyes filled up, and he shed tears.

"Yes," I said, "it was."

Our church was on a hill—behind it was the graveyard. It was perched on the absolute summit—and in several rows, gravestones were set east to west along the crest. Many of the graves were decorated with shells. Those of the Clevelands—father, mother and son—were strewn with horseshoes. . . .

It was the May of '69, and besides the red cedars and pines, the oaks, hickories and chestnuts were flourishing, as well as plantings of roses, azaleas and lilies. And I thought of how I now knew the names of the flowers. . . .

The cemetery was especially bright and well cared for, as it had been graveyard workday only a few weeks before, when we in the community had congregated early, and remained until evening—that all the landscaping should be cared for, and all the stones scrubbed. I remember that the few stones that had toppled had been set right, and the picket fence had been mended—to keep out the animals. And, as that evening had been a kind one, and the dinner on the grounds had been ever so pacific and tranquil, I felt in myself, as well as, I fancied, in those around me, a renewed sense of peace with this place of earthly rest.

There must have been many hymns sung that day, but what I remember most clearly was "Jerusalem, My Happy Home," a song for which I had always had a strong affinity. It was such a beautiful song that even without a high emotional state like that, many, and certainly myself, would be with tears streaming down their cheeks—

> *Jerusalem, my happy home, name ever dear to*
> *me! When shall my labors have an end, in*
> *joy and peace, in thee? In joy and peace, in thee?*
>
> *O when, thou city of my God, shall I thy courts*
> *ascend, where congregations ne'er break up, and*
> *Sabbaths have no end? And Sabbaths have no end?*
>
> *There happier bow'rs than Eden's bloom, nor sin nor sorrow*
> *know; blest seats, through rude and stormy scenes I*
> *onward press to you, I onward press to you.*
>
> *Jerusalem, my glorious home, my soul still pants for*
> *thee; then shall my labors have an end when*
> *I thy joys shall see, when I thy joys shall see.*

It was so very moving to see the sky and to hear that song. . . .

The grave marker was to be made by Mister Meckseper, a German carver in Frickerham. It was to be the same as those of the

Clevelands, which he had also tooled. His markers were large, though plain sandstone, with a carving on the back of a heart rising from the earth and flowering into roses. I had opted that it be placed in three months, whereupon there would be a second gathering at the grave. On that occasion, the pastor would read letters from all over— including one from the tool boy, Max Vicar, who, like many others, was grateful for my aunt's good works, kindness and healing ways—

She had in her the love of mother earth.

After the funeral procession, when we were gathered at the gravesite, Pastor Miles spoke in the voice of a man who had shared too many sorrows. He read aloud from the bible, then he looked up at all of us, and removed his glasses. He wiped them, and slid them into his pocket, and then, squinting for the sun, he said—

"We have prayed for our sons, our husbands, our brothers, our fathers. We have prayed for our daughters, our wives, our sisters and mothers. And sometimes, our prayers have been answered. Let us say today that our prayers will deliver Bettina Flynt Evans, posthaste, to paradise. And let us say today that our prayers have delivered us another daughter."

I felt the sun on my hair as the men lowered the coffin into the earth. It was a simple pine coffin—but made with wooden pegs rather than nails. The old men shoveled the soil, which had dried in the noon. There was Mister Nielson, Joe Sharpless, Horatio Cooper, Stewart Valentine, Doctor Esterbrook and the pastor himself. William Ditzler was only recently returned, and it was the first I'd seen of him in some time. He'd come back with his cousin Sam, whom I had met all those years ago at the Ditzler Mill at Frog Falls in Virginia. Even though Sam Ditzler had never known my aunt, he also helped with a shovel. He had a wooden leg. I heard him wonder if a girl would marry him. He did seem to fit right into the congregation, as tall as he was. Kentuckians are known for their height.

Sam had another bag of marbles for me. He was ashamed to present them, as it was not much of a condolence. He choked on his own words as he spoke. I had been crying, but was all cried out, so I told him I would like to have a new bag of marbles, especially if they were like the old ones, made by his brother. His late brother, he corrected me—Sam was now the tallest in the family.

"Even on one leg?" I smiled, sadly.

"Even on one leg." He smiled, sadly.

Then I asked for the bag of marbles. He gave them to me. Later, his cousin, William Ditzler, thanked me for taking them. He said that it might be hard to believe, but that actually, Sam had guarded those marbles for a long time, and they had been a hard thing for him to give up. The glass shop was gone, William Ditzler said—the one in which Sam Ditzler had grown to manhood. There were no more marbles like that. William Ditzler said it was ever so gracious of me to receive them, even though I was too old for marbles, and the occasion was not at all fitting. But I told him I liked Sam—and I wasn't too old—and the occasion was right. And actually, I did like marbles. And I liked *those* marbles. And I did too.

I didn't have a pocket, so I carried them. I didn't let anyone carry them for me—not even Sam himself, when he offered. He said he should have waited till after the service was over. And I told him no, it was better that he didn't wait. . . .

At the sermon's end, people lined up and wished me their sympathies—and I said that I would miss my aunt, but that I would not look on her death as a tragedy, because I had known my aunt's life, and it was a long one, and a full one. And I said that I knew her spirit would enrich me, and them. But it was still an emotional day, and all bound up in my tight black dress, standing under the sun, I felt faint on several occasions, and had to sit with my head between my legs, so as not to fall unconscious.

Miss Cleveland invited me to come live with her in the schoolhouse. And that night was the first I spent there, in a bed she had prepared for me in the library. She said I would be finished with my higher levels in a year anyway, and then I would be eighteen, and old enough to be on my own. In the meantime, she would help me to look out for my best interests, and to guide me in practical matters.

Some days later, when I changed the sheets and bedding for sheets and bedding that I had fetched from my aunt's cottage, I saw that the cover on the mattress was made from the cloth of Miss Cleveland's green dress, the one that I had seen her wear the very first time I saw her—when she so impressed me. That would have been at the Cleveland estate, in the autumn of '59, when I was seven years old, and John Warren was ten. And for all that had divided him from me—my aunt and his family were buried less than twenty feet apart. . . .

Robin.

Tucker Boyd was a big man. Perhaps that is how he came to learn his trade as a blacksmith. Even as a youth he had been so large as to be a great help around a metal shop—moving enormous things with enormous ease. He, his wife and his son had built a small shop by the new railroad station, and after a year, they had added a stable to the shop, and after another year, they had added a house to that. It was the first freedman owned business in Cotterpin. And he endured greatly to achieve it. It could not have been easy at first—the three of them living and working in that shop—for they were all particularly large individuals, of peoples originally hailing from the White Nile area of Northeastern Africa. For two generations, their people had lived in New Orleans—it was there that Tucker Boyd's owner, a young man who had been bequeathed Tucker in his father's will, and who had known Tucker for his entire life, as they had grown together, allowed Tucker to operate his own business, and then, to eventually buy his own freedom, as well as that of his wife, for a reasonable sum.

Tucker had started out as a kind of a farrier—making horseshoes for all the horses in the locality. He'd travel around his part of the world, from here to there, with all his equipment in a cart. And he'd fix all the shoes around—it was careful work, and work for a man who'd gain your trust—and all that, he did. For years, even in Cotterpin, he'd still make his rounds, attending horses that needed their shoes reshod, whether they had grown out of them, or the shoes had grown thin, or the hooves needed trimming. I'd watched him once or twice, and saw how very patient he was with his pinchers and farrier's hammer. The shoe would have to fit just so—without any light showing between the shoe and the hoof. He'd choose every nail for the comfort of the horse, and set them in place with considerable exactness, as each one passed through the wall of the hoof. Sometimes he'd set studs in the shoes to prevent slipping when jumping or schooling, especially in fall and spring, when the ground tended to be wet. Mister Boyd always had it in his mind to keep track of all the horses in the area. He always had shoes ready for them when they were needed. Sometimes he'd time it to the very day, having a good idea of when this horse would wear out that shoe, and having asked about the training regimen beforehand. . . .

Early in the spring of '69, Mister Boyd had requested Miss Cleveland's assistance in finding his nephew, Morgan Stanfield. Morgan was the son of Tucker's sister, Beth, and only recently had Mister Boyd learned that Beth and her husband Alec had passed from this life. The boy was alive, Mister Boyd had learned, but he did not know where, and he hoped Miss Cleveland could help him in locating the child. Miss Cleveland sent out a number of inquiries, and with summer, she received a letter that stated that the boy could be found in Frickerham, which, as chance would have it, was as close a poorhouse to Cotterpin Creek as there was. Miss Cleveland had met Tucker Boyd when she had taken the schoolbell in to be repaired. The tong had cracked and the bell no longer rang—it just clanked. It was in return for his repairs on the bell that Tucker Boyd had asked for Miss Cleveland's help. She had replied that she would have helped him anyway. To this, he replied that he would have fixed the schoolbell anyway.

Mister Boyd had a way of talking without ever changing the expression on his face. He was a hard man to figure by looking at him. He seemed to make a good living, but he always wore a rope instead of a belt. When Miss Cleveland asked him why, he said, "Rope works good, ma'am." He was not necessarily a stern man, said Miss Cleveland, for she saw him play a prank on his son. He gave him an apple that was already cut into slices on the inside. He tapped the fruit a few times with his big knuckles, twisted it this way and that, and the peel of the apple snapped, and there it was, cut into neat slices, like an orange. Miss Cleveland said that she suspected he had achieved the effect with a needle and a wire—by stitching the apple inside the peel, and then pulling out the wire. His son Buddy, however, was only six, and duly puzzled by the result. He looked to his father, but even to Buddy, it could be near impossible to know what Tucker Boyd was thinking. Still, no one doubted Tucker Boyd's hard work, and he was well respected for it. If you brought him in some horseshoes to work on, his wife would brew you a cup of coffee and he'd be finished before you had a chance to drink it all. And if you brought him in a bigger job, he'd say—"Come in this time tomorrow." And only very occasionally, he'd say—"Come in this time, day after tomorrow." Mister Boyd could fix just about anything, whether it be removing wax from cloth, or cleaning grease spots, or oil stains, or fruit stain, or removing stains from marble, or taking ink from cloth, or even wood. He'd fix wagons, or porcelain dolls. He'd polish silver, or brass, or gild a picture frame in gold or silver, or plate a lucky rock. He'd repair the silvering of a mirror, or remove egg stains from spoons (caused by boiled eggs) or clean coin collections. He'd restore the power of horseshoe magnets, remove rust from anything—and as a rule, if it had anything to do with metal, no man in Kentucky could fix it faster.

That was the reason Tucker Boyd had a good many customers. But it was also an interesting story to hear how he secured the funds to go into business. During the difficult years that this country faced, it had been nearly impossible to obtain travel permits, and thus, even small distances could sometimes divide families. Being a freedman, Mister Boyd was allowed passage where others were not—and by that (delivering letters, procuring passports for travel) he'd fostered a great many friendships and resources. And so it was that when the hardest years were passed, he raised the capital to build his shop.

On the day of our visit to the poorhouse in Frickerham to pick up the Stanfield boy, Nora Mae arrived at the schoolhouse toward 6 A.M.—just as Miss Cleveland and I were eating breakfast. Nora Mae had already eaten, though she did sit down for a glass of fresh milk and three muffins. Sam and William Ditzler arrived shortly, bringing with them Miss Cleveland's battle horse and a sturdy horse of their own. For the time, Miss Cleveland had been boarding her animal and carriage with William Ditzler, who was happy to keep the battle-scarred old lodger. The pair of horses drove a horse-cart, which, from the looks of it, could have barely made the journey from the Ditzlers'. But it was reliable, that cart, and I had seen it in service for more than six years, looking none the worse for wear than the first time I laid eyes on it. Its appearance was always one of a ramshackle thing, and yet William Ditzler had once found a scrap of paper flattened between two boards that suggested it was more than thirty years old. For the poorhouse, we had some clothing that Miss Cleveland and Missus Esterbrook had gathered, as well as two crates of roof tiles provided by Horatio Cooper. All was packed into the feeble seeming cart, and Nora and I made ourselves as comfortable as we could— back with the provisions and a few blankets for softness. William Ditzler also sat in the back with us. Then Miss Cleveland and Sam Ditzler sat themselves on the bench in front, and Sam cried out to the horses and rolled the reins and we were off. We arrived in Frickerham toward noon—and we were all relieved that Miss Cleveland had packed us some cheese sandwiches, as none of us could have brought ourselves to eat a meal at the poorhouse—for it would have been taking food out of the mouths of orphans. We stopped and ate by the roadside, taking some water from the Frickerham River. Even so, I imagine that we were all middling ashamed of ourselves, greedily indulging our appetites before we arrived at the poorhouse. I believe we did not want to eat before the eyes of those who had seen so much hunger, and who had lived in such destitution. But Miss Cleveland said it would help nobody if we starved.

The poorhouse was a fine, large building, much more prosperous than I had imagined, and when we arrived, we climbed down from the horse-cart, crossed the lawn, and knocked at the large double doors. We were then received by the steward's sister, Miss Sylvania Parvin. She took us to the kitchen eating room, where we saw several women and lots of little children running around. We could plainly see that some of them were weak-minded. I stuck close to Miss Cleveland, for fear of the crazy people. We next went upstairs, to be received by the steward, Johann Parvin. While we were standing at the landing, a feeble girl with a crust in her hand came up to me and put her hand on my shoulder. I was frightened—for I did not know what she was going to do. But she just shook the crust and walked away. Miss Cleveland and the Ditzlers spoke at length to Johann Parvin, and eventually, Nora and I were excused. We did not want to insult Mister Parvin, by showing our fear. So we quietly went down the stairs and sat in the nursery, where there were mothers with their children. There was one delicate looking older woman sitting on the floor, leaning against the wall with a baby in her lap. She would not let anyone else care for the child, though she was obviously in an exhausted condition. We saw several other such women—elderly and thin. And a great many were making themselves useful in some capacity. There was a good deal to do—with all the small ones climbing about. My heart would give a big bound as I looked at each of those limpid eyed children, many of whom were infected with whooping cough. I could see how any outbreaks of it could become rather serious. . . .

Morgan Stanfield, Tucker Boyd's nephew, was working in the barbershop, and a child was sent to fetch him. Morgan Stanfield was large, like his uncle. He did not know his own age, but he was no older than twelve, and possibly much younger. It was strange to think that only ten years before, I had been likewise delivered to my aunt. At first, I did not believe he knew how lucky he was, but then, when we delivered him to his uncle in Cotterpin, I could see that he did. First, he expressed his gratitude to Mister Boyd. Then he thanked Miss Cleveland and the Ditzlers, and even Nora Mae and me, for having made such a long trip for him. I realized then that his silence on the trip had been prudence—as he did not know any of us, nor did he know of our political opinions. He seemed to be a bright boy.

In the years to come, Morgan would become like a brother to little Buddy Boyd. Buddy was filled with an absolute awe and admiration for his cousin, who, entirely through self-reliance, had outsmarted a hundred run-ins with death or worse. And for his part, though Morgan was an uncommonly polite and correct child, he protected his young cousin with a fierceness, and a total fearlessness that few were tempted to test. . . .

Morgan grew into a man much like his uncle, quiet and direct—but also silent and mysterious. Buddy grew into a man of unfaltering trust and friendliness. Today, the shop still stands. It is manned by Tony and Kermit. Tony is Morgan's oldest, and Kermit is Buddy's oldest. And I would not be surprised to learn that the Cotterpin Blacksmithery will stand yet—for three generations to come. And I would expect a Boyd to still be there, amid flying sparks, and the clang of hammer and anvil. . . .

 It was so bitter cold outside that one could hardly breathe, and I had not been to town for nearly two weeks. Miss Cleveland and I had been invited by Nora Mae's family to attend their Christmas repast. And it was only on account of the Mayfields' holiday dinner that I made the trip to town at all. I had spent the morning at my aunt's cottage, practicing pumpkin pies. And though for the Mayfields' pies, which I would bake the next day, I had all the ingre-

dients from my own garden and the Mayfields' cow, Shirley, I had a sudden desire to provide the Mayfields with candles for the tree. To do so, I would have to journey all the way to Mister Kinsey the bee-keeper, in Frickerham—either that or pay more for them at Mister Cooper's store by the railway. I had the scent of those candles in my mind. The gentle smell of honey. The living smell of bees. Also, I wanted to purchase candleholders for the tree—so as not to set the Mayfield house on fire. For those, I would need to go to Mister Cooper's anyway. So, while Mister Cooper charged more for Mister Kinsey's wax candles than did Mister Kinsey, I decided that I would lose far more by being away from my business for a whole day than I would save by journeying to Frickerham.

And even with the frigid cold, it was an ever so charming walk to town—the pine trees all strewn with moss, and bright poinsettias all set in windows. Within the houses, people were burning Yule logs, and through the glass, I could see rooms lit by the colored fires.

After I had picked up my decorative candles, which were bundled up in a fragrant brown package that I held under my arm, I crossed the muddy road and gravel railway from HORATIO COOPER'S STORE FOR EVERYTHING to the post office. Mister Cooper had told me that he thought I had a letter waiting for me. The postmaster, old Joe Sharpless, told me that I didn't have a letter, but there was a note for me at the telegraph office at the railroad. So I crossed the road again, and was surprised to find that indeed I had received a telegraph.

It was from Max Vicar—the tool boy from years ago.

> WILL BE RETURNING TO KENTUCKY ON BUSINESS. WOULD LIKE TO ENJOY YOUR SOCIETY. HAVE REQUESTED THE AC-COMPANIAGE OF HESTER ESTERBROOK. SHE HAS SET ASIDE JANUARY 19. IF AMENABLE, PLEASE SCHEDULE.

That was the telegraph, and it was a peculiar one to me. Why had he gone to such lengths? And what was his object? Surely it was expensive to send such a wire. And surely it could have been posted. It was thrilling to be the recipient of such technology, though the profound urgency of it unsettled me.

Though I did not anticipate January 19, I did make a note of it, and when it arrived I was ready. I had spent the morning at my aunt's cabin, baking corn muffins and opening a few jars of the summer's peaches. . . .

That morning, Miss Cleveland had left at the cock-crow with Pastor Miles and Sam and William Ditzler. Sam and William had started working at the Cooper Mill, as they knew lumber and were reliable men who needed a new start. Mister Cooper was donating more lumber to the poorhouse in Frickerham. And as he was too old to tote lumber around, Sam, William and Pastor Miles had asked to do the charitable work. Miss Cleveland was also making the trip, as she had gathered up another collection of old toys and clothing. The four had set out to deliver the goods in Mister Cooper's lumber wagon, led by some rather fine horses—bred from stock that, years ago on the Cleveland Equestrian Farm, the late Somerton Cleveland himself had brought into this world. I was still living with Miss Cleveland behind the schoolhouse, and while she would have preferred to chaperone me herself, because she would not be available, she did not object to my meeting Mister Max Vicar at the old cottage, as Doctor Esterbrook, in person, had assured her of Mister Vicar's good character, and Missus Esterbrook would be in attendance.

Max Vicar was much changed. Whatever youth had been left in him when he and his father ventured west, it had flowered in the new country. And despite all expectation, the boy had become a man. He was still thin, but where he had been gangly, he was now graceful. And where he had been wiry, he was now svelte.

He wore a tailored brown suit, a rabbit fur hat and rabbit lined gloves. When he removed his hat, his hair was neatly combed back. It looked wet, though it was not. He no longer wore glasses, and explained later that the muscle of his eye had restrengthened, so it would not wander. I noticed he did not limp.

"You don't limp anymore."

"No," he said, looking to his shoes, "I have had these made by a doctor in San Francisco. One is half an inch higher than the other."

"You wouldn't know it to look at them," I said.

"No," he agreed, "you wouldn't."

He asked to see the porch that had been extended as a result of his breaking his leg when he was just a tool boy. He had not seen it painted—and he had not seen it furnished. . . .

I had painted and furnished it with my aunt, and even with the oppressive feel of time that had passed, and the snow that was starting to fall, the air on the porch was refreshing, and the rocker and swinging bench were pleasant to recline upon. The snow and sky were both so white that we could not tell one from the other, and it was as if we had sat out to watch the sky find the woods. . . .

He agreed that the porch was an enjoyable respite, and though it was cold, I sat on the bench, and he, on the rocker. We watched the sweep of downy flakes, and I said he was much changed. He said I had not changed.

"Really?" I asked, because I knew that I had changed.

"Well," he corrected himself, looking at his shoes, planted evenly on the wood, "your body is different. But your spirit is the same. It has always been the same. Some people are just born . . . whole."

"Or," I ventured, "they become so very young."

"Yes," he agreed, "perhaps that is the case."

Missus Esterbrook had been seated beside me on the bench. But she said she didn't feel too fine with it swinging back and forth. In fact, it was making her a touch queasy. Besides, it was too cold for her on the porch. She said she would be inside, by the fire.

Max Vicar had hired a carriage which had taken him from the railway to the Esterbrooks', whence he and Missus Esterbrook had made their way out to Cotterpin Bend. Although it was an enclosed carriage, it was cold enough to chill a body, especially a slightly older body. I had noticed that the carriage driver's beard was nearly a sheet of ice—so Missus Esterbrook went out to fetch him. It was silly for him to wait out there. He came in, but he sat in the corner, and wouldn't say a word. He would drink a cup of hot cocoa, though.

So, while Missus Esterbrook and the driver retired to the house, Max and I remained on the porch, watching the light snow fall. I had bundled up in my aunt's beaver coat. Max Vicar was already bundled up, and he buttoned his wool overcoat, and pulled on his fur gloves. I put my hands in my pockets.

The sky dropped its snow. I watched his breath freeze up out of his mouth, as he said he and his father had started a mining company in the West.

"Oh," I said, "you mine for gold?"

No, he answered, he and his father sold miner's tools, and now they refined gold, and sometimes silver and other ores. They had made their way west selling watches, and once they had arrived, they had only spent one day working in the mines. Then they had opened a supplies store, which was the basis of their current industries. Max had only returned from the West to diversify their investments. Mostly, they were taking property in the East.

"That's interesting," I said.

Then I realized—"Is it your house, by the big rock?"

"No . . . and . . . well," he confessed, "to be honest, we are investing in property, but it's not really in the East. It's in the West. This land isn't North and South anymore. It's East and West. And the West—that's the future of this country."

"Then why are you here?" I asked.

"To marry you—

"I mean," he knelt on his knee and produced a box, an open box, with a gold and diamond ring in it—"will you marry me?"

Hester Esterbrook had appeared in the door to the porch—she had a rag and a pot in her hand, which she was polishing. She watched me as I stared at the ring. It was all gold with one great stone—bright, and friendly. There was something so easy about every facet of it . . . easy, and . . .

"I'm sorry," I said, "I won't marry you." I looked up, and Hester was gone. I heard pots banging in the kitchen. She was straightening up. It was straight already—but she was doing it again.

"Is it the West?" he asked. "You'll love the West—"

"It is not the West."

"Is it me?"

I didn't answer at first, because I didn't know.

"No," I said, finally sure that I was honest, "it isn't you."

I had feared the rest of the afternoon would be tense and uncomfortable. But that was when Missus Esterbrook called us in from the cold porch to drink the cocoa by the fire. I didn't know how she had found the cocoa, but she just said lightheartedly that she could find the cocoa in any kitchen. Old people sometimes seem so sleepy, and I often make the mistake of thinking it means they don't have energy. But it's not true—they reserve energy, like lizards in summertime. Sometimes they sit quietly, and sometimes they burst with speed and fire—the sun they've saved up in their bones. And that was the kind of fire Missus Esterbrook had that day. She made us laugh and joke as she told some quite extra-ordinary tales she had heard about or even been witness to in her years in France. The time she had spent with Doctor Esterbrook with the Indians was also of great interest. Like her husband, she did not share in the popular opinion that the tribesmen were savages. . . .

But even so, once, the conversation did return to the subject of Max's journey, and he took my hand and said to me, "I will be very busy with work in the years to come, Alma, and I want you to think about this . . . marriage. Think as long as you like."

I nodded my head, but did not let my eyes look to his.

"And if you don't love me," said Max Vicar, his chin shaking, "think if you could learn to love me. . . ."

And though Missus Esterbrook made the afternoon pass quickly and lightly—like the snow on the windows—I am sure that the night was long, not only for me, but for Max. It was long like the snowfall that came to Cotterpin Creek. And I hoped that it would last no longer than the snow on the ground.

But it snowed again, and I did not know when the new snow melted over the old snow, or when the old snow melted under the new. And then the ground was cold and wet. And then the ground was wet. And then there was moss, grass and flowers.

And because I had planted them the previous autumn, the flowers were licorice flowers and vanilla flowers.

And the flowers were white, like snow on the ground. . . .

Or perhaps I just remember it that way.

Spring '70

rolling. horse.

After my graduation, I moved back to my aunt's cottage—preparing for my higher levels there. I moved things around a little—switched the bench for the writing table, and the stool for the candlestand. But mostly, I left things just the way they were.

In the time I had been living with Miss Cleveland, the townspeople had been coming to me to fix their stuffy heads and sore throats. I knew all of my aunt's recipes, so even though I had been living at the schoolhouse, I'd spent many afternoons at my aunt's stove with herbs that I had gathered in the forest.

One day, Doctor Esterbrook came out to the creek to tell me that my remedies were wonderful for the health of the townsfolk, but that it was high time I stopped taking eggs, butter and pies for payment. He himself had recently adopted a fair set of prices, and he would help me to do the same.

As a result of the doctor's advice, I soon found myself with my business thriving. Nora Mae didn't have much of a head for figures or for remembering the recipes of things, but she was my best friend and a good old time, so I took her on as my assistant. . . .

And in return, Nora Mae gave me the first pick of her cat's litter. I named my kitten Socrates. He was a calico cat.

But even though everything seemed to be going very well for me, I was sometimes lonely in the old cottage. Every morning when I woke up, the first thought that popped into my head was—*I should go wake up Aunty Betta.*

So, late one night, when I was having trouble sleeping, I packed up an overnight bag, took Socrates into my arms and crossed the creek to the new house in the field by the big rock.

I had been spending more and more time at the big house anyway—reading books and making sandwiches for myself and Nora Mae. The house was almost completely furnished now—decorated with carpets, curtains and pictures. I had bought dishes and pots and pans for the kitchen. I had even bought a bed for the bedroom.

I had only meant to sleep in the new house that one night. But one night turned into two, which turned into three, which turned into four, and then I forgot to count, and forgot to think about my sad old bedroom in my aunt's cottage.

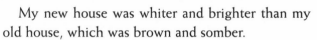

My new house was whiter and brighter than my old house, which was brown and somber.

The rich garden, woods and hot fire made my aunt's a good place to conduct my business, so no one but my cat Socrates knew that I had moved completely into the house by the big rock.

But one day, in the autumn of '70, the lawyer, Mister Pimpernickel, whom the doctor had sent to me with a very swollen toe, did notice that the old cottage was full of cobwebs.

He had been sitting in the green rocker with his foot soaking in hot apple cider vinegar with a tincture of lobelia. It was September, so I had the flower fresh, and the tincture was made up of the whole plant—the stems, petals, leaves and seeds, which were crushed. He was drinking hot apple cider with honey, and I had just prepared a tea for him to take home. Mostly, the tea was skullcap, valerian and yarrow—to help with the pain and to clean out his innards.

Rocking back in his chair, Mister Pimpernickel sipped the cider from his cup and stared at the ceiling.

"Alma," he asked, suddenly surprised at the circumstance of the wooden beams, "are those cobwebs?"

"Oh yes," I said, blushing and attacking the cobwebs with a broom, "I'm sorry, I just don't seem to have the time, and they're so fast. If I had so many legs I'd—"

"Oh, don't be sorry," said Mister Pimpernickel. "It's just rather unlike you, Alma. I wanted to be on the safe side, so I did peek into the new house—it seems to be in excellent condition."

"Oh yes," and I turned back to the stove, and the balm I was mixing for his gout—"I do check in at least once a day."

I was sitting on the back porch of my aunt's house, watching the spring arrive. It was late in a day that I had enjoyed for the sole reason that I had not worn a coat. It was the first day like that since the previous autumn. . . .

There was sun and grass. And the bugs had come to life, navigating the edges of warm leaves, thick bark and moist soil.

It was then that Doctor Esterbrook poked his head around the corner of the house and said, picking his way through the flowers, "I thought I might find you back here."

The doctor joined me on the porch, and wouldn't let me get him anything. In fact, he insisted that he go into the house to get two glasses, which he walked down to the stream for some cold water and a few sprigs of mint. He told me the news of Miss Cleveland's engagement to Sam Ditzler. They would be married at a small service performed by Pastor Miles at the end of the summer. Sam and his brothers had sold the mill at Frog Falls and were going in with William Ditzler to help Caroline Cleveland bring horses back to the estate. The old Cleveland estate had been divided into six lots. Of the four that had been sold, the Ditzlers had bought back two. There were two lots unrecovered, and the one of them belonged to the Mayfields, who were willing to work in tandem, while the other was the lot beside my lot—the lot with the big rock, and the big white house. The Ditzlers had approached Mister Pimpernickel, but the owner, an elderly dance hall operator from the Northeast, wasn't selling. It was a loss but not an insurmountable one, and William and Sam and Sam's brother were working on the barns already. They were living between the one barn that they had finished and William Ditzler's place. The Ditzlers lived in a two room cabin with an open hallway and gables angled front and back. It was the type of cabin called a dogtrot, and it was a good thing they'd added on a second story, as Fanny Ditzler had just had her fourth child (though little did we know she would have seven more). For the crowding, Miss Cleveland and Sam were soon to vacate the homestead, and the Ditzlers were thinking to erect a house for Caroline and Sam during the summer. The cousins were also looking to settle into something more permanent, but as none of them were yet married, they weren't made a priority.

As the doctor joined me on the porch, he was saying, "Folks will be getting together in May or June to help him with that house. It won't be anything like the old Cleveland place, or even anything like your big white house, but it'll be a good start. It's something to feel good about—and to look forward to. These are the beginnings of better days, Alma. I sure hope they are. And it'll be nice to see all those people out and together again. Won't it be nice for you to meet some of the new people who're making roots here? I like that young brother of Sam Ditzler. And there's a nice boy from Arkansas who's helping his family with a new farm—"

I interrupted the doctor, asking him about his wife.

"Oh, she's fine," he answered. "Yesterday, today, every day's pretty much the same."

He was getting on in years, and I asked him how he had made the trip.

"Oh, I took the horse. You know I rely on that old mare."

"But," I asked, "if you don't mind me being inquisitive. It is a long trip and I—"

"Oh yes," said the doctor, "of course. That's one of the nice things about being old. You have time for everything. Or you think you have time for everything. It's funny, how in a lot of ways, it's the young people who have to worry about time. Well, I must be wasting your time." The doctor laughed. "So, are you asking me why I came out here? As a matter of fact, there was one item on the agenda. There's a social with a few people from nearby towns. They'll be rolling some logs early in the day and then, well, I hear they've got two fiddles and a banjo for the occasion, and I hear the boys who play them are powerful good. They can tune and tune. Jigs. Country breakdowns. Now, that might not be exactly to your liking—but that's good enough fun for anyone. And it's just over in Frickerham, and I thought we could get Mister Cooper's nice-looking horse and hitch it up to the carriage for you and—"

"Doctor Esterbrook," I asked, "what are you trying to say?"

"Well," said the doctor, "that Valentine boy is spending an awful lot of time out at the Mayfields'. Harmon's young, but he'll grow up. He can barely say his own name with Nora Mae in the room—and she doesn't seem to mind it. Some say they make a nice couple—"

"Are you telling me to get married?"

He stared out at the sun on the dandelions.

"Yes."

A few minutes passed.

He added, "I suppose I am."

Then we both looked at the dandelions—and I thought about how they were such a modest flower, but always in bloom. There were very few flowers in bloom all the time, and none of the most pretty. . . .

I fought back tears, because I did not want him to see me cry. But I needn't have feared, as he didn't look at me, because he didn't want to see it either.

I dabbed the wrist of my sleeve against my wet eyes—"Who sent you here?"

"They all did," he sighed. "Everyone did, Alma."

"Miss Cleveland too?" I asked.

"Yes," he said, "Miss Cleveland too."

So, with all the good things and the bad things a body might feel, I spent my nights in the big white house with my hands clutching at my white night-gown—holding on as if that was all it meant to keep a hope held in. And my days—I spent burying myself in that rather solitary act of attending my Aunty Betta's garden. The vegetable garden especially. It seems that through about a year I'd be likely to find myself sitting on the bench we'd set out there—either that or digging or planting. It's so hard to recall one year in particular—to separate out that one from all the others. So even now, when I think of it, I know that a garden couldn't be so very lush, and that in describing my garden I must have joined one spring to the next, and thus, one year to another—and thus, all the years and gardens since. But still, I remember that garden like this—

Out in the back, behind the cottage by the creek by the big rock, my aunt had her garden. There was just the slightest pitch to the clearing—southeastern for good sunshine. It was a squarish garden—but also an all over kind of garden, with lettuce and impatiens all along the side of the house—where the lettuce could stay warm, and the impatiens could take up the shade. Near that path was an inlet from the stream, just down a little slope through the bank—so it wasn't too far for water. We had a brick checkerboard laid out—with darker and lighter bricks to enclose the plots. The bricks were laid three or four high—the soil packed within them, making big tubs for the vegetables. (My aunt'd had Mister Nielson mortar in the boxes.) The raised beds would thaw earlier in spring, warm easier in summer and drain faster in rain—and also, my dear aunt had it like that so she wouldn't have to bend over all the time. There'd been clay pathways between the beds, but I'd had Harmon and Pitney load a farm-cart for me, and they and a couple of horses hauled some bricks from the old town to set into pathways. I always found a weathered brick to be the most pretty—resounding as it was with every color on its face, not so much with history, but memory. . . .

In months just gone by, I've reread my aunty's journals. I've treasured them for so long, and read them time and again—but this time, I read them close, and more than ever, they revealed things I'd not seen before. Years ago, I'd started my own journals, keeping a log of all my successes and failures. And reading over all, I think now to pass them on to my granddaughters and nieces—so that they might retain our family memory. I know, being an old woman in a faster world, that nobody has the time for old journals anymore, so maybe I'm including here some of what's most important. All this . . . it's just what I remember, and I've decided that's the best way to do it—for what's remembered *is* most important. . . .

My Aunt Bettina would say that what one needed for a good garden was a good head (and though I may not yet have had that, I had my aunt's journals), good soil (and ours was, especially that year, as Miss Cleveland had resumed the horse trade, and I was supplied with all the manure I could send a farmer for, in trade for his bad stomach or the like), a strong hand and back (and I still had those) and a stout digging fork and shovel (and we had all that, along with a few other things, like a spade, hoe, rake, wheelbarrow and, naturally, a watering can, which had been gained in trade from Horatio Cooper). The only thing I might have added to that list was a good sunbonnet, lest I become as red as an Indian. I always wore mine, though my aunt had never seemed to mind too much—going in'jun.

What did it mean to say it was an all over kind of garden? Well, my aunty's garden was a kind of living, breathing thing—brought into this world by all the preferences of nature. It was those secrets that ordered our garden. What should benefit from what—what soil from what plant, what plant from what soil, what plant from what light, what plant beside what plant and what plant after what other plant. Such was more important than any system of geometry. It was the wild truths that patterned our garden—

Marigolds, or "injun buttonholes," grew well with just near everything—so they popped all about. Particularly kind to tomatoes and potatoes, the flowers were also rather deadly to pesky critters like nematodes and whitefly. There were always nettles about, as they were good for cover, and for preparing new ground—to fatten soil. Chamomile was a nursemaid to sick plants, and rather wonderful for the flavor of mint. I would take it up when it grew too large, and use the flowers to line the clay path along the side of the house, as for medicinal use, chamomile could only be harvested once a year—at noon on midsummer's day. So, the chamomile was beside the mint, the mint was beside the cabbages (along with some thyme and rosemary too), as, to my way of thinking, the flavor of cabbage needed the help. Parsley was a benefit to the bees, increased the scent of roses, mothered asparagus shoots and repelled greenfly. But while parsley was good for asparagus, asparagus didn't seem to do too much for the parsley—so that made it a little easier to get the parsley near the roses. Many of the herbs were delicate, so were kept in barrels on the porch by the kitchen door—that way, they were easy to move when frost threatened. Of course, mints were of more benefit in the garden, and wouldn't take to the barrels anyway, as I used a bonfire ash in the soil, which wasn't much good for mint. . . . Out in the shady valleys between the tomatoes grew the cauliflower—the squash vines ran among the cornstalks—the salad greens under the sunflower clump—the spinach shaded by a trellis of beans. (Planting beans with Nora Mae, we'd drop a pinch of horsehair into each hole before the bean—for a healthy soil.) There were several other trellises in the garden, for I employed them where I could—them being petite, and pretty, and just right for ripening fruits and vegetables—fast and even. Carrots, peas and turnips—these were best planted together, as they were all beneficial to one another—though only the carrots could be planted near the onions and garlic, whose good taste might be harmed by the others. (The garlic cloves had to be crushed a little before planting, to sweeten the result.) And the carrots, along with the radishes, they had to be placed where they wouldn't get too much water and bust open. And the rue—it had to be so far away from just about everything that I didn't plant it at all! Gladiolas were no good either, and I was careful not to let a single ash tree sprout up within sight of the house. It was also a thing that Mister Nielson told me, and that I noticed over the years, that nut trees of different varieties were not to be planted together, or even too close, as one would kill the other. . . . I had a few of the vines planted in hills—soil mounded to stay warmer and drier toward the center. Vine hills were good for squash, cucumber, melon, pumpkin, gourds and the like. And . . . when I *was* orderly, planting in rows, it was in wide rows—I'd carve a trench along the ground with the edge of the hoe, and seed those round, red carrot seeds all along the furrow (sowing generously, as, if not, all that labor might be wasted). I'd use the hoe to cover, then thin out the seedlings as the season progressed—the tangles of pea vines and carrots and radishes. And then I'd mulch between the rows to prevent weeds. Though it was not often spoken of, in those years, we planted with the waxing, and never a waning moon—that was the way for farmers back then. . . . And with the harvest, there'd often come a new planting, and as I didn't like to plant the same twice in the same place (because it tuckered the soil, for one thing, and the weather had changed, for another), it'd be a brand new crop. And so . . . my aunt's garden really was a thing alive unto itself—ever changing, growing and shrinking with each season. (And not only were there those things, but eleventeen others to consider!) And, with every rotation, the garden would become both wilder and more logical—as it was quite a challenge to maintain what should be where and not to have any of the same things in the same places! (I also moved to keep ahead of the bugs, lest they get too comfortable anywhere.) And just as there were friendships and romances between neighboring plants—so it was between consecutive plants. The nightshades (eggplants, tomatoes, peppers and potatoes) were best followed by mustard (cabbage would do) or a bean. Whenever I could, I liked to sow as I reaped—to pick a radish or carrot and in its place drop a seed, or maybe a little seedling in an eggshell. And in that way, I could plant to be sure to have fresh food in every season—to eat, pickle or trade. (More often than not, I traded with Mister Cooper at his Store for Everything.) And . . . as the days were long, and I was without husband or children, and with some respectable income from my trade in root therapies, and well nigh no money going out, as I was meeting my needs by bartering my garden . . . well, I was able to begin my own savings. And with my experience in gardening and in trade growing as much as my garden, I learned to plant more and more varieties of miniatures—as those fruits and vegetables took up less space in the garden, and they fetched a higher price at the market—as the more affluent preferred them for their exotic natures. And though they were small, so was I, and what came outside the harvest, either too early or too late—it was quite enough to feed me. Besides—miniature plants were better suited to my miniature hands. And anyway . . . that was how I grew *my* garden. . . .

So . . . every season had its blessings—the first green salad was a spring enchantment! And to smell the first rare-ripe peach . . . the fragrance of it, the weight, the soft skin, the sweet juice and delicacy on the tongue—surely that was a fruit in Eden! And what more for transport could there be but to sit for a supper of the first ripe tomatoes? And . . . there were the first ears of corn, and the melons, which, with the cucumbers, might be stored for several weeks if packed in a tight box and placed deep in a barrel of dry sand. Fall too had its luxuries—like buttercup squash and collard, neither of which matured into their full savor until fingered by frost. And every one of those pleasures, along with the beets and turnips—they were good until the ground froze. (The cabbage as well, though it was hardly a pleasure.) And the late season carrots, they were ever so sweet—and good in the ground through much of the winter, or even all of it, with a little luck and a thick blanket of mulch. (I remember once digging my beets out from under six inches of snow.) Of course, there were other joys of winter, like Willa Mayfield's raspberry vinegar and sour cherry jam. My aunt wrote out recipes for both her mushroom and tomato catsups. (I don't know that any of your girls, my girls— daughters, granddaughters and great granddaughters—I don't know that any of you are desiring to make catsup the old-fashioned way, but if you are motivated so, do know that the tonics should not be made in copper pots, but earthenware, as the process erodes the copper, and turns the brew to poison.) And, as far as winter pickling— there were onions, walnuts, beets, carrots, cucumbers and everything else. My aunt had done some of her own pickling, but I had more or less left it, along with the preserving and saucing, to my neighbors, who would trade my vegetables or remedies for their jars. I wasn't too fond of indoor activities, as, if I wasn't outside, I liked my time quiet—probably with a book. And while it was true that I was never too fond of the winter cabbage, I did adore the winter squash—baked and softened with honey and cream. . . .

But the garden wasn't just edible—it was bright and colorful, and just as memorable to me as any lady's flower patch. The great, ponderous purple eggplants—and their lavender flower. The rhubarb's green leaves and their so very red stems. And the ever so agreeable purple snap-beans dangling from the house! Pumpkin vines and nodding cornstalks—and the heart shaped leaves of the sweet potatoes on their vines. The flowers of potatoes like foam in the field. The globe artichokes rising skyward until harvest. (Sometimes I could not resist just allowing them to blossom into their blue.) All those ruffled rosettes of lettuce leaves, the ferny tufts of carrot tops, the shining red peppers, the yellow and round okra blossoms, the feathery foliage of the asparagus—all that was my English garden! And back in those days, when the most of us grew our own food, there were so many varieties of everything—blue corn, or red, yellow or white. . . . All was traded between neighbors, friends and family—and I remember in our community especially, there were a dozen dozen varieties of eggplants—tiny white ones, long peppermint striped ones or just gargantuan ones. Tomatoes, peppers and potatoes—all had their multitudes. Miss Cleveland's, or rather Missus Caroline Ditzler's nut potatoes were no bigger than a child's thumb, and as rich and sweet as chocolate. Caroline, my aunt and myself—between us three, a great many of those delights were preserved. And today, a great many of them are being cared for and nurtured by Mary—Caroline's Mary, Caroline and Sam's second grandchild. (Caroline and Sam had their first child that very year.) Just this past summer, the nut potatoes came up true—exactly as I remembered them from all those years ago. . . .

And what else was there for a girl to do in her garden?

I could turn near any white flower red with the juice of Virginia pokeweed. And I crushed up charcoal to make red roses redder, or to give white flowers red and violet veins and hues. (Doctor Esterbrook asked if my petunias were from a *French* variety of seed!) And the roses that season—they were wonderful, as I'd been told by Mister Cooper to bury some trimmed fat with their roots—though it also brought foxes and badgers. I'd some success offsetting the smell with a perfume of herbs, along with the smoke and ash of rue. I'd also some trouble with skunks getting at my flower bulbs, as the skunks, evidently, found them quite delectable (just as the deer indulged in nibbling the buds off roses—their own particular treat). That summer, I had the Ditzler cousins out to weave me a new fence, as the old had softened to beyond repair. The new, like the old, was a wattle type of fence, made of willows, vines and saplings—the willows and vines woven between the thicker, upright saplings. Besides being good for deer, dogs and children, a fence like that was also good for rabbits, skunks, badgers, foxes, opossums and such, as virtually no space was left through which they might clamber. The cousins left the upstanding saplings rather long, so that over the years, as they rotted and went to mush at the bottom, I could just pound them a few inches farther into the ground. Even so, there were other enemies, like gophers and woodchucks and birds. But that was just the way with a garden—the forest gave so much of itself that it had to take a few things back. For the crows, starlings, sparrows and the whole motley assortment of winged pirates, I employed a few twisty wooden snakes made of carved joints, and a couple of painted wooden owls which fit on the ends of vertical branches. (I'd move those snakes and owls quite frequently—to make it seem they'd moved themselves.) I also tied threads of black yarn into the pear tree, and as long as the wind was blowing, they did do a part in keeping the birds off—or at least at bay—or at least from overrunning everything. . . . For clubroot, I'd bury a stick of rhubarb here and there. . . . But nobody could win every battle—and there'd occasionally be flea beetles in the eggplant leaves, wireworms in the carrots or hornworms in the tomatoes. It makes me sigh to think of it—no matter how tidy one kept a garden, there'd sometimes be cabbage loopers in the cabbage. And though I know that none of God's creatures were truly my enemies, I did dislike the loopers—unappealing as they were—soft little cigars. But I could just about thwart all the silkworms—with a drop of mineral oil inside the hood of each ear of corn. . . . And there were various herbal applications against the bugs—I could kill the thrips on the melons and the cucumbers with tobacco water and a decoction of elder leaves. My aunt had always used a decoction of hot peppers, garlic and a few other things, to rid herself of pests—and so many of my neighbors swore by that recipe that I continued to use it myself and to make it for them. And onions cut and open to the air—they were good against not only human ailments, but bug ailments, such as scale and spittle bugs, and tree and frog jumpers. There was pruning too, not only to strengthen plants and growth, but for the battle against the insects—to kill them, and to prevent them from jumping from leaf to leaf. (But one had to know when to use a knife and when not to—as some plants were peculiarly opposed to the blade.) The common way to kill flies back then was a dish set out with a beat egg yolk, a tablespoon of molasses and black peppercorns finely crushed. I don't know what exactly did it, the eggs, the pepper or the combinations—but the flies would die soon after. . . . To banish flies from stables, I sold an application of geranium and slipper flowers—and to keep flies off the horses themselves, I recommended smartweed rubbed on the entire body—especially the legs, neck, ears and tail. Pennyroyal was well suited to keeping the mosquitoes away, as well as fleas—and that was an application much utilized by people. To get fleas out of mattresses, I used chamomile flowers. In fall, I was called upon to rid all the schoolchildren of head lice with my aunt's remedy of larkspur. It was funny to think about bugs and flies all that season, as I remember quite distinctly that Max Vicar . . . Well, he must've sent me a hundred presents that I refused to accept or even open, before finally, old Joe Sharpless at the town post office, he said to me—

"Oh come now, Alma. What's so wrong with Max Vicar? Last I saw, there was no flies on him."

Squitch grass could be choked out by turnips planted in thick crops—the turnips would be small, but to any mind a better harvest than squitch grass. I was a believer in the use of mulch. Spread deeply between the onions, the onion shoots would come up and the weeds would not. It was always wise to use straw as mulch, not hay, as hay itself brought weeds. A cross laying of dried out daisies and their stems proved rather solid for a bottom layer, and I'd use it in winter when protecting harvests from the cold. Occasionally, I'd use sawdust from Mister Cooper's mill, but only when I had someone to tote the supplies for me, for as neat as it was, it was heavy, and really more trouble than it was worth. The slugs were also rather fond of strawberries, and I protected my fruits with planks smeared in railroad soot and oil—for no slug would pass over it. There were traps I used as well, for slugs and pillbugs—a bit of sweet coffee or ale in a pickling jar laid on its side. And, I'm afraid, as the strawberries were also my favorite, I would rather efficiently drown those bugs and slugs in that very same jar—filled up with salted water. Even today, the secret to the tartness of my strawberries is pine needles, spruce needles and crushed pine and fir cones. And the secret to the intensity of those berries is the near proximity of borage, which has some medicinal uses besides, and adds a peppery taste to green salads. It was near that time that the borage seeds were sent to me all the way from England by my grandmother's sister's daughter, my cousin Obelia. Though I'd not met her, we exchanged seeds all winter. Rather vivid is my memory of packaging melon seeds for her—separating out the good from bad in a glass of water, as good seeds float, and bad, sink.

And . . . there were all the ways of guessing at the weather—before rain, flies would come indoors, and bees would stay in their hives. And indeed, there was just watching the darkness and thickness of the clouds. And there was the threat of frost if the air was crisp and still, and the skies were clear. But I knew that even if the frost did come, I probably wouldn't have too much trouble with it, for I'd just bury the sprouts in some more earth, and then they'd stay warm, and just come up again in a day or so.

And so the seasons went. . . .

And when the time came, I tried to get started as early as possible with the cool weather crops like peas, salad greens, root crops, cauliflower and broccoli. (I'd already had enough cabbage.) My method for testing the soil was to lay my cheek upon it—thinking that if it was comfortable for me, it would be comfortable for a seed. (Though I'm sure my thinking was correct, on several occasions, it made me quite a sight to visitors!) My onions and potatoes, I liked to plant them at the same time—and I also liked, in spring, to plant the slow growing crops like parsnips and rutabaga. I'd presprout my beans in dampened cloths, to get ahead of the season, for if there was one thing I'd ever learned in housework, in gardening and in life—if there was one rule, it was—*don't get behind*. Also, I'd prepare the soil a week or so before the last frost, or as near to it as I could guess—so the weeds would come up, and I could pull them before I planted. Amaranth was a weed with purplish or greenish flowers—and it was a grain that ancient people had grown in America for food. (There was a myth that there was a type of amaranth flower that never faded.) There was also lamb's quarter, chickweed, ragweed, purslane and some crab and squitch grass. And I remember, in the days when I was pulling up weeds, I accepted a package at the post office from Max Vicar—it was several yards of an Italian brocade, which I took

to Missus Valentine, who was a fine seamstress, that she might fashion me a cloak with a hood. And thus . . . after the last risk of frost,
my modest crops were planted, and into the summer months I made
my harvests. The greatest labor was watering. Just down by the okra
was the inlet for the creek—years ago, somebody had stoned it in
against the bank, and it occasionally required a little movement and
adjusting of the stones. Though not too far off, those buckets could
still be quite a load—one after another. So, along with using mulch
to smother weeds and warm the garden, I'd use mulch to soak up my
watering, to retain it and cut down on the buckets required (though
mulch decomposed so fast in the summertime it was always needing
replacement itself). I'd start harvesting as soon as I could—summer
squash, cucumbers, pole beans, okra and asparagus—that all would
continue to grow and I'd continue to harvest. I'd always try to get in
two growing seasons if I could—be it with beans, squash, tomatoes
or a great variety of things. And, just in consideration of taste and
texture, it was better in many circumstances to harvest a young plant.
I had asparagus all along one of the garden paths (as when the season
was over, the foliage was so bright and full), and I'd pluck the shoots
soon after they emerged, that they wouldn't get too tough to eat. The
okra too—I liked to pick it while it was still tender and fuzzy, just a
few days after the flowers fell off, otherwise it might become too hard
and wooden. And the radishes, they could get wooden, and drawn-
out and poor in flavor—if allowed to remain in the ground beyond
their time. I'd found that the cucumbers could grow just as big as wa-
termelons (well, very *nearly* so) but that they wouldn't have any taste
at all if they were any bigger than a cucumber. And I remember that
just about the time of my early harvest, I was posted a comb and mirror set by Max Vicar. When I picked it up at the post office, it looked
so like a package I had made poor Joe Sharpless send back on a previous occasion, that Joe seemed to sigh with relief when I signed for
it. He said he was rather glad I'd taken it on my own, for he'd been
instructed by Missus Esterbrook to impress upon me the giver's insis-
tence and honorable intentions. And I did take it, not so much for

those rather limp reasons, but for the even less stalwart rationale that I had liked the Italian brocade. The package was ordered from Boston—within was a canvas covered case, with my initials set in gold. And the canvas in turn was fitted with a snap button over a leather case, which was also set in gold with my initials. Inside the case, nestled into a blue silk, was a comb and mirror set, consisting of a brush, a suede brush, various toiletries (for teeth and nails) and a number of soaps, scented oils and powders. The jars were of a very pretty glass, and they had silver tops—and the handles of the combs and mirrors were silver inset with pearl inlays. All the metal was silver, except for my initials, which were set in gold—and on every single thing! And I always meant to send the all of it back, as it was too fine. But I was unduly impressed by such things—such things as this that I had hardly seen. And it makes me want to cry to this very day, the way I swallowed, and put the set to use (upon a stool in my bedroom, beside the mirror and a wooden chair) and decided to return it soon, as I could keep it new, and I was just too busy—too very busy with my crops. . . . For food I liked to eat, I'd spread out my harvest by spreading out my planting, but for that which I planned to deliver to Mister Cooper, I did my best to harvest all at once. For a share of the spoils, Nora Mae would share in the picking, and Pitney Zooks or Harmon Valentine would help me pack up and take a cart into town. And it was near the time of the beans that I received, from Max Vicar in San Francisco, a bunch of five silver boxes from Egypt. They were all very small, and I liked small things—from vegetables to silver boxes. There was a seashell, a chest, a diamond, a crescent moon and a seahorse. . . . The tomatoes, peppers, salad greens and the like would stay good in the ground for some time, and I'd bring out more mulch to spread over the carrots and the other roots, that I might leave them all fall, and even into winter. I'd have collard in late fall to early winter—and that'd be my last crop but for the multiplier onions. For the storage onions, I'd wait till about a week after the growth was dead, and then store them. I had a nice variety of artichoke, and as I'd let a few flower, I took the seeds for Obelia, my English cousin. (And

297

that was a good thing too, for now I have them for you, Mary.) They were so blue, those artichokes, so brilliant blue—just the color of the dress on Max Vicar's porcelain doll, which he'd had sent to me from Paris. . . . I'd have my root crops in winter. And otherwise, there was not much more to do but lay the compost, take in the last of the cabbage and maybe the mustard greens. And it was then that I accepted another addition to my bounty—a chiming clock from Switzerland. What I was doing accepting such gifts I cannot say—perhaps merely that I was a foolish girl who, to her own way of thinking, had never had things so fine to call her own. And there was always the thought, the near assurance actually, that I would return everything in spring. And so I had my little horde, and I worked on my garden notebook, taking stock of my previous season and preparing seeds for the next. . . . Soon after, I received another gift—and were it not so seemingly modest (for that precious kind of gift) perhaps I might have returned it and maybe even everything else along with it. The music box came from China. . . .

And to one way of thinking, I must acknowledge that there was no excuse for taking such prizes—but to the other, I had heard told that my soldier had fallen sick in Mexico, and that he was perhaps even . . . by then . . . Missus Caroline Ditzler had heard the same. And my heart was so bent and stretched and twisted over the years—and everyone seemed to know about the gifts, and they told me to take them—Sam and Caroline too—and I was really just a girl—still just a girl . . . and I . . . I . . . I too was growing, and was all alone, and I had never had such nice things. . . .

And perhaps it was their wealth, or their wish, that helped me to feel less alone. . . .

And it's as clear to me as if the wind just took it away yesterday—I was sitting in the garden, or lying there, to watch the insects do their insecty things—and I was thinking that even among them, there seemed some good and some bad. Of course, I knew that none were really good, or for that matter, evil—but for the garden, the praying mantis was doubtlessly an ally—an eater of all things insipid. I knew that the hunters tended to move fast, and if a bug moved fast, it was a safe assumption that it was upon other bugs that it dined, and not the garden. So did I learn that ladybugs ate bugs, as did lacewings, which ate caterpillars. . . . But even in that good act, the eating of a caterpillar, I began to see some sadness—some tragedy. For it seemed a rather cruel way to go, and a cruel thing to do—that is, to lay an egg in a caterpillar, so that when the egg hatched, all the hatchlings would devour that hapless caterpillar, who, after all, was a vegetarian himself, a vegetarian who had never dreamed of eating a relative, not even a distant one. . . .

And sadly, tragically, I even began to see some of that cruelty in myself, that cruelty of grown men and women that I had always thought should . . . well . . . just skip over me. But children always seemed to go wrong somehow—going from being innocent one day, to just . . . well . . . not so innocent the next. And one morning, I woke up, there in the big white house, feeling that I too was lacking my innocence. And the thing I remember as if it happened no more than an hour ago, or half an hour ago, or even just a few minutes or seconds ago, it was this—

I had picked a caterpillar out of the tomatoes, and between my thumb and forefinger, I held the soft and gently rolling body—the legs feeling and flimmering. And then I felt a teasing and a pinch at my neck, just under my collarbone, and with my left hand I reached up to my chest, unbuttoned my shirt to the breast, and pressed my hand within to extract a mite. And thus, I was kneeling at the tomatoes with a caterpillar in my right hand, and a mite in my left. So I looked at them, then I fixed the mite to the head of the caterpillar.

And then I left them there on the ground . . . together.

OXEYE
DAISY

Caroline Cleveland's wedding was a simple affair, with none of the spectacle it would have been afforded in days of yore. . . .

Still, it was a cheerful occasion, which sparked a spirit that had been dulled by years of need and regret.

299

The betrothed spent the day at the church, where they talked to the pastor and their families.

The reception, it took place in the evening, out at the Cleveland estate—where there was a new group of barns, and the most of a house. It was lucky the weather was supportive, as it would have been a rather cramped service indeed, were it to have taken place in Caroline and Sam's half built drawing room. The service was a lovely one—and I was overjoyed to be maid of honor. Nora Mae stood with me, as did Dahlia Swanson—and Doctor Esterbrook called the three of us pixies.

Once, we were all very much amused when he tripped over a chair, and he looked up at us and said accusingly—

"It's more pixies!"

Mister Cooper was there, and as we sat in the garden waiting for the ceremony to start, he told us a very interesting story about how he got his start as a storekeeper—

"When I was a young man—well, I am young," Mister Cooper corrected himself and smiled at us, and we giggled, and he went on—

"So—when I was a *younger* man, I was a wheat farmer, in Minnesota, and my whole crop got ate by grasshoppers. They just dropped out'a the sky above, and the ground was thick with'em as far as the eye could see. Nothing to do but listen to 'em crunching. Just a few days, the earth was bare—all but for the eggs, which'ed come up grasshoppers next year. So I was flat put out, and for wheat next year—be a waste a' time. Only good come a' any of it was the chickens got fat. I'da good number of them, and it was some solace to see'em, accustomed to lowering their heads to sort of chase grasshoppers, they'd snap about delightedly and have grasshoppers jump right into their mouths! So all summer, I just planned for winter—lived off chickens and the land. And I made my chickens big, and sold all that farming nonsense, and bought more chickens—and because I killed only the cockerels, and kept those hens happy and plump, by the time the grasshoppers hatched, I had hundreds of young chicks around the place. And then they grew plump and happy, on those grasshoppers, and soon enough, I had more chickens than grasshoppers—until finally, I had no grasshoppers. And then I hired out my chickens to my neighbors, to eat their grasshoppers—until all of them grasshoppers were ate. And then I took those chickens and sold every one of them, and at a good price, for all the crops had been ate by grasshoppers. And my land too, I sold it at a good price, because there were no grasshopper eggs on it, or on the land around it—and all them other grasshoppers from 'round farther than that had marched west, as grasshoppers do.

"And," said Mister Cooper, grinning humbly, but from ear to ear—"that was how I became a storekeeper, for I couldn't see how any man could get rich by farming."

And then we all laughed at that, for he had certainly gotten rich by farming! And only shortly thereafter, the ceremony began—

William Ditzler's youngest girl, Maya, had been made flower girl, and ever so slightly, I could not help but to be envious of her and her basket of petals. She followed Miss Cleveland through the service, sprinkling a trail of roses. . . .

As a wedding gift, Miss Cleveland's dress was commissioned by Missus Esterbrook to her seamstress—for it would have been bad luck for Miss Cleveland to sew it herself. That was the new thing she wore. For the old, borrowed and blue—she wore a brooch of her mother's, which she had saved, and the veil which my aunt had worn at her wedding and a blue pair of shoes (with a coin inside the one of them). Luck was much the preoccupation of the day, and the hazy sky gone sunny was a particularly good omen.

We girls, Nora Mae, Dahlia and I, were so conscious of luck that we barely put any food on our plates—for fear the others would accuse one of taking the last portion on a serving dish (which was said to be a spinster's trait). Nora Mae had caught the bouquet, but Dahlia was quite sure *she* would be the next married—having been recently spit on by a grasshopper. She tried to blow all the down off a thistle, and told us that meant Pitney Zooks was in love with her. She spent the rest of the afternoon dropping dishcloths, pretending to make accidental rhymes and walking about with her shoe unbuckled. I was tempted on many occasions to tell her that rather than such superstitions, she'd serve love better by sitting a few minutes with Pitney himself, instead of tormenting him by flirting with other boys—as well as several grown men! She even spoke encouragingly to Mister Pimpernickel—all while looking over her shoulder at Pitney. She was a selfish girl, and I believed a foolish one, who thought too much about her grandmother's money, and her sassafras love potion, which was no more magic to me than . . . Well, I had no use for it. And I hoped for Pitney's sake that she was wrong about him—though it would turn out she was not. They would be married at Christmas. (She would not have a need for finishing school—as to her mind, she was finished.) She was right too in thinking that she would be married before Nora Mae, though within two years, Nora Mae and Harmon Valentine would also be wed. Of course, by the time of Nora's marriage to Harmon, Dahlia Swanson Zooks would already have two children, both of them angels—while she herself would be a changed and better woman, as a result of the lessons of motherhood. And I must say that I would not love her the more for it.

Dahlia was to be married at eighteen—Nora at nineteen. I was more than a year older than Nora. . . .

The dawn following the wedding of Sam and Caroline, the Ditzler cousins went out in their carriages and gathered everyone onto the front lawn of the newlyweds' house—then we woke them with banter and music until the couple finally invited us in for drinks and refreshments. If they had not been cooperative, Sam would surely have been dragged out and dropped in the well! The shiv'ree was so hearty and crowded with friends that the couple felt loved indeed! And then we would not leave until we were each given a penny. . . .

The newlyweds were soon repaid however, as we all contributed to the pounding—bringing food and furniture, and helping generally to establish the household of a family. . . .

And . . . I felt life as an orphan again. For I did not want anyone but John Warren. For I did not think my heart could be so divided that I would love twice.

I remember a barn dance that very New Year's Eve, when the fiddlers were fiddling and the running set was commencing with a call of "Cage the bird!" Harmon danced with Nora, and Pitney danced with Dahlia, who turned back to me, smiling truly. And meaning well in her own way, she cried out over the music, "Find yourself a man!" And then she nodded like she knew something, as if I was without a partner not for want of suitors, but because I did not encourage any—

"Alma," she called out, "find yourself a man!"

And sometimes at night, all my resolve in my breast would drain out of my toes—and I would stare at the crossbeams, and think that I did not want to be alone. That I did not want to grow old without a love to give. . . .

Good days begin with good nights. So it was on a morning in early fall—

After having slept deeply with the comfort of the cooling night, I rose to prepare myself for the arrival of Doctor Esterbrook, who would accompany me to some ways outside Cotterpin, or what might be considered the outskirts of Cotterpin, where we were to join Max Vicar at a hunting stable thereabouts. Max had returned from San Francisco to attend to several business concerns, and he had stopped at Frickerham for some riding and to call upon myself. I was quite flattered by the attention—and all the loneliness and youth and vanity in my own body ached that I should not spend all my days without admirers. I was encouraged by the doctor and his wife as well, and when Doctor Esterbrook arrived, he partook in a bowl of oatmeal with dried cherries, honey and cream, as well as a deep mug of coffee—and then we set his horse to his paces and took the Esterbrooks' light carriage out into the morning. It was a good road, and on account of that and the mild weather, we arrived sooner than might have been expected.

Max Vicar was there to meet us, and I must say I was rather surprised to find how glad I was to see him—and to see how glad he was to see me. Doctor Esterbrook was blushing and set all aglow by the reunion.

The stables were seemingly sound, but quite unremarkable—though the smell of them was vivid to my memory, and my ensuing recollections were rather acute. I remembered John Warren, and his family stables—I remembered him sauntering and smiling with his hands full of all kinds of this and that—and his pockets bulging, stuffed with turnips, fat carrots and sugar cubes. He was ever ready, as I recalled, and Max seemed much the same. Though perhaps of slightly more Western habits, Max had an attitude that was rather reminiscent. And it was his method of catching—walking up to the horse with a halter hidden behind his back and a tidbit in his outstretched hand. He watched the animal's expression carefully—for any sign of nervousness or fear—then he'd carefully fit the halter. Tacking up, he fit the saddle from above the withers and slid it down—making sure that the hair ran in the right direction. Then he'd give the saddle a few shakes left and right, to settle it, and to be sure that the horse wasn't pinched at all underneath. After that, he'd smooth out the girth, and the hair under it. And all the time he'd be quietly talking to the animal, keeping everything calm and easy—just as John Warren had, so long ago.

Max had a more Western style of mounting a horse than did John Warren—it reminded me of the way John Warren mounted poorly behaved horses—standing at the neck, twisting back the stirrups, stepping in and swinging up and over. John Warren had always been a bit of a performer, and he'd often mount with a vault, that is, right up into the saddle without putting a foot in the stirrup—as he said that disturbed the saddle less than pulling it down from one side while mounting. Later in the day, I saw Max at it too. But John

Warren, he'd also do it from a run—or from behind, right over his horse's rear and into place. Sometimes he'd even vault right up over Pegasus' hind and stand there, up on the animal's hips—and maybe even urge Pegasus to take a few steps forward! I thought of all those fun and childish things that John Warren and I once did together (as I had learned some of those tricks as well). And then, when the good doctor, Max and I were all mounted, we tightened up the girth, and maybe adjusted the stirrup length a bit—and I was overcome by the physical memory of those acts. And though I rode out with Max and the doctor, I could not help but dwell upon former days. . . .

Just as we left the pastures, we saw some of the stable men longing stallions they were going to take out—in order that the animals wouldn't be overly energetic. And I remembered longing young horses with John Warren—leading the horse in a circle and lengthening the rope—either that or with one of us leading the horse and the other anchoring the line at the center of the circle. Regardless, the horse would get the knack of it soon enough. But, as I remembered, the trainer had to have the knack as well—that the circle wasn't so big he'd lose control of the animal, or so small that it strained the horse. John Warren would try to keep an even rhythm, not too fast or slow—and he'd always have that concentrated look on his face—with his lower cheeks sucked in. He had to know not to talk so much that his commands became indistinct—as well as to avoid scolding. Longing on two lines, one from the head and one from the hind, he had to keep the tension even. He also had to know restraint with the whip, and I remembered that he'd use a buggy whip, which was short enough to keep a good distance from a horse. And . . . he'd teach the horse to trot, to stop and to step over bars. Then he'd longe the horse from one circle to another—and then he'd free longe all about, then, without a line, just voice commands and the short whip. I watched John Warren longe a horse even before I had ridden one—and that was the way he made me comfortable with the pony he had chosen as my mount. And, soon after, he was longing with me on that pony. I remembered that it was a stumpy pony—

short with an enormous head! But she was gentle with children, inexperienced ones especially. And John Warren was a patient, cheerful and encouraging teacher—at least to me. And that was enough, for I did learn—as much from all his knowledge as from his giving spirit. I would follow behind Pegasus and John Warren on my chestnut pony, who was named Placid, and rightfully so—for her awkward appearance, she had not only a tranquil persona, but rather smooth paces. (As homely as she was in many ways, she had a rather appealing white star which reached down to just below her eyes.) For practice, John Warren would longe me on her—sometimes without hands, or without stirrups, or even without a saddle, to improve my balance and deepen my seat. . . .

Once, I had been run off with—I was riding a larger pony by then, a more handsome but also more excitable animal whom I had, evidently, excited. He bolted with me on his back and John Warren shouted out instructions, "Run in a circle—in a circle!" I knew that he meant that I should turn into an ever decreasing circle, but I was already trying, and as I couldn't get my pony to turn at all, John Warren cried out anew, "Up the hill—the hill!" And that I did manage to do, veering the beast up a hill until he tired and stopped. And then John Warren and I were both rather amused by it, and I . . .

I found myself rather distracted during my afternoon with Max Vicar and Doctor Esterbrook. Max rode a larger bay horse (who himself had the most adorable white snip right on the end of his nose) and I rode a little palomino, just for safety, as, having been run off with once, I had come to prefer to take an animal I had to urge more than hold. On the few little jumps that we did take, I just grabbed the mane, for though it was not elegant, I would rather it than tear at my horse's mouth. I knew I could do without grabbing the mane, but it was an unfamiliar horse to me, and I was an unfamiliar rider to it—and besides, I didn't see any judges around. Mister Cleveland used to say, "Don't you hurt my horses—better the mane than the mouth!" I also did my best not to thump down on my horse's back upon landing—as there were two higher jumps on the trail, both of hay bales. Each of the four times we came upon a jump, two going out and two coming back, Doctor Esterbrook chose to walk his gray around them. And when Max Vicar asked him why, the doctor just groaned. It was rather amusing! We were nearly returned to the stable when a squirrel scurried underfoot and my palomino jumped. Next I looked up, I was sitting in the wet grass and my horse was snuffing and blowing through his nose. With his childlike voice and big face, it was so much like laughter that I could hardly keep from laughing myself. He'd a kink in his tail and I wondered if it had been there before, for if so, I should surely have taken note of it, as it meant—"Take care, I'm frisky—it's playtime and I'm feeling rather fine." He was clearly guilty of that "joy to be alive" kind of outlook—and perhaps nothing more. As I sat up, I found myself startled but not hurt—and pleased to see I still had the reins in my hand. . . .

"I *was* paying attention!" I said, for I saw the look on the men's faces. But then, Max Vicar and Doctor Esterbrook were rather gallant about it, though I could see they were also amused—and even while they said it could've happened to any one of us, which I knew was the truth, I still would have preferred it wasn't me.

For not having ridden a horse in some years, I seemed to remember fairly well, even if my body had changed. I was also quite relieved that between Max and his Western habits, which considered sidesaddle riding quite absurd, and the changing trends among horsemen, I was permitted to pursue my tom-girl style of riding, as I knew nothing of riding sidesaddle. Throughout all my years of riding with John Warren, I had been wearing the pants and boots that he had grown out of—and to be perfectly direct, the thought of teaching me to ride sidesaddle was about as foreign to him as the idea of riding in a dress was to me. So, it was a good thing that Max Vicar and his stables were of a Western influence, for when he asked me if I could ride, it did not occur to me that my riding might be unlady-like. Doctor Esterbrook hardly took notice at all, and I was quite surprised that in such a few years, from before the conflict to after, attitudes could change so much. Perhaps the matter, after such a time as that, was impossible to view as anything but simply trivial, or even silly. . . .

Having returned the horses to the care of their handlers, we enjoyed tea in a pleasant stone tower above a curving brook. The servants brought salted cucumber sandwiches. And the tea, I don't know how they kept it so very hot! Max Vicar spoke rather seriously of his future, and I was impressed by his good sense and practicality. Doctor Esterbrook was impressed as well, and when, later that evening, he left me at my cottage, he commented that Max Vicar seemed an intelligent, devout and handsome man. And it was at that time Doctor Esterbrook presented me with a reading lamp that Max Vicar had given him to give to me—and he lit it for me and set it on the table by my rocking chair. Max had included a rather breathtakingly colorful bead lamp-mat—with a bead fringe. And I supposed that all Doctor Esterbrook said of Max Vicar was accurate—and that it had been a good day, in that I'd had a good night before. But I must say that I soon had my misgivings, as, though a good day began with a good night, so did a good night begin with a good day—and so on, and so on. . . . And my night was not good, for I dreamt that John Warren's horse had charged—and a man on foot had casually thrust a sword into the horse's shoulder, and that the man had then swung his blade at John Warren, who was struggling with his colt revolver, for the gun had been emptied. And then the horse reared—maybe even to protect his master—so the horse took the blade again, this time in the stomach. And then the horse charged back across the field, trampling at the man with the sword, and another man who had appeared—his rifle trained on my soldier's head. And so did Pegasus run. And when he came to that very last fence, it was as high a fence as he had ever jumped, and as was his fault, he jumped too early—and he did not clear it. And he went head down, hind up—flipping full over. And on the ground, he sighed with his horse's sigh that said, "I'm sorry, I'm not getting up again, and it hurts, it hurts so very much." And so did my soldier fire his colt revolver again—once, and once more, and once more. . . .

And then . . . did my soldier run. . . .

Field glasses

I met Missus Esterbrook at the Esterbrooks' house in the old town, which was now growing over into countryside. And shortly, Stella had us eating her hazelnut and pecan shortbread. By afternoon, we were on our way to Frickerham. We took the Esterbrooks' good carriage, which was quite comfortable, especially as the Esterbrooks had hired a driver. I scarcely needed help climbing up between the wheels into my seat—and I, ever so lightly, just touched the tip of my mittened hand to his gloved one. And whether it be the driver, the road or the Esterbrooks' fine carriage, there was nary a jolt all the journey. We spent the night at the Mule Muscle Inn, which was elegant indeed, and I began to feel rather spoiled. The next morning, we were up early, and after a light breakfast and some discussion about the fine qualities of Max Vicar, we were off again—but this time to complete our journey. We'd been invited to watch the first foxhunt of the fall, in which Max would be participating. I had not seen him in some weeks, as he'd been attending business in Washington—though I'd promised that we should see each other the very instant he returned. He was in fine health and spirits. Missus Esterbrook and I took our place in the gazebo atop the hill, where several spyglasses had been assembled. The glasses were hardly needed, however, as it was such a clear crisp day that one could see all the way to Virginia on the one side, and Ohio on the other. And the air was so sharp and crisp that I could easily believe that were my own name called out from either of those states, I would turn my head, perhaps to say, "Excuse me?"

But I must add that besides my eyes and those of Missus Esterbrook, I felt the sight of another—for the news in Cotterpin had been confirmed by word from New Orleans, my soldier was departed from us. I had not been to a foxhunt since I was no more than nine years old, and he was twelve. And though he had been in the back of the field, and it had been an off-season, and therefore less formal, hound's hunt, with fewer requirements of attire and such—he had ridden Pegasus with the courage, confidence and restraint of an experienced foxhunter. And Pegasus, he'd been such an excellent field hunter! For he could see the ground and the horizon both with equal clarity—and he could move freely with long, even strides, which seemed well nigh effortless—as if he could quickly and gracefully cover much ground without ever straining himself. Usually, a horse that foxhunted and jumped with some composure while in the company of other horses was not much for performing in the ring. One might have a quiet hack—a horse that foxhunted well enough and could show a little—or one might have a horse that could be shown and jumped but wasn't much good in the company of a foxhunt—whether leading or falling behind, or both. Most horses specialized, like people, and just couldn't be good at everything. Mister Cleveland would say that few fishermen could fish equally well out of both fresh water and sea. But once in a great while there was a horse that could do everything well—exceptionally well. Such was John Warren's horse, Pegasus, with his bold yet calm disposition. . . . Perhaps his stride, to an educated eye, was not completely perfect—but to any rider, the good flow of his paces was as much as any could ask. And over the time I was to see Pegasus perform with his rider, I would gradually come to accept that the two could handle next to anything—trick, turn, gait or speed. And for all of that, Pegasus seemed to like to do it—to do everything. He'd just give that "let's get to work" kind of roll and snort, and set about his pleasures. If there was any true fault to the animal, it was that Pegasus may have been, officially, more a pony than a horse. We'd always hear that Pegasus was fourteen hands three inches—but I'm not sure I believed it, and if he were any less than fourteen hands two inches, he would be classified a pony. Still, that was a big pony, and ponies matured faster and seemed to learn faster anyway, and were often better jumpers—and Pegasus was such a natural jumper that he'd sometimes bound three or four feet over a little one foot jump. Or sometimes he would jump almost the moment he saw a fence, and thus, far too early. But he would still sail over it with such immense ease that it was hard to think much of it. John Warren would eventually manage to control (more or less) when Pegasus would take off, but it would take some settling to give him an idea of how hard he had to work. It was just too easy for Pegasus, and he'd always spring way too high over little jumps—just like a deer, with his legs tucked neatly up behind him, and his head and neck extended. For foxhunting, I'd learn that Pegasus worked fine in the back of the field, but was really spectacular up front—showing the way with all his easy courage and flying leaps! Ordinarily calm for such a small horse, the foxhunt seemed to animate Pegasus as much as it did his rider. John Warren had always conducted himself well, I remembered, in the field. . . .

And as he watched from the eyes of the eagles above, in the breath of the trees, I could hear him saying—

"I loved you, and I loved this."

And I thought on what had happened to that boy, and that horse. . . .

A foxhunt always sent shivers up my spine—but the opening foxhunt of the season was an event of enormous pomp and fanfare, and I confess that the commotion succeeded in arousing my expectations. A number of the horses even had braided reins—indeed, there was a reporter from the *Lexington Daily*. And there were other surprises—for though I had hardly seen the likes of it before, and this was such a formal setting, there was one lady who was participating as a foxhunter. And just as Max had foretold, the world had changed, for there she was—riding astride. She was very fine looking in her black coat and tan-colored breeches, and on her black horse—with a white blaze on his nose. It was said that she had grown up in the West. Max on his great bay was also quite a sight—to see him riding on a horse with ears pinned back in the wind. It brought back many familiar impressions. . . .

The master of the hunt was also riding a dark bay, a cousin of Max's horse—one with a white star, stripe and a snip on his nose. That was the face of a fashionable mount! As the man was huge, so was his animal—probably seventeen hands high. Still, as imposing as he was, he was a rather gracious host. It had been up to him to decide upon the country—his reasoning founded on weather, foxes, and his field of hunters. This meet was in an area of mixed terrain, with good flats and grasses for thoroughbreds, and thicker country for horses of a stockier variety. Along with fields, there were hedges, ditches, rails and streams. It was up to the huntmaster to oversee everything—to make sure the sport was good, and that the damage was little. And for what damage there would be to the local farmers and landowners, it was up to him to compensate them from the club treasury. As the foxhunters arrived, they were all certain to greet him, tipping their hats and saying, "Good morning." The huntsman was another man afforded some respect, as he was in charge of the hounds. It was with his voice and his horn that he controlled his animals—and much of the action of the day. His two men were called the whippers-in—and they aided him in controlling the hounds with whips. The field master kept the field from getting too close to the hounds—and no one was permitted to pass him.

As excited as the foxhunters were the horses, for they also loved the thrill of hound-work. Even sluggish animals would come to life at a foxhunt—sometimes showing enthusiasm they'd seemed hardly to possess. Bold and keen—the animals were ready for their adventures. And there were no buffalo or sheep, these were neat looking horses—trimmed and polished. I had not seen such a collection of horses like that since Somerton Cleveland had his estate! The riders were also well dressed—and exactly dressed, wearing their tweeds, breeches and boots, all in their different colors that meant their different things. Max, like many of the more prestigious members of the foxhunt, was outfitted in gold buttons with grinning fox faces. It seemed that many of the foxhunters had the idea that the foxes liked the foxhunt—but I wasn't so sure of that. I was sure that the foxhunters liked it, though. I remember rather specifically the pride of the men in their black jackets and yellow vests. Puffed up just like rock doves. And all had their spurs and hunt-caps (John Warren's velvet hunt-cap, I thought, must've burned up). Scarlet jackets were for those of great importance—and those jackets, despite their color, were called "'pinks."

The horses and riders began by just walking around—the horses greeting and introducing themselves to the other horses, and the riders doing the same. Everyone had to be comfortable with one another. Throughout the day, there was an effort to keep the horses well spaced—not to have one animal on another's tail. (And it was rather significant to know that any horse wearing a red ribbon might kick.) Nevertheless, all of the mounts were trained well to take orders from their riders—rather than to rely on their own herd instincts. And though neat, not all were pretty, as it was ability, not looks, that mattered in a field hunter—for any crudeness, all were fit and ready animals. It made me think of Missus Caroline Ditzler's battle horse, who'd likely been a field hunter years before. And I remembered what Mister Cleveland had once said about it—that even if a horse wasn't much to look at, if he brought you home in the evening, he was better than any empty headed beauty. . . .

As a guest of the foxmaster, Max was invited to ride toward the front of the field. The hunt was to begin at noon—and down the road between a double row of hemlocks, and over a footbridge, and then back up the lane, the hounds arrived at the chosen spot to draw. The horses rode slowly until the hounds got up a fox. Searching for scents, their heads bobbed up—then down. It had been a moist night, and with all the dew, expectations were high, as any fox's scent would linger on grass, twig, bush or tree. The hounds thus cast, they rushed into the fox's covert. The huntsman asked for silence, and the hound Ginger was the first to challenge on finding the line—which is to say (in that funny foxhunting way of saying things!) that she was the first to speak (as, to a foxhunter, no hound would ever bark). On this occasion, the hounds caught the scent near a bush of honeysuckle—and then, the fox was flushed out, viewed away, and the foxhunt was on! The huntsman blew "gone away," meaning that the fox was racing off with the hounds in pursuit, and the field was quick to catch up. And as sudden as had been the start—so quickly did the foxhunters gallop. They'd quite a burst for a few minutes! All disappeared down a woods trail. It was a rough path, Max Vicar later told me—though the horses were galloping anyway—fearlessly and easily. There were cries of " 'Ware hound!" as one of the hounds had gotten left back, and the lead horses had to take care not to trample him as he came up behind them. And then there was a cry of " 'Ware hole," which passed all the way back the line. And then, as the horses and riders emerged from the wood, I could see that there was a jump almost right off—a fence at the end of a field. But as rapidly as they were moving, each foxhunter took care at the jump—being sure that he should be the next to go at the fence, and that he shouldn't cut anyone off who might be coming from another angle, and that he didn't take the fence at an angle himself, and thus risk collision with another rider. The foxhunting style of jumping was rather different back then than it is today—leaning back, stirrups long, legs pushed forward. And though that may seem an extraordinarily dangerous kind of approach today, the riders did their best to lessen the risk—slowing their horses before the jump, as well as after—for the other side of a fence might pose hidden dangers, whether they be ditches, soft ground or rocks. Moreover, it could well be a farmer's field on the other side—and this master in particular was doing his best not to do any more damage than was necessary. The foxhunters also took care not to collapse any fences, and to enact some repairs if they did. Gates had to be closed—and the cry, " 'Ware gate!" which was passed back to the last man—it was a courtesy taken seriously! A farmer who had lost his livestock could be rather unpleasant, and even dangerous, as relations between the foxhunters and farmers could often be . . . well . . . strained. There were fifteen hounds, which to a hunter was "seven and a half couple." And shortly, those hounds were settled to the line, and because they were close to the fox, the line was said to be hot—burning. And the hounds, they worked the line until they came to a stream, where it was said they "lost." And, after checking, the hounds "found." And the hound Mercy's stern soon feathering, she cried out. But, as I was informed, Mercy was known to fling her tongue (that is, would sometimes cry without reason). So, though she had already spoken, the huntsman waited for the other hounds to own to it—to confirm her find. The hunters were then off again—the hounds in full cry, the huntsman cheering them on. I've heard it called "hound music," and though it may have seemed a lot of babble to me—to the huntsman, perhaps it was music, as even the slightest difference in it reflected a change of inclination in the hounds, and thus, the fox. So did the huntsman soon discover that all were rioting, and not chasing a fox at all, but something else. Probably a deer, said Missus Esterbrook. The huntsman then lifted the hounds to another location, where they found again—though we in our gazebo lost sight of the action. The only riders we could see at all were the ones in the backfield who had lost the hunt entirely—they were out of the chase for at least an hour. As Max Vicar told it, upon sighting the fox, there were the screams of "Tally ho!" And then, silence, as the fox had already been sighted, and nobody wanted to confuse the hounds, who were precious close on their now reeling, staggering prey—this poor, wee creature crawling through the woods. The fox then reappeared on a sand bar, and finally went to ground along the bank of a stream. The hounds pushed through the pussy willows and went in to dig him out, as the huntsman had some new entry (hounds that had never been blooded) and he wanted them in on a kill. The fox turned out to have gotten into a hole, so the huntsman sent for his terrier—and when the terrier arrived, it went down the hole after that fox, who was shortly torn to pieces among some ferns—Max Vicar said the ferns too were shredded in the frenzy. Fortunately, I couldn't see anything from the gazebo. Still, everyone agreed that the animal was killed fairly (though it hardly seemed fair to me—all that after one little fox). Later in the afternoon, Max agreed with me that it was really too bad to kill the fox, and said that often they wouldn't kill a fox—though that this fox had been accounted for, it being the first hunt of the season and all. The foxhunters prized the fox's face, which was called a mask, as well as the tail, which was called a brush—as these made sporting trophies. I heard some of the men say that the farmers needed foxhunters (and shouldn't complain so) as foxhunters rid farmers of the foxes that ate their chickens. But I had once heard Mister Nielson himself say that it wasn't the case, as foxes were more likely to be eating mice than chickens—and even so, controlling the mice at the cost of an occasional chicken seemed, to many, a fair trade. A farmer just had to keep the chickens well protected—by dog and by coop. . . .

Afterward, Max Vicar thanked the master and said good night to him, though it was earlyish yet. Max told us that the foxhunt had been just the kind he liked—fast and exciting. And I did agree that it had been rather thrilling—all but the demise of the fox. Missus Esterbrook and I returned to the inn, where Max eventually joined us, after having worked with his horse and cleaned himself up. He joined Missus Esterbrook and me for a dinner at the inn. When the woman rider and her husband stepped into the dining room (he had also ridden that day) we invited them to seat themselves at our table, and they did. Like Max, they had also had an exhilarating day at the foxhunt, and were now enjoying their evening. Max arranged that we be served a roast of venison, as the foxhunters especially were hungry. I had a bite of venison, and though I enjoyed it, I could not eat too much of it, as the taste of it was rather gamey to me—and the more so the more I ate. I had told Max I enjoyed venison, however, and (in a lump of napkin, under the table) slipped a great hunk of it to Missus Esterbrook. I didn't know what she would do with it, but later that evening, she told me in confidence that along with her own, she had disposed of it with a quick toss out of the window behind her—what aplomb she had! The young couple lived near Lexington, and owned an instructor's school for riders. I do not remember their names. They seemed a rather direct couple. Max and the Mister shared a fondness for grouse hunting.

In the coming weeks, Max Vicar and I went riding many times—and then, for the second time, he proposed marriage to me. Mister Esterbrook was standing across the field, watering his horse at a stream, and Max Vicar was kneeling in the yellow grass. And I took the ring, just to hold it in my hand—although my throat was seized, and I could not speak. He told me that I should keep it for one week—just one week, he said. I did not reply, and he asked if then I could tell him no, that I would not marry him—and since I could not do that either, I agreed, in a scratchy whisper that caught in my throat—

"One week."

Over that week, I was visited by Mister and Missus Esterbrook, Mister and Missus Mayfield, Horatio Cooper and Joe Sharpless, Mister and Missus Nielson, Mister and Missus Valentine, William Ditzler and his wife, as well as Sam and Caroline Ditzler. Only Mister Nielson told me that my age was no matter, and that I should marry only if Max Vicar was a man who set my belly afire—although, even Pastor Miles agreed that—

"It might be time."

Max Vicar told me he would love me as long as birds flew. He said he would give me anything—that he would reach into his own ribs and pull out his heart, like a plum from a pie, if that was what I should want. . . .

And all that, I knew it was true.

We would be wed in spring. Max Vicar had to return to the West to prepare my arrival, to buy a house and to ready, as he said, "the entire state of California."

I was amazed at Max for riding so regularly on the railroad, as trains often wrecked. It was a dangerous way to live, I thought, but he assured me that he would come back as soon as the winter broke (early March or so) and he implored me to wear his ring, and I did, in company—though I could be a solitary girl. . . .

 The winter was not hard, as I had my garden journals and herbology to occupy me. I would have liked to exchange more correspondence with Max Vicar, but he did not seem much of a letter writing sort (I did receive

several cables, furthering our plans) and the few I did receive were rather practical. I returned practical letters to him, and felt rather comfortable in this, as I had always been rather practical. There were a few letters I wrote that were not of a practical nature, however, and those did not find their way to post. I was tempted instead to take them out to the collection of Cleveland gravestones on the hill behind the church—but, on the one hand, I thought that any heavenly spirit could read a letter meant for him, and, besides, in this earthly realm, maybe those rents in our country, and within my rib cage— maybe they were better forgotten. . . .

It was in March, just into that cheering sigh of spring, when Max Vicar returned. Missus Esterbrook was spending a great deal of time at the poorhouse, giving her assistance there, and around the whole area, in fact, collecting contributions. And so it was she who accompanied me to Frickerham, where Max and I were scheduled to reunite. From then until the wedding in San Francisco, it had been agreed that Missus Esterbrook would not leave my side. Doctor Esterbrook would be making the trip to San Francisco as well, and it was really quite amazing that what a few years before had been almost inaccessible terrain was now a path possible for an elderly couple who planned for themselves a spectacularly beautiful vacation— all since the railroad route had been completed in '69. Missus Esterbrook and I stayed the first night at an inn called the Mayflower, and when we woke in the morning, Max Vicar had arrived to breakfast with us in the parlor. He and I were rather frenetic at the sight of each other, and we were soon out into the town preparing for the wedding—or so we said—though I suspect now it was more folly, and desperation. To Max, such spending could hardly make a difference to his wealth, not one way or the other, but the spending of money was his answer, then, to love—and I am quite ashamed that his attitude was so infectious. We bounced around Frickerham like children in a candy store . . . or, perhaps, more like rubes from the country in a big city. And perhaps that's why I was so comfortable with it—because I really was no more than a girl from the country.

I was wearing my new cloak of the Italian brocade, and Max Vicar was exceedingly fond of it, but insisted it needed a fur collar. So the first stop we made was to the tannery. I was warned that the sights and smells of the tannery might prove . . . intense. But I did not want to stand outside, and besides, I wanted to choose my own piece of fur—so the three of us made our way into a rather large room. There, several women were scrubbing rabbit skins, while several others were softening them up, pulling them back and forth through a roller. The skins were then set on stretchers. In another area, women were cleaning new skins by rubbing them with moistened bran. A great vat of lime water was filled up with hat feathers, which were cleaned by that method. And it was true that though I had smelled something of the place outside the door, the odors were surprisingly strong. We purchased some ermine, though it made me feel a little sick. Max teased me about it some, for it would look good on that cloak—though I'd only wear that cloak one more day. . . .

Next, we stopped at the tailor's, where the ermine was fitted for my collar. It would be ready in several hours, they said, and Max Vicar gave me his coat to wear. He said he was warm enough in just his jacket, and as the day was not cold at all, but merely cool, even just invigorating, I believed him.

Next, we stopped at the wine-maker's, where we purchased some gooseberry wine for Mister Nielson, and some ginger wine for Doctor Esterbrook, and some fine grape wine for Missus Esterbrook, who shared in a glass with the storekeeper, as he had a bottle open. Max and I partook in the festivities, as Max ordered us each a glass of *Julianna's Effervescing Lemonade.*

At the cheese-maker's, we purchased three wheels of cheese, one for the Esterbrooks, one for the Valentines and one for the Mayfields. The Mayfields made their own cheese, but we bought them one for a special treat. And though we Vicars and we Flynts did not make our own cheese, I did not buy one for myself, as I was not overly fond of cheese, and besides, was sure to be adequately supplied by the Mayfields. And while we would not be selling my aunt's cottage until after the wedding (upon our return we would attend to such details) I was already thinking to clear out what I could. . . . I could see into the back room of the cheese shop, where there were long, rectangular tubs in which curd was gathered from the milk—and the walls were hung with dried and salted calf stomachs, which they called rennet. The smell there was also intense, but somehow clean as well, and not unpleasant.

Next stop was the shoemaker's, to pick up Max's riding boots, which had been blackened with a paste of ivory black and molasses. Also, some trim or other had been added, which bore some significance to his place in the foxhunt—though the niceties of foxhunting always left me a little befuddled.

Each breath at the perfumery was rich with the scent of flower and musk. For me, we purchased a charming crystal bottle filled with essence of narcissus. The smell of it was just magical, as fresh and true as of the flower itself! We also purchased some perfumed soap (almond, honey and orange flower) and some powder (pearl powder and a red rouge called "Bloom of Roses," neither of which would I ever wear once, though I kept them till they hardened). For Max, we purchased *Gouffe's Eau de Cologne*, and also a birthday present for the pastor, even if he'd never wear it. It was a precious little bottle of *Farina's Eau de Cologne*, which was much spoken of back then. . . .

While Max Vicar and I stepped into the pharmacy, to further accouter ourselves, Missus Esterbrook was a few doors down choosing herself some fabric. We were to meet her there shortly, as, in her own words, she left the pharmacy to her husband—"Just the sight of all that muck makes me queasy." The lawyer, Mister Pimpernickel, was there at the pharmacy, which was not so much of a surprise—firstly because he was a consistently sick man, and secondly because he spent much of his time in Frickerham (and even in Lexington). He greeted me more cordially than I thought he had it in him, and then, with a near demented glimmer in his eye, he asked if I was accompanied by Missus Esterbrook.

"Yes," he said, "I thought so. I did speak to her rather recently you know, and during our conversation, as short as it was, she told me of your engagement, and I believe, your meeting here today—ah, and, incidentally, I realized that I would be representing a client here around the same time—but, uh . . . Well, let me extend my congratulations, and my fondest wishes. And as for your employer, well, I believe he'll be sorry to lose you. . . . Ah yes, well, also convey my greetings to Missus Esterbrook—and do tell her that I looked into the matter of that Cleveland boy, and as I suspected, there was some basis to that rumor he was in New Orleans, and indeed, in Mexico as well, but none to substantiate that he'd been . . . uh . . . demised. . . . From my researches, he was last sighted in rather good order—though I'm afraid I have not much more to add. . . . Word is that he's somewhere afloat in the Caribbean—sugar cane, I believe I heard—hard work, you know. . . ."

And for a moment, as that grotesque man spoke of my angel, I felt that I would collapse—and if not that, I felt that I would run away. I had the feeling, for the first time in my life, that I knew what it felt like to be a 'coon treed by a tabby cat—in flight and in a corner all at once. . . .

There was something malicious to that man, I thought. Or was it—was it that he really was just glad to see me? And then, I could see that he was just glad to see me, and that there was nothing wrong with his heart, just—and I'm repentant as I admit it—just his smile, as I found everything about his body repulsive. I realized that Missus Esterbrook had probably wanted to find out for me if my soldier was truly dead, and that she would do that to me, and that Mister Pimpernickel would join her in it—going to all that trouble—I knew I should be touched. And yet, I couldn't help that I didn't feel that way. Shakily, and I believe, rather abruptly, I told the lawyer that I would deliver the message—and then I was overcome by a kind of a mania. After Mister Pimpernickel took his leave, I was just brimming over with . . . not happiness, but cheerfulness—and as Max Vicar became himself all caught up in it, I shortly forgot all about the news of my soldier. . . .

The pharmacist was sugar coating pills with a low flame, sugar and a porcelain pan, when Max and I climbed onto the two stools at his soda counter. Max asked if I had ever seen so many flavors for soda water. I had, I told him, but I had not tried them all. Nor had he, he reflected—and so we set about to drinking it until we were nearly bursting, both with soda and with laughter. The elephant spout of the soda fountain was quite remarkable, we decided. We tried lemon, ginger, wild cherry and so many other flavors (my favorite was something called a sassafras flip). All were topped off by a frothy head engineered by the druggist. And we were soon so full that we were both quite relieved a lavatory was available to us—it was indoors. All around us, as we sat at the soda counter that day, there were all kinds of the old scientific devices and curatives. There were hundreds and hundreds of shelves—stacked to the ceiling with *Moore's Fluid Extract of Vanilla*, *Stewart's Simple Syrup of Rhubarb*, *Goddard's Aromatic Blackberry Syrup*, and *Wine of Wild Cherry Bark*. Sometimes the packaging was simple, like *German Foot Rot Ointment*, or *Cooley's Corn Plaster*, and sometimes it was quite colorful and elaborate, like *Dr. Thompson's Bitters*, and his *"Number Six."* Perhaps *Parrish's Aloes and Mandrake Pills* were leaning against *Griffin's Tincture for Coughs*. Perhaps dusty packages of *Devil Plaster* were stacked high, and *Mrs. Wheeler's Nursing Syrup* was almost falling off the shelf. I remember there were pills, *White's Gout Pills*, *Becquere's Gout Pills*, *William's Gout Pills* and many others, though I knew that for there to be so many of them, and for so many people to come to me for help with their gout, none of them could work very properly. *Bailey's Itch Ointment* was only one of about a million and eleven itch remedies. Up on the counter, there were honey drops and balsams of all kinds. There were sweets and *Nora's Pastils*, of every variety. There was *Angelot's Pastils for Bad Breath*, and incense—and under the glass, *Spackman's Worm Syrup*, *Pieste's Toothache Essence*, *Grosvenor's Toothpowder*, *Mexican Tooth Wash* and more cures for baldness than I could count, which made me think that, like the gout and itch remedies, they were perhaps not so very effective. *The New French Remedy for Baldness* was an elaborate package indeed, green with yellow vines, and *Pomade Contre L'alopécie*, it was also very elegant—black with tall, silvery letters. The pomades were in a shelf behind the counter—*Dupuytren's Pomade*, *Soubeiran's Pomade*, *Wild Rose Curling Fluid*, and *Hungarian Pomade for the Mustache*. *Erasmus Wilson's Hair Wash*, *Morfit's Hair Tonic*—there were dozens of shampoos, and I believe we did buy one or another. That summed up our faith in the science of Frickerham. . . .

And . . . for all those things, I suddenly realized that there was nothing to cure me. I'd graduated from complacent to compliant to complicit. And I suddenly discovered that I'd smiled until my smile was gone. It was a moment that came all at once, when my smile was used up—for as for John Warren, perhaps that had been a childish matter that I had taken too seriously, but, as for Max Vicar, I knew that it was a serious matter, which I had not taken nearly seriously enough. And there came then a silence and utter stillness, of Max not laughing and smiling, and myself not laughing and smiling. I heard a whifflet out in the street—and that whelping cur was about the only sound there was. I'd seen the dogs about that town, and they were a strange lot—all mottled black and pink, and without any fur at all, except for an orange tuft between their ears. I'd heard that the Chinese had brought the dog when they came with the railroad, and that, as it was not a big dog and could feed itself (and not get eaten itself!) there were still a few of them about town. That dog's crying was a lonely crying—the crying of a dog fed out of the back of the saloon—the crying of a dog who ate while being splashed with boiling water, all for the entertainment of the clientele. And I knew that it was a fitting kind of cry, as I was sitting there, I'm sure as pale as could be, with no more humor on my face—just naked fear. A fear to hurt another, a fear to be alone, a fear of having done wrong. . . .

And Max? He had stood and backed away, as it is quite amazing how people just know sometimes. As Dahlia would say it— "Sometimes a person just knows when the jig is up." And it was that way then. The jig was up—

Max Vicar asked, "Do you love me?"

And I looked up, and from his sugar coated pills, the pharmacist looked up—and then I whispered, "No, but . . . maybe I can learn."

Max Vicar took a step back, holding his chest and staggering some, as if he'd been struck by an arrow. Then he cleared his throat and screwed up his eyes, looking at me rather directly—

"I'm sorry then, Alma, I can't marry you."

"Why?" I asked, feeling my own lip quaking.

But when he didn't answer, and just stood with his feet steady and his eyes watering, I answered myself—

"I'm sorry," I said, "I know why."

A few minutes passed, with no sound other than the nervous scraping of the pharmacist. He pushed his pills around the pan, that they shouldn't stick—and he shook them occasionally. . . .

"Oh," said Max, "please do pick up the cloak, and as far as anything else, I'll take care of it."

I had begun crying then, and with the tears streaming down my face, I could hardly think of doing anything, or of taking the long carriage ride home without a cloak—

"Or, no—I'll—I'll need that cloak," and I said it, maybe a little hysterically, and just as I was thinking that I had been such a fool, and such a cruel fool—that I'd been a cruel thing, just like some cat with a woodchuck—

"Or, or, maybe I don't deserve it . . ."

"Oh Alma, it's no more you than me, it's just, well, us children brought up poor, we have to learn what the rich already know. . . ."

Max turned his hat in his hands—feeling around the hat rim. He said—

"One can't buy everything."

"No," I said, my sleeves at my eyes—and then I was fumbling in my pockets, for I had a kerchief—and then I let it be, for it had been given to me by Max Vicar. So I just sat there with my hands folded in my lap, and my eyes streaming. . . .

"No," he affirmed, this time more solemnly, shaking his head and turning to go, "I suppose not."

I had not seen him limp since he was just a tool boy, but as he moved, I saw him limp then, and it made my body ache, and my tears pool as they rolled from my chin and dropped into a crease in my green dress. The material was a thick cotton. . . .

"Oh—" he said, turning back, as Max Vicar was always a gentleman, "would you like to keep my coat, for now?" He had started to put it on, but was already taking it off again.

"No," I said, "I'll be fine—really, it's no colder for me than it is for you."

And then Max looked at me concentratedly, and thoughtfully, and he tipped his head to the side, pulled on his coat and hat and said—

"Well, whatever you say, Alma."

Missus Esterbrook was coming in as Max was going out, and I averted my weepy eyes, as did the pharmacist, who was a bit teary himself. "What happened, dear?" she kept asking, "What happened?" But I couldn't really talk about it, and just cried all the way back to Cotterpin. In fact, I couldn't have talked even if I wanted to. It was just endless, the crying. It was as if there were years of it, a hundred years of it—as if I were crying for myself, my aunt, my mother, my father— and everyone who had tears to shed that had not been shed. . . . Missus Esterbrook cried too, "I'm sorry dear, I don't know for what, but I am sorry—and look at me, crying like a young girl myself." Missus Esterbrook returned the engagement ring—I don't know how she went about it. Max asked her that I keep it, but I would not. I really did want to return every last thing that he had given me, but he had made a point of saying to Missus Esterbrook that whatever it might be, I should keep it, or throw it away, as it would be cruel for me to even attempt to return it. And Missus Esterbrook conveyed his idea to me, and I sorrowfully acknowledged that he was right. I'd already taken it, after all. And all those things, I could hardly bear to use them, hide them, sell them or even throw them away—for all the shame I had about them, and the waste they were. So they just sat there, like a penance of sorts, like objects made of the guilt that I felt inside me— that I should have to look at it outside me. And that guilt, at times I could hardly separate it from my own worry and fear (would I be alone?) and what I sometimes thought was regret. Max Vicar was an intelligent man, and a devout one, and a handsome one. . . .

Horatio Cooper's store was fuller of more things than one could ever imagine. . . .

Even just a few years ago, *any* merchandise was so scarce, but now . . . the bolts of fine fabric. The fine and shining tools for farming. The buckets of every imaginable nail, and every imaginable candy. The sacks of salt. The sacks of sugar. And—

I was there at the Store for Everything, buying sewing needles, when Horatio Cooper suggested I buy a new dress.

"Excuse me?" I asked, my eyebrows perhaps lifting—

"A store-bought dress?"

He explained that he had ordered it by accident, and that he just wanted to cover some of the cost, seeing as it wasn't for me, originally. Then he named a very small sum.

"Is that all?" I asked.

"Well," he said, "I could charge you more for it."

"Ah," I said.

He pointed to the dress, which was hanging in the light by the window. It was a blue afternoon dress. It had sloping shoulders and seams at the waist that made a triangular torso. The crinoline hoops were rather wide. It was a fashionable dress, he said, and I agreed that it was. It was a wool and silk blend.

"Go ahead," he said, "take it for barter. I can't sell it next season anyway."

"Barter?"

"Yes, barter," he joked, coughing. "I'll try to get sick."

I felt at first that I shouldn't take it. But then I did—for I did not want to hurt Mister Cooper's feelings, and I'd suddenly had the idea that he had ordered the dress for me. And as barter was not uncommon in those days, and in fact, Mister Cooper conducted almost all of his business in barter, I thought that was not so extraordinary, and it would be ever so nice to have a new dress—and this was not a gift from Max Vicar, but from an old man who did not want a young girl to feel . . . disquieted. And though it maybe did hurt me, I smiled, as I liked the dress, and . . .

All through the summertime, it had been a pleasant walk from my aunt's cottage to the town by the railroad tracks. It sometimes took an hour—it sometimes took an hour and a half, depending on the speed and length of one's gait. As autumn had come on Kentucky, the walk was a more burdensome and chilly one, and then with winter, it would not be pleasant at all, unless one were in a rather peculiar mood. But it was not yet winter, and though Kentucky was well into autumn, there was still the memory of the summer, and I was not yet ready to let it go, as I had purchased my new dress only several weekends ago. . . .

So I made the slow walk to town. I always forgot the prettiness of the turning leaves—as it was not something I remembered to antici-pate. So all those colors—those reds, golds, yellows, oranges and greens, were blessings I was surprised and grateful to receive.

At the post office, I had received a letter.

The stamp on the envelope was from San Francisco. The writing on the card was of a fine and even hand—

Mister Grover Vicar

Mister and Missus Nathan Hall

announce the marriage of their children

Max David

and

Emarine Ann

on a joyous Saturday, the sixth of July

Eighteen hundred and seventy-one

at

The Wiston Street Church

San Francisco, California

I folded the thing into the palm of my hand, clenched it, and turned into a stony lane to cross the railroad tracks. I heard children crying out with youth and good humor—and then there was silence (perhaps they were whispering) and a voice called from the alley between the telegraph office and Mister Cooper's lumberyard—

"Thou shalt not suffer a witch to live."

At first I halted, and I felt almost as if my soul had fallen right out of the bottom of me—right from my stomach to my feet, and then out into the gravel and dirt of the ground. And then I recognized the voice—it was a child's voice. . . .

I turned, lifting my dress and giving chase down the alley—I saw four children running, all young—but the very youngest, the speaker, was unable to clear the wood fence into Mister Cooper's lumberyard.

One of the children who was running off behind the fence called out—

"Old maid."

And there was laughing, because poor little Trumble had been caught by her—by me.

"Trumble! Trumble Ditzler, you turn around."

I felt the salty tears running down my face, just as if they'd returned from that carriage ride back from Frickerham, and when Trumble, a middle Ditzler boy, turned around to see me crying, he began crying too.

"Trumble," I asked, "what did you call me?"

"I'm sorry," he said, "ma'am."

And there was no more laughing or children's laughter—though I'm sure those other children were watching from somewhere nearabouts.

I tried not to sound angry. "Trumble, do you know what a witch is?"

"Yes ma'am. I didn't want to say it ma'am, they told me to say it, and I'm the littlest . . . and . . . and . . ."

He began crying afresh, wiping his eyes with the sleeves of his little blue jacket—with its sheep lining and collar.

"Do you know that your older brother came to me in that jacket when he had the dengue fever—that your mother brought him to me?"

"No ma'am. I . . . I . . ."

"Trumble," I said, "you know I've seen you push your peas around your plate as if that made it look like you ate more?"

"Yes ma'am," he said.

"Would you and your friends like to ask Pastor Miles what a witch is?"

And I said that loud enough for the other children to hear, because it was not easy to anger Pastor Miles, but it was possible—and this was the kind of thing that might do it—and, as a child especially, to have Pastor Miles's wrath descend upon you was to have the entire community punish you—for as long as Pastor Miles might demand it. He might say, "Well, those children . . ." And until he said they'd been God-fearing as of late, and they'd atoned for their misbehavior, they were as good as closed off to the better things in life. . . .

So Trumble didn't say anything.

"You know I'm no witch, don't you?"

"Yes ma'am," he said, "I know you're no witch ma'am, for a witch can't go over no bridge that passes over water, and you live by a creek with a bridge, and you cross it well nigh every hour . . . and . . ."

"I pray to the same God as you."

"Yes ma'am. I know ma'am."

"Do you think you'd like to ask the pastor?"

He was looking down. "No ma'am. I don't need to ask him, neither, ma'am."

"Who are your friends?"

"It was—"

"No, don't tell me, Trumble."

"Yes ma'am."

"I'm not that much older than you," I said.

And then, Trumble looked down silently—and I felt all the others, wherever they were, looking down, silently, because I was. . . .

Time can pass. . . .

Time can pass like cold honey from a spoon.

It can pass like a day before a day awaited.

It can pass like bad days after good.

It can pass with success, and fine things to fill the days—but no things may fill the night. Perhaps that's what it is to be grown. It is to look at a toy—whether it be a book or poems or a picture in a frame—and to feel no inner joy that might distract one from all the aloneness. No marionette makes company.

So time can pass.

Eyes can grow big. Eyes can narrow. All in darkness. Voices we know may whisper to us in sleep. Perhaps we do not recognize them, but we feel them as we feel a held hand. Or we may feel what it is to feel a hand dropped.

Thus, time passes.

And I mean not to paint a sad picture, for I was not sad. My days were filled and bright. My friends were many. Yet still, there were days I wished for night—*night, night*. As if it might bring more than just colder air, and a bluer world.

And thus, did two years go by. . . .

And I might stand at a window, or sit on the back porch of the big white house, and watch the passenger pigeons roll their way under the clouds—and I would think how scripture says life is but a shadow. And so life and the people in it sometimes seemed to me—mere shadows. And not shadows of towers or great monuments, but shadows of flying birds. And thus the birds would fly away, leaving neither bird nor shadow.

Summer '73

*I*t was a late night in May when I heard a horse and carriage cross the bridge with the heart shaped rails. The wooden planks rattled under the hard wheels. The hooves of the horse made a clopping sound which echoed on the water of the creek.

I lit the lamp.

Then I stood transfixed, and I listened, and I looked through the glass bowl—the salt in the kerosene, which was there to keep the kerosene from exploding. And I looked at the yellow and pink strips of flannel in the salt, which were there to be bright. The yellow flame burned, and the glass chimney of the lamp reflected it. And I listened, and the hard wheels rolled off the bridge and onto the hard packed soil. . . .

I had my aunt's pistol in the big house, and I took it, and loaded it. I hated it, but I kept it, as my aunt had kept it before me, for occasions just such as this. My aunt had carried that five-shooter all the way back from the West—back from her years in Kansas. And for seventeen years, she had kept it without the occasion to use it. But, like her, I would use it if I had to. And I wasn't ashamed anymore of living in the big house—as, at twenty-one, I was deemed by many an old woman, and that was quite enough for me to be who I was—to be good and gentle and pure, and to let those who liked me like me, and let those who didn't not. But still, I felt the threat, and when I pulled back the purple curtain at the window, I saw the riders in the carriage, and was much relieved to pack the gun back in its case before I went to the door. . . .

Mister Pimpernickel was at the reins of the horse. Another man was riding beside him. He was a young man wearing soft city clothing, which was wrinkled. His body was so trim, and his skin so smooth and white, and his hair was cut so just-so, that I could not remember having ever seen a man anything like him. On his feet, he wore a pair of black leather slippers.

Their horse was not riding fast. But it was not riding slow either. When it neared, I closed the curtain and went to the door. The lawyer was tying up the horse. The young man was tugging a wooden crate out of the back of the cart. He lost his footing and fell in the mud. Then he stood up and took off his very impractical jacket. I was standing on the front porch, and called down to him—

"You should tie it around your waist."

The young man did so. But he still had trouble getting any traction in the mud—because of his impractical slippers.

I called out, "Why are you wearing slippers?"

The man called back, "These are not slippers. These shoes are sold in the finest store on Broadway."

"Yes," I said, "they very well may be. But they are very impractical for the country."

"Yes," said the young man, "I know. I know they are impractical for the country—but these are the only shoes I have."

In fact, the young man did look like he was wearing the only clothing he had. It looked like expensive clothing, like the kind of clothing one would wear in a big city building, or the kind of clothing one would wear to have tea with a general, or even a president. It must've been machine made cloth. But that young man and his machine made cloth suit had come so far, and he was so wearied and footsore, that he looked like he just didn't care about his clothing anymore. It was as if he had just walked out of his office one day for lunch time, and he had never gone back. . . .

I called to Mister Pimpernickel, who had tied up his horse, "Why are you here? It is too late for me to prepare a remedy. Is this young man sick? If he is, it is because he is not wearing shoes, but slippers—"

The lawyer interrupted me. "Alma—"

But then the young man interrupted the lawyer. "Alma? Is that you?"

"Yes," I said. "Now why are you here? It doesn't appear entirely proper."

"No," sighed the young man, "I can see that, and I apologize. But this is my house."

"It's your house?" I asked. "I thought you were old."

"I'm not so old," he said.

"Well, it may be yours," I said. . . .

But I had picked out the curtains. I had picked out the fabric for the sofa. I had lit the candles. I had polished the wood. I had even hammered the knocker onto the front door. I had worked on the house for so long that I had almost forgotten it belonged to someone else.

My lip began to quiver. "Is that true, Mister Pimpernickel? Is it true?"

"Yes," said Mister Pimpernickel, "it is."

"But he hasn't lived here for seven years," I said. "Is it really still his? Maybe there's some law. Maybe I can keep it. It isn't fair! It can't be right!"

"I'm afraid, Alma," said Mister Pimpernickel, "there is nothing like that, nor should there be. You have been the caretaker of this property, and the owner is now assuming residence. Besides, Alma, you have your own house."

But at that particular moment, I did not like the looks of my puny, rotten cottage across the creek—

"You built it too close to my house anyway," I said, and I ran into the new house—then back to the front door, dragging a train of men's boots by their laces. I cried out—

"And you haven't had anything to do with this property for seven years. In this whole house, this is all that's yours. Twenty-eight size 10 boots for the right foot!"

I was throwing boots off the front porch as the young man pried open his crate. As soon as he opened it up, he dumped the contents out into the mud.

They were twenty-eight size 10 boots for the left foot.

"It's true, Alma," the young man said to me, "I don't know very much about boots. But I know a little. I know that you can never have too many boots. I know that because that's what you told me seven years ago."

Then I recognized that young man. . . .

"I am the soldier," he said to me, "who you met in this field, by that big rock, a long, long time ago."

His voice was quaking—

"I am John Warren."

Cricket

I emptied out my closet, gathered up my cat and dragged everything back across the creek in a wheelbarrow.

No, I yelled back to the two men, I didn't want any help.

The old house was stuffy, so I opened all the windows.

The old house was dusty, so I went outside and shook out the carpets and bedding.

I found the old feather duster, and dusted.

I found the old broom, and swept.

I found an old cinnamon candle that my aunt had made, and I burned it.

Then I called Socrates, and we went to bed in my old bed.

There was a storm during the night. I heard thunder in the sky. I saw lightning flash in the windows. I heard rain patter on the roof.

There were more leaks in the old house than there used to be.

✳ ✳ ✳

Through the night, I got to considering, and by morning, I'd become more lucid in my thinking. I'd developed a picture in my head of that boy's life, that soldier's life, John Warren's life—

He'd gone from a privileged child with an incidental gift for numbers to an accountant in some giant city. He'd gone from being a star in the country sky to a cloud of city dust—and it must have felt like that, in some stingy office in New York City. That's how I imagined it—a stingy prison of an office with a million ledgers and maybe no window at all. And with his salary, he had not enjoyed himself with leisure, but rather, he had lived as frugally and ascetically as possible. Maybe it was in another stingy room, one in a boarding house, whence he dreamt of returning home. Maybe it was from there that he invested cautiously, and sent every penny he earned back to Cotterpin to build the house by the big rock. . . . And I would later learn that I was not far off—that it was a stingy office, though it did have a window and was slightly bigger than I imagined. But what I had not imagined was that he worked a second job—his employer, John McGurk, besides employing him as an accountant, made John Warren a bookkeeper in his evening establishment, Suicide Hall. (And that was an office that did not have a window.) And when Mister McGurk had his dealings at the horse market, he would sometimes rent a room for John Warren at the Bull's Head Hotel, that he might work and be on advisory call all at once. John Warren sometimes worked sixteen hours a day, and, sometimes, for days on end in the employ of Mister McGurk. And John Warren would be grateful to that man for his entire life. It was as a bookkeeper that Caroline Cleveland had won Mister McGurk's trust years before, and when Mister McGurk had first hired John Warren, it was discreetly, and sight unseen. And as for John Warren's life outside the office, I had been too generous when I imagined his sleeping quarters. In order to conserve his savings, John Warren did not live, but merely subsisted through his years, sleeping in a bunkhouse with many other men, who were likewise sending their money to far away places—though, among them, there were also several no-accounts and transients. Additionally, John Warren had borrowed much of the balance necessary to build the big house, and therefore, he was not sending his pay home, but bearing the burden of a larger debt. To think that an outdoor boy like John Warren had endured a young life behind a small desk in a small office, performing numerical operations that must have seemed to his free spirit and his curious mind an excruciatingly small occupation—that was a melancholy vision! It was even sadder to think that, maybe, he'd passed those seven years thinking about his lost family, and the lost life they'd once lived.

So, while I perhaps was not yet apprised of the particulars, it was through my own sense of intuition and application of simple deductions that I grew to envision John Warren's years of poverty and exile—perhaps he would stand on the roadside, watching wealthy people pass in their fine carriages. . . .

And, of his crumpled clothing, I had suspected correctly—he had indeed left his employ quite suddenly. On his way to his office one morning, he'd decided to settle his affairs and depart—realizing that if he did not leave right then, he would never leave. His employer was fair and understanding, as John Warren Cleveland had been a steady worker for seven years. . . .

And it was as I was thinking about the trials of John Warren's life that I began to think about my aunt. Lying in my bed, looking up at the ceiling, I thought how odd it was that not a one of the cracked planks had seemed to change—while it had been several years since my aunt had passed.

Then I realized it had been to that very day—and perhaps even to the hour, or the minute—it had been four years before that my aunt had left this life. The first year that followed her death had been very hard—filled with instances of such loneliness that it felt as though there were a blank that time could not fill. But the years since had been much more serene. I remembered that first year—to the day my aunt had passed from this world of trouble—it had also been raining.

But it had been a heavy rain, accompanied by a heavy wind—so much so that for a number of days our community was storm-stayed. The rain this year, however, the rain this night, was much more tranquil than that—and so seemed the emotions brought on by the memory of my aunt's death. I hoped that she was in a better place—a place that no one would ever want to return from—but still, the loss of her remained acutely vivid to me.

I did not know all of my aunt's life, but I knew that she had suffered greatly in Kansas, years before, when she had lost her husband. She had never remarried, and I assumed it was not just because of me, but because she had loved the man greatly. And yet I knew that I could not view that as an affliction, as my aunt would certainly say that, years ago, she had loved the man so completely that this part of her life had been fulfilled. My aunt could bear no ill against anyone, and she had quietly given herself over to caring for me, her brother's daughter—though she had not, at the time of his death, communicated with her brother for more than two years. They were not at odds, they were just quite different, and they had forgotten the civilities—they had simply grown apart. Yet she had taken on my upbringing, and my safety, during a time that she must have known would be enormously difficult. She had hidden me away in a house in the woods, so that I might grow without breathing the undiluted poison—the hatred that overtook us all. . . .

And hardly a word had ever been spoken of her husband, or the circumstances of his death, and until then, I was aware of her loss by only the conversational slips of friends and acquaintances. And, in the twilight of John Warren's return, as I stared up at the ceiling, I wished she were there to tell me about the man—her man.

Had he been a spelling champion? Did he like his apple pie with ice cream or melted cheese? Did he prefer a huckleberry to a blueberry? Did he ever lie on his stomach by the edge of a creek, to watch the long legs of the scoot-bugs skate across the water?

I knew that if I had asked my aunt about him, she would merely have sighed and told me all there was to tell. She could never hold anything back that might be to my betterment to hear spoken of. But what more—what more could she have told me? She could have told me to love, if I loved. She could have told me that no sadness or pain should keep one from love—no sadness or pain had kept her from me. She could have told me that in every storm, in every hurricane, each drop of rain was a fallen tear. Tears had filled the oceans, tears had filled the skies. And it was tears that filled the lakes and streams—and tears that filled our own bodies, every moment we were alive. . . .

Of all the many things my aunt had taught me—the profession she had given me, the honesty and forbearance she expected from every relationship—I thought at that particular moment, what was most important was that I should embrace the storms and hurricanes which changed the face of landscape—for what would come would be no less beautiful than what had gone.

And outside, the rain splashing on the ground—it was weeping. And inside, the rain, dripping in the house—it was weeping. And the whole wide world, and my own little world—all wept my aunt's tears of forgiveness.

And I heard every drop, every splash was a second, or an instant—or every pause or half breath taken between John Warren's departure and his return. And there were a million and one of those halved and halved again moments between the night and the morning—between the time that I had departed from John Warren, and the time I might return.

And the swirling wind, I heard that too. And it was gently saying to the land, as it had since the very first rain—*forgive, forgive, forgive me.*

And . . . since I am now occupied by the passage of time, and I am nearing the end of my story, I will pause to tell of the people of Cotterpin. I could not leave these pages without mention of their lives, and how they progressed. Of course, it is here that you will begin to recognize these as the people in my life—and moreover, you will also recognize where you entered this world. I must say that I have not filled a composition book in nearly fifty years, and I feel rather silly, at my age, doing so. Yet all of this is for you, my daughters, and you, my granddaughters. You have asked me of my youth many times, and I so much have enjoyed the telling of it. The idea that I write it down was ever so flattering, and as all things change, and what's passed fades with time, I was inspired to do so. Some of you have come up in places more country—and some, more city. But that matters not. And the picture of little ones gathered around me—curious to hear about a time in their nation both simple and turbulent—that is one I am warmed to think will continue for many years and childhoods yet. But I fear there will come a day when their curiosities wane, or my voice grows faint. So—I am as much guilty of recording these hard years as an act of vanity as I am loath to withhold a history from the dear children who are born to it. Nevertheless, I could not cheat any mind from its birthright—and certainly not through sheer sloth or false modesty. Thus, I have embarked, and am nearly accomplished in my task.

Pastor Miles was much beloved in our part of the world. He had married and comforted and extended a helping hand to everybody a person could think of. He died at sixty-four. He had been fixing the furnace in his parlor, when he was taken with a fainting spell. His headache and spells progressed, and he died several days later. There were nearly two hundred people at his funeral, which was a great many, on short notice, in the wintertime. That was almost twenty-five years ago. William Ditzler and Fanny Ditzler passed away some years later. They were a loving couple, and are remembered fondly by their many children. Their eldest son, Flynn, married Guenevere Stamp, and they and their grown children are still living in Cotterpin. Flynn owns the Equestrian Supply Store, and was recently elected to his second term as Cotterpin's mayor. Sam Ditzler and my teacher, Caroline Cleveland, were dedicated friends and business partners for all of their marriage. Theirs is a beautiful family. We were sorry to see them pass—Caroline in 1904—Sam in 1906. Stewart Valentine and Cassie Valentine moved to Frickerham, where they opened a paper mill. Stewart lived a long life, and passed away only a few years ago. Nora Mae and Harmon Valentine moved to Atlanta, where Harmon, surprising everyone, took up educating himself with great vigor. He taught mathematics at university for many years. He and Nora had five sons. Twenty years ago, with the passing of Nora's mother, Willa Mayfield (her husband Frank had died sixteen years before of bad circulation), Harmon and Nora returned to her old house down the creek. Sadly, like his father-in-law, Harmon also died at fifty-eight, of pneumonia. In recent years, Nora Mae and I have resumed something of our girlhood friendship. . . .

I might also say that Pegasus' brother was returned to the Cleveland estate after ten years of absence. He'd grown into a fine animal, and he sired many fine horses. Several other horses from Somerton Cleveland's former estate were also recovered. Caroline Cleveland's battle horse lived for another eleven years after his arrival. Mister Nielson died in '83, while mixing mortar. He was at least ninety-five years old. He joined his wife in the graveyard behind the chapel. She had lain alone for nine years. Hetty Esterbrook died in the autumn of '76. She asked her husband, Doctor Esterbrook, for a last hug, and then she quietly passed from this life. He died four days later. Their nurse Stella was remembered with an annuity, and she moved on to live with her grandson in Virginia. He was a reverend, and had gone to a good deal of trouble finding her. I might also say that Horatio Cooper died, but let me say instead he made a great fortune for his family, and left behind many good works in the lives of the people around him. Mister Pimpernickel died in the summer of '74, while trying to fix a wagon wheel. He was only thirty-six years old. I had thought he was much closer to fifty. Joe Sharpless, the postmaster, also died that summer—but of old age, in his bed. He passed peacefully one night, as had my aunt. He was looked for when he did not report for work in the morning. He had never been late or absent that anyone could remember. As for the other schoolchildren—most are alive and well, and still living in Cotterpin. It is interesting to note that Pitney Zooks and Loren Mayfield, Nora's brother, opened a studio for still pictures and have been quite successful at it. (Dahlia and Pitney are both with us still.) And—as for

Max Vicar, I have not heard of him, nor his father, nor his wife again. I have already mentioned the history of Tucker Boyd and his family, and there is little to add—except perhaps to say that his sons both married and were blessed with good women and good children.

The only other soul I have to account for is my cat Socrates. He too led a good life, and at one time disappeared for a two year adventure, and then reappeared. It is peculiar how when one matures, vast amounts of time can sometimes be contained in the time it takes to close and open one's eye, or even just turn one's head. So clearly do I remember lying in bed with my cat Socrates, looking up at the cracks in the wooden planks of the ceiling, that it could have happened only a moment ago. . . .

Back on that night, in the May of '73, I listened to the light rain patter on the roof. Socrates lay beside me—curled up on his side. He lifted his head to look at me, and I stroked his head with my hand, as I thought about the boy John Warren, my Aunt Bettina, and the future, and the past—and I thought about tornadoes, hurricanes, storms and just misty rains—and I thought about flower petals, and snail shells—and I thought about rainbows, and the ripples in a pond.

Perhaps no shape in nature was more common than that, spheres, circles, spirals—a shape unto itself, a shape forgiven. Sabers did not sprout from hillsides—bricks did not shine in the night, or rise in the morning sky. . . .

Who would I be to say a boy could not return in a man—and a man could not return home?

Sunflower

When I woke in the morning, the sky was clear. There was dew on the flowers.

I stacked wood in the old stove.

I brewed tea in the old kettle.

I heated up oatmeal in the old pot, and added berries from the old garden.

I ate at the old table.

Then I heard a knock at the door.

It was the young soldier. He was still young, but not so young as he used to be. And I was not a little girl anymore.

I answered the door rather angrily. "What do you want?"

But then the soldier looked so silly in his thin city shoes that looked just like slippers, that I began to laugh.

He was holding his boots in his hand. "Do you think I should wear them today?"

"Yes," I said, "today is a good day to start."

"I think I need some clothing too."

"Yes," I said, "that would be a good idea."

He began to put on his boots.

"Well, Miss Flynt," the soldier cleared his throat—"you did such a practical and tasteful job with the boots, and the house, that I was hoping . . . Well, you see, Mister Pimpernickel met me in Frickerham, as I had some papers to notarize. And I hadn't seen the new town, and I was hoping, well, that perhaps you could show me where to shop . . . in . . . in the new shops, at the railroad crossing. . . ."

"Walk you to town?"

"Yes, that would be wonderful—or, if you don't have the time, perhaps you could just point me in the right direction."

"I'd better walk you."

"Yes. Thank you. That would be much better."

"May I call you John Warren?"

He had just finished tying his boots.

"Yes," he said, "I am no longer a soldier."

I saw that he still had his scar on his lip, though it had healed to be no more than the faint touch of memory. I asked if later I might show him around his new house. Yes, he said, that would also be very nice.

He was crying a little bit.

I said, "Are you crying again? You cry very often."

"No," he smiled—"I do not."

✳ ✳ ✳

It was a bright morning.

The sun was very white and the dandelions were very yellow. There were birds in the woods and spring peepers in the creek. Ladybugs picked their way over delicate leaves.

Soft Rush grows on the riverbank

John Warren and I walked side by side through the field by the big rock.

The grass had grown tall and green.

He asked, "Is the town far?"

"No," I said, "it is not too far."

And from that day forward, John Warren and I were always together.

Postscript

Hummingbird
Trumpet

And so I rest and tell no more, as that would begin another story, the story of when your parents were but newborn babes, or the yet unborn siblings of newborn babes. And after you would come your children, and your children's children, and my tale would be no more than the childhood of a grandmother's grandmother, and indeed, a distant thing—

So . . . of course there were days of rain and tears, as well as days of sunshine and exuberance.

And there were long journeys and short ones. And there were frequent journeys, and years without journeys at all. And there were world journeys, and hammock journeys.

And there were journeys behind eyes that were closed, and journeys behind eyes that were open. . . .

And there were porch sitting days, family loving days, and battle fighting days. (I cannot help but recollect my struggles with the American Medical Association, and in particular, that one butcher, Doctor Robert Battey.) And of those porch days, family days and fighting days, what can I say except—we were well prepared for that.

Author's Thanks

Giles Anderson and Jacob Hoye—for your faith.

Also, for their faith—Paul Auster, Lillian Ball, Clove Breuer, Jill Brienza, Darcy Cosper, Elyse Cheney, Airié Dekidjiev, Dimitri Falk, Pearl Fessler, Fran Gordon, Paula Huston, Carol Irving, Mark James, Alexis Katz, Matthew Lenski, Yeardley Leonard, Carole Maso, Josephine Meckseper, Gabriel Morgan, Alex Orlovsky, Dale Peck, Daniel Pinchbeck, Beverly Reed, David Reed II, Pamela Reed, Raul Rothblatt, Andrew Stuart, Irving Tenenbaum, Scott Waxman, Nina Wiener, Bethany Yarrow and Sebastian Gross-ossa.

For their ongoing efforts—Kate Miciak and Theresa Zoro.

For her illustrations—Judy Rifka.

And everyone who's contributed their knowledge and talents—Fiona Capauno, Elizabeth Epley, Pam Feinstein, Sally Fernandez, Zoe Fishman, Anna Forgione, Virginia Norey and Honi Werner.